THE MAN WITH THE

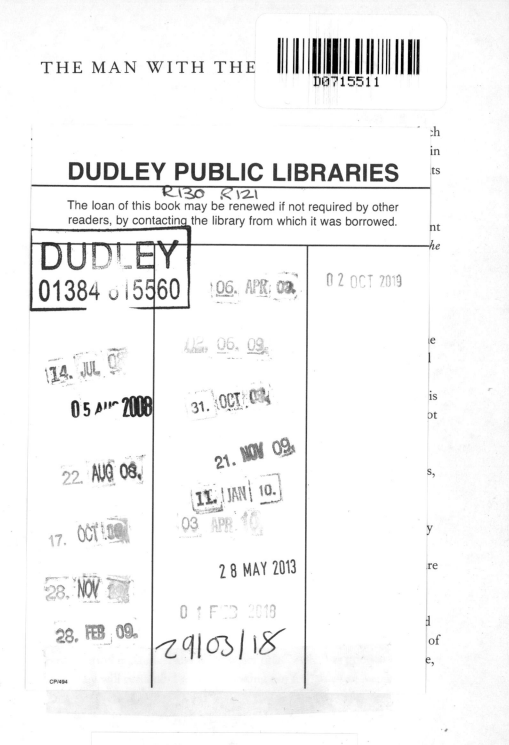

THE
MAN WITH THE
LEAD STOMACH

GALLIC

Also by Jean-François Parot

The Châtelet Apprentice

THE

MAN WITH THE LEAD STOMACH

JEAN-FRANÇOIS PAROT

Translated by Michael Glencross

GALLIC BOOKS
London

This book is supported by the French Ministry of Foreign Affairs as part of the Burgess programme run by the Cultural Department of the French Embassy in London
www.frenchbooknews.com

Liberté • Égalité • Fraternité
RÉPUBLIQUE FRANÇAISE

A Gallic Book

First published in France as L'homme au ventre de plomb by Éditions Jean-Claude Lattès

Copyright © Éditions Jean-Claude Lattès 2000
English translation copyright © Michael Glencross 2008

First published in Great Britain in 2008 by Gallic Books, 134 Lots Road, London SW10 0RJ

A CIP record for this book is available from the British Library

ISBN 978-1-906040-07-9

Typeset in Fournier by SX Composing DTP, Rayleigh, Essex

Printed and bound by Butler & Tanner, Frome, Somerset

2 4 6 8 10 9 7 5 3 1

For Marcel Trémeau

CONTENTS

Background to *The Man with the Lead Stomach*

In the first Nicolas Le Floch investigation, *The Châtelet Apprentice*, the hero, a foundling raised by Canon Le Floch in Guérande, is sent away from his native Brittany by his godfather, the Marquis de Ranreuil, who is concerned by his daughter, Isabelle's, growing fondness for the young man.

On arrival in Paris he is taken in by Père Grégoire at the Monastery of the Discalced Carmelites and on the recommendation of the marquis soon finds himself in the service of Monsieur de Sartine, the Lieutenant General of Police of Paris. Under his tutelage, Nicolas is quick to learn and is soon familiar with the mysterious working methods of the highest ranks of the police service. At the end of his apprenticeship he is entrusted with a confidential mission, one that will result in him rendering a signal service to Louis XV and the Marquise de Pompadour.

Aided by his deputy and mentor, Inspector Bourdeau, and putting his own life at risk on several occasions, he successfully unravels a complicated plot. Received at court by the King, he is rewarded with the post of commissioner of police at the Châtelet and, under the direct authority of Monsieur de Sartine, continues to be assigned to special investigations.

DRAMATIS PERSONAE

NICOLAS LE FLOCH : a police commissioner at the Châtelet

PIERRE BOURDEAU : a police inspector

MONSIEUR DE SAINT-FLORENTIN : Minister of the King's Household

MONSIEUR DE SARTINE : the Paris Lieutenant General of Police

MONSIEUR DE LA BORDE : the First Groom of the King's Bedchamber

AIMÉ DE NOBLECOURT : a former procurator

The VICOMTE LIONEL DE RUISSEC : a lieutenant in the French Guards

The COMTE DE RUISSEC : a former brigadier general and father of the vicomte

The COMTESSE DE RUISSEC : the vicomte's mother

The VIDAME GILLES DE RUISSEC : the vicomte's brother

LAMBERT: the Vicomte de Ruissec's manservant

PICARD : the major-domo of the Ruissec household

ARMANDE DE SAUVETÉ : the vicomte's betrothed

MADEMOISELLE BICHELIÈRE : an actress

TRUCHE DE LA CHAUX : a Life Guard at Versailles

PÈRE MOUILLARD : a Jesuit, Nicolas's former teacher in Vannes

JEAN-MARIE LE PEAUTRE : a fountaineer

JACQUES : Le Peautre's deaf-and-dumb helper

GUILLAUME SEMACGUS : a navy surgeon

CATHERINE GAUSS : Monsieur de Noblecourt's cook

PÈRE GRÉGOIRE : the apothecary of the monastery of the Discalced Carmelites

CHARLES HENRI SANSON : the hangman

OLD MARIE : an usher at the Châtelet

PELVEN : the doorkeeper at the Comédie-Italienne

RABOUINE : a police spy

LA PAULET : a brothel-keeper

GASPARD : a royal page

MONSIEUR DE LA VERGNE : the Secretary to the Marshals of France

MONSIEUR KOEGLER : a jeweller

I

SUICIDE

'The laws in Europe are ferocious towards those who kill themselves: they are made to die twice, as it were; they are dragged in ignominy through the streets; they are branded with dishonour; their property is confiscated.'

MONTESQUIEU

Tuesday 23 October 1761

Carriages were streaming on to Rue Saint-Honoré as Nicolas Le Floch advanced cautiously over the slippery cobbles. Amidst the din of the vehicles, the shouting coachmen and the whinnying horses, a coach arrived at great speed and almost overturned in front of him, one of its metal wheels sending up a shower of sparks. Nicolas negotiated his way with some difficulty through the forest of blazing torches, which a host of manservants was waving aloft in the darkness to provide their masters with as much light as possible.

How much longer, he thought, would such ostentatious and dangerous displays be tolerated? Candlewax ran down clothes and hairstyles; wigs and hair were in danger of being set alight – there had already been numerous fatal incidents. The same scene would be repeated on the steps of the Opéra at the end of the performance, but then there would be even greater chaos with the wealthy spectators trying to hurry home.

Nicolas had made his thoughts on the matter known to Monsieur de Sartine, who had merely rejected his remarks in a way that was both evasive and ironic. However committed he was to the common good and to public order in the capital, the Lieutenant General of Police had no desire to antagonise the Court and the Town by regulating a practice that he occasionally found convenient himself.

The young man pushed his way through the crowd blocking the steps of the great staircase. There was an even greater crush in the confined space of the foyer of this grand edifice, which had been built for Cardinal Richelieu and in which Molière himself had performed.

Nicolas always experienced a thrill on entering this temple of music. The audience recognised and greeted one another. They spoke of the forthcoming performance, as well as of the latest news or rumours, which in a time of war and uncertainty were the subjects of animated debate. On this particular evening, talk was divided between several topics: the recommendation that the bishops of France were due to submit to the King concerning the Society of Jesus,[1] Madame de Pompadour's fragile state of health, and the generals' recent military successes – in particular those of the Prince de Caraman, whose dragoons had pushed the Prussians back beyond the Weser that September. There was also mention of a victory by the Prince de Condé, but the news had not been confirmed.

All these people, shimmering in silk, waded through dirt. There was a disconcerting contrast between their luxurious clothes, and the foul-smelling remnants of wax, earth and horse droppings with which they were soiled.

Trapped in the middle of this throng, Nicolas felt his usual disgust at the mixture of odours filling his nostrils. The stench wafting up mingled with the smell of face powder and poor-quality candles but still did nothing to cover up the sourer and more obtrusive smell of unwashed bodies.

Some women looked on the point of passing out and were frantically waving their fans or sniffing perfume bottles to revive themselves.

Nicolas managed to extricate himself by slipping behind the French Guards on duty on the staircase. He was not attending the Opéra for pleasure but had been sent on official business. Monsieur de Sartine's orders were to watch the audience. It was no ordinary performance that evening. Madame Adélaïde, the King's daughter, together with her retinue, was due to attend.

Since Damiens's attempt on the King's life, a general sense of anxiety had haunted the royal family. In addition to the spies positioned in the theatre stalls and the wings, the Lieutenant General of Police wanted to have his own man on the spot who was totally dedicated and enjoyed his complete trust. It was Nicolas's role to hear and observe everything whilst remaining visible to his superior in his box. As a commissioner from the Châtelet he was entitled to call in the forces of law and order, and to take immediate action if necessary.

To carry out his duties Nicolas had chosen to stand near the stage and orchestra where he could be sure of a full view of the auditorium without losing sight of the stage, another possible source of danger. This location had the incidental advantage of putting him in the best possible position to judge the quality of the orchestra, the performance of the actors and the tessitura of the singers, whilst avoiding the vermin that infested the woodwork and the velvet seats.

How often on returning home had he needed to shake out his clothes over a bowl of water to rid himself of those wretched jumping and biting insects . . .

No sooner had the young commissioner taken up his place than the match-cord began to rise up slowly, like a spider swallowing its thread. Once it was high enough, it moved across the candle wicks of the great chandelier, lighting them one after another. Nicolas loved this magical moment when the auditorium, still dark and buzzing with conversation, emerged from the gloom. At the same time a stagehand lit the footlights. From the boards to the flies shades of gold and crimson appeared in all their splendour, along with the blue of the French coat of arms decorated with fleurs-de-lis, which dominated the stage. Coils of dust, now made visible, filtered the light that spread softly across the clothes, the dresses and the jewellery, in a silent prologue to the magic of the performance.

Nicolas berated himself. When would he grow out of his habit of daydreaming? He shook his shoulders. He needed to keep an eye on the auditorium, which was filling up now, the volume of noise rising.

*

One of Nicolas's main concerns on duty at the Opéra was to establish exactly who was present or absent, as well as to spot any strangers and foreigners. This particular evening he noticed that, unusually, given the generally blasé nature of the public, the boxes were nearly all taken. Even the Prince de Conti, who often made a point of arriving, with the majestic indifference of a prince of the blood, when the performance was already under way, ~~with the majestic indifference of a prince of the blood,~~ was already seated and talking with his guests. The royal box was still empty but servants were busy making it ready.

Nicolas only fulfilled this duty when members of the royal family attended a performance. On other evenings his colleagues were assigned to this task. The police's priority was to seek out and keep a watch on agents suspected of trading with or spying for countries currently at war with France. England in particular was flooding Paris with hired emissaries.

Feeling a light tap on the shoulder, Nicolas turned and was pleased to see the friendly face of the Comte de La Borde, First Groom of the King's Bedchamber, dressed magnificently in a pearl-grey coat embroidered with silver thread.

'What a doubly happy day! Nicolas, my friend, I am so pleased to you again!'

'And may I ask what other agreeable event is implied by your greeting?'

'Aha! You devil . . . What about the pleasure of an opera by Rameau? Does that mean nothing to you?'

'It certainly does, but you're rather a long way from your box,' said Nicolas, with a smile.

'I like the smell of the stage and enjoy being near to it.'

'Near to it, or near to someone?'

'All right, I'll confess. I've come for a closer view of a most gentle and graceful creature I admire. But, Nicolas, I must say we feel you're being very elusive at the moment.'

'We?'

'Don't you try to beat me at my own game. His Majesty enquires about you often, in particular during the last hunt in Compiègne. I do hope you have not forgotten his invitation to join the royal hunt. Because he never forgets anything. Show your face soon, for goodness' sake! He remembers you well and frequently mentions the account you gave of your investigation. At his side you have a most powerful advocate: the Good Lady thinks of you as her guardian angel. Believe me, you should make use of such rare influence and not cut yourself off from your friends. Such elusiveness harms nobody but you, as your friends will not easily tolerate it.'

He pulled a small gold watch from his coat pocket, looked at it and went on: 'Madame Adélaïde should be here very shortly.'

'I thought our princess and her sister Victoire were inseparable,'[2] said Nicolas. 'However, if my information is correct she is attending tonight's performance alone.'

'How very astute of you. But there has been a row between the King and his second daughter. He refused her a set of jewels and out of annoyance Madame Victoire retorted with some biting remark about how the King would have treated a similar request from Madame de Pompadour. There's a Court secret for you, my dear fellow, but as you are the soul of discretion . . . That said, Madame Adélaïde will not be alone; she will be chaperoned by the Comte and Comtesse de Ruissec. Members of the old military nobility, as stern, pious and doddering as you could wish. They are part of both the Queen and the Dauphin's entourages, which says it all. Though the comte—'

'What a sharp tongue you have today!'

'The Opéra inspires me, Nicolas. I assume our friend Sartine will be coming?'

'He will indeed.'

'Madame will be well protected. But nothing ever happens when our lieutenants of police are present. Our performances are so uneventful. Only the cabals and the claques liven them up a little, and *Les Paladins* by the esteemed Rameau should not cause a storm. Both the Queen and the King's corners will be content.[3] *Le Mercure*'s account says that it combines Italian and French tastes very skilfully, even if the daring mixture of comic and tragic may go beyond propriety.'

'It won't go too far; the passions in it are quite innocent.'

'My dear friend, have you ever been to London?'

'Never. And with things as they are, I fear that I may not have that opportunity for some time.'

'Don't be too sure. But what I was going to say is that a visitor from France is always astonished when he enters a London theatre to find there is no police presence. Of course, the price of this freedom is uproar and fighting.'

'It must be the sort of country our friends the philosophers dream of; they say our theatres have the "foul smell of despotism" about them.'

'I know who said that and the King did not appreciate the remark,' said La Borde. 'Discreet as ever, Nicolas, you did not name him. But please excuse me: I am off to pay court to Madame Adélaïde. And quickly, because the object of my attentions appears in the prologue.'

He sauntered across the stalls, bowing this way and that to the beauties of his acquaintance. Nicolas was always pleased to see the Comte de La Borde. He recalled their first meeting, and the dinner when La Borde had kindly rescued him from an awkward situation. Monsieur de Noblecourt, the elderly procurator with whom he lodged and for whom Nicolas was like a son, had often emphasised that such heartfelt affection was a privilege and could be useful. The young man went back over the rapid succession of events since the beginning of the year. The First Groom of the King's Bedchamber would always be associated in his mind with his extraordinary meeting with the King. He knew the secret of his noble birth; he knew that he was not only Nicolas Le Floch but also the Marquis de Ranreuil's natural son. However, he remained convinced that this fact had played no part in La Borde's spontaneous friendship for him.

A loud roar brought him back to reality. The whole house had risen to its feet and was clapping. Madame Adélaïde had just appeared in the royal box. Fair-haired and shapely, she had an air of grandeur. Everyone agreed that she was far more beautiful than her sisters. Her profile and eyes resembled the King's. She smiled and gave a courtly bow, to even louder cheers. The princess was very popular: her affability and friendliness were well known. She seemed to be enjoying the prospect of an evening on her own and, after bowing, continued to nod graciously. Nicolas saw Monsieur de Sartine enter his box after accompanying the King's daughter to her own.

The curtain rose for the prologue, and La Borde hurriedly rejoined Nicolas. To the accompaniment of a triumphant chorus, the goddess of Monarchy appeared on the steps of a classical temple. Young children held her train, which was decorated with fleurs-de-lis. Suddenly the figure of Victory, in breastplate and helmet, emerged on a chariot pulled by the spirits of war; she stepped down from it to crown the goddess with laurels. The chorus rose to a climax and repeated its refrain:

We pay this homage
Worthy of our King,
To crown his glory
And proclaim his might.

Deities waved palm branches. Monsieur de La Borde squeezed Nicolas's arm.

'Look, the fair-haired girl on the right ... the second one wearing a tunic. That's her.'

Nicolas sighed. He knew as well as anyone the sad fate awaiting these young girls from the Opéra. They began their careers in the chorus or as dancers, but then, still barely more than children, fell prey to a world in which loose morals and the power of money prevailed. Unless they managed to navigate the dangerous waters of libertinism, which required skill and caution, and reached the privileged status of kept women, inevitably once the charms of their youth had faded they were condemned to lives of squalor and degradation. At least this pretty little thing might fare rather better with a decent sort like La Borde. Perhaps.

The splendid strains of the prologue continued to ring out. This style of composition had gone out of fashion years ago: Rameau himself had ended it, replacing this standard device with an overture linked to the entertainment. Nicolas had been surprised by this spectacular opening, which lauded the monarchy and glorified its military successes, when the reality was a series of short-lived victories and uncertain setbacks, hardly a reason for bombastic celebration. But carried away by force of habit, everyone continued to pretend. It was not a bad policy in the view of those in authority who looked on from the shadows for any hint of public disaffection. The curtain fell and Monsieur de La Borde sighed; his goddess had disappeared.

'She will be on once again in the third act,' he said with a sparkle in his eye, 'in the dance of the Chinese pagodas.'[4]

The performance resumed and the plot of *Les Paladins* followed its tortuous and conventional path. Ever attentive to the music, Nicolas noted the overlap with vocal elements already used in *Zoroastre*,[5] the importance given to accompanied recitatives and the clear reference to Italian opera in the extensive use of ariettas. Carried away by the orchestration, he paid little attention to the plot: the depraved love of the elderly Anselme for his ward, Argie, herself in love with the paladin Atis.

In the first act Nicolas delighted in the dance tunes, whose gaiety was enlivened by the virtuoso horn accompaniment.

At the end of the second act, during the singing of the aria 'I

Die of Fear', Nicolas, keeping a watchful eye on the auditorium, noticed that something was happening in the royal box. A man had just entered it and was whispering to a military-looking old man sitting to the right behind the princess and who must have been the Comte de Ruissec. Then the elderly gentleman himself leant towards an old lady with white hair and a black lace mantilla. She became agitated and Nicolas saw her shake her head in disbelief. Although from a distance this whole scene appeared to be taking place in silence, the King's daughter became concerned and turned round to learn the cause of the disturbance.

At that moment the curtain fell for the end of the act. Nicolas then saw the same man enter Monsieur de Sartine's box and speak to him. The magistrate rose to his feet, leant towards the auditorium to peer into the stalls and, after finally spotting Nicolas, summarily signalled him to come up. The commotion was growing in the royal box and Madame Adélaïde was dabbing Madame de Ruissec's temples with a handkerchief.

Later, going back over these moments, Nicolas would remember that this was when the whole monstrous mechanism was set in motion, to end only once destiny had been sated with death and destruction. He bade farewell to Monsieur de La Borde, then hurried to join the Lieutenant General of Police as quickly as the public, now on its feet and talking in tightly knit groups, would allow.

Monsieur de Sartine was not in his box. He must have gone to the princess's. After parleying with the officials of her Household, Nicolas managed to gain admittance. Madame Adélaïde was speaking to the Lieutenant General in a low voice. Her beautiful, full face was scarlet with emotion. Monsieur de Ruissec was kneeling at his wife's feet, fanning her as she sat semi-conscious in her seat. A man in black, whom Nicolas recognised as a police officer from the Châtelet, was standing stock-still against the partition wall, looking terrified. Nicolas drew near and gave a deep bow. The princess, taken by surprise, replied with a slight nod of the head. He was moved to see in her youthful face a close resemblance to the King.

Monsieur de Sartine resumed: 'Your Royal Highness may rest assured that we shall do everything necessary to accompany the comte and comtesse back to their mansion and attempt to settle this matter discreetly. However, some observations do need to be made. Commissioner Le Floch here will accompany me. The King knows him and holds him in high esteem.'

A royal look fell upon Nicolas without seeming to notice him.

'We rely on you to do your utmost to allay the distress of our dear friends,' said Madame Adélaïde. 'And above all, sir, have no concern for my person but deal with what is urgent. The officials of our Household will watch over our person and besides the Parisians love us, both my sisters and myself.'

Monsieur de Sartine bowed as the elderly couple – the comtesse trembling uncontrollably – took their leave of the princess. They all left to return to their carriages. It took some time to gather up the coachmen, who had gone off for a drink or two. A court carriage set off with the Ruissecs, since they had come in procession from Versailles with the princess. It was soon followed by Monsieur de Sartine's coach. The flames from the sputtering torches cast flickering shadows over the houses in Rue Saint-Honoré.

The Lieutenant General remained silent for some considerable time, lost in thought. A disorderly jam of carriages brought the vehicle to a standstill and the young man took advantage of the moment to venture an observation.

'One day, sir, it would be useful to introduce regulations with respect to vehicles waiting outside theatres and opera houses. It might even be appropriate to force them to go one way only, in order to make our streets less congested and easier to negotiate.[6] If the roads were also better lit, safety would definitely improve.'[7]

The observation elicited no reply. Instead the Lieutenant General drummed on the windows of the carriage in apparent irritation. He turned towards his subordinate.

'Commissioner Le Floch . . .'

Nicolas stiffened. He had learnt from experience that when the Lieutenant General of Police addressed him by his title instead of calling him by his first name, as he normally did, it meant that he was not in a good mood and that trouble was brewing. He listened carefully.

'We have before us, so I believe, a case that requires particular tact and lightness of touch,' Sartine continued. 'I am, moreover, hostage to the promises I gave to Madame Adélaïde. Does she think this kind of procedure is simple? She knows nothing of the world or of life. She gives herself over to her instinct for kindness. But what relevance have feelings of sorrow and pity for me? Have you nothing to say?'

'First, sir, I would need to have a little more information on the situation.'

'Not so fast, Nicolas. It suits me far better to let you know as little as possible. Otherwise I am only too well aware what the result will be. Your lively imagination will immediately start to run wild. We've seen what happens when I loosen your reins. You take the bit between your teeth and bolt. Suddenly we're off in all directions, picking up bodies on every street corner. You are shrewd and throw yourself into your work, but if I am not there to put you back on the right track ... I want you to retain a completely open mind so that I can benefit from your initial impression. We must not put the hounds off the scent!'

After two years of working for him, Nicolas was accustomed to Sartine, who could at times be monumentally unfair. Only Monsieur de Saujac, the president of the Parlement of Paris, whose reputation for unfairness was legendary, could have taught him anything on that front. So Nicolas was not taken aback by his comments, which another might have found hurtful. He was well acquainted with the sudden mischievous twinkle in his superior's eye and the involuntary twitching to the right of his mouth. Monsieur de Sartine did not believe what he was saying: it was just an affectation, his particular way of imposing his will on people. Only the less perspicacious let themselves be taken in, but he treated everyone in the same manner. Inspector Bourdeau, Nicolas's deputy, claimed that it was his way of manipulating his puppets to check they remained loyal to him and agreed with what he said, however outrageous it might be. What was more surprising was his tendency to prove cantankerous and irascible to those close to him when he had a reputation for being a gentle, secretive and extremely courteous man.

Monsieur de Sartine's apparent mood was a cover for his distress and anxiety. What would they find at the end of their night ride through Paris? What drama lay ahead of them? The Comtesse de Ruissec had looked so distressed . . .

Whatever spectacle fate had reserved for them that evening, the young man vowed not to disappoint his superior and to take careful note of everything. Monsieur de Sartine was once more locked away in a gloomy silence. The effort at concentration that showed on his face further emphasised the lines in his angular features, which had lost all their youthfulness.

They stopped outside the half-moon gateway of a small mansion. A large stone staircase opened on to a cobbled courtyard. Monsieur de Ruissec entrusted his distraught wife to a chambermaid. The comtesse protested and tried to hang on to her husband's arm but he freed himself firmly from her grasp. This scene was played out by the light of a candelabrum held by an elderly retainer, but Nicolas was unable to work out the layout of the broader premises, which were still cloaked in darkness. He could barely even make out the wings of the main building.

They climbed the steps leading into a flagstoned entrance hall with a staircase at the far end. The Comte de Ruissec staggered and had to lean against an upholstered armchair. Nicolas studied him. He was a tall, wiry man, somewhat stooped, despite his concerted efforts to stand straight. A broad scar, now red from emotion, ran across his left temple, probably the mark of a sabre. He was biting his inner lip, his mouth pursed. The austerity of his severe dark coat further emphasised by the cross of the Order of St Michael hanging from a black ribbon, contrasted with a single note of colour, the insignia of the Order of St Louis fastened to a bright red sash, which hung over his left hip. The sword he wore to the side was no ceremonial weapon but a sturdy blade of tempered steel. Nicolas, well versed in such matters, remembered that the comte had been escorting Madame Adélaïde and might in certain circumstances have had to protect her. Monsieur de Ruissec straightened up and took a few steps. Whether it was the result of an old wound or the effect of age, he walked with a limp and sought to conceal this infirmity by raising and thrusting forward his whole body with every stride. He gave his old retainer an impatient look.

'We do not have a moment to lose. Take us to my son's bedroom and give me your account of events on the way.' The authoritative voice was still young, its tone almost aggressive. He led the small group, leaning heavily on the bronze handrail.

Wheezing, the major-domo began his story of the evening's events.

'Your lordship, around nine o'clock in the evening I had just taken some logs to your rooms and had gone back downstairs. I was reading my Book of Hours.'

Nicolas caught the wry look on Monsieur de Sartine's face.

'His lordship the vicomte arrived. He seemed in a great hurry and his cloak was wet. I went to take it from him but he brushed me aside. I asked him if he needed me. He shook his head. I heard his bedroom door slam, then nothing more.'

He stopped for a moment, short of breath.

'That wretched bullet again. Sorry, General. As I was saying, then nothing more until suddenly a shot was fired.'

The Lieutenant General intervened. 'A shot fired? Are you quite sure?'

'My major-domo is a former soldier,' said the comte. 'He served in my regiment. He knows what he's talking about. Carry on, Picard.'

'I rushed up but found the door shut. It was locked from the inside. There was not a sound or cry to be heard. I called out but there was no answer.'

Having gone down a corridor at the end of the landing, the procession was by now in front of a heavy oak door. Monsieur de Ruissec had suddenly become stooped.

'I was unable to force it open,' Picard went on, 'and even if I'd had an axe I would not have had sufficient strength. I went back downstairs and sent her ladyship's chambermaid off to the nearest guard post. An officer came running but despite my pleas he refused to do anything unless someone with greater authority was present. So I immediately sent for you at the Opéra.'

'Commissioner,' said Sartine, 'please find us something with which to open or knock down this door.'

Nicolas seemed in no hurry to obey. Eyes closed, he was carefully going through his coat pockets.

'We are waiting, Nicolas,' said his superior impatiently.

'To hear is to obey, sir, and I have the solution to hand. There is no need to go in search of tools to force an entry. This will do the job.'

He was holding a small, metallic object similar to a penknife, which, when opened, revealed a series of hooks of various sizes and designs. It had been a gift from Inspector Bourdeau, who already possessed one himself and had confiscated another from a bandit and given it to Nicolas.

Sartine raised his eyes to the heavens. 'The thieves' picklock comes to the rescue of the police! The designs of the Great Architect often follow crooked paths,' he murmured.

Nicolas smiled inwardly at this Masonic parlance, knelt down and, after carefully deciding on the most suitable hook, inserted it into the lock. Immediately a key was heard to drop on to the wooden floor of the bedroom. He studied his hooks again, chose another and set to work. Only the wheezy breathing of the comte and of his major-domo, and the sputtering of the candles, disturbed the silence of the scene. After a moment the lock mechanism could be heard creaking and Nicolas was able to open the door. The Comte de Ruissec rushed forward but was just as swiftly stopped in his tracks by the Lieutenant General of Police.

'Sir,' the old man said indignantly, 'I will not allow this. I am in my own home and my son . . .'

'I beg you, your lordship, to permit the officers of the law to proceed. Once the initial observations have been made, I promise you that you will be able to go in and that nothing will be hidden from you.'

'Sir, have you forgotten what you promised Her Royal Highness? Who do you think you are to disobey her orders? Who are you to oppose me? A petty magistrate who has barely emerged from his ancestors' herring-barrels and whose name is still redolent of the grocer's shop . . .'

'I shall not tolerate anything that breaches the law and I take my orders from His Majesty alone,' replied Sartine. 'I vowed to deal with this matter with discretion and that is the only promise I made. As for what you have said to me, your lordship, were it not for the dignity of my office and royal condemnation of the practice, I would challenge you to a duel. The best thing you can

18

do is to proceed immediately to your apartments and wait for me to call for you. Or rather I shall come to fetch you myself.'

Eyes blazing, the elderly nobleman turned and left. Nicolas had never seen Monsieur de Sartine look so pale. Purplish rings had appeared under his eyes and he was furiously twisting one of the curls of his wig.

After taking a candle from the candelabrum Picard was carrying, the young man stepped cautiously into the room, followed by his superior. He would remember his first impressions for a very long time.

At first he could see nothing but immediately felt the chill in the bedroom, then detected the smell of brackish water mingled with the more irritant odour of gunpowder. The flickering flame shed a dim light on an enormous room decorated from floor to ceiling with pale wood panelling. As he moved forward he saw on his left a large, garnet-red marble fireplace topped by a pier glass. To the right an alcove hung with dark damask stood out from the gloom. A Persian carpet and two armchairs hid from view what seemed to be a desk, placed in the corner opposite the doorway. Here and there were chests covered with weapons. These and the disorderly state of the room showed that its occupant was a young man and a soldier.

It was when he neared the desk that Nicolas noticed a figure stretched out on the ground. A man lay face up, his feet pointing towards the window. His head seemed shrunken, as if out of proportion to his body. A large cavalry pistol lay beside him. Monsieur de Sartine moved closer and then recoiled. It was truly a sight to shock the most hardened individual.

Nicolas, who had not flinched when he leant over the body,

suddenly realised that his superior had had few opportunities to witness death in its more gruesome forms. He took him firmly by the arm and forced him to sit down on one of the armchairs. Monsieur de Sartine let himself be led like a child and did not utter a word; he took out a handkerchief and mopped his brow and temples whilst airing his wig, then slumped down, his chin drooping on to his chest. Nicolas was amused to note that Monsieur de Sartine's pale face had now turned a greenish colour. Having scored a point over his superior – he allowed himself such little victories – he resumed his examination of the scene.

What had horrified the Lieutenant General of Police was the dead man's face. The military wig had slipped down on to his forehead in the most grotesque fashion. It further emphasised the already glazed look in the eyes that seemed to be staring at death itself. But where a gaping mouth should have completed the expression of horror or pain, all that could be seen were sunken cheeks and a chin that almost touched the nose in a twisted grin. The face had been so disfigured that it immediately brought to mind an old man who had lost all his teeth or the contorted features of some sculpted monster. The wound that was the cause of death had not bled, but it was too soon to draw any conclusions from this. The bullet seemed to have struck the base of the neck at point-blank range and to have singed the fabric of the shirt and the muslin of the cravat.

Nicolas knelt down beside the body to look at the wound. It was black, and the tear in the skin, the width of the bullet, seemed already to have been closed over by the epidermis; a little congealed blood was visible but it had mainly spread out into the flesh. The young commissioner noted down his observations in a small notebook. He described the way the body was lying and added that the victim was wearing civilian clothes. He was struck by the state of the hands and the fact that they were clenched. The fancy boots were muddy and all the lower part of the body was soaked with foul-smelling water as if the young man had crossed through a pond or an ornamental fountain before returning home to put an end to his life.

Nicolas walked over to the window and studied it carefully. The inner shutters of light oak were bolted. He undid them and noted that the window was also shut. He put everything back in place, picked up the candle and lit the hurricane lamp on the desk. The room suddenly emerged from the half-light. A voice behind him made him turn.

'May I be of assistance, sir?'

The door was still open and on the threshold stood a young man, wearing livery but wigless. Monsieur de Sartine had not detected his presence since the back of the armchair hid the stranger almost completely. His uniform was neat and buttoned up but Nicolas was surprised to see he was in stockinged feet.

'May I ask what you are doing here? I am Nicolas Le Floch, a commissioner of police from the Châtelet.'

'My name is Lambert and I am the manservant and factotum of Monsieur the Vicomte de Ruissec.'

Nicolas was shocked by his slightly provocative tone of voice. He did not admit to himself that he hated tow-coloured hair and eyes of differing colours: on his first day in Paris his watch had been stolen from him by a brigand with just such eyes.[8]

'And what are you doing here?'

'I was asleep in the servants' quarters when I heard Madame

the comtesse's cries and so I quickly dressed and hurried here. Please forgive me,' he said, nodding towards his feet. 'In my haste . . . my eagerness to be of assistance . . .'

'Why did you come here first?'

'I met old Picard in the entrance hall. He explained what had happened and his fears for my master.'

Nicolas rapidly made a note of everything he was told, registering the possible contradictions and the contrasting impressions that the valet's words had on him. The fellow's tone of voice held more than a hint of mocking sarcasm, something unusual for a person of his station when addressing his betters. The man was not as straightforward as he at first appeared. He claimed to have dressed in a hurry, whereas his uniform was immaculate down to his knotted cotton cravat, and yet he had failed to put on his shoes. Nicolas would need to check which way he had come and compare his statements with Picard's. Was it necessary to go outside and then through the courtyard to get to the vicomte's rooms or was there a secret passage via the staircases and corridors connecting all the buildings in the Ruissec mansion? Lastly, the man seemed quite unmoved, though admittedly he might not have seen the corpse as it was hidden by the armchairs and by Nicolas himself. As for Monsieur de Sartine, he remained impassive and silent, and was contemplating the back-plate of the fireplace. Nicolas decided to get straight to the point.

'Do you know that your master is dead?'

He had moved closer to the manservant, who screwed up his pockmarked face into an expression that could have been interpreted either as a fatalistic acceptance of the fact or as a sudden feeling of sorrow.

'My poor monsieur. So he finally kept his word!'

As Nicolas remained silent, he went on: 'Over the past few days he had become sick of life. He had stopped eating and was avoiding his friends. A disappointment in love or at cards, or both, if you ask me. All the same, who would have believed he would have done it so soon?'

'He kept his word, you said.'

'His promise, to be more precise. He kept saying that he would create a stir, one way or another. He had even mentioned the scaffold . . .'

'When did he make such a strange remark?'

'About three weeks ago at a rout with his friends in a tavern in Versailles. I was there to serve them and supply them with drink. It was quite a party!'

'Can you name these friends?'

'Not all of them. I only really know one of them: Truche de La Chaux, a Life Guard at the palace. He was a close friend, even though he is only gentry.'

Nicolas noted that failing common in footmen of adopting their masters' prejudices. In this way contempt for others was to be found at all levels of society, permeating the nobility and their servants alike.

'When did you see your master for the last time?'

'Only this evening.'

At his reply, the Lieutenant General of Police jumped out of his armchair; Lambert recoiled in surprise at this pale apparition, leaping up like a jack-in-the-box, with a ruffled, precariously perched wig on his head.

'Well, Monsieur, please tell me about this evening in detail.'

23

Lambert did not ask who he was dealing with and recounted his story.

'My master was on guard last night. The Queen and many of her entourage were at cards. After coming off duty he rested until midday. He then went for a walk around the park on his own, instructing me to be in the forecourt at four o'clock with a carriage. He wanted to spend the night in Paris, so he said. We arrived this evening at about nine o'clock, without incident. He then told me to leave as he no longer needed me. I was tired, so I went to bed.'

'You were due back on duty tomorrow morning, were you?'

'Yes, indeed. At seven o'clock I would have brought hot water up to his lordship.'

'Was the weather fine in Versailles?' Nicolas interrupted, to the evident annoyance of Monsieur de Sartine, who did not see the point of this digression.

'Misty and gloomy.'

'Was it raining?' He stared at the manservant.

'Not at all, sir. But perhaps this question relates to the state of my poor master's clothes. I suggested he change before leaving Versailles. Lost in melancholy thoughts, he had slipped during his walk and fallen into a small drainage canal. That was the explanation he gave me when I expressed my concern at the state of his clothes.'

Nicolas was trying hard not to give in to his instinctive mistrust of the manservant. He kept repeating to himself that to judge somebody on first impressions always carried the risk of serious error. He recalled Inspector Bourdeau's words. In his youth the inspector had usually trusted his initial judgements. He had attempted to correct this tendency, but as he had grown older experience had taught him the value of his first reaction – when instinct alone had its say – and he had returned to the habits of his youth as a surer means of discovering the truth about a person.

Annoyed by this introspection the young man decided to wait until later to marshal his thoughts. At present it would not be justified to hound the manservant when the case seemed a clear-cut one of suicide. He merely needed to clarify the circumstances in order to understand what had led the unfortunate young man to commit the fateful act. So with Monsieur de Sartine's agreement Nicolas dismissed Lambert, advising him to remain in the corridor; he wanted first of all to question the major-domo.

At this point some police officers appeared. He asked them to wait until the initial investigations were complete and instructed them to keep an eye on Lambert and not allow him to speak to anyone.

When he went back into the room, Sartine was again slumped in the armchair, apparently grappling with his thoughts. Nicolas did not disturb him, but returned instead to the body.

Candlestick in hand, he examined the scene, starting with the wooden floor. He spotted a few recent scratch marks, which could have been caused either by gravel sticking to the sole of the boots or by something quite different.

His attention was then drawn to the desktop. Under the hurricane lamp in the middle of the desktop leather he found a sheet of paper and, scribbled in large capitals, the words: 'FORGIVE ME, FAREWELL'. To the left of this sheet lay a quill next to an inkstand. The position of the armchair behind the desk indicated that the person who had written this message had then stood up, pushed the chair back and made off to the right towards the door, presumably to go round the front of the desk and to end up where the body now rested.

He looked at the corpse once more, paying special attention to the hands, and tried unsuccessfully to close the eyes. He then had a thorough look around the room and noticed to the left of the entrance a huge, elaborately carved wardrobe that almost reached the ceiling. Its doors were ajar. He pushed one open and looked inside; it was dark and cavernous, reminiscent of the box beds of his childhood in Brittany. A strong smell of leather and earth filled his nostrils. In the bottom part was a collection of boots, some in need of a good brushing. He pushed back the polished door of the wardrobe, then drew a plan of the apartment on a page of his notebook.

Continuing his inspection, Nicolas spotted a break in the moulding of the wainscoting. To the left of the alcove a door opened on to a dressing room with deal half-panelling and an adjacent water closet. The room was tiled in Lias[9] and black marble. The walls were hung with wallpaper depicting exotic birds. It was lit by a bull's-eye, which he checked was closed. He stood in thought for some time before the dressing table and its fine porcelain bowl, admiring the toilet case with its razors and mother-of-pearl and silver-gilt instruments carefully laid out on a white linen towel. He also subjected the brushes and combs to the same scrutiny, as if mesmerised by the sight of such splendours.

When Nicolas returned to his superior, Monsieur de Sartine was pacing to and fro in the bedroom, carefully avoiding the corpse. His wig was straight again and the colour had returned to his bony cheeks.

'My dear Nicolas,' said Sartine, 'I am in the most terrible predicament. Like me, you are convinced that the young man took his own life, is that correct?'

Nicolas was careful not to answer and, taking his silence to be tantamount to assent, the Lieutenant General carried on, though not before checking in the pier glass that his wig was properly back in place.

'You know the procedure in such cases. The assumption is one of suicide, and the commissioner who has been informed goes to the scene without his gown and draws up a report without the least fuss or publicity. Then at the request of the grieving relatives, but equally to preserve the conventions, the magistrate requires the parish priest or requests him via his bishop to conduct the funeral service for the deceased and to bury him quietly. As you are also aware . . .'

'Until recently the bodies of those who committed suicide, since they were deemed to be their own murderers, were tried and sentenced to be dragged along on a large timber frame attached to a cart. I know that, sir.'

'Very good, very good. However, notwithstanding this appalling public ordeal on the hurdle, the body was hanged and denied burial in consecrated ground. Fortunately a more enlightened philosophy and our more compassionate times now spare the victim and the family such distressing and shocking excesses. However, we have just such a tragedy here. The elder son of a noble family with a promising future ahead of him has just died. His father is close to the King, or rather to the entourage

27

of the Dauphin. Foolishly – because one should not speak of death to royalty – Madame Adélaïde was informed of the vicomte's suicide and quickly gave in to the Comte de Ruissec's entreaties. Without weighing her words she gave me some recommendations, which I pretended to take as orders, though in fact she is not entitled to give me any. However, it is difficult to deny her wishes and I need to deal carefully with a family that has her support. Nevertheless . . .'

'Nevertheless, sir?'

'I'm thinking aloud here, Nicolas. Nevertheless . . .' The tone was again warm and frank, the Lieutenant General's usual way of speaking to Nicolas. 'Nevertheless, on behalf of the King, I am also responsible for law and order in Paris, which is no easy task. Too strict an application of the rules could lead to trouble. The wise thing to do would be to make the body presentable, send for a priest and a coffin, and spread the word that the young man mortally wounded himself while cleaning a firearm. The funeral Mass would take place, the princess be obeyed, the parents grief-stricken but their reputation intact, and I would have no more problems, having satisfied all concerned. Can I in all conscience act in such a way? What is your feeling? I trust your judgement, even if you are sometimes overhasty and your imagination runs away with you.'

'Sir, we must give the matter careful thought. We are accountable to both the ideal of law with justice and of wisdom with prudence.'

Sartine nodded approval of this carefully worded preamble.

'Since you do me the honour of asking my opinion I feel it appropriate, given the current state of the investigation, to sum up our dilemma. We know that suicide is an act that offends against the divine order, a misfortune that visits opprobrium on an honourable family. The body we see before us is not that of a man of the people, not a pauper driven to this extreme by hardship. Here we have a gentleman, a young man of good education, who knows perfectly well what his actions will mean for his parents and close relatives, and who without further reflection performs the irrevocable deed without offering his family any means of escaping the shame. Do you not find it strange that he did not write to you, as many do, in order to avoid any difficulties after their death?[10] All he left was this.'

He picked up the sheet of paper on the desk and handed it to Sartine.

'Lastly, sir, I have to say that it will be very difficult to keep the news quiet. It has already spread to the Opéra and around town; it will soon reach the Court. The princess will certainly have mentioned it and everyone will repeat her words. A dozen or so people have already been informed: police officers, servants and neighbours. No one will be able to stop the rumour and uncertainty will only make it grow. It will be a godsend for the hawkers of handbills.'

Monsieur de Sartine was rhythmically tapping the wooden floor with his foot.

'Very well put, but where does it get us and how will all your meanderings extricate us from this maze? What do you suggest?'

'I think, sir, that without divulging any details and without dismissing the idea of an accident or a fit of madness, we should have the vicomte's body taken to the Basse-Geôle[11] in the

29

Châtelet to be opened up and examined in the greatest secrecy. That will in the first instance allow us to gain some time.'

'And in a few days we'll be back in the same position but with a scandal blown up out of all proportion. Not to mention the task you've presumably left me of informing the Comte de Ruissec that I'm going to hand over his son's body to the medics. For goodness' sake give me a more convincing argument.'

'Sir, I do not think you have taken in the full implications of my proposal. If I am suggesting that the Vicomte de Ruissec's body should be opened up it's precisely in order to preserve his memory and the honour of his family, because in my opinion the examination will show that he was murdered.'

II

RECONNAISSANCE MISSION

'The truth is perhaps what you do not want to hear; but if I do not tell you it now there will be no point in my revealing it to you on another occasion.'

QUINTUS CURTIUS

Monsieur de Sartine did not immediately reply to this calmly delivered statement. He reacted only with a doubtful expression followed by a sort of wince. He took a deep breath, put his hands together and, having cleared his throat, finally spoke.

'Monsieur, I might well have been perplexed by the gravity of what you have said, and, I make no secret of it, my initial reaction should have been to put you back on routine duties. However, I have not forgotten that the reason for your presence here was precisely to deal with matters that are out of the ordinary. Besides, your suspicion takes a weight off my mind. As usual you will not give me any explanations and will save up your dramatic effects until your magic lantern suddenly lights up the truth, which until that moment will have been apparent to you alone . . .'

'Monsieur . . .'

'No, no, no. I am not listening and wish to hear no more. You are a commissioner and a magistrate, and as such I am entrusting this investigation to you. I am leaving it to you, putting it entirely in your hands and will have nothing further to do with it. And do not try to drag me into one of those complicated demonstrations you specialise in because you think you know it all and want to show you do. Whether you are right or wrong does not matter for the moment. I plan to leave you and make my way quickly to Versailles to deal with more urgent aspects of the case. I shall alert Monsieur de Florentin[1] in order to use my modest influence to combat the storm that the Comte de Ruissec will undoubtedly stir up. But we have one ace up our sleeves. Not so long ago Madame Victoire called our minister "a fool"; as always at Court the remark was repeated to him and however meek and mild he may seem he's bound to be pleased at the prospect of going against her sister Adélaïde and saying the right things to the King. His Majesty has total confidence in him and does not like the normal course of his justice to be impeded. No, no, do not interrupt . . .'

Nicolas disregarded the Lieutenant General's order. 'You will not find Monsieur de Saint-Florentin at Versailles.'

'What do you mean? Who are you referring to?'

'The minister, Monsieur.'

'So not only have you made up your mind about this suicide but you also claim to know the minister's whereabouts.'

'I am your pupil, Monsieur, and your obedient servant. Nothing that happens in Paris escapes me. The contrary would be proof that I neglect my duties and then you really would have cause to complain about my ignorance and lack of zeal. So I can tell you that this evening Madame de Saint-Florentin is with the Queen since, as you know, she is Her Majesty's favourite confidante. As for the minister, he left Versailles at around three o'clock, using Madame Adélaïde's visit to the Opéra as an excuse to meet the lovely Aglaé.'

'The lovely Aglaé?'

'Marie-Madeleine de Cusacque, Langeac's wife, his mistress. At this very moment he is paying her his respects at her mansion on Rue de Richelieu. There is, therefore, no need to rush off to Versailles, Monsieur.'

Monsieur de Sartine could not stifle a laugh. 'All right, that will save me a sleepless night. I hope the minister will pardon my intrusion and that in such charming company he will listen to me carefully so that the prospect of going against the princesses will encourage him to be less accommodating than he tends to be to the parties in dispute.'

Nicolas chanced his luck one last time. 'You do not wish to know the motives—'

'The less I know, the better, for the time being. It would jeopardise my ability to argue a case with which I am not yet fully acquainted. I must keep a low profile and appear to adopt a matter-of-fact approach to a tragic incident, where everything points to suicide. If it is something else ... Oh, do not look so pleased, Monsieur. I do not believe it is a case of murder ... I am handing the investigation over to you and you will inform Monsieur de Ruissec that I have been called away to the Court on urgent business and am leaving you in charge. In fact, tell him what you like! I am sending you Inspector Bourdeau. You will give me a report by tomorrow. Be accurate. Nothing fanciful or imaginative. Just be methodical. Have I made myself clear? Behave like a parrot: move carefully and only let go of one bar when you have grasped another. Do not hesitate to lay mines, to play the sapper, but above all do not trigger any explosions except on my express orders.'

'What if the comte is against having the body removed?'

'You are a magistrate. Issue an order, an injunction, a warrant. Good day to you, Monsieur.'

Alone now in the room, Nicolas sat down in an armchair to reflect on his superior's attitude. He had to make allowances and to take into account the Lieutenant General's subtle approach, caught as he was between powerful interests whose whims and secret designs he had to reconcile. Between the King, Monsieur de Saint-Florentin, the royal family, the parlements, the Jesuits, the Jansenists, the philosophers and the members of the criminal fraternity, his task was not an easy one. Added to this were the problems of wartime and a fear of foreign powers and their machinations.

Nicolas certainly understood all this, but he still bore a grudge against Sartine for continuing to treat him as he had done when he was only an apprentice, which the young man had been until quite recently. Sartine too often forgot that his protégé was now a commissioner and no longer the provincial lad freshly arrived from the countryside. He dismissed this unworthy thought immediately, realising it was an unfair criticism of the man to whom he owed everything. Once more the main thing was that he had been given a completely free hand to solve a tricky case.

Having been profoundly insulted by the Comte de Ruissec, Sartine was only too happy to hand things over to Nicolas in order to teach the comte a lesson. He had not discussed Nicolas's interpretation of events simply because he was not interested in the preliminary stages. As Bourdeau put it, a starving man doesn't care how his dinner was made. The Lieutenant General of Police was not bothered about the trivial details of an investigation. He had a lofty view of his role and the only thing that counted was success. He did not voice an opinion on the ins and outs of his subordinates' doings. He expected evidence and results.

As far as evidence was concerned, Nicolas had none. He let his imagination be his guide. And even Sartine had not picked up on what could be the main objection to Nicolas's theory: the indisputable fact that the vicomte's room was locked from the inside and that there was no other escape route for a potential murderer.

However, Nicolas was sorry not to have had the time to explain to his superior why he was convinced it was murder. It had come to him as he was looking at the body. His experience, backed up by conversations with his friend Semacgus, the navy surgeon, and his own work with Sanson, the Paris executioner, had not been wasted.

He got up and went over to look at the dead man once more. He had never seen a face so appallingly contorted and disfigured. But, above all, the state of the body and of the wound was inconsistent with the very short period of time that had elapsed between the shot heard by Picard and their own arrival in the Ruissec mansion. There was also something else that disturbed him, a vague feeling he could not quite pin down.

So now his investigative work was entering new territory, the realm of the unconscious. Occasionally his dreams, or rather his nightmares, had provided him with solutions to questions troubling him. The important thing at such times was not to think too hard, to let ideas develop naturally until they came together, once the doors of sleep were open. He still needed to remember the contents of his dreams and all too often something would suddenly rouse him from sleep just at the crucial moment.

Nicolas walked around the room one last time. He came across a second door in the wooden panelling, parallel to the dressing-room door. It opened on to a windowless closet containing a library. From a quick inspection he was struck by the disparate nature of the titles and vowed to come back for a closer examination. He noticed in passing the dead man's tricorn, which had been thrown on to the bed and lay upside down beside his cloak.

Nicolas thought about what he still had to do. This initial examination of the scene remained superficial and limited. It did, however, provide a starting point for his work, using his intuition and the unconscious side of his mind. The case was under way and God alone knew if the route they were taking would lead to it being solved. For the time being he put his ideas together and prepared his campaign.

A thought struck him: no close relative of the vicomte had so far seen the body and confirmed its identity. Lambert, the manservant, had not gone up close to the body; everything suggested that he had assumed it was indeed his master, and both he and Sartine had acted as if there could be no doubt of that.

It was appropriate, therefore, to make doubly sure. Nicolas would first put the question to the major-domo and at the same time clear up another point: had Lambert really met Picard, as he had stated, before reaching the vicomte's rooms, and thus learnt about the evening's events? Once this fact had been established, the body ought to be removed and the door to the rooms officially sealed.

He considered whether to inform Monsieur de Ruissec that the body was to be removed. He looked again at the dead man's face. Could he really force a father to endure such a grisly sight? Knowing the old man's personality, his grief and other feelings would lead to an argument that Nicolas could not be sure of winning by simply using his authority. So the elderly retainer's co-operation was essential in order to avoid any slip-up: he would understand the reasons for preventing a father from seeing his dead son and would help Nicolas confine Monsieur de Ruissec to his rooms until the removal was completed. Then and only then would he summon the comte and explain to him the steps he had taken. The comte would no longer be able to stand in his way even though his reaction was bound to be fierce.

Then, when night fell, Nicolas would ask for a lantern and examine the area around the buildings, beginning with the gardens beneath the windows of the vicomte's rooms. At first sight there seemed no real need for such a search: the windows were shut and all the indications were that the vicomte had returned via the main corridor, but the very fact that it was so obvious meant that it was worth checking. Having done that, he would leave the Hôtel de Ruissec and not resume his investigation until the following day.

Lost in thought, he was startled to feel a hand on his shoulder, then reassured to hear Bourdeau's familiar voice.

'Here you are at last, Nicolas, having a delightful tête-à-tête, I see. This elderly gentleman doesn't look too good.'

'He's not an elderly gentleman, Bourdeau, but the young Vicomte de Ruissec. I quite understand why you were misled by appearances. That is precisely the problem. I'll tell you the whole story, but first you tell me how you got here so quickly.'

'Monsieur de Sartine's messenger caught up with me at the Châtelet as I was about to go home. I requisitioned his horse and the old nag finally got me here, though it almost threw me off a dozen or so times. With all these new building plots in Grenelle the mansion really stands out among the wasteland and gardens. Is it a murder?'

Nicolas explained the situation. Having worked so closely together the two men understood each other implicitly. As Nicolas spoke, the puzzled expression on the inspector's ruddy face grew until finally he lifted his short wig and scratched his head in his usual way.

'You do have a knack for getting involved in strange cases . . .'

Nicolas liked the comment. He knew he could count on Bourdeau to do everything in his power to help him. He asked the inspector to fetch the major-domo and make sure he had no contact with the vicomte's manservant.

When the old retainer appeared, Nicolas regretted making him come upstairs. Picard had difficulty breathing and was leaning against the casing of the doorway to get his breath back. A strand of yellowing grey hair fell across his forehead, disturbing the meticulous arrangement of his hairstyle with the regulation pigtail, coils and lovelocks of a former dragoon. Nicolas thought his eyes looked clouded as if a grey-blue membrane had been stretched across them. He had observed the same phenomenon in his tutor, Canon Le Floch, in the last years of his life.

The major-domo mopped his brow clumsily with his gnarled hands. The young man led him towards the corpse while partly shielding him from a full view of the body, then stepped aside.

'Do you recognise Monsieur de Ruissec?'

Picard thrust his hand into the right-hand pocket of his jacket and, having removed a snuff-stained handkerchief, pulled out a pair of spectacles. He put them on, leant over towards the body and instantly recoiled, his stomach heaving.

'God forgive me, Monsieur, I've seen some sights in my time but that face, that face . . . What have they done to Monsieur Lionel?'

Nicolas noted the affectionate way of referring to the vicomte. He did not reply, preferring to let the old man have his say.

'Even on the eve of the Battle of Antibes in '47, when our sentries were abducted and tortured by a band of Croats, I never saw a face as contorted as this. The poor soul.'

'So it definitely is the Vicomte de Ruissec, is it? You recognise the body as his? Beyond the shadow of a doubt?'

'Alas, Monsieur, who is better able to recognise it than I?'

Nicolas gently led the old retainer towards an armchair.

'I would like to go over the events of the evening with you. I noticed that you brought fresh firewood to your master's bedroom. Does this mean that Monsieur de Ruissec was expected to return to his mansion this evening? The way you put it clearly implied that you were expecting him.'

'I certainly was hoping he'd be back this evening. The general is far too old to be going out like this. He and Madame had left for Versailles yesterday to accompany the King's daughter to the Opéra. When they go to the palace they sleep in a damp attic, too hot in the summer and too cold in the winter. Madame has always complained about it. Monsieur doesn't say anything but his war wounds play up every time he spends the night in the palace. When he comes back I have to rub him down with vintage schnapps like an old warhorse.'

'So you couldn't be sure of them coming back this evening, could you?'

'The princess usually says they are free to return to their mansion. She has her retinue of servants to accompany her back to Versailles. That's what I hoped would happen. But Monsieur does not like turning his back on his duties in such a way.'

I've established one thing at least, thought Nicolas, whilst noting that it did not prove whether or not the Ruissecs would have returned home.

'Is your eyesight poor?' he asked.

Picard looked at him in amazement.

'I heard you say that you were reading your Book of Hours. With these same spectacles?'

'Oh, I can see but my eyes tire quickly. Too much marching in the sun . . . I used to be able to hit a bottle with my pistol from twenty yards but now I can't see more than a few inches ahead of me and my sight is becoming increasingly blurred.'

Nicolas resumed: 'Did you remove your spectacles when the vicomte arrived?'

'There was no time to remove anything. Though if I'd done so my sight would have been even poorer. In any case he rushed past and climbed the stairs four at a time.'

He took off his glasses. 'To tell you the truth, Monsieur, I only wear them for reading my Book of Hours and Monluc's *Commentaries*, which Monsieur gave me. That marshal really was a brave—'

Nicolas interrupted him, disliking nothing more than the ramblings of witnesses.

'Was it usual for him not to speak to you when he returned home?'

'Not at all, Monsieur. He was always affable, with something kind to say, always enquiring about me and my old war wounds. It is true though that he'd seemed a little out of sorts to me for some months now.'

'Out of sorts?'

'Yes, a bit ill at ease, wrapped up in himself, putting on a forced smile. I even said to myself, "Picard, something bad will come of this." I've got a feel for this sort of thing. One day in a little village—'

'What in your opinion was the cause of this gloominess?'

'It's not for me to say. I just felt it.' Picard was clamming up. He bit his lip as if he had already said too much.

'Out with it. I'm listening.'

'I've nothing more to say.'

He seemed sad and was playing with one of his lovelocks. Nicolas felt he would get nothing more out of him for the moment.

'Picard,' he said gently, 'I need your help. I don't want Monsieur de Ruissec to go through the ordeal of seeing his son in this state. Here's what I suggest. While my men are removing the body, you will make sure that your master remains in his rooms. As soon as they've finished I will let you know and I will then inform the comte of the arrangements that have been made. Up until then I require silence and discretion.'

Picard was staring at him, his eyes clouded with tears.

'What are you going to do with Monsieur Lionel?'

'All you need to know is that if his parents do have to see him again we shall ensure that it is not too horrific a sight. May I rely on you?'

'This old soldier hears you, Monsieur, and I will carry out your orders to the letter.'

Nicolas was about to dismiss him, then changed his mind.

'This Lambert,' he said casually, 'he seems an honest and faithful servant . . .'

Picard looked up and his mouth tightened. His lower lip pouted as if to signal his disagreement with the police officer's words.

'That's for my masters to decide.'

Nicolas noted that this form of words seemed to exclude the Vicomte de Ruissec.

'But what do you think of him?'

'If you must have an answer it's that I expect nothing good from the two-faced rogue. A spoilt child grown into a spineless adult; he gives in to anyone who does him favours and is easy to lead down the slippery slope.'

'Does the comte know your feelings?'

'Huh! What could a poor man such as myself have done against such privilege? How could I fight against someone of such worth? Monsieur Lionel doted on him. Unfortunately, the master who becomes his valet's servant is quite the fashion nowadays, Monsieur. And speaking to the general is no easy task . . .'

'Did you see him this evening?'

'Who? Lambert? Yes I did, Monsieur. When the Lieutenant General of Police requested my master to withdraw to his rooms, I accompanied him, then went back downstairs to wait in the corridor. Some time later I saw Lambert appear. He told me he'd been woken by the noise. He came up to speak to you.'

'Are there several ways of getting from the servants' quarters to the interior of the mansion?'

'Either you go through a door opening on to the main courtyard then up the steps to the front entrance, or you go over the top.'

'The top?'

'Through the attics in the roof space, where the washing is put to dry. There's a small staircase that links up with the workrooms on that floor. It's used at night when everything is shut and a servant is sent for.'

Nicolas wrote down all these details in his little notebook.

'Did Lambert seem his usual self to you?'

'More or less. But I don't often see him.'

'Did anything about his appearance strike you?'

'Monsieur, you now know my eyesight is poor: I could barely make out his outline, like a shadow.'

'Thank you, Picard. You have been most helpful.'

The major-domo thanked Nicolas with a soldierly nod of the head. He hesitated before withdrawing and finally added: 'Monsieur, find the person who brought our child to this.'

'I will. You may be sure of that.'

Nicolas watched him walk away in an attempt at a military gait but which merely betrayed his stiffness and pain. He recalled another old soldier: one who had hanged himself in a cell in the Châtelet and whose death meant that Nicolas's nights were sometimes haunted by feelings of remorse . . .

Picard's interrogation had indeed proved helpful. The dead man's identity had been confirmed. The major-domo's remarks about the vicomte's melancholy matched Lambert's. The fondness that Picard clearly felt for the vicomte did not affect his judgement. Lastly his view of the manservant's character tallied with his own. So Nicolas would have to be even more cautious before coming to a definite opinion. The fact remained that Lambert exerted a considerable influence on his master but whether it was for better or for worse had yet to be seen. However, there was nothing to suggest that the servant had been informed of his master's death before reaching the first-floor rooms.

All that remained for Nicolas to do was to have the body taken away as soon as possible, after one last formality: emptying the dead man's pockets. He proceeded methodically, trying not to look at the horrifying spectacle of the face, but his search did not prove very fruitful: a few crown coins, an empty silver snuffbox, a piece of pink ribbon and a red wax stamp. In the pockets of the cloak on the bed he found a wet and still folded handkerchief, and round the hem a few specks of a powdery, coaly substance that had resisted the damp. The hat, which he carefully shook out and examined minutely, yielded nothing of particular interest.

Nicolas met up with Bourdeau in the corridor and, after allowing Lambert to withdraw, took the inspector off into the bedroom.

'Have you found anything?'

'A spoilt child, a shady servant who was a bad influence,' replied Bourdeau. 'But it does seem that he learnt of his master's death directly from the major-domo.'

The inspector kept some of his observations to himself, which might be of use to him in the future.

Then it was time for the unchanging ritual: the body was lifted up, placed on a stretcher, covered with a brown blanket and taken away. After a final look at the scene of the crime and having extinguished the candelabrum, Nicolas closed the door and affixed the sealing wafers, which he signed carefully. He put the bedroom key in his pocket, where it joined the items he had picked up and the pistol found near the body. He undertook all this without much thought as to what he was doing, like an automaton. In the course of his short police career he had already followed these procedures on various occasions but each time he was aware of their sinister meaning, the end of a human life.

He sent Bourdeau out to check that the coast was clear and then had the bearers go downstairs, telling them to make as little noise as possible. He hoped that the Comte de Ruissec would have no inkling of what was happening. He remembered that when they had reached the Hôtel de Ruissec the shutters on the façade had seemed closed. The police carriages were waiting in the street: the rumble of the cart would not be heard from inside the high walls of the building. He decided to wait until all was quiet again and to take advantage of the silence to broaden the scope of his investigation. He wanted to explore the grounds behind the main building, beneath the wing containing the vicomte's rooms. He left Bourdeau to keep guard and had Picard show him the door that led outside.

The major-domo had lent him a lantern but the moon was bright enough. To the right he could make out the wing he was looking for. It was a very simple construction on two levels, a ground floor with wide oval carriage entrances allowing a glimpse of stables or sheds for carriages, and a first floor where the vicomte's rooms were situated. Everything was identical to the main building with a double-pitched mansard roof above it. Nicolas headed towards the wing. He opened one of the doors; he knew where he was by the strong stable smell and the prolonged neighing of those horses that were awake. The entrance was cobbled and climbing roses were growing up between the two doors. He crouched down and carefully examined the ground beneath the vicomte's windows, then stood up again and beamed his lantern towards the wall. He stayed there for some time, then tried to gain a more precise idea of the layout.

The irregular shape of the garden – a trapezium with its apex extending beyond the stables – was disguised by the symmetry of two long rectangular parterres that ended in a *rond-point* decorated with trellises. The other parts were made up of patches of greenery interlinked by small grass pathways planted in the shape of a maze. Each of the two parterres was decorated with stone corbeils. The central alley ended abruptly at a large circular marble pond ornamented with a group of lead cupids and tritons that acted as water spouts. A cobbled alley formed a sort of terrace in front of the steps leading to the large rooms on the ground floor. A small door, through which Nicolas had come out, was situated in the right angle where the buildings met and was half hidden in a sort of sunken rotunda.

Nicolas turned left again and discovered a closed carriage gateway, which must have led on to an adjacent lane perpendicular to the road on which the Hôtel de Ruissec was situated. He walked all the way round the boundary wall, stopping here and there and crouching down several times in the dead leaves. He ended his walk in a tucked-away corner where, behind a hedge, he discovered a garden shed full of tools, watering cans, a ladder and seedlings in pots. He went back towards the central pond and, as he drew near, the smell of stagnant water became stronger and stronger, mingled with the heady aroma of boxwood. An impression flashed through his mind and then was gone.

After a last glance at the parterres full of rosebushes, Nicolas met up with Bourdeau and Picard, who were talking together. He was always surprised by his deputy's ability to gain the immediate trust of ordinary people. He asked the major-domo to inform his master that Nicolas needed to see him. Picard obeyed and came back without saying a word; he opened the door of a large drawing room, lit some candelabra and asked Nicolas to enter.

The gentle, flickering gleam of the candles filled the room with enough light to reveal a wall with a *trompe-l'oeil* vista of an imaginary landscape. A large archway led the eye towards a park, suggesting the countryside in the background. To extend the perspective the painter had placed two incomplete marble banisters halfway, which appeared to flank the beginning of a flight of steps and gradually disappeared into the distance. The archway, resting on two Ionic columns, also had pilasters that supported an attic whose panel was decorated with musician cupids sculpted in the round. The open windows on the right and left of the work added to the illusion, increasing the suggestion of space beyond the real room. Nicolas admired this surprising blend of painting and sculpture. He was lost in contemplation before it, rediscovering in this life-size work of art one of the themes of his childhood dreams. The few engravings that discreetly decorated Canon Le Floch's austere interior in Guérande had provided plenty of scope for his imagination. He had spent hours gazing at the scenes they depicted, especially the one of Damiens's ordeal in the Place de Grève, until he felt caught up in the events themselves. Then in a sort of waking dream he would invent endless adventures, whilst deep down always secretly worrying that he would never return to a peaceful and protective existence. What he could see in this reconstruction of real life both fascinated and attracted him with its baroque extravagance and opera-like décor. He held out his hand as if trying to enter it.

An angry voice rang out, bringing him back to reality.

'"Shall the throne of iniquity have fellowship with thee, which frameth mischief by the law", taking pleasure in the wickedness of the images?'

Nicolas turned. The Comte de Ruissec stood before him.

'Psalm Ninety-four. You are, Monsieur, or so I assume, neither a Huguenot nor a Jansenist. I have known two men who were accustomed to quoting the Scriptures: one was a saint and the other a hypocrite. Here indeed we have his master's sleuthhound, lost in contemplation before this graven image that is a mere parody of life.'

'And yet it is what decorates the drawing room of your mansion, Monsieur.'

'I acquired this house from a ruined farmer of taxes, who took great delight in such illusions. For my part I have little liking for them and will have them covered up with paintings or tapestries. But we have not a moment to lose. For the last time, Monsieur, I command you to let me see my son.'

He stood with his hands on the back of an armchair, gripping it so tightly that his knuckles had turned white.

'Monsieur, it is my duty to inform you that the Vicomte de Ruissec's body has been removed from this house and taken to a place of justice for a special inquiry.'

Nicolas was expecting an explosion of anger from the comte, but it did not come. The comte's expression remained intense and full of hatred, his jaw twitching tensely. He sat down and, for a while, remained silent.

'This is most cruel and quite incomprehensible.'

'I should add that if such a decision has been taken it is in order both to spare yourself and Madame the comtesse an unbearable sight . . .'

'Monsieur, I am used to the spectacle of war.'

'. . . And also to consult physicians as to the nature of your son's wounds.'

He did not wish to go into too much detail and feed the comte's imagination; there was no point.

'Are you telling me that they intend to open up my son's body?'

'Much to my regret, Monsieur. The procedure might be necessary in order to establish the truth.'

'But what truth do you hope to establish, given that my son killed himself in a room that was double-locked? You opened it yourself. What purpose can it serve to inflict such treatment on a lifeless body?'

'Remember, Monsieur,' Nicolas replied, 'that this examination may provide precious information and prove, for example, that your son may have injured himself while cleaning his weapon, thus removing the stain of his having killed himself deliberately.'

Nicolas thought that this effort to justify the examination would make no impression on the comte. Sometimes in extreme circumstances mental torment can lead people to cling desperately to the slightest hope. Yet Nicolas felt that the comte would not contemplate the idea of an accident, as if he was convinced that it was indeed suicide.

'As soon as the examinations have been carried out,' Nicolas continued, 'with, I can assure you, the utmost discretion and in total secrecy, your son's body will be properly prepared and returned to you. This is, I think, the best arrangement, one that does not prejudge future developments and leaves open every possibility of preserving your family honour.'

He thought that this comforting promise to make the corpse presentable was quite risky, given the state of the body.

Suddenly the comte stood up. The effect that the announcement of the removal of the body had not produced was suddenly triggered by the word 'honour'.

'Who are you, Monsieur, to speak of honour? What do you claim to know about it? Honour is something, Monsieur, that one needs to have been born with to be able to speak of it. Honour comes from the purity of the blood line, uncontaminated by commoners. It goes back to the dawn of time, nourishes generation after generation, and is earned by the sword in the service of the King and of God. How dare you allow this word to cross your lips, Monsieur Police Officer?'

Nicolas held back a childish and conceited desire to remind him of his precise official title, momentarily raising his left hand slightly, then lowering it. It was at this point that the comte laid his eyes on the emblazoned signet ring that the young man was wearing.

It had been sent to him by his half-sister, Isabelle, after the King himself had explained the mystery of his birth, and it bore the coat of arms of the Ranreuils. He had not wished to take up a title that was his by right but he kept this ring in memory of his godfather, whom he only dared to call his father in the secret recesses of his heart. This signet ring was like a bond with what lay beyond the grave. As a child he had admired this time-worn blazon a hundred times or more and now it was his.

Eyes flashing with fury and his mouth twisted in anger, the elderly comte continued, pointing to the ring: 'How dare you speak of honour and presume to display the arms of a Ranreuil? Yes, my sight is good enough to recognise the blazon of a nobleman who served with me and I still have enough energy to express my outrage at the sight of a hireling forgetting his place in this fashion.'

'Monsieur, I am of the Marquis de Ranreuil's blood and lineage, and I would advise you to moderate your language.'

Nicolas had been unable to restrain himself. It was the first time he had proclaimed his birth after declining to take up its privileges.

'And so the fruit of sin finds pleasure in contemptible occupations. What, though, does it matter? Such are the times we live in. A century when sons rise up against their fathers, when aspiring to good leads to sinking into the mire of evil, an evil that is everywhere in the highest and the lowest ranks of society.'

The Comte de Ruissec's white face was a picture of hatred. As he put his hand to his forehead, Nicolas noticed his curved and scored fingernails. The elderly man pointed towards the door.

'Enough, Monsieur. I note that as a true and worthy servant of Sartine's you neither comply with the wishes of a father nor show the respect that my position should inspire in you. Get out. I know what there remains for me to do.'

He turned round to face the *trompe-l'oeil*, and for a moment Nicolas thought that he was going to fade into it and disappear into the grounds it depicted. This impression was enhanced by the comte leaning against the wall and placing his hands flat against one of the marble banisters.

There was nothing to keep Nicolas any longer in the house, which was now just a place of mourning. His footsteps echoed along the stone floor of the entrance hall, then he felt the cool air of the courtyard, with its smell of dust and decaying plants. A light wind was blowing, sending the leaves swirling across the cobbles. He went over to the cab, which had presumably been sent by Monsieur de Sartine. Bourdeau's horse was tied to the back of the vehicle by its halter. In the lantern light he could see the outline of Inspector Bourdeau, lying back with his mouth open, fast asleep. As he went to take his seat, Nicolas turned, as if something were holding him back, and looked up. On the first floor of the mansion the silhouette of a woman holding a candlestick appeared at one of the windows. He sensed that she was staring at him. At the very same moment a discreet cough called his attention. Without a word, Picard slipped a small square envelope into his hand. When Nicolas looked back up at the window he thought he must have been dreaming: the figure had disappeared. Unsettled by this, he climbed into the cab, which creaked under his weight. The coachman cracked his whip and the horse and carriage clattered out of the courtyard of the Hôtel de Ruissec.

Nicolas held the envelope in his hand, resisting the temptation to open it immediately. Beside him the sleeping figure of Bourdeau was jolted around with every bump of the cab. The road, which had only recently been marked out and laid, went through a half-wrecked countryside of waste ground, building sites and gardens. Nicolas wondered what could have persuaded the Comte de Ruissec to acquire this new mansion in such an isolated spot. Had it been a cheap purchase, a compulsory sale to pay off the debts of a bankrupt farmer of taxes, or was there some other reason? Perhaps the simplest explanation was its closeness to the Versailles road. It suited a courtier whose functions were divided between the town and the Court, requiring him to be not too far away from either place. And, as Picard had suggested, it also enabled the elderly nobleman to enjoy the comfort of a home after the rigours of life in military camps. We need to look into this whole family, he thought to himself.

His conversation with the Comte de Ruissec had given him a glimpse of the comte's bitterness, a strange reaction that did not seem appropriate for someone grieving over a dead child. He needed to take the Comte de Ruissec's interrogation a stage further, but this would have to be done skilfully if he were to get round the wily old creature's defences. His forthright character seemed resistant to charm of any kind. Nicolas had not been convinced by his ostentatious show of almost Puritan piety or his outburst about honour. The conversation had left the commissioner with an almost tangible impression of a cruel and dissembling character.

He was holding the small square of paper so tightly that it hurt his hand like burning coals: the sensation roused him from his thoughts. He lowered the carriage window and the chilly, damp air hit him straight in the face. He leant out to make use of the lantern light and broke the wax seal. The light revealed a few lines of large, shaky handwriting – probably a woman's – with curved, overlapping letters. The text was short and to the point:

> *Monsieur,*
> *Tomorrow at four o'clock be in the Lady Chapel of the Carmelite church on Rue de Vaugirard. Someone will be waiting for you there who desires to have the benefit of your knowledge.*

Instinctively, he put the message to his nose and breathed in the scent. He had already smelt this perfume on elderly ladies, the dowagers of the upper echelons of Guérande society who frequented his guardian, the canon, or whom he met in the Marquis de Ranreuil's chateau. He recognised the lingering scent of face powder and *eau de la Reine de Hongrie*. He examined the paper: it was an almond-green colour, laid paper with no engraved monogram or watermark, which observations led him to make a connection between the writer of these lines and the face at the window of the Hôtel de Ruissec. The message, handed on by the faithful family major-domo, came most probably from the Comtesse de Ruissec and was clear evidence of her wish to tell him some secret in confidence. One detail, however, intrigued him: the purpose of the meeting was less a desire to enlighten him concerning the vicomte's death than a supposed request for advice. He reassured himself with the thought that these two things were perhaps not totally unconnected.

Bourdeau was snoring discreetly, giving little groans as he breathed out. Nicolas tried to rest a little, but even the rocking carriage could not lull him to sleep. He was beset by unformed thoughts. Several ideas that had occurred to him now eluded him; he was tormented by this, annoyed with himself for not noting them down as they came to him. Irritated, he gripped the notebook that never left his side and in which he jotted down his thoughts and observations. He had not forgotten that he would have to write a report and give an account to the Lieutenant General of Police. He could hear Monsieur de Sartine's starchy tones harping on as ever about 'precision and concision'. But Nicolas had never had any difficulties in this respect and his superior valued his brisk, businesslike approach. He could thank the Jesuits in Vannes for perfecting his written style, but also the notary with whom he had begun his career, who had taught him the importance of weighing up his words and choosing them with care.

In the course of these cogitations Nicolas forgot what it was he was trying to remember. It was then he realised he had not checked if there was a duplicate key to the vicomte's bedroom. He bit his lip; he needed to make sure. He continued to worry about this but then took comfort from the thought that if a copy really had existed, Picard would have told him rather than let him pick the lock.

The carriage came to a sudden halt amidst shouting and the neighing of horses being roughly reined in. In the sudden shifting flicker of lights he heard the coachman arguing. In these times of war, entering and leaving the capital at night was strictly controlled. Nicolas had to make himself known in order to be let through the gates. From then on progress was quicker through a deserted night-time Paris. He dropped Bourdeau off at his house near the Châtelet and set off again towards the church of Saint-Eustache and Rue Montmartre to return to Monsieur de Noblecourt's mansion. The house, in which he had received such a generous welcome one desperate morning, was always a comforting sight. 'Mansion' was in fact rather too grand a term for the sturdy bourgeois dwelling whose ground floor on the street side was occupied by a bakery.

Nicolas always liked to be greeted by the warm smell of the night's first batch of loaves. It drove away the cares of the day and the troubles of a mind always exercised by suppositions and calculations. It enveloped him like a familiar and reassuring presence, and provided the transition between a hostile outside world and his return to a friendly and protected space.

He decided not to take the hidden staircase that led directly from the inner courtyard up to his bedroom, and instead opened the door beneath the archway of the carriage entrance. A wriggling furry ball jumped into his arms: Cyrus, Monsieur de Noblecourt's dog, always welcomed him warmly. Cyrus was yelping with pleasure at the sight of a friend he had taken to from their first meeting. After this outpouring of affection he became once more the procurator's dignified lapdog and, raising his head like a proud steed, preceded Nicolas into the house, only his irrepressible wagging tail still showing his pleasure.

He headed towards the pantry, regularly checking that Nicolas was following him. The young commissioner deduced from this that Monsieur de Noblecourt was already asleep. Increasingly afflicted with gout, the elderly magistrate enjoyed talking to his protégé, even when Nicolas came back late. He was always eager to hear the police officer's account of his day's activities and just as curious to find out the news and the gossip about the town and Court. As he entertained frequently he was one of the best-informed men in Paris; as Nicolas had often been in a position to observe, his advice and opinions enjoyed considerable favour. When he waited up late in his wing chair, Cyrus was the messenger given the task of intercepting Nicolas and leading him to his master.

One meagre candle lit the pantry dimly. On a low chair, near the stove, a slumped figure heaved peacefully with every breath. Nicolas recognised Catherine, the cook. On seeing her, the pedantic schoolboy in him was awakened and he recalled

Boileau's line: 'Upon her breast her double chin does droop'. He immediately told himself off for this joke at the expense of someone who had proved unfailingly loyal to him.

After the fall of the Lardin household,[2] Catherine Gauss had at first been given shelter by Dr Semacgus in Vaugirard. But the surgeon already had his own cook, the African Awa, and even though the two women had become friends he could not keep Catherine on. Nicolas had found the solution. Marion, Monsieur de Noblecourt's housekeeper was getting on in years and had been delighted for Catherine to take charge of the cooking. Nicolas, now comfortably off thanks to his position as commissioner and the extra emoluments accruing from this post, had himself engaged his old friend and therefore shared in the expenses of running the Noblecourt household. The elderly procurator had protested as a formality but he had been touched by Nicolas's kind gesture.

Cyrus tugged the bottom of Catherine's skirt, making her wake up grumpily. As soon as she noticed Nicolas, she wanted to get up but he prevented her from doing so.

'I nodded off waiting for you, my little one,' she sighed.

'Catherine, how many times do I have to tell you not to wait up for me!'

'You were at the Opéra. Nothing could happen to you.'

Nicolas smiled at the thought of how his night had started in Grenelle. But Catherine was already busy, laying the table and producing a delicious-smelling pie.

'You must be hungry. I have cold pâté and a bottle of Irancy that the master had a sip of for his supper. He ate heartily.'

Nicolas sat down at the table for one of those ample and

succulent late-night meals that Catherine was so good at, thanks to her Alsace upbringing. The golden crust of the pastry was still warm and the bouquet of red wine and bay leaves made his mouth water. She looked at him apprehensively, waiting for his slightest reaction. The tender meat melted in the mouth.

'You've kept this dish a secret from me, Catherine. It's quite delicious! Is it from your region?'

'Not at all. That one's a pie. The meat is chopped and marinated in white wine. This dish is from Champagne. You cut pork and veal, and most of all you add fat to make it tender. You let it soak in good red wine with spices, salt, pepper, two days, no more. You make the pastry. You wipe your meat. You line the dish then spread the meat on top and you cover with a round of pastry brushed with beaten egg. You keep it in the oven for a good two hours. It's better warm or cold. It can also be done with rabbit without needing to bone it. Where I come from we would draw lots for who was going to have the head. Yes, that's what we did!'

Once he had eaten enough, Nicolas watched Catherine extinguish the stove and put the leftovers of the meal away in the sideboard. He smiled gratefully and wished her good night. He went up to his room and without undressing lay down on his bed before immediately falling into a deep sleep.

III

THE WELL OF THE DEAD

'Misfortunes often form a chain.'

RACINE

Wednesday 24 October 1761

Nicolas was woken by a scraping sound. After looking at his watch he realised that it was Catherine, placing a jug of hot water outside his bedroom door. She had done this every morning since her first day at Monsieur de Noblecourt's house. She had probably decided to let Nicolas sleep in a little. It was already past seven o'clock. Since his earliest childhood he had got up at six, winter and summer alike: as a boy, whilst barely awake he would serve Mass for the canon, his guardian, in the cold and damp of the collegiate church of Guérande.

He discovered to his amusement that he had slept fully clothed. Fortunately his wardrobe had increased considerably since his arrival in Paris. His tailor, Master Vachon, who also dressed Monsieur de Sartine, had seen to that. Nicolas fondly recalled the green coat, originally made for another customer, that he had worn at Versailles on being first presented to the King.

He felt refreshed and full of energy until the events of the previous day suddenly came flooding back. A rare moment of early morning happiness gave way to the preoccupations of the hunter planning the chase. He noticed his tricorn on the floor. Fortunately he had not slept with it on, as that was said to bring bad luck. This fleeting observation stirred some vague memories that he could not quite pin down. Bare-chested, he had a thorough wash in the water that was already cold. In the summer he used the pump in the courtyard and splashed the water all over himself, but now autumn with its early morning chill was on the way. He reminded himself of what he had to do.

First he must go to the Hôtel de Gramont and give Sartine a detailed account of what had happened since his departure the previous evening. Perhaps his superior would be able to clarify how those in high places wanted the case to be handled. It was even possible that they might not want it dealt with at all. He must prepare himself for an encounter with a very angry Lieutenant General of Police.

Then he would quickly return to the Châtelet. He muttered to himself about the inconveniently long distance between the two most important police buildings, a situation that, in his opinion, slowed down work. Inspector Bourdeau would be dispatched to Grenelle to take a fresh look at the scene of the crime and to enquire about the existence of a duplicate key to the vicomte's bedroom. He wondered whether his deputy had already begun to open up the body with Sanson, the public executioner. Nicolas felt slightly uncomfortable about calling on Sanson's skills and experience, as it was not normal procedure, but he was only too aware of the routine methods and incompetence of the forensic doctors attached to the Châtelet. So he preferred to do things this way, enabling dreadful discoveries to be kept secret.

Nicolas would also have to discuss with Bourdeau the

arrangements for his meeting with the stranger in the church of the Discalced Carmelites. He was increasingly convinced that Madame de Ruissec was the author of the note.

Lastly, it would be useful to go fishing for information about the vicomte amongst his superiors and fellow officers in the French Guards.

Satisfied by this plan of campaign, he finished his toilet by brushing his hair vigorously and tying it with a velvet ribbon. He wore a wig only on very rare occasions, as he disliked the constriction of his head and the clouds of powder required.

The distant strains of a flute could be heard in the house. If at such an early hour Monsieur de Noblecourt was already eagerly 'playing the penny whistle', as he often put it, this spoke positively of his state of health: his gout could not be troubling him too much. Nicolas decided to bid him good day. These morning conversations with the former procurator were always very instructive, full of the wisdom that comes from experience and an understanding of the human soul. He went downstairs to the first floor and into a handsome room with pale green panelling set off with gold, which Monsieur de Noblecourt used as his bedroom and to receive guests.

As he entered he saw the magistrate firmly ensconced in his armchair, his back stiff, almost arched, his head leaning to the left, his eyes concentrating and half-closed. His purple skullcap was askew, his left leg resting on a damask pouf, while his slippered right foot beat time. His nimble fingers fluttered along the holes of a flute. Cyrus, standing upright on his back paws, the tip of his pink tongue sticking out, was listening to his master in fascination. Nicolas stopped to savour this delicious moment of domestic bliss. But the dog was already leaping towards him and Monsieur de Noblecourt abruptly stopped playing on seeing the young man. Nicolas, tricorn in hand, greeted him by bowing slightly.

'How pleased I am to see you looking and sounding in such good spirits so early in the morning!'

'Good morning, Nicolas. I am indeed better. The pains in my left leg have almost gone and I shall be on my feet for supper if I manage to master this tricky sonata.'

'I'll wager you composed it.'

'Oh, you rascal, you flatterer,' the procurator spluttered. 'Alas, I did not. It's a piece by Blavet, first flute of the Royal Academy of Music. Unless you have heard this virtuoso perform you can have no idea of how best to position the lips, to hold a note or move the fingers: his is a truly prodigious talent.'

He put down his instrument on a small card table in front of him.

'Enough of all this. I was indeed hoping to see you at breakfast.'

He rang and Marion, the housekeeper, suddenly appeared as if out of the shadows. It had been agreed that the elderly servant would retain the privilege of serving her master his first meal of the day. Catherine brought the heavy tray as far as the bedroom door and then handed it to Marion, who was grateful for this kindness.

'Marion, my morning feast. You have yet to see what it is, Nicolas, as I tasted it for the first time only two days ago. The same for Nicolas, please.'

His triple chin wobbled with laughter and his eyes were screwed in wicked delight.

'Monsieur, what a thing it would be if for the sake of your tendons and muscles you sentenced this strapping young man to your measly breakfast!'

'What do you mean, "measly breakfast"? Show a little more respect for a diet that Fagon drew up for the great king who was our sovereign's grandfather.'

Marion went out, only to reappear immediately with a large tray tinkling with silverware and china. She set down in front of her master a dish of cooked prunes and a cup of amber-coloured liquid. Nicolas was allowed his customary whipped chocolate, soft bread rolls from the bakery on the ground floor and a jam pot brimming with a bright red jelly. Monsieur de Noblecourt stirred in his armchair and carefully placed his left foot on the floor, letting out a few groans as he did so. His large, ruddy nose seemed to quiver as the pleasant aroma of the exotic beverage wafted towards him.

'Might it not be right . . . given the improved state of my legs – to allow me, my dear Marion, some respite from sage and fruit compote?'

Marion grumbled loudly.

'All right, very well,' sighed Monsieur de Noblecourt. 'There's no point in making a scene about it. My arguments are of little weight in this domestic court of law. I see that I am straying from the regulations and that no one will agree with me. I submit, I give in, I surrender my weapons.'

The servant also sighed and, with a mischievous smile to Nicolas, disappeared as fast as her elderly legs would allow.

Monsieur de Noblecourt composed himself once more and contemplated the young man.

'Either I am very much mistaken, Nicolas, or there's something new afoot. You look as pleased with yourself as a pointer about to go off with the hunt. First, Monsieur, you came home very late. Not that I am spying on you but with my insomnia I heard the carriage entrance slam.'

Nicolas looked mortified.

'Secondly, as performances at the Opéra do not end so late I assume that one of those pretty creatures who display their charms at the very back of the stage set became an object of detailed study or that you were detained by some unexpected police matter.'

'You know how great my respect is for you,' said Nicolas. 'I have always admired in you, Monsieur, a wisdom matched by your sensitivity . . .'

'Do get to the point. I am burning with curiosity and desperate to know all your news.'

Nicolas launched into a detailed account of the events of that night, which his host listened to, eyes closed, arms folded across his paunch, with a blissful smile on his lips. He remained silent after the account was finished and Nicolas thought he was dozing. But that was to underestimate Monsieur de Noblecourt. Neither the sage nor the story had sent him to sleep; he was meditating. Nicolas had had many opportunities to observe how the former procurator's conclusions were always unusual and revealed an unexpected and sometimes surprising way of seeing the world. He opened his eyes.

'At this point being honoured does not mean a great deal, as it is not the same as being honourable.'

This cryptic comment was followed by the lengthy tasting of a few prunes.

'My dear boy, you are confronted with the worst sort of courtier, a breed that shamelessly combines false piety and ambition, apparently proud figures who grovel before the powerful. Remove their masks and they disintegrate.'

As he spoke these weighty words, Monsieur de Noblecourt was slyly moving his spoon towards the jam pot. Cyrus leapt on to his master's lap, bringing the manoeuvre to a sudden end.

'The Comte de Ruissec is not the figure you describe, an elderly nobleman steadfast in his convictions and his obsession with honour. I have often heard him talked about in society. He comes from a Huguenot family but he renounced that faith at a young age and is careful never to mention his origins. In the army he showed great bravery. But who does not? That sort of man knows no fear.'

'One can know fear and overcome it,' the young man interjected. 'For my part I have often been afraid.'

'How touching, Nicolas. Long may God preserve this frankness of yours – such an endearing quality! As I was saying, Monsieur de Ruissec had the reputation of being a fine soldier, but hard and cruel to his men. His career was blighted by rumours of looting and he never reached the high rank for which he seemed destined. He was said to be in league with army commissaries and tax collectors. The profits supposedly supplemented his income. He left the army, sold his estate in the Languedoc and the family chateau. "The walls of towns are built from the ruins of country homes." He settled in Paris, first in the Place Royale, then quite recently in Grenelle, where he bought the mansion of a bankrupt farmer of taxes in rather murky circumstances. Today people say he is immersed in the world of finance and speculation, where his insignia impress people. Alongside these secret activities he leads what is on the surface a perfectly well-ordered life. He is a supporter of the pious party, introduced to it by his wife, who is in attendance to the King's daughters. He has obtained a position in Madame Adélaïde's household. What better cover could there be? Thanks to that he has had access to the Dauphin who, going on appearances, has taken him into his confidence and allowed him into his inner circle.'

'What does he expect from him?'

'A good question. All those who harbour a grievance against the Court support the heir to the throne. Thus, unwillingly and even unwittingly, the Dauphin now finds himself at the head of a group of malcontents. The King, seeing his son surrounded by religious devotees, sincere or otherwise, who constantly criticise the sovereign's conduct and condemn his favourite, has gradually become estranged from his son and treats him coldly. Madame de Pompadour considers him her enemy. You have met His Majesty, Nicolas. He is entering old age a tired man. No one can predict the future but everyone is already planning for it. As for Madame Adélaïde, she is good-natured but light-headed. It is hard to tell whether she prefers the lure of piety or the pleasure of hunting deer with her hounds. Nothing is denied to someone who is an expert huntsman. This is also one of the Comte de Ruissec's assets. As for his sons . . .'

'His sons?'

'What, didn't you know that the suicide victim had a younger brother? This is news to you, then. The Vidame[1] de Ruissec was always intended for the Church without his father ever consulting him as to his own wishes or his religious vocation. After finishing his studies he was relentlessly harassed and soon had no choice than to enter the nearest seminary to escape his father's obsessions. Nothing is decided. He is still only a candidate for the ministry and has not yet been fully ordained. He is charming and beguiling, and in all he has said and done he has always made clear his aversion for the priesthood, which is being forced upon him. And, dammit, I can quite understand him! He's said to have very loose morals but he probably overdoes it deliberately. They say he is dissolute, thoughtless and unprincipled, and indulges in acts of violence and behaviour that are as inimical to his family honour as to the mere decency of a man of the cloth.'

'Is there any proof of this?'

'Nothing definite. There is a lot of talk in the salons about this young coxcomb who is an ideal subject for rumour and tittle-tattle. People claim to have seen him in many an alleyway . . . But the question is: is he just a hothead or truly depraved? His brother, compared to him, seemed dull. He was said to gamble a great deal but *sub rosa*. He was supposed to be engaged but I don't know to whom. That's a mystery even to the salons. As for their mother, she is, so they say, a discreet and retiring person, overshadowed by her husband and deeply pious. That, my dear Nicolas, is the modest contribution that a gout-ridden man confined to his armchair can make to the early stages of your investigation.'

He wrapped himself in his floral-patterned chintz dressing

gown and took a melancholy look out of the window at Rue Montmartre, hearing the roar of the city below.

'Men of my age are not particularly fond of autumn, and sage tea is not a very great remedy.'

'Come, come, if your condition improves you will be entitled to a splendid glass of Irancy. In any case, you are like Persephone: you reappear even more radiant in the springtime.'

Monsieur de Noblecourt smiled. 'Probably, but before that I must cross the kingdom of Hades, the god of the dead. "I shall see the Styx and greet the Eumenides."'

'But I know another version, in which Persephone, beloved of Zeus, gives birth to Dionysus, the god of wine and pleasure. I can just imagine you crowned with vine leaves and surrounded by cupids playing the pipes!'

'Oh, you devil! You're a clever fellow who wants to cure a hypochondriac! The Jesuits of Vannes may congratulate themselves on the education they gave you. Besides, if things carry on at this rate there will be little else left for them to do. Well, you've managed to cheer me up.'

Nicolas was pleased to have brought a smile to his old friend's face and to have lifted the momentary gloom darkening his sunny temperament.

'One last word, Nicolas. You know how accurate my presentiments are. Be careful where you tread. These pious malcontents are the worst kind. Take precautions, reinforce your security and do not act alone as you are only too inclined to do. Cyrus and I are very fond of you.'

On this affectionate note Nicolas took his leave. On Rue Montmartre he looked for a sedan chair to take him back as quickly as possible to Rue Neuve-Saint-Augustin where the Hôtel de Gramont, the Lieutenant General of Police's residence, was situated.

The narrow streets were already crowded and bustling, which slowed down his vehicle and gave Nicolas time to think about what he had just learnt from Monsieur de Noblecourt. He stared unseeing at people shopping and the myriad incidents of street life.

His cheerfulness had by now given way to a vague sense of anxiety, all the more disquieting because he could not identify its cause. He eventually admitted to himself that it was in large part due to injured pride. He was annoyed that he had been too quick to judge the Comte de Ruissec, labelling and dismissing him as a mere puppet. His inexperience – Monsieur de Noblecourt would have called it innocence – amounted to naivety. The elderly nobleman, however aggressive and insulting he had been, had still impressed him; his usual sense of intuition had not worked. He had set off on the wrong tack, overawed by the comte's haughty references to the qualities and privileges of the nobility, a class familiar to him from his Breton childhood. The brigadier general, a Life Guard to Madame Adélaïde, had given him a polished demonstration of the cunning of the courtier, albeit disguised by the usual bluffness of the military man, and he had been taken in by this performance. He found it impossible to imagine that this father might harbour a grievance against his own son, if the suicide theory were disproved. But it seemed Monsieur de Ruissec was keeping plenty of secrets to himself.

Nicolas would need to find the younger brother as soon as possible, to complete the family picture. He was also annoyed with himself for failing to obtain this information and having to learn it from the former procurator. The position the comte held at Court might have very serious implications for the case. Nicolas ran the risk of offending powerful interests. He knew from bitter experience that Monsieur de Sartine was not always in a position to cast a protective shadow over him. There remained the King. After all, he thought, the sovereign was the one who had wanted him to be assigned to special investigations. Did the matter he was embarked upon belong in this category? He needed to proceed with caution but not hesitate to call upon the source of supreme authority. It was with this reassuring thought that he entered the Hôtel de Gramont.

A footman led him directly to the office of the master of the house. Often when he came to receive instructions or to give the latest report on a case, Nicolas had the opportunity to admire the large wardrobe containing Monsieur de Sartine's collection of wigs of all shapes and origins. This innocent foible was the talk of Paris, and the magistrate's every change of hairstyle was an eagerly awaited event. Even the King's ministers in foreign courts were constantly being encouraged and requested to provide him with new models. This was a sure way of being well thought of and favourably looked upon by a man who, despite his reputation for being incorruptible nevertheless enjoyed the immense privilege of a weekly audience with the King, and could ruin a reputation and destroy a career with one word.

When Nicolas entered the room, Sartine was not alone. A glance was enough to tell him to stay back and listen closely.

Nicolas observed the scene. Standing behind his desk, the Lieutenant General of Police was thoughtfully examining several wickerwork heads of dummies, covered with wigs. Nicolas assumed he had been interrupted during his morning selection procedure. Sartine looked at once deferential and exasperated. A stocky, pot-bellied man, dressed in a russet velvet coat, sat in an armchair, talking away in a loud voice that suited the size of his German-style wig. His French, though perfect, was marked by a strong foreign accent, which Nicolas assumed to be Teutonic. On his left hand he wore a ring with a large diamond that sparkled each time he emphasised his words with an imperious wave of his arm. Nicolas listened carefully.

Monsieur de Sartine sighed.

'Your Excellency, may I present Commissioner Nicolas Le Floch, whom I intend to put in charge of the business to which I owe the honour of your visit.'

The man barely turned, gave the young man an angry glance and immediately resumed speaking.

'I shall therefore have to repeat myself . . . What happened to me is most distressing and I want you to understand how regrettable it is for me to have to inform you of an incident I did everything possible to prevent. Yesterday evening between six and seven o'clock I was returning from Versailles when my coach was stopped by some minor officials at the Porte de la Conférence. One of them came up to the door to tell me that he knew my carriage was full of smuggled goods. You can imagine my surprise. I said to the man – a police officer, I believe – that all he had to do was to follow me and that I would have the carriage searched in his presence and if any smuggled goods were indeed found he could simply confiscate them. So he accompanied my coach and it was then, during the journey, that I made the decision, first to write to Monsieur de Choiseul about the treatment meted out to the Minister of the Elector of Bavaria in Paris, and secondly to seek an audience with you, Monsieur, to make you aware of what happened to me and to request the imprisonment of any of my men who might be guilty, in order to force them to reveal the provenance of the smuggled goods.'

The Lieutenant General was shaking his head whilst simultaneously raising and lowering it in the manner of a horse trying to rid itself of a bridle.

'And what was in fact the truth about such an unlikely and insulting assumption?'

'After returning to my residence I left the police officer to his search. My valet, who had accompanied me from Versailles and had questioned my coachman, assured me that the latter had admitted to being the sole guilty party. The officer in question asked to see me and informed me that my coach was full of tobacco and that the said coachman accused the papal nuncio's postilion of having passed it on to him. It proved impossible to get any other information out of him. In the meantime my coachman had fled. As for the nuncio, whom I immediately went to see, he categorically refused to hand over his postilion.'

Nicolas noted that his superior was in the process of moving objects sideways on his desk, like a chess player deciding to castle in anticipation of an attacking move by his opponent. This was undoubtedly a sign of his growing irritation.

'So what exactly can I do for Your Excellency?'

The minister, aware of Sartine's little game, continued, in a calmer voice: 'This is the present state of affairs, the tedious details of which I would have preferred to spare you. But I felt I had no choice. If ever anyone deserved to avoid such unpleasantness I am that person because of the care I have taken to order my men never to let me enter my carriage without their first having checked it. I insist, Monsieur, that you seek out and arrest my coachman. It is most unfair that I should find myself somehow compromised and exposed to spiteful talk because of the action of such riffraff. I beg you, Monsieur, to pursue this as a matter of urgency. If Monsieur de Choiseul believes that I am entitled to some form of redress, I like to think that he will kindly offer it.'

'Ambassador, I can do no better than to request Your Excellency to enable Monsieur Le Floch, here present, to have access to your staff. He will act on my behalf and will be answerable to me alone. I am only too aware of the concern this incident has caused you and will do all in my power to solve it. I can also assure you that we certainly do not suspect any foreign minister of playing the least part in this act of smuggling. The necessary measures will be taken to find your coachman and to discover the true instigators in this damnable business.'

There followed a series of carefully executed movements, forwards and backwards, half bows and courteous whisperings. Monsieur de Sartine accompanied his guest back to the steps of the Hôtel de Gramont and returned, looking quite red in the face.

'Damn that confounded bore! What a start to my morning: first my barber cuts me, then my tongue gets burnt on hot chocolate and now I have Baron Van Eyck pestering me.' He was unwinding the curls of a frizzled wig. 'And to crown it all the weather turns damp and ruins my wigs.'

There was a tap at the door.

'What next?'

A footman entered and handed him an envelope. Having examined the seal, he broke it, read the message and then repeated it out loud to Nicolas.

'What did I say? Listen: "Versailles, 24 October 1761. You will soon be informed, Monsieur, of an incident that befell Count Van Eyck on his return yesterday from Versailles. The King desires you to pursue this matter as swiftly as possible in order to discover who was responsible and for you to keep me fully apprised of your progress." Signed: "Choiseul". All this fuss, as if we had gone and spoilt the King's supper with such a trivial affair.'

Nicolas could already imagine what would happen next. He tried to parry the blow.

'Monsieur de Noblecourt, who is very knowledgeable on the ways of society, told me this morning . . .'

But Monsieur de Sartine was not listening. He was feverishly flicking through the pages of a leather-bound volume embossed with his armorial bearings, the famous 'sardines' that were a testimony to his ironic attitude towards his origins and his contempt for Parisian sneerers. He found what he was looking for.

'He's not a count; Choiseul was flattering him, as I might have guessed. "Baron Van Eyck, special envoy of the Elector of Bavaria and of the Cardinal of Bavaria and Prince-Bishop of Liège." Hmm . . . he lives at the Hôtel de Beauvais on Rue Saint-Antoine. The *Almanach Royal* is irreplaceable. Nicolas, you are going to solve this case for me and immediately find a way to placate Monsieur de Choiseul, satisfy the baron and put an end to all this fuss about a few packets of poor-quality tobacco. Good heavens, zealousness can sometimes do more harm than good!'

'May I point out, Monsieur, that there is another inquiry that requires further urgent investigation and—'

'And nothing, Monsieur. I want you to go to Rue Saint-Antoine: the matter in question can wait.'

Sartine suddenly looked down at the frizzled wig and stared in dismay at its ruined curls. It only remained for Nicolas to take his leave and go.

He went to the stables to choose a mount. The time was long past when his superior's strictures limited him to the use of a mule or donkey. Now the finest horses were always at his disposal, a sign of how far he had risen.

He was greeted by joyful neighing. A large chestnut mare was pawing the ground and tossing its long head in its stall as it looked towards him. He went up to it and stroked the warm silkiness around its nostrils; he felt it straining with impatience to stretch its legs. Its whole body rippled, like water gently stirred by the wind. A stable lad saddled the animal, and after a few prancing steps on the cobbled courtyard it calmed down but the pricking of its ears showed its still frisky mood. Nicolas dreamt of open spaces and of galloping away at full tilt, a fantasy that would never come about in this built-up city.

Once in the saddle, Nicolas let his mind wander in the golden glow of the autumn morning. A light mist veiled the prospect: large patches of dappled light crisscrossed the view, casting triangular shadows over the façades facing the sun. More trails of dust were thrown up from the ground in columns, then scattered and disappeared. He reached the banks of the Seine. The river bed was obscured by thicker mist pierced in places by barges and ferries. Towards the bridges the mist grew denser, as if hemmed in and trapped under the dank arches. The houses on Pont au Change overlooked the whole scene, seemingly suspended in the air. A woman hanging out the washing at her window suddenly disappeared, swallowed up by resurgent wraiths of mist that spread out in a tree shape. Nicolas veered off towards the Great Châtelet and, after handing over his horse to a young groom, went along to the inspectors' office.

Bourdeau was smoking a pipe while he waited for him. Nicolas quickly glanced through the duty book. In addition to a few routine incidents he noted the report on the interception of the Minister of Bavaria's coach at the Porte de la Conférence. There was also the usual list of drownings, the remains of fished-out bodies caught in the nets at Saint Cloud, severed limbs and foetuses, all destined to figure in the same grisly exhibition on stone slabs in the freezing vaults of the Basse-Geôle. He was indifferent to all this: it was the daily round of life and death in Paris.

His conversation with Bourdeau was brief: a concise account of the meeting with Sartine and various instructions. The inspector did not believe their superior's apparent lack of interest in the case: nothing was more misleading than this display of detachment in the early stages of an investigation.

They considered their priorities. Bourdeau would go back to Grenelle to clear up the matter of the duplicate key. He informed Nicolas that Sanson intended to open up the Vicomte de Ruissec's body in the evening. The executioner's day was to be spent extracting confessions under torture from some counterfeiters.

As for the meeting in the Carmelite church, they decided to dispatch Rabouine. One of the most discreet and effective of police spies, he had displayed all his skill and diligence in a recent case. He would keep a watch on the surroundings of the monastery and be on the alert for any development. In this way, Nicolas would have someone nearby to come to his assistance if necessary, who could also act as a messenger when required.

He suggested to Bourdeau that they met up for lunch at half-past twelve, on Rue des Boucheries-Saint-Germain. It was a good choice, halfway between the district of Saint-Paul and the plain of Grenelle. In addition it was close to the Carmelite church where Nicolas's mysterious correspondent would be waiting for him. They were both regular customers at one of these establishments famous for good wine and hearty food. Old Madame Morel, who ran a tripe-house, would be delighted to give them a good meal. The first to arrive would wait for the other. After two hours each would be free to go about his own business again. This seemed a sensible arrangement as neither knew in advance what the morning's investigations held in store.

Having agreed this, Nicolas bid good day to old Marie, the elderly usher, for whom he felt great affection. Once back outside he found the young groom again. With the reins under his arm, he was busily rubbing the mare down, his face red from the effort of it; the animal seemed to be enjoying it and was breathing down the boy's neck. His reward was a handful of sous, which he accepted with a toothless grin.

Nicolas went back along the Seine, crossed the Place de Grève and reached the Port Saint-Paul. As on every other morning, it was a hive of activity and a colourful throng was crowding aboard the river-coaches. These large covered boats, pulled along the river banks by horses, set off at times and days arranged for the convenience of passengers and trade. Nicolas had enjoyed the privilege of taking the royal coach, which went upriver every day to Fontainebleau. He halted the horse, stood up in the stirrups and gazed at the huge collection of boats lining the bank. A few moments later he had reached the Hôtel de Beauvais, the Minister of Bavaria's residence, not far from the church of Saint-Paul. He remembered that it was in this holy place that the prisoners who died in the Bastille were buried. The turnkeys of the State fortress carried the coffins and only members of staff were allowed to be present at the services and burials.

A huge doorman, whose arrogance was presumably intended to be appropriate to his master's status, greeted him disdainfully and then came and went several times before opening the carriage entrance to allow the horseman to enter the Hôtel de Beauvais's inner courtyard. Nicolas's eye was immediately drawn to the activities of a blond young man, wearing a shirt and breeches but barefoot. With bucketfuls of water, he was washing down a muddy carriage that bore the arms of Bavaria. Nicolas was shown into an antechamber by a major-domo with a thick accent. He seemed to Nicolas to be lacking in politeness. Nicolas was becoming increasingly irritated, but fully aware that there was nothing to be gained from losing his temper, he resolved to put up with everything and remain cool and resolute. The man reluctantly told him what he already knew: that the suspect, the plenipotentiary of Bavaria's coachman, had fled and that no one knew where he might have taken refuge. As Nicolas had neither the possibility nor indeed the intention of questioning Baron Van Eyck again, he asked to speak to the footman who had accompanied the carriage on the journey to Versailles. With a look of disgust the major-domo pointed towards the man in the shirt who was at work in the courtyard. He called the man over and ordered him to answer 'the gentleman's' questions. He stayed there, wanting to hear the conversation, but was disappointed when Nicolas took the servant off in the direction of a shed.

He opened his snuffbox and handed it to the man, who, after wiping his hands, clumsily took a pinch, all the while shifting from one foot to the other. He had a big, open, ruddy face that betrayed his unease at having to deal with someone in authority. Nicolas helped himself in turn and breathed in the snuff on the back of his hand. There followed a short session of shared sneezing. Nicolas wiped his nose in one of the fine cambric squares that Marion ironed for him each day with obsessive care. The man hesitated briefly and then did the same but used his shirt, without too much embarrassment. He was gaining in confidence and feeling less self-conscious. You cannot overestimate how reassuring and friendly it is to have a good sneeze with someone, Nicolas thought to himself. One day he had raised the subject with his friend Dr Semacgus. The navy surgeon considered that this evacuant reaction was 'a useful social convention'; like playing cards or eating, it cleared the mind and removed depressive vapours and humours. The pleasure it induced boosted mutual confidence.

Whatever the case, the footman's face was now beaming and he listened with evident interest to Nicolas's cautious preliminaries. After a few diversions to sidetrack him, Nicolas questioned him about the area he came from, Normandy, and launched into a lengthy commendation of the region, especially its horses, its cows, the lushness of its pastures and the beauty of its women. Then he finally got to the point.

'Are you the driver of this coach?'

'Good Lord, no, Monsieur. I'd like to, Monsieur, but for the moment I am at the back. Yes, my word, I want to for them boots and all that braiding from head to foot.'

His eyes lit up at the impossible prospect of fiery horses, the cracking of whips and the headlong rush along lanes and streets. He pictured himself enthroned on his box, looking down at the road.

'He's bolted, curse him. But he'll be replaced by someone just as puffed up.'

'Puffed up?'

'From being sat up above the others some do think themselves cleverer than the rest. But they's still on their arses, begging your pardon, Monsieur.'

He stopped, seeming to consider these strong words, then continued, looking thoughtful.

'He were the best paid of us, and what with bringing in tobacco he could make himself a goodly sum.'

'Did you know about his trafficking?'

'We all did, but there ain't none who'd talk about it. He would have had us thrown out. It was his word against ours.'

'Would you mind giving me your account of what happened yesterday evening?'

'I can't say no to a gentleman what's so kind and has tobacco what's so nice.'

Nicolas took the hint and invited him to help himself. Several sneezes followed, along with more staining of the shirt.

'We were coming back from Versailles along the Paris highway,' the man continued. 'Guillaume, our coachman, looked ill at ease. Maybe his conscience wasn't clear, what with that tobacco. But there was also the lead mare on the right: just as we were leaving the palace she had got her foot caught by the nuncio's carriage wanting to get past. The flesh was raw. When we got to Pont de Sèvres the coachman asked the master if we could go to the river to wash the wound; the poor thing was hobbling. Then we went and got stuck in the mud. I jumped down after taking off my shoes and turning up my hose. There was muck and filth everywhere, stinking like a sewer. I ruined a nice pair of stockings.'

Nicolas was listening intently.

'It was getting dark. Near the river we come up against another vehicle. Two men were plunging a body into the water. He looked in a bad state. Guillaume asked what they were doing. They were coming back from a rout. Their friend had had too much to drink and was unconscious. He must have downed a bit to be in that sort of state, as stiff as a poker. I reckon that them coxcombs weren't up to much good. They quickly lifted the fellow back into the carriage and made off in a hell of a hurry, begging your pardon. The animal was better; the water had helped. We set off back to Paris and at the Porte de la Conférence we were stopped by the watch and they found the tobacco. I'll bet my wages that it's all that mud I was washing off the carriage when you arrived what did for us. Have you ever seen an ambassador's carriage what got muddied like that between

Versailles and Paris? The excise men were bound to jump at the chance.'

'All this is very clear,' said Nicolas. 'You have recounted it well.'

The man felt flattered, puffed out his chest and tugged at his shirt, looking very pleased with himself.

'Did you get a good look at those people you disturbed on the river bank?'

Eyes half closed, the man seemed to be trying to gather his thoughts.

'It was getting dark.'

'Did they seem troubled or upset?'

'No. But then it being dusk I couldn't make them out properly. Cloaks and hats was all I saw.'

'What about the drunken one?'

'I saw nothing, except a wig out of place. One thing's for sure. In his state even the dark would have given him a headache.'

Nicolas was thinking. Unformed ideas raced through his mind once again. An inner mechanism had been set in motion but the fragility of its cogs and wheels meant that nothing should be done to hamper its mysterious workings. The purpose of his investigation came back to him.

'What about your coachman?'

'The police officers brought the carriage back here. No sooner had we unhitched it than Guillaume suddenly bolted. I thought it was a scalded cat, he disappeared so fast.'

Nicolas felt he had done his duty. The investigation had been carried out quickly; a report would be given to Monsieur de

Sartine, who would then give an account of it to Choiseul. Assurances would be made to the Minister of Bavaria and everything would be in order again. A minor excise incident would fade into oblivion; its cause had been simply pride and wounded feelings and, blown up out of all proportion, it would be deflated just as quickly. There was nothing more to it. The name and description of the coachman would be circulated to the commissioners and the intendants of the kingdom, and with a little luck the man would be caught and sent to the galleys. Nicolas returned to his mare, who was munching the heads off a few late-flowering roses along a whitewashed wall.

The horse took him safely via Pont Neuf and Rue Dauphine as far as the crossroads at Bussy. On Rue des Boucheries-Saint-Germain Nicolas was back on familiar ground. A quarter-past one had just struck. In the small tavern with its worn and knife-scored tables, old Madame Morel clasped him to her ample bosom. His new status as police commissioner at the Châtelet had in no way diminished her affection for him. She was pleased to have him as a regular customer and, possibly, also pleased to know someone whose help she could call upon if need be. She secretly served pork offal in violation of police regulations and of the privileges granted to pork butchers. She knew his tastes and immediately brought him a glass of cider accompanied by a plate of crackling cut into strips, which tasted crisp and crunchy. Bourdeau appeared a few moments later.

Making the choice of what to eat was something they both took very seriously. The mistress of the house reappeared and they asked her advice.

'My dear boys,' she said with the motherly familiarity that was one of her charms, 'I've been keeping two dishes for you on the corner of my stove, without knowing when you'd be coming. First a soup of lamb giblets—'

She broke off to rearrange her décolletage, which had been disturbed during her show of affection.

'I'm going to let connoisseurs like you into the secret. Into the pot I put four or five pounds of nice beef, whatever cut you like . . .'

'Chuck?' said Bourdeau.

'Chuck, if you like; it's a good part, nice and tasty. When it's been well skimmed I add some fat and the lamb giblets. You mustn't skimp on salt, nutmeg, thyme and even some lettuce hearts or handfuls of sorrel – though this herb tends to alter the colour – and of course a few white onions. After skimming and reducing it well, I give it body and flavour by adding a few egg yolks diluted in some good vinegar. And it will warm you up into the bargain, because it's starting to get pretty chilly despite that impudent sun.'

'And what's there to follow?' said Nicolas.

'For your main course, one of my very special dishes: pork faggots. I'm a good soul and I'll tell you exactly how I make them: I chop up liver with a third part of fat, herbs, a crushed clove, pepper, nutmeg, garlic and three egg yolks. I make the meat balls, which I then wrap tightly in caul. I cook them in an oven dish with a little melted fat and a dash of white wine. Add some mustard and it makes you want to lick your fingers.'

The two friends applauded and the hostess disappeared. They could now talk freely.

'Did your visit to Grenelle yield anything new?' asked Nicolas.

The inspector looked doubtful. 'I was given a very rude reception by the master of the house, as arrogant as ever, just like the picture you'd painted of him. Had it not been for Picard's help I would have come away with almost nothing. As to the key, things are not very clear. There was indeed a duplicate but it's thought to have been lost during the work carried out after the mansion was bought. So on that score nothing's definite.'

'Any other observations?'

'Not really. I did a general inspection of the vicomte's rooms again. It's impossible to enter or leave them except, as you might expect, through the door or the windows. I even checked the chimney flue, at considerable risk to my uniform.'

He rubbed the front of his doublet, which still bore some blackish marks.

'On the other hand I was struck by the titles of the books in the library closet. They were an odd assortment for a young man, works of piety and theology.'

'So that struck you as well, did it? We'll have to look into this.'

'As for the dressing room ...' Bourdeau did not finish his sentence but gave Nicolas a knowing look.

Old Madame Morel reappeared carrying a piping hot tureen. They leapt on the food and for a considerable while thought of nothing else.

'There's just one thing missing from this meal,' said Bourdeau, 'a good bottle of wine. Cider is a very poor accompaniment to these tasty morsels.'

'Our hostess isn't allowed to serve any. As she's already looked on with suspicion by the pork butchers she doesn't want to get the wine merchants' backs up. She told me in confidence that they sent in their spies to check whether her establishment was sticking to the rules.'

'I have the feeling,' said Bourdeau, 'that she keeps aside some pitchers of decent wine for certain customers.'

'Not for us. She thinks she's really got us by the throat on this one . . .'

'I know how keen you are on her pig trotter fricassée. And for the law to break the law . . .'

'It's probably my position that intimidates her, and where wine is concerned she doesn't dare take the risk.'

Bourdeau sighed. The calm look on his face, which some people were too easily taken in by, was a picture of contentment. He enjoyed these feasts with just the two of them.

'Let's get back to our case, Nicolas. What do you expect to find in the Carmelite church?'

'Everything points to the message being from the Comtesse de Ruissec. It's a well-formed female hand. Who else would it be?'

'As I left Grenelle the comte asked for his horse and carriage to go to Versailles.'

Old Madame Morel brought in a large earthenware dish containing the faggots that crackled in their golden brown caul.

'So, my boys, what do you think of this? And here's the mustard.'

'We think it's delicious as usual, and my friend Bourdeau was also saying that it deserved to be washed down with some wine . . .'

The hostess put a finger to her lips. 'The day has yet to come when I take the risk on a pitcher of wine that could attract some unwelcome attention. Not that I suspect you of wanting to get me into trouble but there's always some evil individual hanging around who'd be only too pleased to catch me out, to the great satisfaction of you know who.' She looked around her fiercely and withdrew.

'You're right, Bourdeau. She didn't take the bait. Where were we? Oh, yes, Versailles . . . That's not a good omen. Our man is going there for news and to complain to his protectors.'

'Unfortunately yes. He has the privilege of eating at Court.'

They remained silent for a time.

'Are you still convinced that we are dealing with a murder here?' Bourdeau asked eventually.

'Yes, I am. I won't say why just yet; I'll wait for Sanson's conclusions. Once we're sure, we'll have scored a point over the murderer and stolen a march on those who would like to stop justice taking its course. Then there will still be much left to do: why, who, how . . .'

The meatballs melted in their mouths; they wiped their plates clean with crusts of bread.

Having eaten his fill, Bourdeau lit his pipe. 'The body is to be opened up this evening at about nine o'clock. Don't forget your snuff . . .'

Nicolas smiled; it was an old joke between them. When a body was to be opened up in the Basse-Geôle the inspector advised Nicolas to make liberal use of snuff.

At three o'clock they went their separate ways. Nicolas decided to ride to the Carmelite monastery at walking pace. As soon as he had arrived in Paris he had fallen in love with the city and enjoyed nothing more than ambling through the streets in a daydream. He had acquired a detailed knowledge of the different districts, which had surprised Sartine on several occasions. This was very useful to him in his job. He carried a map of the great city inside his head. In a trice he could transport himself there in his imagination and find the smallest blind alley. By going through Rue du Four and Rue du Vieux-Colombier he reached Rue Cassette, went past the Benedictine nunnery of the Holy Sacrament and entered Rue de Vaugirard, on which stood the main entrance to the Carmelite monastery. The sound of his mount's hoofs echoed along the deserted street. He stopped, moved by the sight of the place where he had spent his first days in Paris. It was from there that he had set off one morning for an audience at the Châtelet with the Lieutenant General of Police.

Rabouine really was still the most discreet spy on his team. There was not the least sign of his presence. Where on earth could he be hiding? He was there, though, watching him. Nicolas could feel it. He had enough time to visit his old friend Père Grégoire. After tethering his mare, he stepped into the familiar corridors of the monastery, crossed a courtyard and entered the dispensary, where the air was thick with the smell of medicinal herbs. An elderly monk, with spectacles on his nose, was weighing herbs on a pair of scales. Nicolas rediscovered the strong odours that not so long ago had befuddled his senses. He coughed and the Carmelite turned round.

'Who dares disturb me? I specifically said that—'
'A former apprentice, a Breton from Lower Brittany.'
'Nicolas!'

He embraced the young man tightly, then made him step back to look at him.

'Clear, bold eyes, head held high, a ruddy complexion. All the humours are in harmony. I heard about your promotion. Do you remember how I prophesied it? I had a presentiment that Monsieur de Sartine would affect the course of your life. I have often thanked the Lord for it.'

They shared their memories of a still-recent past. Nicolas explained to Père Grégoire his reason for coming to the monastery and learnt from his friend that the Comtesse de Ruissec was a frequent visitor and that one of the Carmelite fathers was her confessor. The time passed quickly and, whilst enjoying this reunion, Nicolas waited for the bells of the church to strike four. He suddenly thought they were not on time. He looked at his watch and was startled to discover that the bells were already five minutes late. Père Grégoire informed him that they had stopped sounding the hour so as not to disturb the peace of one of the brothers whose life was drawing to a close.

The young man arrived at the church quite breathless, having run all the way. It was empty. He was relieved; he was first to arrive. The smell of incense and extinguished candles and the more insidious odour of decomposition reached him. He examined the four side chapels; they, too, were empty. In the crossing of the transept he admired the beautiful white marble sculpture of the Virgin modelled on a statue by Bernini, or so Père Grégoire had often told him. Above him he recognised the painting in the dome in which the prophet Elijah was depicted being taken up to heaven in a chariot of fire. In front of the altar the well into which the bodies of the dead monks were lowered was open. Nicolas knew the place; it was from here that holy water was sprinkled down into the crypt.

Nicolas was getting breathless again: incense often had this effect on him. He sat down on a prayer stool and tried to overcome the choking feeling. He was alerted by a sudden cry and the sound of hurried footsteps. They echoed through the building but it was impossible to determine where they came from. They soon faded, giving way to a silence so deep that he could hear the sputtering of candles and every creak of the woodwork. There was more shouting; then Père Grégoire appeared suddenly, red in the face and followed by three monks. He spoke incoherently.

'Something has happened . . . Oh my God, Nicolas, a terrible thing . . .'

'Calm down and tell me from the beginning.'

'When you left me . . . Someone came to inform me of the death of our prior. In the absence of the abbot I am the one who makes the arrangements. I asked for the crypt to be prepared for the funeral. Then, then . . .'

'Then what?'

'Brother Anselme went down there and discovered . . . He found . . .'

'What?'

'The Comtesse de Ruissec's body. She had fallen down the well of the dead.'

IV

OPENINGS

Around the bodies stripped of life
By violent and cruel blow,
The shifting shadows come and go.

PHILIPPE DESPORTES

Nicolas felt as if a gaping chasm had opened up in front of him; he was overcome with anxiety. How would Sartine react to this news? Nicolas could not in all truth deny that the corpses began to pile up as soon as he became involved in a case. However, he soon pulled himself together, ready to respond as a consummate professional to all the demands of the situation.

First, he needed to reassure Père Grégoire, who was choking with emotion and had turned alarmingly red. Next, he must weigh up all possibilities without coming to any hasty conclusions, having carefully examined the circumstances of the tragedy. But most importantly he had to establish whether Madame de Ruissec was dead. If this was not the case, he needed to calm the monks and make arrangements to send for help.

He shook to awareness a dazed Brother Anselme, who was absently crossing himself, and instructed him to take him down to the crypt. They had to go outside, then back in through a side entrance and down a small staircase. A dark-lantern, which was lying abandoned on the floor, served to light their way. At first Nicolas found it hard to recognise where he was, but after his eyes had adjusted to the dark he saw that he was surrounded by coffins piled one on top of the other. The air was rarefied and the flame of the lamp was guttering so perilously that he was afraid he might be left in total darkness in the middle of the sepulchre. Brother Anselme must have been having the same thought as the lantern was trembling more and more in his hand. Its light cast shifting shadows across the stone walls and revealed recesses containing the skulls of monks long deceased.

After they had taken two or three turnings, their surroundings disappeared into the shadows. The focus of their attention was now a pool of light coming straight down through the well of the dead. On the marble slab where the dead were usually placed lay a body as limp as a rag doll, showing no signs of life. Nicolas moved closer and asked the friar to give him some light, which he did, trembling wildly all over. The young man grabbed the lantern in irritation, put it down near the body and asked the friar to go to fetch help, a stretcher and a doctor.

Once alone, he carefully examined the body and the area around it. In a black satin gown – worn either in mourning for her son or in order to be inconspicuous – the Comtesse de Ruissec looked as if she had been snapped in two, facing upwards with arms outstretched. Her head, covered in a black veil held in place by a large jet comb, was at a strange and gruesome angle to the rest of her body. There was absolutely no doubt that she was dead.

Nicolas knelt down and gently lifted the veil. The elderly woman's face seemed oddly turned to the left; it was pale with traces of blood on her lips; her eyes were open. He touched the base of her neck but there was no pulse. He took out a pocket mirror and put it in front of her mouth; it did not steam up. Gently and respectfully Nicolas closed the elderly lady's eyes. He shuddered; her skin was still warm. He examined the body all over without moving it. There was no sign of any wound other than the obvious fracture to the neck.

He stood, summed up his observations and then carefully wrote them down in his little notebook. The comtesse seemed to have fallen into the well of the dead. So it must have been open. Why? Was it always open?

Given the position of the well there were two possibilities: perhaps Madame de Ruissec had failed to see the gaping hole in the semi-darkness of the sanctuary and, distracted by the prospect of her meeting, had fallen by accident. But in that case, thought Nicolas, a fall of twelve or more feet ought to have caused more fractures to the legs or injuries to the face, given that the rim of the well was low and that she would have fallen head first. Also the body should have been face down but in fact Madame de Ruissec was lying on her back, her legs unscathed. Or else she had fallen backwards but this could only have happened if she had been between the well of the dead and the chancel, or in the process of admiring the painting of the Presentation of Christ in the Temple. In that case the position of the body made sense. The fact remained that the body and especially the head should have caught on the circumference and rim of the well. He checked under the nape of the neck: there was no sign of injury.

As he straightened, his eye fell on a small square of printed paper on a cotton and pearl alms purse hanging from Madame de

Ruissec's left arm. He had not noticed it until then. He took it and held it up to the lantern. Much to his surprise he discovered that it was a ticket to a performance at the theatre of the Comédie-Italienne.

He checked the alms purse was properly shut. In fact the drawstring was tight in her clenched hand and nothing could have fallen out of the bag. He extracted it from her grasp and, trembling as always when he disturbed the personal effects of a victim, began to list its contents. He found a small silver mirror, a piece of purple velvet with some pins, a phial of spun glass containing what appeared to be perfume and more specifically *eau de la Reine de Hongrie* – he recalled detecting this smell on the note inviting him to the meeting in the Carmelite church – a small metal purse containing a few *louis d'or*, a rosary and a small leather-bound devotional work embossed with the Ruissec family arms.

The list disappointed him; there was nothing unusual for a woman of her age and status. He put everything back in the purse. The theatre ticket continued to intrigue him as it seemed out of keeping with everything else. This ticket could not have ended up in the crypt of a monastery by accident and as it was clean and intact it could not have been brought in stuck to the underside of a shoe. Given where it had been found, it could only have been placed on the body after the fall.

He heard the sound of footsteps. Nicolas tucked the ticket into his notebook. Père Grégoire, having recovered from the shock, appeared suddenly, carrying a candle. He was followed by two men and two stretcher-bearers, whom Nicolas assumed to be police officers. One of the men held out his hand; Nicolas recognised him as Monsieur de Beurquigny, the police commissioner for the district, whose offices were on Rue du Four. He was pleased to be dealing with this affable and well-respected figure. Nicolas's youth, his rapid promotion and the persistent rumour that he was Monsieur de Sartine's protégé had not endeared him to certain sections of the police force; he was very lucky to have come upon this kindly, older colleague.

Père Grégoire introduced the other man to him. He was Dr Morand, from Rue du Vieux-Colombier, who was the Carmelites' sole physician and whose name was given with an accompanying, meaningful wink and an even more telling shrug of the shoulders.

'Monsieur,' said Nicolas, 'I fear your assistance is unnecessary. The victim is dead. On the other hand I should be grateful to have your opinion on the cause of death.'

The doctor leant over the body and performed a similar examination to the one Nicolas had already carried out. He listened carefully as he turned the head from one side to the other; he observed the comtesse's neck after removing her wig; lastly he examined the well of the dead.

'Before giving you my opinion,' he said, 'could we go back up into the chapel?'

'I'll come with you,' said Nicolas. He added in a whisper: 'I, too, wanted to see if there were any traces up there.'

Dr Morand nodded. 'I see, Commissioner, that you have not wasted your time.'

They went back up into the church in silence. They learnt nothing from the well of the dead and its rim.

Morand thought long and hard. 'I make no secret of how

puzzled I am,' he said at last. 'If we go by appearances everything points to the lady dying as a result of falling into the well.'

'You used the word "appearances".'

'Indeed I did. I shall come straight to the point as I suspect you have understood the whole situation already. If the comtesse had stumbled against the rim of the well, it would have been difficult for her to fall. And had she done so she would have hit her neck in the process. You might object that the wig would have acted as a cushion but in that event it would have been dislodged. However, you have noted that it was still in place and, moreover, the victim is face up. I note that there is an unnatural freedom of movement between the head and the rest of the body and that the head makes a cracking sound when handled. There are traces of blood on the lips, the result of internal bleeding from a wound. Thus I deduce and maintain that the victim was attacked, that her neck was broken and her body thrown down the well of the dead.'

He moved towards Nicolas, and standing behind him placed his right arm over Nicolas's chest, putting his hand on the young man's left shoulder. He then grabbed Nicolas's head with his left hand and twisted it to the left.

'This is how it was done. If I press harder I can break your vertebrae although you are a healthy young man; but the comtesse was an elderly woman . . .'

A thought crossed Nicolas's mind but he kept it to himself. The doctor respected his need for silence. He must make up his mind quickly. There was a crucial decision to reach and he alone could take responsibility for it: he felt the absence of Bourdeau, whose advice would have been useful.

Once again he was dealing with a murder. Someone had been

determined to stop the comtesse talking to him. He felt somewhat sad that he had not been able to prevent this tragedy. However, he sensed that nothing could have been done to avoid it: had he been the first to arrive at the church, then Madame de Ruissec would probably never have got there. It was time for action, not for remorse, which would return soon enough during his sleepless nights. The main thing was to act quickly.

Duty required him to hand over the case to a magistrate, then have an official statement drawn up and hold a witness hearing. The terms of the royal ordinances of 1734 and 1743 flashed through his mind. Making the crime public would involve opening up the body in the Basse-Geôle. He was fully aware of the risk this would entail, given the obvious incompetence of the doctors attached to the Châtelet. Additionally, as this new case was connected to the death in Grenelle there was great potential for muddle and confusion.

I really am the special investigations officer, after all, he concluded. He simply needed to convince Dr Morand and the commissioner to treat the crime for the time being as an unfortunate accident. In this way they might avoid arousing the murderer's suspicions.

Nicolas took Dr Morand off into the crypt. The monks were praying around the body. He motioned to Commissioner de Beurquigny to join him.

'My dear colleague, I shall be blunt. The doctor's observations confirm my own. The victim did not fall by accident; she was thrown down the well after someone had deliberately broken her neck. I was due to meet her about another criminal case involving the interests of a family close to the King. Making the murder public may jeopardise the investigation into the first crime. I'm not asking you to abandon this case but to delay its disclosure. In the interests of justice, people must continue to think it was an accident. I will officially free you from all responsibility and Monsieur de Sartine will be duly informed this evening. May I rely on you?'

Commissioner de Beurquigny held out his hand and smiled. 'Monsieur, I am at your service and your word is enough for me. I understand your concern. I shall do everything in my power to ensure this temporary version is believed, that goes without saying, and I trust you on this point. But you may be unaware of the consequences of a murder taking place in a church.'

'I am indeed.'

'The place ceases to be consecrated and Mass cannot be celebrated there. Just think of the scandal.'

'My dear colleague, I greatly appreciate your understanding and what you tell me about the church confirms me in my decision.'

'Remember, I joined our organisation in 1737 and for a long time my deputy was an inspector you know well.'

'Bourdeau?'

'The very same. He has spoken of you so often and with such warmth, especially for someone as mistrustful as he is, that I feel as though I know you quite well.'

Bourdeau always proved helpful in so many ways . . .

'What about Dr Morand?'

'Leave him to me. He's a friend of mine.'

'I would like him, moreover, to draw up an official statement which all three of us will sign and that you will keep in your

possession pending further information. There's one other thing
– but I feel I am taking advantage: would you be able to have the
comtesse's body taken to her mansion in Grenelle and go there
yourself? I have good reason for not going personally. She came
to the Carmelites for confession so no questions or explanations
are needed: it was a dreadful accident.'

Trusting the word of the two magistrates, the doctor agreed to
hold his tongue; he drew up and signed the document as
requested. The body was removed and taken under escort to
Grenelle.

Nicolas went to see Père Grégoire in his dispensary. Still in a
state of shock, he was trying to calm himself with some lemon
balm liqueur, one of the monastery's specialities. Nicolas confirmed the theory of an accident. The monk was most upset,
saying that nothing similar had ever happened before. The well
had been opened in preparation for the forthcoming funeral of
one of the friars.

'Father, are there other entrances to the monastery apart from
the door on Rue Vaugirard?'

'Our wall has plenty of gaps, my poor Nicolas. Besides the
main entrance, there are doors leading to our outbuildings,
gardens, orchards and vegetable plots. In addition there are several
exits on to Rue Cassette, and finally we share a door with the
Benedictine nunnery of the Holy Sacrament. Not to mention the
one that opens on to the estates of Notre-Dame de la Consolation.
From there you can easily reach Rue du Cherche-Midi. Our
monastery is open on all sides and in any case what would we have
to protect apart from our novices' virtue … for whom this
location remains a temptation. Why are you asking me this?'

Nicolas did not reply; he was thinking.

'Who was Madame de Ruissec's confessor?'

'The prior, who has just died.'

Nicolas did not respond but left his old friend to his thoughts, surrounded by his alembics. He still needed to find out what his spy Rabouine had seen from the outside of the monastery. After retrieving his mare, who showed her impatience by snorting and neighing, he went on to Rue de Vaugirard and began to imitate a blackbird, the agreed signal, to bring the man out of his hiding-place. A carriage gateway opposite the entrance to the monastery creaked open and Rabouine emerged, wrapped in a baggy cape. He was sharp-featured but had a friendly twinkle in his eyes. He would have gone to the stake for Nicolas. He stayed in the shadows while his superior, the horse's reins around his arm, came closer then stopped, pretending to tighten the saddle-girth. The mare stood between them, hiding Rabouine from view.

'Let's have your report,' said Nicolas.

'I arrived at three o'clock. At half-past I saw you go inside. A few minutes before four—'

'Are you sure? The bells didn't ring.'

Nicolas heard the discreet sound of a repeater watch striking. He smiled.

'As I was saying, at five minutes to four a vehicle arrived and an elderly woman alighted and entered the church.'

'What about the coachman?'

'He didn't move from his box.'

'Then what?'

'The street remained empty until a monk rushed out in a panic before coming back with two men in black.'

'Thank you, Rabouine, you can stop watching now.'

He took out a silver coin from his coat pocket and threw it over the saddle. It was caught in mid-air because he did not hear it fall.

Nicolas set off at a fast trot. He needed to see Monsieur de Sartine as soon as possible and give him an account of events in order to justify his very serious decision. The main reason for bending the rules in this way was to avoid antagonising the Comte de Ruissec and his protectors. He was also aware that the comtesse was lady-in-waiting to Madame Adélaïde. Any scandal was bound to tarnish the monarchy's reputation and, in these times of war, in full view of the enemy. The more he thought about it the more convinced he was that he had taken the right decision and that his superior would approve.

Monsieur de Sartine was not on Rue Neuve-Saint-Augustin. A clerk told Nicolas in confidence that the Lieutenant General of Police had been called away to Versailles by Monsieur de Saint-Florentin, the Minister of the King's Household. He led his mount to the stables and instructed the groom to give it a double peck of oats, then he set off in the gathering dusk towards the Châtelet.

The dim, poorly lit outline of the ancient prison loomed up before him, as did the statue of the Virgin above the doorway, eroded by the elements and blackened by the city smoke. After exchanging a few words with old Marie, Nicolas went to the duty room to check the latest reports and to write a note to Monsieur de Sartine relating in detail events in the Carmelite monastery. Having crossed it out and rewritten it several times, he sealed it with the Ranreuil family arms, the only concession to pride that he allowed himself, and entrusted it to the elderly usher, asking him to have it delivered as quickly as possible; there was always a reliable young boy loitering under the archway in anticipation of some paid errand.

Nicolas decided to have a nap and, pulling his tricorn over his eyes, soon nodded off. When Bourdeau came to find him for their meeting with Sanson he saw he was still dozing and reluctantly woke him. The young man was startled to see Bourdeau.

'Nicolas, you're like a cat. You sleep with one eye open.'

'Yes, sometimes that can save one's life, my friend. But right now I was sleeping like a log.'

He gave him a detailed account of recent events. The inspector's face was tense with concentration.

'What a strange theatre ticket and, knowing you, I assume . . .'

'That tomorrow I'll be paying a visit to the Comédie-Italienne, as the crypts of monasteries do not tend to issue these sorts of things spontaneously.'

Once again Nicolas was lost in silent thought; this theatre business evoked a vague memory. But he must stop thinking about that for now. If it was going to come in useful, something would spark off the recollection later on.

They were now deep inside the cellars of the ancient fortress. The torture chamber next to the court record office was where bodies were usually opened up. Every time he approached this place of suffering, Nicolas felt a deep sadness well up within him, even though he had by now managed to overcome his feelings of revulsion once and for all, strong in the knowledge that his job required him to set aside any sense of compassion.

Bourdeau took out his pipe, then thrust his hand into his coat and pulled out a snuffbox. Despite the coolness of the room and the salting down of the corpses, nature was still at work, and the insidious odour of decomposition, combined with the reek of sweat and blood from the torture victims, produced a more powerful smell than the damp coming from the walls covered in mould and saltpetre.

They soon emerged into the examination room lit by torches fastened to rings on the wall on which the shifting shadows of two men were outlined. The younger one, wearing the inevitable puce-coloured coat, had on a white wig, and was pointing at something that the other, older and bulkier, man was examining, bent over, hands on knees. The object of their attention lay on a large table. These men were Charles Henri Sanson, the public executioner, and Dr Semacgus. The latter, a navy surgeon and seasoned traveller, was a friend of Nicolas's, to whom he owed a special debt for having rescued him from a very difficult situation. Nicolas had established the surgeon's innocence in a murder case when all the evidence was against him: his reluctance to talk, his carelessness and even his liking for the fairer sex.

'Here,' said Nicolas, 'we have experience backed up by medical knowledge.'

It was traditional for the tone of these encounters with death to be detached and ironic. It created the necessary distance by hardening the outer shell of those who were witness to such cruel scenes. The two men turned. Sanson's youthful face, with its gentle expression, broke into a smile as he saw Nicolas. He waited for the commissioner to hold out his hand before shaking it. Normally one did not shake hands with the executioner but the warmth of feeling between them from their first meeting made this gesture acceptable. Dr Semacgus's full and florid face broke into a broad smile on seeing his friend.

'Doctor,' Nicolas resumed, 'I am destined to always find you roaming the underground passages of the Châtelet.'

'Monsieur Nicolas,' Sanson interjected, 'I am the one who asked our friend for assistance in a case that I will readily admit certainly taxes my modest abilities.'

'Nicolas,' said Semacgus, 'surely you aren't going to pretend that you haven't noticed the extraordinary nature of this subject?'

There was a mischievous and contented sparkle in his brown eyes. He took a clay pipe out of his pocket and asked Bourdeau for some tobacco.

'You might even say it's a very weighty subject,' he added, bursting into laughter.

Seeing the bewildered expressions on Nicolas and Bourdeau's faces, Sanson, after a long look at the fingernails of his left hand, took it upon himself to explain the doctor's words.

'What Dr Semacgus wants you to understand,' he began, 'is that the corpse we have before us has a specific density that bears no relation to a member of the human species. We both lifted up the remains, or rather we tried to do so. We succeeded only after a huge effort, beyond anything we are used to when handling bodies. My assistants had also mentioned it to me.'

Sanson tugged at the lapels of his coat, as if wanting to hide his black waistcoat with its jet buttons, and stepped back a pace into the shadows.

'What is your explanation for this phenomenon?' asked Nicolas. 'I did not notice that the body was wearing a breastplate or that his clothes were weighted down with anything.'

Sanson moved forward a pace and nodded in the direction of Semacgus, who was pulling on his pipe.

'Have you examined the dead man's face, Nicolas?'

'I have never seen such a grisly sight. It looked like one of those shrunken heads I saw depicted in a work concerning the savages of the Western Indies written by a Jesuit father; I read it one day in Monsieur de Sartine's library while waiting in his antechamber.'

'Our friend Nicolas even manages to curry favour with the disciples of Loyola while he's waiting for an audience,' joked Semacgus. 'The monstrous appearance struck us too.'

He disappeared into the shadows and reappeared holding a lancet that he delicately inserted into the corpse's mouth. They were all leaning over the body and all distinctly heard the instrument make a metallic, clinking sound. Semacgus pulled out the lancet, then rummaged in his coat pocket for a pair of small tweezers that in turn he introduced into the corpse's mouth. The observers shuddered as they heard the teeth gnashing on metal. The doctor persisted in his task for some time. When he removed the tweezers he had succeeded in collecting a sample of a grey-black substance that he raised above his head.

'Heavy and ductile! Lead, gentlemen. Lead.'

With his other hand he struck the dead man's chest.

'This man has a lead stomach. He was killed, tortured, slaughtered even . . . He was made to swallow molten lead, which burnt up his insides, made his head shrink and destroyed his entrails.'

There was a heavy silence, which Nicolas eventually broke, his voice trembling slightly.

'What about the bullet,' he asked, 'and the pistol shot?'

Like a well-practised dancer Semacgus stepped back a pace and nodded to Sanson to come forward and explain.

'There is indeed the impact of a firearm,' he said. 'The doctor and I have probed the wound. The bullet is lodged in the vertebrae, but it was not the cause of death for the reasons that have been outlined.'

'But still . . .' said Nicolas.

'It's up to you to tell us what you observed.'

Nicolas took out his notebook, turned over a few pages and began to read aloud: '"Face shrunken, convulsed, horrifying. Shot point-blank. Muslin fabric of tie and shirt burnt. Dark wound. Aperture as wide as bullet half closed on skin. A little congealed blood visible, but mainly bruising."'

Semacgus applauded.

'Excellent. I'm taking you on as my assistant. What a keen eye. Master Sanson, what are your conclusions?'

The executioner looked at his left hand once more and after this inspection pronounced his verdict.

'Dear Monsieur Nicolas, I share my colleague's – I mean Dr Semacgus's – feelings. He is the expert, and has written authoritative works on the subject.'

He blushed. Nicolas understood his embarrassment and felt sorry for him. Sanson's sole colleagues were the public executioners of the other great cities of the kingdom, all entrusted with the same gruesome task and sentenced to the same solitude . . .

'Such perceptive comments make our task easy,' Sanson

continued. 'It is almost impossible to confuse wounds inflicted shortly before death with those caused several hours after.' He leant over the body once more. 'Look at this retraction of the wound and how the aperture to the skin is closing up. You noticed, I believe, the signs of bruising, which go to show that the bullet wound was inflicted shortly after death.'

'Could you specify this time lapse?'

'A few hours, six at most. I should add what we already know, that the wound cannot have been the result of suicide. A shot was fired at point-blank range into a body that had choked from absorbing molten lead. I have seen many things in my life and have inflicted terrible torture in the service of the King, but this is beyond me . . .'

He paused, white-faced, and mopped his brow. Nicolas thought of the terrible account Charles Henri Sanson had given him of the ordeal of Damiens, the regicide, when they first met. The man was a mystery with his gentleness and sensitivity. Bourdeau seemed impatient for Nicolas to intervene.

'I can see that our friend Bourdeau is urging me to tell you what I really think, which is probably what he thinks too. I'm going to give you the full story.'

He glanced round, though no one else could hear them in the dark entrails of the Great Châtelet, and began: 'Once I had entered the vicomte's bedroom and examined the body I immediately noted, apart from the horribly disfigured face, that the shot had struck the base of the neck on the *left* side. At first I did not attach too much importance to this. Next I discovered something written in capital letters – I emphasise in *capital* letters. The position of the piece of paper, that of the hurricane lamp and of the quill to the left of the note did not in the first instance surprise me. Things became more complicated when I visited the dressing room. I stood for some time in front of an elegant dressing case of silver gilt and mother-of-pearl. Something intrigued me and I let my mind wander. I thought that it was only the beauty of the object that had made an impression on me . . .'

'Our sleuthhound had caught the scent,' said Semacgus.

'It's my hunter instinct and the result of following the pack. In short, after a moment it was the brushes and razors that gave me the answer and then I understood. I'm sure that Bourdeau will be able to tell you the rest.'

Nicolas wanted to give the inspector the pleasure of doing this. He knew he could count on his loyalty. An old police hand, his deputy had accepted the unbelievable rise of a young man twenty years his junior without any apparent reservations and with good humour. He had taught him the job, revealing its hidden workings, and had even saved his life on one famous occasion. He felt not only fondness but also respect for him. What meant little to Nicolas would give Bourdeau a certain satisfaction; it was a way to build the self-esteem of a man convinced of his own worth.

'What the commissioner wants you to understand,' said Bourdeau gravely, 'is that brushes and razors are usually placed on the side most convenient to the hand that uses them, in particular when they are laid out for daily use by a manservant. Well, the dressing case in question – brushes and razors – was actually laid out for the right hand. But, Monsieur, please, I beg you, finish your excellent demonstration.'

'It would appear, gentlemen, that the vicomte really was killed in the way that we have established. His body was returned to his parents' mansion in circumstances of which we are not yet aware, then an unknown person fired a shot into the body to make it look like suicide but the shot was to the *left*. That person then wrote a false confession, without even having to imitate the vicomte's writing because he used capital letters. There, too, he made mistakes: the quill to the left, the hurricane lamp to the right. The Vicomte de Ruissec was right-handed. He could not have committed suicide by shooting himself on the left.'

'I have checked this point with Picard in Grenelle,' said Bourdeau. 'He confirmed that the position of the dressing case was indeed intended for someone right-handed.'

'This seems quite conclusive. The corpse has nothing more to teach us, gentlemen. I think it inappropriate to carry out any further exploration of the body.'

'Nevertheless,' said Semacgus, 'it looks as if your man was plunged into water. It cannot have been rain. I discovered some traces of algae – you know botany is one of my hobbies.'

'Seawater?' said Nicolas, whose Breton sea-going instincts resurfaced at the most unexpected moments.

'Certainly not, Monsieur Le Floch. Freshwater. From a pond or a river. I'm giving you the information for what it's worth. Use it as you wish.'

Nicolas remembered that he had been struck by the unusual smell on the vicomte's clothes.

'Of course!' said Bourdeau, 'the body was weighted so that it would remain at the bottom. But they must have changed their minds or been forced to change their plans.'

'There are easier ways of disposing of a body,' Semacgus remarked.

'Are there?' said Bourdeau. 'Immersing a body in water, if it is guaranteed to sink, must remain the surest method. Imagine dropping the body into the Seine without weighting it: it would most likely end up caught in those nets at Saint Cloud, which are stretched across the river to retrieve victims of drowning.'

Nicolas was thinking. The facts were coming together. The soaking body that the Minister of Bavaria's men had seen by the river . . . He was just about to put his thoughts into words when a noise like a clap of thunder resounded. The three men looked at each another in surprise. Sanson merged back into the walls cluttered with instruments of torture. The sound of hurried footsteps echoed through the vaults of the ancient palace. As the noise drew nearer a bright light could be seen. Then a group of men burst into the Basse-Geôle, some carrying torches, others a coffin on a stretcher.

The person leading the procession and wearing a magistrate's gown turned to Nicolas and said: 'Monsieur, you are, I assume, one of the doctors on duty.'

'No, Monsieur, I am Nicolas Le Floch, commissioner of police at the Châtelet, in charge of a criminal investigation.'

The man bowed.

'Is the opening-up of the Vicomte Lionel de Ruissec, lieutenant in His Majesty's French Guards, now complete?'

'No,' said Nicolas icily, 'I was simply making some preliminary observations. Look, Monsieur, at this frightening sight.'

The man examined the face of the corpse, even more terrifying in the light of the torches, and recoiled in horror.

'So it has not begun. That is most fortunate. I have to inform you of the decision taken in the King's name by Monsieur the

111

Comte de Saint-Florentin, Minister of the King's Household, with responsibility for the City and Generality of Paris. It requires the provost to suspend all investigations and inquiries and any opening-up of the body of the aforesaid person, and to restore it to the representatives of his family. I assume, Monsieur, that you will not countenance disobeying the King's orders.'

Nicolas bowed. 'Certainly not, Monsieur. Please proceed. You will see for yourself that the body is, dare I say it, intact.'

The men put the stretcher carrying the coffin down on the ground. They removed the lid, parted the shroud that had been placed inside, then with no attempt to disguise their revulsion at the horrific sight, lifted the body with great difficulty. Nicolas heard the bearer nearest to him swear and mumble: 'This fellow must have been guzzling stones.'

'Monsieur,' continued Nicolas, 'would you be so kind as to inform me what has led to this decision?'

'I see no objection to that, Monsieur. Monsieur the Duc de Biron, a colonel in the French Guards, was alerted by the family and intervened with the minister himself. Both of us belong to the same administration, so I can tell you in confidence that Monsieur de Ruissec has come forward with new information. It turns out that it was in fact an accident that occurred during the cleaning of a weapon. Anyone can make a mistake.'

Nicolas fought to restrain himself. Bourdeau looked at him anxiously, ready to hold him back. The young man had momentarily felt tempted to grab the magistrate by the arm and thrust his head into the coffin in order to bring him face to face with the brutal truth. The procession reformed and, after bowing again, disappeared from sight as its sound faded into the distance.

Semacgus's deep voice broke the silence. 'A judge's duty is to administer justice; but his job is to defer it. Some judges both know their duty and do their job!'

As Nicolas remained silent, Bourdeau responded: 'If the dead man had been a member of the bourgeoisie, it would all have been over and done with and the law obeyed. One day justice will have to be the same for all, whoever they may be.'

'My friends,' said Nicolas, 'I'm sorry we cannot continue, but fortunately the essential work had already been done thanks to you, and I have found out what I wanted to know.'

'You're not going to continue your investigation, are you?' said Semacgus. 'That would be like sticking your head in the lion's mouth.'

'I know, I'm not doing what my job requires: I'm just being stubborn. I've received no new instructions from Monsieur de Sartine, and this pantomime is not going to divert me from my task. I shall find out who is guilty of this heinous crime.'

'So God be with you! And, Bourdeau, my friend, I'm leaving him in your care. Look after him.'

They walked back up to the entrance arch. Semacgus made a vague suggestion about restoring their spirits with something to eat and drink. Sanson was the first to decline politely, before bidding them farewell and disappearing into the night. Nicolas was concerned for the doctor, who had to return to his house in Vaugirard. He might not be allowed through by the watch. But he quickly realised that the sprightly surgeon had no such intention and must have some amorous rendezvous planned in town. The doctor wished him good night and urged him to be careful. Then he too disappeared into the shadows, alone and in a hurry.

*

Nicolas stayed and talked with Bourdeau for some time. He assured him that he would see the investigation through to the end unless the Lieutenant General of Police categorically ordered him to abandon it. Until such time, he considered that he had a free hand and he would not veer from his chosen course even if he had to change tack to succeed. Like a ship that is making headway, he was set and nothing would stop him.

The inspector, who saw no objection to this, remarked that if it was now certain that the vicomte had been murdered, the field of investigation had to be widened because the motives for such an appalling act were still just as unclear, and in any case the mystery of the body brought back into a locked room was as yet unresolved. Added to this now was the comtesse's death.

When presented with a complicated knot, Nicolas thought that unless one happened to be Alexander the Great, the solution was to pick out the loosest thread to try to untangle the whole thing. That was how they would proceed. He would go fishing for clues at the Comédie-Italienne, casually, without drawing attention to himself, and using whatever pretext first came to mind. After all, the theatres were within the Lieutenant General of Police's jurisdiction. He would ferret around and make people talk. It was not by accident that the theatre ticket had happened to be on the Comtesse de Ruissec's person. This elderly and pious woman, a member of the Household of the King's eldest daughter, might accompany a princess to the Opéra by royal command but would never have lowered herself to the entertainment provided at the Comédie-Italienne.

Lastly Nicolas told Bourdeau where he suspected the vicomte's body had been put in the water. It was essential that they track down the Minister of Bavaria's runaway coachman. And most importantly he needed to avoid meeting with Sartine. His superior's intelligence service was sufficiently well organised to be able to find him if he was needed and until then he would make the best use of the time pending a possible suspension of the ongoing investigation.

As for Bourdeau, he had been given a particularly delicate mission at the Hôtel de Ruissec. He was to go there once more on the innocent pretext of removing the seals from the vicomte's rooms. Nicolas was sure that this would already have been done, but it was just a way of gaining access. He trusted the inspector to carry out a discreet search. He had sufficient experience and cunning to cope with the inevitable difficulties and objections he would encounter, as they presented themselves. Nicolas wanted him to draw up a complete list of the books in the vicomte's library.

He offered to accompany Bourdeau home. The inspector refused, urging him to take an immediate and well-earned rest. He never mixed professional matters and family life. And yet Nicolas remembered that one day, when he had been thrown out on to the street, Bourdeau had offered to take him in without any hesitation. They went their separate ways. Everyone was essentially alone, thought Nicolas; in this world it was what people most had in common. Everyone experienced the effects and sorrows of that solitude. For Sanson it was the horror of his work, for Semacgus his unbridled taste for pleasure-seeking, for Bourdeau the perpetually open wound of his father's unjust death. As for himself, he did not want to dwell on the subject too much.

These bitter-sweet thoughts occupied his mind until he reached Rue Montmartre. In the Noblecourt residence everyone seemed to be asleep, including Cyrus. Only Catherine had stayed up and was preparing a rabbit pâté. She wanted him to have supper but the events of the evening had upset him and put him off his food. He listened for a moment to the cook exhorting him never to use a knife to cut a rabbit. The right way was to slice the flesh through to the bone and then twist the bone to break it in order to avoid the danger of splinters. She illustrated what she meant by snapping off the head.

Nicolas hurried up to his bedroom, exhausted by the day's emotions but then tossed and turned for a long while before finally falling asleep.

V

COMMEDIA DELL'ARTE

This is the place of sweet delight,

Of joyfulness and fancies bright.

Here too doth reign the goddess Love,

With all her suite in heav'n above,

Whence cast they spells from up on high

To make poor mortals sob and sigh.

RÉMI BELLEAU

Thursday 25 October 1761

Nicolas hacked away at the mob with his sword. He cut and thrust, yelling at his assailants, who in turn began to scream. They were done for and fell on top of each other, either wounded or dead; those who did escape fled up the tower's narrow staircase. He felt the same satisfaction as he did felling a tree, but then suddenly found himself sliding down into a bottomless pit, ending up in a dazed state on the edge of a pool, whose surface stirred with slow, strange movements. On an island covered with seaweed, a young man wearing a puce coat and an iron mask was stacking bundles of wood around a stake. An elderly woman with the head of a rabbit, which had been half severed from her body, held out her arms to Nicolas. He wanted to wade into the water. He had barely dipped his toe in when he began to fall again and found himself at the foot of his bed.

He was astonished to see that dawn had long since broken and that sunlight was slanting into his bedroom. His watch showed it was past nine o'clock. The jug of hot water outside his door was now cold. He decided to go to wash himself quickly at the court-yard fountain. The temperature was still mild in the sunshine.

Having washed and dressed, he went into the pantry. Marion had been worrying about his unusual lateness and scolded him: how could he soak himself in cold water? He would catch his death! She served him his chocolate and soft bread rolls. Monsieur de Noblecourt had left early in the morning with Poitevin. He had to attend the meeting of the Saint-Eustache parish council, for despite being a long-standing disciple of Voltaire he held the august position of churchwarden. She grumbled that a man of his age should go out so early in the morning, whilst also recognising that such an expedition proved his attack of gout was over.

Nicolas asked after Catherine. She had already gone off to the fish market to have her pick of the freshly arrived catch, and would be wading around the newly opened barrels of seawater looking for a choice specimen. The previous evening she had promised her master she would make *sole à la Villeroy*. With Marion's help she intended to celebrate the procurator's convalescence. Apart from fish the recipe required Parmesan cheese, mussels and prawns. Marion hoped that Nicolas would be able to attend the evening meal because he always finished everything on his plate, thereby limiting her master's greediness. She was counting on his good nature and his appetite to spare Monsieur de Noblecourt too many temptations.

With half an ear to Marion's chatter, Nicolas reread what he had written in his notebook. He was still feeling the effects of his nightmare. In Semacgus's view an empty stomach was as bad for the health as too much food. He was paying the price for going to bed without supper. That evening Catherine's feast would be just what he needed, as long as nothing unexpected prevented him from keeping his promise. Marion was surprised to see him lingering over breakfast. He was taking it slowly, relishing some leftovers of pâté that the housekeeper had felt duty-bound to fetch from the storeroom to satisfy the young man's voracious appetite.

Full at last, he took refuge in Monsieur de Noblecourt's library. However obsessed he might be with his collections in general and his books in particular (which included several valuable items that even the King would have been proud to possess), the former procurator to the Parlement had given Nicolas free access to his library.

Nicolas knew what he was looking for. Occasionally he settled in a *bergère* to read some venerable tome in greater comfort. On this occasion he jotted several things down in his little notebook. Feeling pleased with himself, he returned everything to its place, carefully closing the grille of the cabinet containing the most valuable books. He then put the key back under a Saxony china figurine that represented the pastoral idyll of a shepherd playing his pipes to charm a swooning shepherdess dressed all in pink. Lastly, as instructed by the master of the house, he closed the curtains, since the bright morning sunlight was 'damaging, ruinous and fatal' for the bindings and engravings. This was one of the procurator's particular hobbyhorses.

Midday was striking and it was time for him to set off for the Comédie-Italienne. Nicolas had learnt from his theatre visits that it was pointless to wander around such places early in the day since the only people to be found there were floor polishers and sweepers. Moreover, actors had a reputation for going to bed late and therefore also rising late. He estimated that at a leisurely stroll it would take him just under an hour to reach the Comédie-Italienne.

Outside, the cool air, made brisker by a slight breeze, drove away the city smells. He gladly filled his lungs with the scents of autumn, which for once were stronger than the stench of filth and rubbish. A mixture of this and decaying animal flesh was what spattered stockings and breeches, leaving them with greasy, indelible stains.

For a moment Nicolas was uncertain which route to take, then with a smile and after quickly glancing around he entered Impasse Saint-Eustache. This dark and dank alleyway led to a side door of the church by that name, which huddled amongst the houses. Experience had taught him that there was always the possibility of being shadowed when he went out so he routinely took steps to foil anyone trying to follow him. This funnel-shaped blind alley had already proved helpful in that respect. Once inside the silent, gloomy interior of the church, and depending on what he thought would be most effective, Nicolas would hurry off towards either a confessional or a particularly dark side chapel where, his heart fluttering with excitement, he would check to see whether he was being followed. Being something of a master of disguise and make-believe himself, he was never fooled by appearances, even by someone who looked like an infirm old woman, as he knew that the least likely looking person was often the one most probably tailing him. Sometimes he also went back out via the side street to avoid following too regular a pattern, which could result in his being caught out at the main door of the church.

On this particular morning he noticed nothing unusual: a few pious souls deep in prayer, a legless man slumped near the stoup at the main entrance and the organist rehearsing a theme on the bourdon stop. Outside he found himself back in the bustling city.

He still felt as surprised as when he had first arrived in Paris. He remained appalled at the danger presented to pedestrians by the traffic on the road. He noted that city life replicated the relationships between individuals all along the social scale. The great looked down on the insignificant, smart carriages ploughed their way through, with a liberal use of the whip. The whips were not always aimed at the horses but only too often struck the drivers of more modest vehicles or even the backs of unfortunate day-labourers pulling handcarts. Had it not been for the boundary posts that the authorities had sensibly placed at the street corners and crossroads, and which acted as the sole obstacles to the murderous frenzy of coachmen, bourgeois, women, the elderly and children would have been mercilessly pressed and crushed against the walls. He was moved by the patience of ordinary people driven to the limits by such lack of respect. There were often harsh words and even exchanges of blows, but as long as there was no shortage of bread the masses put up with a great many things. If the day came when there was no bread in the shops, then anything might happen.

Rather sooner than expected, he reached the corner of Rue Mauconseil and Rue Neuve-Saint-François, where the annexe of the Hôtel de Bourgogne now housed the Comédie-Italienne. Having shaken the grille and banged on the glass with a piece of wood, he eventually saw a vague figure appear. He heard a key turn in the lock and the door open slightly; then the grille was pulled back and a hoarse, angry voice shouted at him to clear off.

In the smoothest of tones Nicolas gave his name and position. The owner of the angry voice cleared his throat noisily and Nicolas was allowed in. Now that the grille had been opened he had time to look at the man on the other side . He was huge and as sturdy as an oak. His face, as rough-hewn as that of a pagan idol, peeped out from a dark blue frock coat with shiny brass buttons done up to the collar. A yellowish wig only partially concealed a bare skull wrapped in a badly tied red headscarf. His left arm was missing and the empty sleeve was pinned to the front of his coat. Was Nicolas dealing with a doorkeeper or some eccentric theatrical figure? The man looked him up and down and stood aside heavily. He was surrounded by a mewing cluster of cats, their tails erect; some of them chased after one another, scampering between his legs. He raised his foot and banged it down on the ground; the felines scattered briefly.

'Filthy creatures!' said the man. 'But we need them to chase after the rats and the mice. Begging your pardon, you look a bit of a raw recruit to be a commissioner. The one in this district has a few more grey hairs than you. But at least you're young enough to fire a few broadsides, I should say.'

Nicolas now saw that he was not dealing with an actor but with one of those old salts who were often taken on by theatres. The skills of former sailors were much in demand as they could change scenery, handle machinery and move around at a height above the stage as well as tie knots and use ropes. This work enabled them to escape the sad fate that befell other veterans abandoned on the quayside.

'Let's steer ourselves to my cabin. I'll give you a drink and in exchange you can tell me what wind brings you to these waters.'

He stopped and turned. 'You ain't like the head of the coppers in this district. He's always dressed like a monk. Tall as a beanpole and pale as a church candle.'

They began walking down a dark corridor lit by an Argand lamp. The man pushed open a door; Nicolas was struck by the smell of stale tobacco and brandy. There was a table, two chairs, a straw mattress and a cooking pot on a roaring stove. A woven mat covered the floor and gave a little warmth to the place, which was in fact perfectly clean. A skylight at head height looked on to the corridor; the cats that had been driven back were congregating and scratched angrily at the glass which separated them from the room. Next to the skylight were dozens of keys in rows on a wooden board. The man went to give his food a stir, then filled two earthenware bowls and put them down on the polished table. He took out two sparkling pewter goblets from under the straw mattress together with a bottle, which once opened released a strong smell of rum.

'Please do me the honour of being my messmate and while

we're eating you can tell me what brings you here. And all in good cheer.'

'It'll be my pleasure,' said Nicolas.

He was somewhat apprehensive about what was being served up but he felt that accepting such a generous offer and eating with the man would simplify preliminaries. He was pleasantly surprised by a good piece of salted pork in a helping of beans. He perhaps would not have chosen to wash down this feast with rum, though late nights at Dr Semacgus's, who had also sailed the high seas, had gradually given him more of a taste for this manly, honest and straightforward tipple.

'My powers are wide-ranging and extend also to the city,' he declared.

The man was pulling at the hairs of his beard while looking at Nicolas, puzzled that a young man should exercise so much power. He was remembering no doubt those young gentlemen scarcely out of school who stood on the poop deck, lieutenants with the captain's authority. Compared to them, Nicolas seemed old and worthy of respect.

'This fills you up and anything salted is healthy,' he said. 'On board most of the time it was ship's biscuit with weevils and meat with maggots. But here am I talking and you need to tell me what you're after.'

Nicolas put a gold coin on the table. The man trembled with emotion; his hand moved forward, then stopped.

'I'm sure you'll make good use of it for your tobacco or this excellent rum,' said Nicolas.

The coin disappeared without a word. A friendly grunt was the only thanks. Nicolas made do with that.

'Here's my problem,' he went on. 'A ticket for the Comédie-Italienne has come into my possession. Is there a way of finding out where it comes from? There's no special mark: no date, just a number. Perhaps it refers to a box or a day. But I'm sure that nothing here escapes your eagle eye.'

Nicolas bit his lip; he had let the words slip out by mistake. Not only was the old sailor one-armed but he was also one-eyed or rather he suffered from leucoma, a white film that covered his left eye entirely.

'From the sail pit to the maintop – this is my domain.'

'Here's the piece of paper.'

The man brought a smoking candle closer and raised the ticket to his good eye.

'Yes, yes, yes, the little madam gets everywhere.'

'The little madam?'

'La Bichelière. Mademoiselle Bichelière. Well, that's her stage name. She's really lived and burnt the candle at both ends from a very young age. A tasty morsel, nice enough to get your teeth into, but a fortune-hunter too. And what an appetite for money – she'll have whatever she can get. She'll clean out anyone who's flush – old fogeys and young dandies. She sets herself up, sponges out her gun, loads up, rams in the charge, gets into position and opens fire; she never gives up and if her target puts up any resistance she just keeps on firing time after time.'

'You were a naval gunner, I assume.'

'And proud of it, Monsieur. I lost an arm at the battle of Minorca in '56 with Monsieur de la Galissonnière on a man-o'-war, a sixty-gun frigate.'

'So this ticket . . .'

'The custom is to give complimentary tickets to the actors, who hand them out to whoever they like. Well ... in small quantities. Mustn't chuck all the money away.'

'But how do you know that this ticket was given by Mademoiselle Bichelière?'

'You're not easily blown off course, are you, my lad? This figure you can see here corresponds to one of the seats allocated to the young lady. When she doesn't have a man on her mind, she's quite a decent girl. Otherwise she's got a real temper.'

'Really?'

'You've no idea! She wears round, comes upon her victim unawares and fires all her guns. In theatrical circles she's known as "Bloody Mary".'

'As bad as that? Who's she got it in for at the moment?'

'Oh, it's already over between them! The poor fellow got a real roasting. Just after last Thursday's performance, in fact. That evening you would have thought part of the set had caught fire. With her there are no half-measures: either the timbers of the whole vessel are creaking with passion or the anchor's being weighed out of sheer anger. As soon as some swell starts kissing her she can't help herself. She's like an alley cat when the moon's full.'

'Would you happen to know the name of this swell, as you call him?'

'As sure as my name's "the Clockmaker".'

'That's an odd nickname.'

'Yes, I've got a clock inside my head. I always notice when someone's late. It wouldn't do for anyone to miss their watch.'

126

'So you know who he is.'

'A pale-looking young thing, all powdered. Only the epaulettes give him a bit of calibre.'

'So he's an officer, is he?'

'I should say so! And not any old regiment but the French Guards. The ones who strut around Paris and are never in the front line. The only attack they ever launch is on the Opéra ball. I don't know his name. And not for lack of asking every time he went past my cabin, but he just sailed straight on. He's a vicomte, I think.'

'Was he very attached to her?'

'Like a limpet to a rock. The poor boy thought it was true love and then last Thursday she sent him packing.'

'Did she have someone new lined up?'

'That's quite possible. I've seen a strapping lad come past several times since.'

'Would you be able to recognise him?'

'No, definitely not. He wasn't looking to be noticed, a very dull fellow. I tried to stop him once; he told me he was taking her a letter.'

'Anything else?'

The man scratched his head.

'I just noticed a yellowy strand of hair sticking out from under his wig.'

Nicolas stood up.

'Many thanks. What you've told me will be very useful.'

'My pleasure, lad. Come whenever you like. I keep an open house. If you need me my name is Pelven, otherwise known as "the Clockmaker".'

127

'Just one more thing: at what time does Mademoiselle Bichelière usually arrive at the theatre?'

Pelven thought for a moment.

'It's two o'clock in the afternoon. She's still at home and won't show her pretty little face until about four. But if you want to see her she has a cosy little place in a house on Rue de Richelieu, at the corner of Boulevard Montmartre.'

Feeling somewhat dazed, Nicolas relished the fresh air that hit him full in the face. His inquiry had suddenly taken a new turn. The description of Mademoiselle Bichelière meant that he needed to proceed with caution. What would she have to say about her affair with Lionel de Ruissec? Why had she left him? Were these events in any way linked to the murders of the young officer and his mother? There were many unknown factors in this plot that brought together the worlds of the theatre and the Court.

Nicolas was lost in thought for a time, and then suddenly found himself back in the bustle of the boulevards. The trees, three or four rows deep, were shedding their last leaves, their fall hastened by the night frosts. In the middle of the thoroughfare a procession of carriages and horsemen trotted past. In many places con artists and quacks had set up stage and were holding forth at crowds of spectators. He noticed the gaudily dressed women with outrageously made-up faces who walked at a slow pace and stared at him. He was always struck by the mixture of town and countryside that still endured. Here there was the odd contrast of popular entertainment alongside mansions inhabited by bourgeois or noble families.

He had no difficulty spotting the actress's house. At the entrance he was stopped by an old hag wrapped in an enormous rabbit-skin jacket. Perched on a stool with a straw seat, she was selling jumping jacks and a whole array of combs, needles, pins and playing cards. She stuck out a fat leg swathed in bandages to block his way. Nicolas was used to women of this type. He did not want to arouse any suspicions by revealing his status. He knew that a show of humility and politeness, a discreet smile and above all a few coins would win her over and allay her suspicions. These were the necessary rules of Paris etiquette. Ogling him in a way that made him blush, she smiled lewdly, showing her rotten teeth and greyish tongue. He learnt that La Bichelière was at home.

On the mezzanine floor, he raised the knocker of a recently revarnished door. It opened and out shot the head of a sharp-featured maid clearly used to receiving visitors without asking any questions. None the less, she gave him an inquisitive glance, which seemed to satisfy her. After taking his tricorn and cloak she showed him into a small drawing room where the strong smell of fresh paint lingered. The accommodation seemed only recently to have been occupied and redecorated. Nicolas recalled the rumours concerning the vicomte's financial problems, his reputation for spending money and losing a fortune at cards. So it was not only faro and biribi that had affected the young man financially. That grasping Bichelière had also played a part in squandering a significant part of his wealth. And all the showy luxury of the décor had not been chosen to be tasteful: it reminded Nicolas of places that made no secret of their amorous function. A servant arrived to take him to the actress's bedroom.

The windows were still closed and only the dying embers of

the fire lit the room, which he immediately found to be oppressive. Nicolas only liked airy places; enclosed and confined spaces always caused him anxiety.

On the right he could make out an alcove with a canopy. The crown of the structure was decorated with white feathers. Had it not been for the pastel shades of the material, this monstrous piece of furniture would have been reminiscent of some fantastical catafalque. On the left side of the bedroom a floral-patterned screen hid part of the room. He noticed the top of a cheval mirror. At the far end of the room, to the right of the window, was an ottoman covered with heaped-up cushions and loose fabrics, and opposite it a pouf where a grey cat sat and stared at Nicolas with its green eyes. Thick carpets muffled every sound. A few engravings hung on the walls, which were papered with a pattern of vases and talapoin monkeys in staggered rows. All this intensified the stifling effect. The maid had withdrawn, with a wince on her mouse-like face, which was presumably meant to be a smile. At last a voice spoke from behind the screen.

'To what, Monsieur, do I owe the pleasure of your visit? If it's about paying a bill to a supplier, please make an appointment for five o'clock.'

And she's chosen that hour for a very good reason, thought Nicolas. Because that's when she's at the theatre.

'That's not why I'm here at all, Mademoiselle. I would simply like the benefit of your knowledge. Just a little information. I am Nicolas Le Floch, commissioner of police at the Châtelet.'

There followed a silence during which he had the impression of being examined from head to foot.

'You are rather young for a commissioner.'

The screen must have had a hole in it for peering through without being seen.

'You yourself, Mademoiselle, are proof that age—'

'Yes, yes. I didn't intend to offend you. But I know one of your colleagues intimately. His office is opposite the Comédie. He loves vaudeville and occasionally sends me bottles of wine.'

The words were spoken in a matter-of-fact way but he sensed the underlying warning: 'I have my protectors, including within the police force, and they are ready to risk their reputations for me. I don't know what brings you here but remember that if need be I know how to defend myself . . .'

'Mademoiselle, would you be so good as to examine a piece of paper in my possession and let me have your thoughts on it?'

A hand with pink fingernails pushed back one of the screen's panels. It revealed a charming sight. Mademoiselle Bichelière was at her toilet. Her hair was arranged like a child's, her flowing light auburn locks pulled back by a ribbon. A loosened linen shirt was arranged so as to reveal her delicate bosom, despite the white muslin dressing-gown thrown over her shoulders. She looked at Nicolas, one foot dipped into a porcelain bowl, the other, hidden by a towel, resting on a small stool. Her small eyes were deep blue. Her pencil-thin eyebrows emphasised her regular features and the perfect shape of her face. The dimples on her cheeks added to the expressiveness of the whole. Her mouth was rather large but mischievous-looking, and allowed a glimpse of small, perfect teeth. She had a slightly snub, upturned nose and without this minor flaw she would have been an example of ideal beauty. But Nicolas was one of those men who thought that a small imperfection added to a woman's attractiveness rather than detracting from it. The dressing table was cluttered with perfume bottles, brushes, combs, ribbons, jars of make-up and powder puffs. By her armchair was a drinks cabinet made from exotic wood and containing a dozen or so small bottles of different colours. The actress's face took on an embarrassed expression.

'Monsieur, you will, I trust, forgive my rather shocking forwardness, but would you be so kind as to help me wipe my foot?'

Nicolas bravely entered the fray, his heart beating a little faster. He picked up a towel from the floor and, kneeling down, held it out to the woman, thinking all the time how strange he must look. She straightened her leg and lifted her foot out of the bowl: as she did so the folds of her shift parted gently. Nicolas, now pink with embarrassment, was squeezing her tiny foot and found it to be very heavy. He indulged her as far as putting her foot in a pink mule. She presented her other foot for him to do the same. He stood up and moved back a step. The young woman put on her dressing-gown and went to recline on the ottoman, inviting Nicolas to sit on the pouf. The cat moved away, growled quietly and in the end jumped on to the bed. Nicolas felt uncomfortable on this low piece of furniture, his stomach cramped and knees raised, all too aware of the beans he had eaten and the rum he had drunk. He was too close to the fire and his back was roasting.

'This piece of paper, Mademoiselle . . .'

She looked up as if in annoyance and began to twist a wisp of hair around her finger. He proffered the ticket; she looked at it without taking it from him.

'I distribute them amongst my friends. I'm entitled to a certain number of seats.'

132

He was desperately thinking of a way to slip the vicomte's name into the conversation. She was almost certainly unaware of his death. He could risk . . .

'To my great regret, I'm afraid this may well displease you, Mademoiselle, but I must confess everything . . .'

Now it was her turn to look intrigued.

'Confess everything? So what do you have to confess?'

'A friend of mine, the Vicomte de Ruissec, gave me this ticket and he'd told me so much about how beautiful and lovely you were that I used it as a pretext to . . .'

None of this made sense. If she asked him what the ticket was a pretext for he would been unable to give an answer. But he had not for a moment imagined the reaction his words would provoke. She rose up as if in the throes of an epileptic fit and tore off the top of her dressing-gown as if she were suffocating. Hair undone, bare-breasted like a Bacchante, the little china doll was transformed into a fury. She jumped up, hands on hips and like a marketplace fishwife began to pour out a stream of insults and abuse.

'Why are you talking to me about that pimp, that piece of filth? A pig: I sacrificed my virtue to him, he fucked me to his heart's content and then dumped me. If I'd known, I'd have let myself catch the pox just to pass it on. Yes, I'd have peppered him. I'll stuff his words back down his throat. Won't I just. He puts on airs and graces, plays the faithful, devoted sweetheart and then runs off with someone else.'

She stopped for a moment to bite her fist. The tomcat had taken refuge under the bed and was mewling desperately. The maid poked her nose in, then scuttled off, accustomed no doubt to her mistress's histrionics. Nicolas was taken aback, but at the same time was closely examining a dirty coffee cup on a pedestal table. He could see a mark made by lips to the right of the fine china handle.

The truce was short-lived. 'And with a rancid Court whore! That Mademoiselle de Sauveté! Oh! I found out all about her. No one's exactly sure where she comes from. I hear that she paints, which says it all. That means she must be frightfully ugly. But she's rich and I predict she'll be even uglier after she's married. As for him, he's broke, he can't pay my debts any more. Does he want me in the poorhouse dressed in rags? I hate him! I hate him!'

She let out a scream and fell on to the ottoman in tears. Nicolas was both pleased with what he'd discovered during this outburst and sorry to see Mademoiselle Bichelière in this state.

Having vented her anger she became more human. Out of sheer kind-heartedness he drew closer to her and stroked her hair, talking to her gently. She was sobbing and clung to him. He clasped her half-naked body, intoxicated by its fragrance. She lifted her face, offered him her lips and pulled him towards her. Nicolas surrendered to his instincts. The ottoman almost collapsed beneath the ardour of their embrace. The cat, terrified by the din, was hissing furiously. Nicolas could not help hearing a first name that his companion screamed out twice as she sank her fingernails into his back . . .

The maid returned very quickly, with a bottle of wine and two glasses. Her arrival prevented any embarrassment between the two of them that might otherwise have arisen. For him this was a tricky moment, when he had to resume his official role in unusual circumstances, even though, like a true gentleman, he had performed to the apparent satisfaction of La Bichelière. But he did wonder whether, with women, appearances were always what they seemed.

'Mademoiselle, at the risk of displeasing you, I must ask when you last saw the vicomte.'

She looked at him in exasperation as if what had just happened should excuse her from all further questioning.

'So you're back to being a police officer again. You weren't quite so curious just a moment ago. You've had what you wanted. What is the meaning of this inquisition?'

'You have given me everything I could wish for, Mademoiselle. I have just a few questions. I admit that my visit here is a result of an . . . The Vicomte de Ruissec has disappeared.'

He would soon see what results a half-truth would bring. Either she had rare strength of character or she had nothing to do with the death of her lover: she made no attempt to show any concern.

'He can go hang. That's the least of my worries. I saw him last Thursday and I told him that I knew he was betrothed and that he'd pulled the wool over my eyes. He wanted to sort things out, he said, so that he could keep me. I would have liked to have seen that! Oh, I know his little game; he would have played the knave at Court with his strumpet and then in his spare time would have slid under my sheets. For free, of course.'

She had resumed her toilet and had drawn the screen again. He could no longer see her. He could hear water being poured.

'What about Tuesday evening?'

'What about it? Are you going to name every day of the week?'

'That's the only one,' said Nicolas, watching the cat playing under the bed with a light-coloured man's wig, near which lay white clerical bands.

'Tuesday evening? Tuesday evening there was no performance. Harlequin was ill and I stayed here to rest.'

She did not, however, look like the sort of person who rested.

'Alone?'

'Monsieur, you are overstepping the mark. Yes, alone. Alone with Griset, my cat.'

At the sound of its name the tomcat emerged from its hiding place and went warily over to its mistress, its tail raised and its eyes trained on Nicolas. There was nothing more to add and Nicolas bade farewell; she did not reply. The maid accompanied him out with due ceremony, then shamelessly held out her hand for her reward. After a moment's hesitation he paid his contribution. The Bichelière household certainly had many faults but modesty of manners was not one of them.

Once he was back outside he began to regret what had happened. How on earth, he asked himself, could I have lost control and surrendered to my instincts like that in the middle of an investigation while questioning a witness in a criminal case? A small voice inside him tried to plead extenuating circumstances: he had not really wanted to do it, the girl was pretty and forward, and anyway was known to be of easy virtue. Added to this soul-searching was an underlying anxiety. The whirlwind of sensations had been so violent that he had taken no precautions. He remembered only too well his friend Semacgus's advice.

Speaking from long experience as a libertine, he had warned him of the dangers of the company of actresses, opera girls and other harlots, too happy or too carefree to be bothered about spreading the poisoned fruits of their licentiousness far and wide. The surgeon had urged him to use a sheath made of sheep gut, more commonly known as a condom, which was a man's best defence against Venus's revenge. Finally, who was this 'Gilles' whose name had unfortunately disturbed the moment of climax?

To take his mind off things, Nicolas walked towards the Place des Victoires. He was always struck by the beauty of the place. He had never had the opportunity to examine closely the monument at its centre. Above the inscription '*Viro immortali*' Louis XIV sat enthroned in glory. Protected by the figure of Fame with wings outstretched, the monarch looked down on slaves in chains, with the globe at his feet, beside Hercules' club and lion's skin. One day as they were crossing the square in a carriage Sartine had rattled off an anecdote, as he loved to do. He told Nicolas how a courtier, the Maréchal de La Feuillade, had built this square, taking his cult of the King so far as to have an underground passageway constructed from the crypt of the church of the Petits-Pères to a vault situated directly beneath the statue in which his mortal remains could pay court to the King for all eternity. The Lieutenant General of Police had also pointed out that this used to be an area of ill repute and that a reminder of its murky past was to be found in the street name Vide-Gousset.[1]

Nicolas got back to Rue Montmartre on the stroke of seven. The normally peaceful household was a hive of joyous activity. Marion and Catherine were busy in the pantry, surrounded by the noise and pleasant smells of the supper they were preparing. He could particularly smell the delicious aroma of fish and buttered croute. The atmosphere in the house helped dispel his lingering sense of melancholy, due as much to a heavy stomach as to his amorous exertions, whose beginning and ending had not lived up to the pleasure he had experienced in between.

Poitevin went back and forth, his arms laden with silverware and bottles which, Nicolas discovered upon enquiry, were to be used to lay the table that had been set up in the library that evening. He asked for some hot water and, still faithful to his godfather's precepts with respect to personal hygiene, washed thoroughly before changing. When he entered the drawing room to be greeted by Cyrus jumping about, he heard three voices express their surprise at seeing him.

'Here comes the prodigal son!' said Monsieur de Noblecourt, on his feet and wearing a magnificent Regency-style wig. 'Hunger has brought him in off the streets!'

Nicolas blushed at the biblical reference. He would have to learn to ignore these innocent jokes since those who made them were unaware of their meaning for him.

'My dear Nicolas, you have arrived just at the right time. Two of our friends have done me the honour of asking to dine with me this evening.'

Glasses already in hands, Monsieur de La Borde and Dr Semacgus were smiling. They had never met and had just been getting acquainted. The company exchanged greetings. Nicolas sat down. The fire was burning cheerfully high; he surrendered to the wellbeing and warmth of friendship.

'Nicolas,' Monsieur de Noblecourt went on, 'we are amongst

friends, the door is well and truly closed. Give us a detailed account of the results of your investigations.'

The young man recounted the course of events, beginning with the evening at the Opéra particularly for La Borde's benefit. Reporting to Monsieur de Sartine meant he needed to be able to explain facts quickly and clearly, avoiding excessive or tedious details. The Lieutenant General would not have tolerated them because he was a model of verbal precision himself. He continued his account, missing out certain details that he wanted to verify first. There was no doubt about his friends' discretion but Nicolas never told everything, not even to Bourdeau. He blushed slightly when he came to the episode with the lovely Bichelière. He suddenly thought that he did not even know her first name and also that he would have to find out about this 'Gilles' fellow who had made such an ill-timed intervention in his love-making. Most surprised by his account of events was the First Groom to the King's Bedchamber, who had only witnessed Nicolas's hurried departure during the performance at the Opéra.

'I now understand,' he said, 'why Monsieur de Saint-Florentin summoned the Lieutenant General of Police yesterday as a matter of urgency. The result of this audience was the order to abandon the investigation and the body was then taken from you. I understand, however, that you had already established a diagnosis . . .'

'I've been giving our problem a great deal of thought since yesterday,' Nicolas said. 'This frightful death resulting from the ingestion of molten lead . . . Lead can be found everywhere. We still need to find those who use it.'

'Printers,' said La Borde.

'Quite right, but also gunsmiths,' added Semacgus.

'Roofers,' said Nicolas.

'And coffin-makers.'

Monsieur de Noblecourt gave a knowledgeable wag of his finger.

'My friends, my friends, I remember an evening with the late Duc de Saint-Simon. He entertained rarely and stingily, being rather tight-fisted but exquisitely courteous. One evening in the year 1730 or thereabouts, he arranged a supper party, which was unusual for him. I was there, listening to the conversation. One of his friends who was visiting Paris at the time, the Duke of Liria, the Spanish Ambassador in Muscovy . . . He was, it must be said . . .'

A long digression was in prospect, one that would considerably delay the main point of the speech.

'. . . He was the son of the Duke of Berwick, himself the son of James II. I can see Nicolas becoming impatient. What it is to be young! In short, the Duke of Liria was telling the Duc de Saint-Simon how it was an old Russian custom to execute counterfeiters by making them ingest molten metal, which, he added, made their bodies explode. They probably did not use lead, which liquefies quickly. In any case, with the unfortunate vicomte it must have required a pipe or a funnel to force this devilish potion down his throat.'

'It seems to me, Monsieur Procurator,' interjected La Borde, 'that there is also a fifth and a sixth profession that handle lead.

First the executioner and, above all, fountaineers. In Versailles the other day I was watching the conduits of Neptune's fountain being repaired. They did not stint on the lead.'

'In a word,' said Semacgus ironically, 'you have a ready-made list of suspects ... But still what could be the reason for this barbaric punishment? What crime could merit such an end? Not so long ago they used to cut out the tongues of informers.'

The four dining companions indulged in lengthy speculation, then turned their attention to the case of Mademoiselle Bichelière. If Madame de Ruissec had been pushed into the well of the dead what was the connection between her death and the actress? Their suppositions were interrupted by Marion who, grumbling, reminded them that it was time to sit down to dinner.

As they were getting up, Semacgus grabbed Nicolas's elbow and whispered in his ear: 'I suspect you, my young Romeo, of taking your questioning of La Bichelière rather further than you would have us believe . . .'

What was originally intended to be a quiet supper turned into a feast, even if, under his housekeeper's watchful eye, the elderly procurator abstained from the morel pie. He made up for it with the *sole à la Villeroy*, which Catherine brought in reverently, but he managed to resist the temptation of a restorative white Mâcon. Had he shown the least inclination to taste it the ever-vigilant Marion would have prevented him, white wine being notorious for exacerbating the symptoms of gout. Meanwhile the assembled representatives of the medical profession, the royal Court and the Châtelet pursued the task in hand methodically, whilst exchanging the latest gossip. Their favoured topics were once again: the war; rumours of negotiations with England; the business with the

Jesuits, who were under increasing threat; and the failing health of the King's favourite, made worse by the rumours of the King's latest fancy who was said to be with child by him. Finally dispatches from Moscow indicated that Tsarina Elizaveta Petrovna's health was declining rapidly.

Monsieur de Noblecourt mentioned a strange event that one of his Swiss correspondents had drawn to his attention.

'In Geneva they saw a shining ball of fire which, as it disappeared, exploded, and everyone felt a short earthquake along with a muffled noise. My friends thought they had been plunged into darkness when the brightness of the phenomenon had passed.'

'What a very philosophical tale!' said Semacgus. 'Your Calvinist friends have been drinking too much Fendant . . . Here they are, imagining night in the middle of the day.'

Monsieur de Noblecourt nodded thoughtfully. 'Sometimes the obvious can blind us to the truth. To return to the case before us, I would advise our young Châtelet commissioner not to attach too much importance to appearances but to seek to discover instead what lies behind them. The present is born of the past and it is always worth disentangling the past of the protagonists in a drama, to find out who they really are as opposed to how they wish to present themselves, who they say they are or what they would have people believe.'

Following these wise words they went their separate ways. For a celebration to end someone's convalescence it had turned out to be a lively evening. Nicolas accompanied his friends outside. He was pleased to see that La Borde and Semacgus were already on such good terms. The two men, though different in character, age and station, had in common their friendship for Nicolas. The First Groom of the King's Bedchamber, having at his disposal a Court carriage, offered to take the doctor back to Vaugirard.

He stepped aside for him and, turning towards Nicolas, whispered in his ear: 'Madame de Pompadour wishes to see you tomorrow in her chateau at Choisy. You will be expected at three o'clock in the afternoon. Good luck, my friend.'

It was on this astonishing note that Nicolas's day drew to a close.

VI

THE TWO HOUSES

'Once the imagination is in motion, woe betide the mind it governs.'
MARIVAUX

Friday 26 October 1761

Nicolas left Rue Montmartre early in the morning. The evening he had spent with his friends had allayed any misgivings. Mademoiselle Bichelière had used him either to satisfy a passing fancy or to ingratiate herself with the police. He convinced himself that as he was not the first person she had given herself to, he was absolved to a degree from having yielded so thoughtlessly to his instincts. He recognised that the experience had been quite pleasurable, and then remembered Semacgus's sniggers.

But Nicolas now had other things on his mind. He could not postpone meeting with Monsieur de Sartine any longer and felt apprehensive about what his superior would say. Would he try to salvage what he could of the situation by covering for his deputy or would he distance himself as he had done on occasion? Would that be tantamount to forbidding him from pursuing the investigation? This possibility worried Nicolas.

The other matter worrying him was the summons from the King's favourite to go to her chateau at Choisy. He could hardly believe it. What requests or orders could she possibly have for him? Admittedly he had recently rendered her a signal service, but why turn to him, a modest link in the police chain, and not go directly to Sartine? Was the latter aware of this summons? If so, what did he think of it?

The venue for the meeting partly answered his question. The marquise had plenty of choice: her apartments in Versailles, her mansion in the royal town, the Hôtel d'Evreux in Paris, the chateau of Bellevue . . . but Choisy seemed most appropriate for a discreet meeting as it was relatively far away, very extensive, with a large number of servants, and thus a place of many comings and goings. The fact that the message had been passed on by La Borde, in whom the King had absolute trust, reassured him somewhat. The sovereign was no doubt aware of everything.

Monsieur de Sartine seemed to be in neither a good nor bad mood. Having tapped gently on his door and crept in, Nicolas found him busy writing, wearing a colourful, shot-silk headscarf. A man-servant was clearing a pedestal table. The Lieutenant General gave his visitor a guarded look.

'Are you Tamburlaine, Attila the Hun or Genghis Khan, Monsieur?' he declared. 'Wherever you go, nothing survives, the bodies pile up, whole families perish, mothers follow their sons on to Charon's ferry. What's your explanation for this – in as few words as possible, please?'

The jollity of his tone belied the strength of his words. Nicolas took a deep breath and replied in similar vein.

'I am desperately sorry, Monsieur.'

'Oh, I am so glad, so glad to have to explain to Monsieur de

Saint-Florentin about the goings-on in our good town. How the body of an unfortunate who has committed suicide, or rather the victim of an accident, was taken away against the wishes of his father and delivered up to quacks and to the . . . I won't mention his name . . . so that they might have the macabre pleasure of delving into his entrails. This is intolerable, Monsieur! How can it be explained or justified? And how do I look in all of this? A lieutenant in the French Guards, the son of a gentleman-in-waiting to Madame Adélaïde . . . As I predicted the father has gone on the offensive and the minister has not weathered the storm. Heaven – or the Devil – help us if you actually opened up the body!'

'There was no need.'

'What do you mean, no need? All this fuss for nothing?'

'Certainly not, Monsieur. Our quacks had time to examine everything and come to a conclusion.'

'Oh, really! Well then, Mister Sawbones, what did they conclude? I am keen to know . . .'

'The conclusion, Monsieur, is that the Vicomte de Ruissec was murdered. Molten lead was forced down his throat.'

Monsieur de Sartine tore off his headscarf, revealing his thinning, already greying hair.

'Good God, Monsieur. That is terrible. This changes everything, obviously. I'll take you at your word and assume that the matter is now beyond doubt.'

He stood up and began to walk up and down his office. After some time he stopped his obsessive pacing and sat down again.

'Yes, beyond doubt: the crime is proven. Ruissec has now seen his son's body and can be under no illusions. That expression on the face still haunts me. So, not suicide ... But what about the comtesse? You're not going to tell me that—'

'Once more I am desperately sorry, Monsieur. Myself, Monsieur de Beurquigny, the commissioner for the district, whom you know, and a doctor concur in all our findings: we have ruled out the possibility of an accident and must conclude that the unfortunate lady's neck was intentionally broken and she was then thrown down the well of the dead in the church of the Carmelites.'

'This is really all too much. The situation could not be more difficult. Is it possible to establish a link between these two crimes?'

'At this stage of the investigation it's impossible to say. However, there is one disturbing detail.'

Nicolas gave a rapid account of the story of the ticket for the Comédie-Italienne and the ensuing inquiries.

'Which means, Monsieur, that you are requesting permission to continue your investigation, does it?'

The young man nodded. 'I am asking your permission to go on searching for the truth.'

'But the truth is like a slippery whore that always escapes your grasp. And if you do catch hold of her she will burn your fingers. In any case, Nicolas, how can I let you continue an investigation when the minister has decreed that no crime was committed?'

Nicolas noted that he was being addressed by his first name again.

'So we must close our eyes, must we? Let the crime go unpunished and—'

'Come, come, stop being childish by putting words into my

mouth. No one is more anxious than I to separate the truth from the lies. But if you persist with this investigation it will be at your own risk. My support will cease as soon as influences more powerful than mine are brought into play. I realise you do not wish to give up the chase and, if I am speaking to you like this, it is because I am concerned for your safety.'

'Monsieur, I am touched by your words but you must understand that I cannot stop now.'

'Another thing: be punctual for your meeting with Madame de Pompadour.'

He glanced towards the clock on the chimneypiece. Nicolas said nothing.

'Monsieur de La Borde told me about it,' continued Sartine. 'Take care not to lose such a precious and disinterested friendship.'

He paused and then went on in a quieter voice, as if talking to himself, 'Occasionally a woman hides from a man the full extent of the passion she feels for him, whilst for his part the man feigns for her feelings he does not have. Yes, be punctual and respectful.'

'Monsieur, I will give you a full report . . .'

'That goes without saying, Commissioner.'

Nicolas bit his lip. He would have done better to have held his tongue.

'And what does Monsieur de Noblecourt think about all this?'

Nicolas noted that his superior apparently thought it quite natural for him to tell the former procurator about an ongoing investigation.

'He talks in maxims. According to him, being honoured counts for little because it does not mean that one is honourable and he advises me to look closely into the protagonists' pasts. He, too, urges me to be on my guard.'

'I see that our friend has lost none of his wisdom. The last piece of advice is good and the others equally apposite. Be off with you, Monsieur. A carriage awaits you. Do not forget the business with the Minister of Bavaria. Find me this damned coachman as quickly as you can.'

Nicolas bowed and refrained from expounding on his theory concerning the incident at Pont de Sèvres. There would be time for that later. He was already at the door when he heard the Lieutenant General of Police's voice once more.

'Don't do anything foolish, Nicolas. And don't brush Bourdeau aside. We are very fond of you.'

Following these kind words, Nicolas found himself in the antechamber. A mirror hung over a chest of drawers showed the reflection of an elegant, well-built young man with a cocksure air, dressed in a black coat and carrying a hat under his arm. The long eyebrows above his grey-green eyes made him look more startled than innocent. His well-defined lips gave the hint of a smile and his auburn hair, tied in a knot, emphasised the youthfulness of the face, despite a few scars. He dashed down the stairs four at a time. Monsieur de Sartine planned things down to the smallest detail when it suited his purposes. It was important for Nicolas to get to his meeting with the King's favourite without incident, so a carriage was waiting for him in the courtyard.

In the end, the interview with the Lieutenant General had gone better than expected from Nicolas's point of view. He had been afraid of encountering a man who was annoyed, hesitant and wanting to distance himself from his subordinate's risky initiatives. In fact he had been given a free hand, admittedly 'at his own risk', but with a veiled expression of concern that came from the heart. He shuddered belatedly at the thought that everything might have come to a halt there and then. No more bodies, no more crimes, no more victims, no more culprits ... Perhaps Madame de Ruissec's murder should have been made public but the result would have been exactly the same: the body would have been removed and the case buried together with the comtesse. That was in fact how things stood for now and he alone held the small clue that might enable the mystery to be solved and thus unmask the perpetrators.

From the comfort of his carriage Nicolas practised guessing the occupations of the passers-by, by trying to read their expressions and imagining what might be going through the minds of this mass of humanity called the people. He stored up images of clothes, outfits and postures in his memory. He would call upon these one day in relation to specific people, to make those mysterious connections that were essential to his intuition. His knowledge of people would gradually increase by consulting these living archives in the course of his investigations. The sight of the gloomy bulk of the Bastille interrupted his ruminations. He had gone there once to visit his friend Semacgus in prison. He could still feel the dank cold of the ancient fortress. The carriage turned off to the right to follow the Seine. He banished the image of the prison from his mind.

Town suddenly gave way to countryside. Having nothing else to do, Nicolas give some order to the various facts he knew about the Marquise de Pompadour. Monsieur de Noblecourt's well-informed guests talked a great deal. In addition to what they said he read publications confiscated by the police or letters opened by the postal censors. Scurrilous tracts, lampoons, obscene poems and insults made up a motley collection. Everyone said she was ill and exhausted by the frenzy and anxiety of the Court. The King, who had never treated her with much consideration, required her presence at late-night vigils, suppers, entertainments and on his incessant travels, especially in the hunting season. Her delicate stomach had been damaged by too rich a diet. Semacgus put forward the theory that to please her lover she had listened to bad advice and made excessive use of stimulants provided by charlatans – not to mention her prodigious consumption of truffles and spices.

But it was generally agreed that what most gnawed away at the marquise was her constant obsession about 'some other woman', one who would discover the secret of this unusual man, so difficult to distract from his ennui. She had even gone to the length of creating her own rivals who were seductive but naïve and who posed no threat to her hold over the King. At present, and despite these precautions, a young girl from Romans was a worry to her; she was said to be scheming and witty.

Monsieur de La Borde, though sworn to secrecy, had agreed to repeat in select company the words of one of the favourite's friends. In an attempt to reassure her she had told her: 'It's your staircase that he likes, he's used to going up and down it.' Thus the time for passion was over, replaced by the gentler waters of friendship.

This fear of losing the King was compounded by the

permanent dread of another Damiens affair. The favourite did not forget that she had almost been pushed aside and exiled during the period when the King had been in uncertain health and the Dauphin and pious members of the royal family had managed to prevent her seeing him. As for what the people thought of her, they viewed the marquise as one of the three calamities afflicting the kingdom, along with famine and war. The streets were full of people hurling insults and threatening to kill her.

Nicolas, who had been in the marquise's presence once before, had thought her unfussy and kind. Monsieur de La Borde, who saw her every day, shared this opinion. According to him the Good Lady was neither a spendthrift nor a hoarder, and her expenditure, though considerable, was put to good use in the arts. It was true that her allowance and income were not commensurate with the needs of her household and this vocation as patron of the arts. It was rumoured that she had obtained permission from the King to make use of treasury bonds as she pleased, without being accountable for how they were spent. She owned numerous estates, ranging from the distant Menars to the nearby chateau of Bellevue, halfway between Paris and Versailles, built on a hillside above Pont de Sèvres. Madame de Pompadour liked to be in a dominant position.

The carriage followed the river. The countryside offered a pleasant prospect of taverns, and small farms that were crowded with herds of cattle, which their breeders fattened for consumption in the capital, selling the manure as fertiliser to the gardeners and fruit and vegetable growers in the neighbourhood. Orchards and glasshouses lined both sides of the road. These rural impressions put Nicolas in a good mood. His reflections had armed him with the necessary facts and information for his forthcoming conversation; for now, the reason for the interview remained a mystery to him, but it was clearly something quite out of the ordinary. The fact that Monsieur de Sartine, normally so eager to give advice, had made no comment on the matter was evidence enough of his own puzzlement.

As they entered Choisy, Nicolas made the carriage stop outside a small, pretty-looking tavern, attracted by its vine-covered façade, which still bore clusters of dried grapes left at the previous harvest. In a whitewashed room he ordered a pitcher of new wine, its recently pressed juice having been clarified by the use of wood chips. He was also served a few slices from a ham hanging in the fireplace and some freshly baked bread to go with it. The wine proved to be a pleasant surprise. He was expecting it to be as rough as usual but it was unexpectedly clear, bright red in colour, fresh and with the slightly wild aroma of redcurrant. Amused by the incongruousness of the image, he eventually concluded that the best comparison was with a redcurrant crushed on the fur of a polecat. The smell of this small wild animal had remained with him since childhood: the Marquis de Ranreuil wore a collar made of this fur on one of his cloaks and there had been no way of removing the smell. Those of his dogs who were unaccustomed to the smell would bark at his heels.

Nicolas suddenly noticed a young man in the uniform of the Life Guards. He was seated at another table watching him, but turned his head away under Nicolas's gaze. Nicolas was surprised to see him there but thought no more of it; the King was not in Choisy but, after all, whoever served the sovereign could also serve his favourite.

At half-past two he set off again and the carriage made its way up to the chateau at walking pace. The vehicle came within sight of a magnificent gate opening on to an immense avenue with a double row of trees. He noticed several forks in the road, leading off into the surrounding countryside. The building rose up before him, its two wings decorated with pediments. To the left a huge building served as the staff quarters and the stables. Nicolas alighted in front of the central main steps, where a man with a staff in his hand who seemed to be waiting for him greeted him with great formality.

'Do I have the honour of addressing Monsieur Nicolas Le Floch?'

'Your servant, Monsieur.'

'I am the intendant of the chateau. My mistress has asked me to take a tour with you. She is a little unwell and will receive you later.'

The man took Nicolas off towards the chapel. There he was able to admire Van Loo's painting of St Clothilde, Queen of France, before the tomb of St Martin. He then visited the ceremonial rooms of the chateau, the main gallery decorated with pier glasses and Parrocel's painting of the battle of Fontenoy. Nicolas thought that the marquise was showing her devotion to the King even down to the decoration of her houses. The dining room was embellished with six views of royal houses, and the buffet room with hunting scenes. The King's particular interests: war, buildings and hunting, were all depicted in this residence. His guide led Nicolas outside to admire the view from the terrace, the most attractive feature of the chateau. The Seine flowed peacefully at his feet. A pavilion that was used as a summer dining room stood at the centre. A breathless servant ran up to them: the Marquise de Pompadour was ready to receive Monsieur Le Floch.

He was shown into a grey and gold boudoir. The curtains had been closed and the room was in semi-darkness. In the great pale marble fireplace dying embers glowed. As he entered he was greeted by a little black barbet who, after inspecting him quickly but cautiously, celebrated his arrival. This little game created a diversion.

'Monsieur Le Floch,' said the marquise, 'I have every reason to believe in your loyalty and I notice that Bébé thinks the same.'

Nicolas bowed, thinking that the smell of Cyrus on his breeches and stockings must have had quite a lot to do with the trust Bébé showed him. He looked up at the marquise. She had changed considerably within a few months. Admittedly there was still the same oval-shaped face, but her chin had become heavier. The skilful application of white powder and rouge probably concealed the other ravages of time. Her eyes, ever inquisitive and lively, watched Nicolas with some amusement. A white lace headscarf allowed a glimpse of her ash-grey hair. A white taffeta cape covered a double-flounced black silk skirt. Long cuffs covered what she considered to be unattractive hands. Nicolas wondered if that was why the King so disliked seeing ladies wearing rings, thereby drawing attention to a part of the body he could not admire in the marquise. The overall effect felt rather sad, even austere to him, in keeping with her new-found reputation for piety, but then he remembered that the Court was in mourning for a German prince.

'Do you know, Monsieur, that on two occasions the King was concerned for your safety?'

This was intended both as a criticism and a piece of advice but it was also a way for her to charm and flatter the person she was addressing. Nicolas was not fooled. There was nothing to say in reply and so he bowed.

'You are too discreet. Remember that for the King you are the Marquis de Ranreuil and all you have to do is to . . . Do you not regret your decision?'

Her look became more intent. Nicolas sensed the trap: the woman who was speaking was not of noble birth.

'The Marquis de Ranreuil, my father, taught me that worth is not something that one is born with. Everything depends on what one makes of one's life.'

She raised her eyebrows and smiled, no doubt appreciating this sidestep.

'Even so, Monsieur, you ought to follow my advice. You are a hunter, so you should go hunting. That is where you will meet your master.'

However accustomed Nicolas was becoming to the manners of the Court, he nevertheless found this a somewhat long-winded preamble. La Borde had already passed on the message that he had to put in an appearance at the King's hunt.

'All this is to say that one is assured here and elsewhere of your loyalty,' continued the marquise.

She motioned to him to sit.

'Monsieur de Sartine has entrusted you with an investigation into the, let us say, unexplained death of the Vicomte de Ruissec . . . I know what happened and also the strange circumstances of his mother's death. I have requested that Monsieur de Saint-Florentin and the Lieutenant General of Police spare the King the details of these deaths. He would be only too inclined to dwell on them.'

She remained thoughtful for a moment. Nicolas remembered the sovereign's morbid curiosity when he had recounted the examination carried out on a body found in the knacker's yard at Montfaucon. This strange interest in macabre details had become more marked, it was said, since Damiens's attempt on the King's life.

'Monsieur, what do you think lies behind these deaths?'

'Madame, I am convinced that we are confronted with two cases of murder. For the time being there is nothing to indicate a connection between the two but nothing either to prove the opposite. In the case of the Vicomte de Ruissec the circumstances are quite extraordinary. I am investigating the victims and their pasts, on the understanding, as you are no doubt well aware, that these murders have not been officially recognised, that the course of justice has been impeded and that my inquiry is personal and undertaken at my own risk.'

She gave an elegant nod of the head. 'Whatever the circumstances you will continue to enjoy my protection.'

'It is of the most precious assistance, Madame.'

He did not believe a word of it. The protection of the King's favourite was good as far as the door of this boudoir. As soon as he left Choisy, a good sharp sword and Bourdeau would be infinitely more useful.

'Perhaps, Monsieur, you would do well to believe that this decision to stop the investigation was merely a device to avoid scaring away the game one wishes to trap.'

This obviously opened up new perspectives. As was often the case – and he sometimes did the same thing himself – Monsieur de Sartine had doubtless concealed part of the truth from him. Or else the favourite had reserved for herself the privilege of informing him. The game was becoming decidedly more complicated. His own side had just castled, he thought, like the good chess player he was.

As he did not respond, she continued, 'That does not seem to come as a surprise to you. You had already thought of it. I must confide to you how anxious I am ... Public misfortunes are causing me great distress. Threats are being made against the King and I am constantly the victim of insults. If only I could withdraw to a retreat ... To Ménars, for example.'

She was interrupted by the crash of a falling log. From what Nicolas knew, Ménars was not a particularly austere type of retreat.

'I am tired and sick,' continued the marquise. 'I might as well tell you, Monsieur. You have already saved me once. Look at this piece of paper that I found on the door of my apartments. And it is not the first.'

She handed him a printed sheet. He read it through to the end.

To the king's whore. God in His ineffable but unerring wisdom in order to punish and humble France for your sins and wickedness that now are at their height has allowed the Philistines to vanquish us on land and on sea and to force us to sue for a peace that they will grant only to our greatest and most humiliating disadvantage. The hand of God is visible in this disaster. He will punish again.

When Nicolas looked up from reading he saw her face was in her hands. The dog jumped on to her lap and whined quietly.

'Madame, leave this rag with me. I shall find the source.'

She raised her head again.

'You will find it is a hydra with heads that constantly grow back. I foresee more insidious dangers. I have reason to fear the Ruissec family whom the King holds in little esteem. It is plotting with the pious, the Jesuits and all who wish to see the back of me. I cannot tell you more. This case must be solved. In truth I fear for the King's life. Look at Portugal: the newspapers announce the execution of the Jesuit Malagrida. He is an accomplice to the murder of the King of Portugal. It is reported that he met Damiens some time ago in Soissons. So many plots! Time and again they try.'

'But, Madame, many people around you and the King are watching over you.'

'I know. All the Lieutenant Generals of Police have been my friends – Bertin, Berryer and now Sartine. But they are taken up by more important matters and their time is divided between many tasks, just like the minister, Monsieur de Saint-Florentin. I put my trust in you, Monsieur le Marquis.'

Nicolas felt that the Good Lady could have spared herself this new attempt at flattery, which was, nevertheless, a good indication of her distress. She could count on him but he would have liked her to give more detail at points where she had clearly held back as she spoke to him She had not laid out all the facts in her possession. It was regrettable that the normal course of an investigation should be subject to so many refusals to disclose information. She held out her hand for him to kiss. It was as feverish as on their previous meeting.

'If you wish to see me again, Monsieur de La Borde will inform me.'

As the carriage moved along the main driveway it passed a rider whom Nicolas recognised as the Life Guard in the tavern. He spent the return journey to Paris deep in thought. His private talk with Madame de Pompadour had left a bitter taste in his mouth. On the one hand he had found an unhappy woman, worried to the point of extreme anxiety about the threats to the King – but Nicolas was sharp enough to see that concern about her own fate also played a part in this anxiety. More generally, he had observed her reluctance to speak of certain things and her ambiguous choice of words, which he felt was a sure sign that she knew more than she would say.

The idea that stopping the investigation was a manoeuvre, a pretence intended to deceive the enemy, seemed too good to be true. It was most probably a ploy slipped into the conversation to encourage him to persevere. In any case it mattered little because with Monsieur de Sartine's blessing he intended to see the investigation through.

One last question remained: did the Good Lady's wishes and orders have the King's approval?

At Porte Sainte-Antoine he ordered his coachman to go to the Châtelet where he was hoping to find Bourdeau. Would he tell the inspector about his interview at Choisy? Should the meeting be kept secret? He thought about it long and hard. The inspector gave good advice and Nicolas had absolute confidence in his discretion. Sartine had urged him not to brush him aside. In any case the coachman would most probably talk, as he was not under instructions. Despite the choice of Choisy as somewhere distant and discreet Nicolas could have been recognised; his rapid promotion had made him conspicuous.

He was held up by a tangle of vehicles on Rue Saint-Antoine, where a carriage had overturned after the horses had become uncoupled. A herd of passing cows destined for the butchers had taken fright; the chaos was indescribable. It was after seven o'clock by the time he reached the Châtelet. He found Bourdeau in a calm mood, smoking his clay pipe.

'Was the hunt successful, Nicolas?' He went over to close the office door.

'I was at Choisy. The mistress of the house wished to see me.'

Bourdeau's face remained impassive. He merely took a few quick puffs of his pipe. He was obviously in the know.

'Did you discuss our case at all?'

'It was at the heart of the conversation.'

Nicolas gave him a detailed account of his talk with the marquise.

'With such influential protectors we'd be very unlucky to fail in our efforts. Even though the Good Lady doesn't have the upper hand at the moment. As Choiseul's influence is growing, hers is on the decline. On top of that the minister is at odds with Bertin on matters of finance, Bertin himself being one of the marquise's protégés. His brother-in-law, the Comte de Jumilhac, is governor of the Bastille.'

'It's both an advantage and a disadvantage for us. Everything is allowed within certain limits that are unknown to you and me. But not everything is appropriate or useful. Monsieur de Sartine told me as much this morning. There are too many higher interests at stake, and they are beyond us. This murder, these murders, conceal something else. That's the marquise's opinion and I'm tending more and more towards it myself. We need to gather more information about the vicomte. We must find out everything about his life, meet his brother the vidame, his betrothed, his commanding officers and his friends.'

'And we need to do all this with the greatest discretion. It will be difficult.'

'And especially hard because if I belonged to his family I would not be fooled into believing we'd given up the investigation. The Comte de Ruissec will not lower his guard. And we have no new evidence at our disposal, none. I assume, Bourdeau, that you were prevented from doing anything in Grenelle?'

'I was even forbidden from entering the courtyard. A mortuary chapel has been set up in the entrance hall. The funeral ceremony should take place tomorrow, in the church of the Theatines. The bodies will then be transported to Ruissec, where the family has a private chapel inside the church. All I could see were the tapers and the mourning band with the family coat of arms.'

'Did you speak to anyone?'

'I didn't even open my mouth when I was being insulted. But the arrogance of these aristocrats, this nobility that crushes—'

He broke off and gave Nicolas an embarrassed look. The commissioner did not pick up on it. He was in fact unsure what he felt about his own origins, given that he had turned down the title.

The signet ring he was wearing was merely the outward sign of his attachment to the Marquis de Ranreuil's memory and he was not forgetting the venerable figure of Canon Le Floch who really was a man of the people, and of peasant stock at that.

'Bourdeau, I'm beginning to think an expedition is in order. I'm going to think aloud, as if I were talking to myself ... We need to go back to Grenelle and find a way of getting into the house. I really need to see certain things again and carry out another search of the vicomte's bedroom. It would be possible at night. I had thought of getting Picard, the major-domo, to help us. I think he's an honest fellow and he was the one who handed me the comtesse's note; but I'm afraid I might put him in a difficult position. We can probably approach that wing of the building from the back but how can we get inside without breaking any glass or making a noise?'

'Through the bull's-eye.'

'What bull's-eye?'

'Remember the dressing room. It has a round window fitted onto a swivel frame. On my last visit I disturbed the mechanism. If no one has noticed – and there's no reason why they should have done as the rooms have been left unoccupied since the vicomte's death – then all you have to do is push from the outside to get in. With the help of a ladder it would be easy, and there must be one lying around the grounds.'

'In the garden shed. Bourdeau, I take my hat off to you. You're amazing!'

'I've just been thinking ahead. Given the turn of events and the complexity of the case I suspected we would be prevented from returning to the scene rather sooner than expected. It was important to retain a means of access. But we need to weigh up the consequences, Nicolas. If we are caught there, we'll be shown no mercy and we'll be ripe for attending the Tenebrae at the Poor Clares' or going to New France to live with the Iroquois.'

Nicolas burst out laughing. Bourdeau was right. It was a risky undertaking and potentially such a scandal that the authorities would be unable to take any action. However, he remained convinced that there were important clues to the mystery to be found in Grenelle. He was annoyed with himself for not spending more time examining the scene when the vicomte's 'suicide' was discovered.

'Bravo, Bourdeau, I can see in this your professional touch and your feel for detail. As for the rest, we'll just have to trust to fortune. I admit I don't like using roundabout methods but here the end justifies the means. That's what reason of state is all about. Let's draw up our plan of campaign. A carriage, a coachman. You and I, perhaps Rabouine as the scout and the lookout. We'll leave the carriage some distance away so as not to arouse any suspicions. We'll decide how to get over the wall once we're there.'

'We could break down the door.'

'We could, and we have got the weapon to do it. But that's not the solution; the door might creak or have a bell. We need to find the ladder again. The rest will depend on our agility and silence.'

'I suggest,' said Bourdeau, visibly delighted with the idea of the expedition, 'we wear hats.'

Nicolas agreed. This was an old joke they shared, dating from the time when the inspector had saved Nicolas's life thanks to a miniature pistol of his invention fitted to the inside wing of his tricorn. He had given his superior an identical copy as a present.

'When shall we set off?' asked the inspector.

'I already have the carriage. Find Rabouine, who can't be far away. Before that I have to make an urgent visit to the Dauphin Couronné.'

'Aha!' said Bourdeau.

'You're wrong there. It only occurred to me on my way back from Choisy that I might be able to gather some useful information about Mademoiselle Bichelière from our friendly madam. La Paulet can't refuse us anything since we saved her from the poorhouse. I visit her regularly and her ratafia from the Antilles is not at all bad.'

'It's a good idea. She knows everything that goes on in her world of pleasure and illegal gambling.'

'As for our little raid,' Nicolas concluded, 'one in the morning would seem to me the ideal time.'

So Nicolas let Bourdeau prepare the expedition. Before leaving the Châtelet he wrote a brief new report for Monsieur de Sartine. He entrusted it to old Marie: the usher was to hand it to the Lieutenant General of Police in person if their raid on Grenelle went wrong. Otherwise he was to return it to Nicolas the following day. Having arranged this, he climbed back into his coach.

Reflecting on the relations he had established with the brothel-keeper, he considered what set a police officer apart from an ordinary citizen. He now exercised his profession without too much soul-searching. Monsieur de Sartine had once made him read Fontenelle's eulogy of Monsieur d'Argenson, one of his great predecessors. In it he had noted this sentence: 'To tolerate an industry of vice only in so far as it might be useful, to keep the necessary abuses within the required limits, to ignore what it is better to ignore than to punish, to enter families by covert means and to keep their secrets hidden providing it is not necessary to make use of them; to be everywhere without being seen and to be the active and almost unknown spirit of the teeming masses of the city.' All these precepts led to close and regular links between the police and the world of pleasure. Each side benefited from the arrangement.

Nicolas had a strange feeling every time he lifted the knocker on the door of the Dauphin Couronné. He had almost died in this house and he himself had killed a man here. He was still sometimes haunted by that look and that face when he could not sleep at night. And sometimes he relived the duel he had fought blindly in La Paulet's drawing room against an opponent whose every move he had had to anticipate.

He heard a cry of surprise and the door opened to reveal the face of the little black girl, who gave him a half-amused, half-frightened look.

'Good evening,' said Nicolas. 'Is La Paulet available to see Nicolas Le Floch?'

'Always for you, Monsieur. You please follow.'

She pointed towards the entrance to the drawing room, tittering behind her hand. It was too early for the usual customers to have arrived and yet snatches of conversations were coming from inside. Nicolas stopped at the door and listened. A man and a woman were talking.

'My dear child, you are delightful. Kiss me, I beg you.'

'I'm only too willing.'

'I was as stiff as a dog while serving at table because of you. I could hold out no longer.'

'That was obvious enough and so I left the table to come and find you.'

'I've got to take you here and now.'

'Yes, but what if your master catches us?'

'What does it matter, for God's sake? I'd shag you on a boundary stone, I'm so desperate!'

Nicolas gently pushed the door ajar. In the large drawing room with its furniture upholstered in daffodil-yellow silk, the curtain of the little theatre was raised. The *trompe-l'oeil* set depicted a boudoir. The only items on stage were a sofa and two chairs. A slovenly dressed young man and a young woman in a négligé were practising their lines. La Paulet directed the performance by waving her fan, her enormous bulk slumped in a *bergère*. She was wearing a red dress and a black mantilla, and was plastered with more ceruse and rouge than a fairground puppet.

'Put a bit more passion into it, you fool. Can't you tell you're meant to be at the end of your tether? I know it's only a rehearsal but we have to think you're burning with desire. And you, slut, less restrained and more provocative. Remember we're dealing with connoisseurs this evening . . .'

Nicolas coughed to signal his presence. La Paulet let out a scream. The two actors drew back and the curtain fell. After recovering from the shock, the madam got up with great effort.

She shouted towards the stage set: 'There's nothing to fear, children. It's Monsieur Nicolas.'

'I see that you have not given up the theatrical arts,' he said. 'Such spirit! Such passion! Such delicacy! Is Mademoiselle Dumesnil, the goddess of French theatre, on this evening's bill with her covey of dashing lords?'

La Paulet was all smiles.

'We have to make a living somehow. I'm expecting only a few tax collectors on the roister who want to enjoy themselves after supper and revive their failing powers of virility by watching my young actors. So we were rehearsing. At midnight there'll be a private performance and then my girls will satisfy . . .'

'With an edifying spectacle.'

'In a way. So Monsieur le Commissaire has not forgotten his old friend.'

'My dear, you are quite unforgettable. As is your ratafia.'

'Would you like a little glass?' said La Paulet, delighted. 'I've just had a shipment from the Antilles.'

While she filled two glasses with an amber liquid Nicolas looked about him. The layout had changed, the carpets now being in different places. He realised that this alteration was meant to hide the part of the wooden floor stained with Mauval's blood. Settling accounts with the past really did take a long time.

'How's business?'

'I can't complain. I always have plenty of customers. The pleasure we offer is varied, of high quality and with no nasty surprises.'

'Any new recruits?'

'Quite a few. Hard times always bring me young ladies drawn by the city lights.'

'As you know everybody in Paris, does the name La

Bichelière, Mademoiselle Bichelière of the Comédie-Italienne, mean anything to you?'

'Doesn't it just! A little slut, quite pretty, with lovely eyes. She's making a pile at the Théâtre des Italiens. She almost came to me but decided she preferred to make her debut elsewhere.'

'But she plays the innocent.'

'She plays it on stage perhaps, but she began her career at a very young age. Oh yes, she can put on airs all right . . . Nowadays there are no morals left in the trade.'

La Paulet began to tell the story. La Bichelière had come up to Paris from the country when she was very young with a group of gypsies that she then left in order to go begging. That was all she could do, that and dance. She had sunk to the depths of debauchery, reduced to earning her living by using her gentle, deft touch at night in the bushes around the boulevards, providing pleasure that was incomplete but without danger, a second best for the shameful and faint-hearted. Then she sold her main asset to a financier, whilst engaging in numerous amorous adventures with ladies' men.

'In fact,' added La Paulet, 'she renegotiated her main asset on many occasions. The customers fell for it.'

'How come?'

'It's like magic. A small amount of miraculous balm, such as "Du Lac's Astringent Ointment" or an application of "Maidens of Préval Specific Water" and then a small pouch of pigeon blood in the right place and that's it. Being gullible and in the right mood does the rest. It works every time. I came across her one day on Rue Saint-Honoré. She thinks she's the cat's whiskers. But mark my words, she'll end up in Bicêtre like the rest of her kind.'

'How about the gambling?' asked Nicolas. 'Is it still doing well?'

The madam looked embarrassed and dubious. Not so long ago Nicolas had closed down the illegal gambling den that La Paulet had added to her list of activities. However, he knew via his spies that betting was still going on. It was tolerated as long as she proved amenable when called upon.

'I no longer have a protector, so I'm keeping my head down.'

'Which means you're doing exactly the opposite. Do you really think I am foolish enough not to realise that you've found a way of keeping your little business going? Come, come, you should know not to try that with me.'

She was wriggling like a worm on the end of a hook.

'Very well, Monsieur Nicolas, I see I can treat you like a friend. La Paulet is a good sort; she knows how much she owes you. What information do you need?'

'I've been given the task of making sure the honour of certain families is maintained, which means preventing some of our young men of quality from falling victim to swindlers and professional tricksters. I have one particular dissolute case in mind and I wonder if you know that person.'

The little eyes, deep-set in their folds of flesh, stared at him impassively. 'I don't know them all by name.'

'Don't give me that, La Paulet,' snapped Nicolas. 'You're too sharp not to find out information when it might be of use.'

'That's what you think. But I have a very mixed clientele.'

'Ruissec.'

'Wait a minute. That does ring a bell ... Yes, a handsome young man. My girls fight over him. What a loss to the fair sex!'

'What do you mean?'

'Yes, he's going into the Church. Oh, of course that doesn't mean much, but still, seeing a strapping young lad like that ... well, it's a real shame, a waste.'

Nicolas realised that La Paulet was referring to the vicomte's brother. Noblecourt had already mentioned this Ruissec forced by his father into a vocation to which he felt totally unsuited. He had not yet taken his vows and his brother's death meant that he was now the elder son and free to take his life in a different direction.

'He never comes on his own,' added La Paulet. 'He's always accompanied by a Life Guard, someone called ... du Plâtre ... No, de La Chaux. Only the other day the little priest was left without a sou and his friend gave him a ring to leave as security on the understanding that he would pay him back afterwards. I was given the job of negotiating it within the fortnight and paying the creditor. And just to show how open I am with you, I have it here and I'm going to show it to you.'

La Paulet rummaged around in her skirt. She carefully took a ring out of a small bag fastened to her bodice and handed it to him. Nicolas was immediately struck by the jewel's unusual appearance. It was clearly a very fine item. A fleur-de-lis of brilliants was set in a field of turquoises. Judging by the size of the ring it must have been for a woman or man with slender fingers. He gave it back to her.

'I would like this jewel to remain in your possession for a few days. It may prove important.'

One thing intrigued him. On several occasions he had been told that it was the vicomte who was the gambler. His manservant, Lambert, had said so first, and this had been corroborated by Monsieur de Noblecourt.

La Paulet looked grim. 'There's no hurry, Monsieur Nicolas. I always said that pretty boy would bring me nothing but trouble. A good many of my regulars would no longer play with him.'

'With Monsieur de La Chaux?'

'No, the other one, the pretty priest, little Gilles. He plays with his left hand.'

Nicolas shuddered. Gilles ... That was the name that had crossed La Bichelière's lips in the midst of their amorous encounter.

'Left-handed, you say?'

'He certainly is! And people don't like it. They say it brings bad luck in gambling.'

'But that was not the case in this instance.'

La Paulet was carried away by the speed of their exchange.

'There was no risk; we had to restore the balance. We certainly saw to that!'

She sniggered, then tried to win him over by winking at him. Nicolas hated her bringing him down to her own level as if they were accomplices.

'Madam,' he said disdainfully, 'cheating has taken place and you dare admit as much to a magistrate in the performance of his duties. This is a different situation altogether. Please hand over the jewel at once. Remember that gambling here is illegal. We tolerate it and you know why we do so. But when the wolves start to fleece the sheep in this establishment, the matter must be taken seriously. Were this sort of crime to be seen as clever and something to boast about, that would spell an end to law and order. You may tell whoever is responsible that police spies have got wind of the affair. But I'm sure you'll find some explanation without too much trouble.'

'This is robbery!' screamed La Paulet. 'This will be the death of me. Monsieur Nicolas, have you no pity for an old friend?'

'I wish my old friend would keep to her usual activities,' said Nicolas, 'otherwise she might become acquainted with some less pleasant places, which she has so far been spared thanks to Monsieur Nicolas. And she would do well to remember that.'

He left, leaving the madam in a state of collapse. His good humour had evaporated. He needed to digest what he had just learnt. He was also slightly annoyed with himself for having treated La Paulet so roughly. Although he understood the need to blackmail houses of pleasure associated with gambling dens, he disliked being personally involved. Monsieur de Sartine kept repeating that gaming was a threat to society, that it was an unproductive way of diverting money from its use in other areas that were more beneficial to the State.

His visits to the Dauphin Couronné had really never done him much good. It was where he had lost his illusions both of being a police officer and a man of honour. There was no deluding himself: in a world of trickery, bullying, blackmail and the underhand use of authority and law, where was the limit, the boundary between right and wrong? The truth was never easily uncovered. What mattered was to succeed and serve the interests of justice by means that would otherwise be considered dishonourable. He wondered, too, if this might explain his refusal to take the

Ranreuil name but then he said to himself that if he had accepted it he would have been barred in any case from entering the police. At best he would have become a soldier, at worst a courtier. For better or for worse he now served the truth. At least that was what he believed.

VII

GRENELLE

The safest place to hide of all
Is in the holes of yonder wall.
LA FONTAINE

Before setting off on their expedition, Nicolas and Bourdeau ate in a little tavern on Rue du Pied-de-Boeuf at the back of the Great Châtelet, where they were regular customers. The innkeeper gave Bourdeau special treatment because they both came from Chinon. This way, the inspector pointed out, they would not begin their adventure on empty stomachs. Nicolas recounted to him in detail his visit to the Dauphin Couronné and passed on the information he had obtained. Like him, Bourdeau was struck by the appearance of the ring Nicolas had confiscated. The investigation was constantly uncovering ever more puzzling facts.

They found themselves suddenly focusing on the vidame. He was left-handed and that was the third time they had come upon this physical characteristic. Everything pointed to him being on intimate terms with La Bichelière, his elder brother's mistress. A possible motive for fratricide was emerging but Nicolas could not bring himself to believe that one brother might kill another for a reason that, although significant, did not in his eyes justify such a sacrilegious crime. And yet . . . He now urgently needed to make the acquaintance of the vidame, as everything seemed to lead back to him, despite his low profile. They also needed to meet the brothers' mutual friend, the Life Guard Truche de La Chaux. So they would have to extend their investigations to Versailles, which was also, according to recent information, where the vicomte's betrothed, Mademoiselle de Sauveté, lived.

As for Bourdeau, the following day he was to go to the church of the Theatines to observe the funeral mass for the comtesse and her son. The inspector remarked that this was all very well but he did not know how to investigate a crime that had not been officially reported and with no legal authority behind him. He would just have to improvise.

After making sure they were not being watched, Bourdeau took a small box out of his pocket. At first Nicolas thought it was a clock, but on closer inspection it turned out to be a dark-lantern, although a third of the size of a standard one. Bourdeau explained that once again he had called upon the services of the elderly craftsman who had so skilfully made the little pistols for their tricorns. With this, observed the inspector, delighted by his latest acquisition, they would be able to prowl around without being hampered by having to carry a lantern. This model, which was equipped with a clip, could be attached to the front of any garment. It would be particularly useful that night because in order to get into the vicomte's apartments they would first have to climb up and then heave themselves in, a risky manoeuvre for which they would certainly need both hands free.

*

They set out at about midnight. Rabouine had been sent on ahead and was already there. They went through the checks at the toll-gate without incident and soon found themselves on the plain of Grenelle. Nicolas looked out once more at this eerie-looking suburb, where remnants of its rural past stood amongst demolition sites, new buildings and a few old farms whose days seemed numbered. They left the carriage in a tree-lined lane with its lights extinguished. The wind had got up, blowing the dead leaves about and whistling in the branches. Its noise covered up the sound of their footsteps as they walked towards the Hôtel de Ruissec.

Everything seemed quiet in the house and all that could be seen from outside was a dim, flickering light coming almost certainly from the mortuary chapel set up in the entrance hall. They made their way stealthily along the path that ran parallel to the outbuildings until they reached the carriage entrance leading into the grounds. A faint whistle alerted them to Rabouine's presence. He came to reassure them that all was quiet. No one had entered the property that evening, except for a priest accompanied by monks. Rabouine had taken advantage of the semi-darkness to feel his way along the boundary wall, and to the left of the door had identified some loose stones that would make the wall easy to climb over. They would just need to be careful with the pieces of broken glass stuck into the mortar to keep away thieves. But a piece of sacking would be enough for them to get over without gashing their hands. On the other side they would have only to jump down and on the way back they could use the ladder.

The plan was for Nicolas to go in through the bull's-eye on his own, as Bourdeau was too stout. He fastened the little dark-lantern on to his chest and checked that he was equipped with matches. Using it outside was out of the question as they would risk being seen. They would benefit from there being just one long gallery running the whole length of the first floor of the main building. It would be extraordinarily bad luck if someone from the mansion happened at that very moment to be looking out at the grounds, which were in total darkness that night.

Nicolas wanted Bourdeau to let him go on alone but the inspector would not hear of it. He needed to be there to help Nicolas carry the ladder and prevent it from slipping, as well as to lend a hand in the event of a hasty retreat. These were very valid reasons but the real one, which he did not mention, was concerned with the young man's safety. Out of friendship for him and in his role as Sartine's obedient inspector, Bourdeau would not leave him. He would wait in the shadows until the visit was over and keep the ladder hidden. Rabouine set off again to keep watch.

They found climbing the wall straightforward because it was built of millstone grit, which made it easy to get a hold, though had they not taken the precaution of wearing gloves they would have grazed their hands. Nicolas put the piece of sacking on the top. Fortunately the broken glass barely protruded from the mortar and he was able to hoist himself up without injury. He sat down carefully, then launched himself into the void. He landed softly on a bed of dead leaves and rotting soil. He moved to one side and Bourdeau immediately joined him. Nicolas motioned to him to follow him along the wall.

They reached the corner of the grounds without incident and

found the gardener's shed. The door was open and Nicolas lit the small dark-lantern after sending Bourdeau inside and then shutting the door. In the dim light they could see tools and potted seedlings. There, leaning against the wall of the shed, was the ladder. They took it and, after extinguishing the lantern, set off again towards the left of the building, making for the wing that housed the stables and the vicomte's rooms. Nicolas recognised the cobblestones beneath his feet and deduced from the smell that they were walking past the first stable door. He had forgotten the rosebushes growing between the two doors. He stumbled and caught his boot in the thorns, almost falling and taking Bourdeau with him. One end of the ladder struck the wall. The silence was broken by prolonged neighing and the clatter of hoofs: they had woken a horse. They held their breath for a moment, then everything went quiet again. Nicolas thought how fortunate it was that there were no dogs roaming the Hôtel de Ruissec or they would really have been sunk. He avoided the second clump of rosebushes just below the dressing room.

They used guesswork to set up the ladder, leaning it against the wall. Nicolas took the precaution of removing his boots, both for his own comfort and to avoid making a noise and leaving footmarks. At the top of the ladder he found he was at the right height straightaway. He could feel the pane of the bull's-eye and, after finding its lower moulding, pushed it gently. The opening was not wide and he realised that it would be impossible for him to get through: the top of the ladder was still too low. After a moment's thought he climbed back down and explained the situation to Bourdeau. The inspector decided to move the bottom of the ladder closer to the wall and further to the left. This way

Nicolas's feet would be level with the bull's-eye and he would be able to get into the room sideways.

The second attempt was successful; by clinging on to the frame, which did not give way, he managed to slip through, then move forward until he could feel the top of the dressing table. His touch rolled some items from their position but he decided he would put them back later. The main objective had been achieved and he could set to work.

Precariously perched on this fragile piece of furniture, he cautiously lowered his legs and put his feet on the floor. He gave himself a few minutes for his heart to stop racing. Then he relit the dark-lantern, found his bearings and pushed open the bedroom door. Nothing had been moved since his first visit. Every item was still in its place except that the hurricane lamp on the desk was now in a more natural position. He walked across the room and on the other side of the alcove pushed the door hidden in the panelling that gave access to the little library closet.

Nicolas began a systematic inventory of its contents, comparing some of the titles with the list of authors he had noted in Monsieur de Noblecourt's library. It was a badly organised collection that contained what one would expect to find in the home of a young man, who was also an officer, from a good family – works on fencing and horse-riding, military memoirs, frivolous and even libertine literature, and books of scholasticism. Nicolas was interested to note that many of the authors were Jesuits. The regularity with which these religious or polemical works recurred intrigued him. Bookmarks or markings in lead pencil indicated passages justifying the legitimacy of murdering kings. He shuddered with horror as he picked out incitements to regicide, underlined in a work written in 1599 and entitled *Du roi et de l'éducation* by a certain Mariana, of the Society of Jesus. The reference reminded him of something: this book had been implicated in the murder of Henri IV by Ravaillac. Continuing his investigation, he was intrigued by a licentious work that did not shut properly. On closer examination he discovered that the lining of the binding had been unstuck and then stuck back down again. He felt something thick underneath. With the aid of the small penknife that he always carried with him he carefully cut out the lining paper. Two sheets of very fine paper fell out. One showed a geometrical drawing and the other was written in such tiny characters that it was impossible for him to decipher with the little light he had available and without the help of a magnifying glass. He returned the documents to the book and slipped it into his coat pocket.

Suddenly he heard the sound of floorboards creaking some distance away. Nicolas hurried out of the library, extinguished the lantern, and listened. Someone was walking along the corridor. There was no time to escape. He remembered the large wardrobe near the door to the room. He opened it and ducked into the huge section where the boots were kept. The wooden floor creaked again, then silence. Was it just a false alarm? In the stillness his heart was pounding, making his head throb. Feeling more reassured, he prepared to leave his hiding-place when there was another loud noise, closer this time. There was no mistaking it: someone was trying to pick the door lock. He himself had done the same when the body was discovered. A slight click confirmed that the lock picker had been successful. The sound of creaking floorboards came ever closer, broken intermittently by long silences. Through gaps in the wooden wardrobe he saw a flash of light, then a flicker. A candle had just been lit. Nicolas slowed his breathing. Straining with all his senses, he followed the visitor's progress as if he could see him. He heard him go past and then into the library to the right. He could made out the sound of shuffling feet, then the faint, regular noise of things falling onto the floor. Surrounded by darkness once more, he was losing all notion of time and the wait seemed unending. Although he was in a fairly comfortable position, he feared his body would become numb from lack of movement or, worse, that spasms brought on by cramp would betray his presence. In that case he would find himself facing either a legitimate visitor or an intruder like himself. And then what?

Objects were still landing on the floor: the visitor was searching through the books, one by one. Perhaps his quest was identical to Nicolas's own, in which case he was looking for the book already in Nicolas's possession. After a considerable amount of time, the stranger left the library. His footsteps were hesitant. He banged loudly on the door of the wardrobe and swore under his breath. Nicolas then had the impression that he was moving around the bedroom; the gleam from the candle had broadened. He wanted to look through a chink in the wood, but it was not close enough and the slightest movement would have given him away. The stranger wandered about the room for a few more minutes. Nicolas feared he would look in the dressing room. The open bull's-eye, along with the untidy table he had stood on, might have aroused his suspicion. Then he heard the door being gently closed and the footsteps faded away. Nicolas waited for a few more moments, then lit his lantern, pushed open the wardrobe door and emerged back into the bedroom. There was no one there, but the library was in chaos. The books lay in heaps on the floor, with bindings that had been torn off, pulled apart and ripped open. Not a single volume had escaped unscathed. Nicolas's horror at the sight before him was mingled with the satisfaction of knowing that the intruder had drawn a blank.

He tidied up the dressing case on the dressing table and was preparing to leave through the bull's-eye when he realised that he would have to go out head first. He was suddenly gripped by anxiety. The weight of his body meant he might easily fall, and a fall from that height – twenty-five to thirty feet – was enough to kill anyone. He had to think quickly. He eventually decided simply to open the window of the adjoining bedroom and call Bourdeau, who would bring him the ladder. At that very moment he heard the inspector's voice and saw his head appear in the opening of the bull's-eye. Bourdeau, too, had been thinking about how hard it would be for Nicolas to get out. He explained his solution. Head first, Nicolas grabbed Bourdeau's shoulder with one hand, drew up his legs, pushed his chest through and, after twisting his whole body, ended up on Bourdeau's back. This was followed by a difficult descent down the ladder. The combined weight of their two bodies made each rung bend and creak. But at last they reached the ground. Nicolas put his boots back on and removed all traces of footprints in the soil around the rosebushes. They returned the ladder to the lean-to. The frame of the bull's-eye was closed and there was no sign of their intrusion. When the ransacked library was discovered, suspicion was bound to fall on members of the Ruissec household.

Rabouine appeared, worried by their long absence. They climbed back into the carriage with him and headed towards the city. Nicolas described his eventful visit, including the mysterious intrusion. Bourdeau agreed with him that it must have been someone from outside the Ruissec family as the comte would not have needed to take such precautions when visiting his son's rooms. However, they still had to check whether the vidame had been at home. He might have had reason to visit his brother's bedroom. In any case, one detail had particularly struck Nicolas: the visitor made the floorboards creak but he had not heard the sound of shoes. Had the person taken the same precautions as Nicolas?

'Bourdeau,' he said, 'the vicomte's manservant, that Lambert fellow ... I questioned him after he suddenly appeared behind me; he wasn't wearing shoes, but in stockinged feet. He even apologised, saying he'd left his room in a great hurry. But I noticed that in fact his servant's uniform was impeccably neat and buttoned up, and his cravat had been properly wrapped and knotted.'

'What do you deduce from that?'

'That without realising, we have perhaps re-enacted what happened in the room that evening. We've solved the mystery of the room locked from the inside, my friend!'

'I don't see how, without the key. But I know you're going to explain what happened.'

'It's blindingly obvious! The Vicomte de Ruissec was killed in circumstances that we have yet to determine. For reasons we do not know, his murderers – and I emphasise the plural because all this presupposes accomplices – bring back the body by carriage. They go through the entrance gate into the grounds and their carriage waits in the lane; I found the tracks it left. They take the ladder, put it up against the wall . . .'

'You make it sound as if you were actually there!'

'I noticed the marks of the ladder's feet in the earth around the rosebushes as I patrolled in the evening, after the body was discovered. Don't forget how heavy the body was, weighed down by all that lead. Besides, remember how we got down!'

'True, and you aren't even full of lead,' laughed Bourdeau.

'The operation required two men to hoist the body up to the window . . .'

'But you specifically said that the windows and their inner shutters were bolted. How could they have got in? It doesn't make sense.'

'Bravo, Bourdeau. Your objection has provided me with the key to the mystery. Since everything was shut – well and truly shut – when the body was discovered, someone must have closed these windows, mustn't they?'

'I'm just not with you.'

'And in order to close them, someone must have opened them first. It's obvious. Bourdeau, Bourdeau, Lambert is one of the murderers . . . Everything fits. Remember the major-domo's evidence. He sees his young master, or rather he dimly recognises him because he has poor eyesight. The vicomte does not speak to him and for a very good reason. Because if he had spoken Picard would immediately have realised that it was not his voice. Why Bourdeau? Why?'

'Because it wasn't the vicomte?'

'Exactly. It wasn't the vicomte; it was Lambert, Lambert wearing his master's sodden cloak. Remember again the major-domo's evidence, that's the basis for my theory. Lambert goes up the stairs, opens the door to the apartments, goes in and locks the door. He throws the cloak and hat on to the bed. I was particularly struck by this detail; where I come from, you know, you never throw a hat on to a bed, especially not upside down.'

'There's a good old Breton superstition for you.'

'Not at all. Ask people in Chinon. Lambert takes off his boots, which are the vicomte's. He opens the shutters and the windows, and goes out and down the ladder to help his accomplice to bring the body up. They drag the body along, leaving suspicious marks on the wooden floor. They put the boots back on the body, write the note and fire a shot at the corpse. One of the accomplices escapes through the window, which Lambert closes again, and then hides himself.'

'That would be far too risky. Why didn't he just escape along the corridor? And where did he hide?'

'You're forgetting about the pistol shot that alerted the whole house. He didn't have time to escape. He was forced to remain on the spot, trusting to luck.'

'Nicolas, it's impossible. He would have been trapped like a rat.'

'What about me? Just now when the intruder came into the bedroom I was in a very tight corner. What did I do?'

'Good Lord!' said Bourdeau. 'The wardrobe.'

'I know all about wardrobes. As a child I used to play hide-and-seek with ... Well, never mind. It was in the chateau at Ranreuil and my favourite hiding place was an enormous wardrobe that was tall enough for an officer in the dragoons to stand up in. In the same way as I did, Lambert must have hidden in that wardrobe, fully dressed but in his stockinged feet because he had put the boots he was wearing on the dead body. After the comte and Picard had been sent away I was alone in the room with Monsieur de Sartine, who had collapsed into an armchair. We both had our backs to the door and therefore also to the wardrobe, which stands to the right of the entrance. The little light there was came from a candle and the hurricane lamp. Lambert sprung up from behind us as if by magic. Clearly it was because he had been cramped up in the wardrobe! That's why we neither saw nor heard him come in. Add to that, Bourdeau, the fact that he was the person who gave us various pieces of information which were intended to put us off the scent. Yes indeed, everything fits.'

'The audacity! How could anyone be so shameless and calculating? He's no ordinary criminal, that's for sure.'

'And that's not the end of it. Just now I took possession of some documents hidden in the binding of a book, which I assume to be what our intruder was also looking for. Why else would the library have been ransacked?'

Bourdeau thought for a moment.

'Nicolas,' he ventured, 'if your theory is right, that Lambert could well have been this evening's visitor. Who else otherwise? The comte is ruled out; the comtesse, his wife, is dead. We know nothing about the vidame. But one thing intrigues me. I can understand that the Comte de Ruissec and his family did not want the scandal of an autopsy. On the other hand I think it's unbelievably strange that a father who must by now be convinced

– having seen the body – of how his son died, is not trying to do everything possible to find and punish those responsible.'

'That is the crux of the matter, Bourdeau. There's something else behind this murder. And we seem to be forgetting that Madame de Ruissec was also murdered. Almost certainly because she knew something and wanted to tell me about it. We have a clue that will lead somewhere. By the way, thank you for your help. I was beginning to wonder how I was going to get myself out of there.'

'For once it was Anchises carrying Aeneas!'

'Except that you are neither paralysed nor blind, thank God!'

They were both impatient to return to the Châtelet in order to examine the documents Nicolas had found. They had to wake the guard and old Marie to get back into their office. Bourdeau looked for a glass lens to magnify the two documents found inside the book. The first was a drawing with coded information. It consisted of small squares placed next to one another, making up what looked like an upside down U; the second, which was handwritten, contained tiny characters that looked as if they had been formed with the point of a pin.

Holding the lens, Nicolas was startled to decipher these words: 'To the King's whore . . .' He could not believe his eyes. It was the original, or a copy, of the printed tract that Madame de Pompadour had showed him at Choisy. How did this text come to be hidden in a book from the Vicomte de Ruissec's library in Grenelle? Was it connected with the information that the King's favourite had been careful not to confide in him? Did she want to set him off on a trail whose mysteries she had already solved?

Bourdeau suddenly let out cry. Having looked at the drawing from every possible angle he had finally understood what it represented. He waved it about.

'I've got it,' he said. 'It's a plan, and not just any old plan. It's a plan of the palace of Versailles, showing the courtyards, doors, guard posts and passageways between every building. Look.'

The inspector indicated different points on the drawing.

'Can you see? Here's "the Louvre", and there's the Princes' Courtyard, and here the Ministers' Wing. This long rectangle is the Hall of Mirrors and over there is the Ambassadors' Staircase.'

'You're right! And the other piece of paper seems to be the original of a scurrilous tract that Madame de Pompadour found in her apartments! This is all very disturbing. It's a plot or something very much like it.'

'I think,' Bourdeau said, 'the Lieutenant General of Police should be informed immediately.'

'By tomorrow morning, or rather in a few hours' time. Until then let's rest a while. It's going to be a hard day. I shall go to Versailles to investigate and you will be my eyes and ears at the Theatines.'

'I really don't like leaving you on your own in these circumstances.'

'Come on, Bourdeau. Nothing can happen to me at Court. Don't worry.'

Saturday 27 October 1761
After a few hours of fitful sleep, Nicolas left Rue Montmartre

very early. He wanted to catch the Lieutenant General of Police at his toilet. After normally rising at around six o'clock Monsieur de Sartine liked to extend his early morning routine by having breakfast, reading the first reports from Court and the city and receiving anonymous-looking emissaries.

Although he was early, Nicolas missed his superior; by the time he arrived his carriage had just left the Hôtel de Gramont. A minor official informed him that Monsieur de Sartine was on his way to Versailles for a meeting with Monsieur de Saint-Florentin. He would be spending the night at the palace as he was due to attend Mass and have an audience with the King as he did every Sunday. Nicolas asked for a carriage. All this was working out quite well: he intended to carry out some enquiries at Versailles. He wanted to find out more about the vidame and Mademoiselle de Sauveté. Both would certainly have stayed behind in Paris for the funeral service for the vicomte and his mother at the church of the Theatines. That would leave him time to find Truche de La Chaux and to question him on some pretext or other. He still did not know exactly what, as officially no investigation was taking place; he decided to leave it to chance, which often presented the opportunity he was looking for.

As Nicolas went over Pont de Sèvres, thoughts of two people crossed his mind: one was the Marquise de Pompadour, whose chateau of Bellevue he could see on the hill, its terraces gleaming in the splendour of the rising sun, and the other was the Minister of Bavaria. From the window of his cab he could see the muddy bank of the Seine, the setting for the strange scene that had been described to him. He urgently wanted to question the coachman but the Minister of Bavaria's servant had not yet been found.

Nicolas reached Versailles late in the morning and directed his carriage to the palace forecourt. He had taken great care over his clothes: a dark grey coat, a delicate lace cravat and cuffs, silver-buckled shoes, a new tricorn and a sword at his side. His carriage was put away and he noticed Monsieur de Sartine's coach and horses nearby. He walked towards the wing of the palace that housed the ministers' offices. He had to push his way through a bustling, noisy crowd of petitioners, minor officials and business-men thronging on the main steps. After submitting to some courteous questioning by an usher he managed to have a note delivered to his superior. In terms intended to intrigue the Lieutenant General, Nicolas emphasised how urgently he needed to meet him and to inform the minister, Monsieur de Saint-Florentin, of an extremely serious matter.

Nicolas knew Sartine well enough to expect a swift response because the commissioner was well known for never sounding the alarm without good reason. And he did not have long to wait. A footman came for him, and led him through a maze of corridors and staircases. A door was opened and he entered a vast office. Two men sat eating at a pedestal table near a window looking out over the grounds. He recognised the minister, to whom he had already had the honour of being introduced, and Sartine. One o'clock chimed on the chimneypiece clock, topped by a figure of Victory crowning a classical-style bust of Louis XIV with laurels. Nicolas gave a deep bow.

'You know Commissioner Le Floch, of course,' said Sartine.

The rotund little man in his tight-fitting coat glanced furtively at the new arrival, then after looking away, cleared his throat before speaking.

'Yes, I do.'

Nicolas found it hard to believe that this shy, blushing figure before him enjoyed the King's confidence and held such extensive powers. The minister still retained the King's favour, despite his unpopularity and the undisguised contempt that certain members of the royal family showed towards him. But one thing explained the other: the man was totally devoted to the King and his lack of brilliance simply added to his merit in the eyes of a monarch who had little liking for new faces and habits. His wife, whom he neglected in favour of his mistress, was well thought of by the Queen and was now her favourite confidante. This double good fortune further strengthened the minister's influence. Yes, who could have believed that this unprepossessing, paunchy little man, next to whom the austere Sartine looked like a knight in shining armour, was the enthusiastic dispenser of *lettres de cachet* and grand master of the King's own justice?

'So, Nicolas, I assume that some matter is sufficiently grave to warrant your pursuing me even here.'

Nicolas assumed that Monsieur de Saint-Florentin was already well acquainted with the details of the case, and he acted on this. He was careful, however, not to put Sartine in a position possibly at odds with other instructions from higher up. He skilfully outlined the unusual circumstances of his visit to Grenelle, knowing from experience that the great of this world rarely stoop to the humdrum details of police operations. He ended by showing the papers he had discovered, making no mystery of the fact that one of them matched the printed tract found at Choisy by the Marquise de Pompadour.

'Aha!' said Saint-Florentin. 'The young man has the ear of our friend the marquise!'

The minister examined the papers. He ordered Nicolas to fetch a magnifying glass from his desk and bring it. Nicolas could not help noticing that the instrument was lying on top of a pile of *lettres de cachet* ready to be signed. Monsieur de Saint-Florentin studied the documents carefully and then handed them to Sartine.

'The tract is nothing unusual,' said Sartine. 'I have a dozen or so like this which are seized every single day. But the drawing is intriguing.'

Nicolas coughed. They looked at him.

'Allow me, gentlemen, to put forward a theory. In my opinion this sketch represents the palace. Look at the cipher in this little square; it seems to correspond to this office.'

Monsieur de Saint-Florentin blinked, deep in thought. He took the document and examined it closely once again.

'Well, well!' he said. 'Your deputy is right, Sartine! This is much more serious. These plans may be an attempt at working out the layout of the palace and moreover, they contain secret information to which we do not have the key but that probably relate to the ciphers. Do you not agree, Monsieur?'

'I fear so, Monsieur.'

'Indeed, indeed . . . I think I'm going to alter the course of these investigations. Listen, Sartine: this must remain secret. I do not want anyone to trouble the King with all this . . .'

Nicolas recognised almost word for word a concern expressed by the marquise.

'However, having had to temper the legitimate ardour of our commissioner, much to my regret and for reasons that you will appreciate, I am anxious for this matter to be resolved. I am said to be conciliatory, a friend of order and harmony, but I value above all common sense and everything I have just heard is precisely that. I will not go back over the measures already taken, instead I shall turn a blind eye and give my approval to investigations based on, let us say, individual initiative – yes, that's a good way to put it.'

He began to laugh, then suddenly appeared serious again, as if annoyed at having let himself go, and he continued with an air of authority of which Nicolas would not have thought him capable.

'Commissioner Le Floch will gather information about this case by the use of any means he may deem appropriate. In particular he will take as proven that the Vicomte and the Comtesse de Ruissec were murdered. He will unravel the motives behind their deaths. Finally, under your authority, Lieutenant General of Police, he will attempt to solve the mysteries surrounding these papers and seek to explain their connection with the crimes we are dealing with. There we are: your task is urgent but needs total discretion. Total and utter discretion.'

He went to his desk, took two *lettres de cachet*, signed them, furiously sprinkled them with powder and then, after shaking them, handed them to Nicolas.

'Finally, here are two blank weapons that you have the authority to charge and use!'

He sat down again and turned to the contents of his plate,

without showing any further interest in Nicolas. Sartine signalled to him that it was time to leave. He bowed, went out and found himself back in the palace forecourt, feeling somewhat dazed. Since the start of this case the authorities, with all their orders and counter-orders, had treated him like a plaything and seemed to have no clear idea of how to proceed. The irony of the situation struck him even more after this last audience with the two most important members of the police force in the kingdom. He had been sent to investigate, then the same authority had taken matters back into their own hands, influence had been exercised from various quarters, blowing hot and cold, and finally he had just been put back on track. His mind was made up: he would do his job without worrying too much about the consequences.

The time seemed right to go off fishing for information about Mademoiselle de Sauveté, the Vicomte de Ruissec's betrothed. According to Bourdeau's sources, she lived on the Paris road, the wide avenue opposite the palace. This still predominantly wooded area offered a vista of grand mansions, more modest town houses, the barracks of the King's regiments and inns, all neatly aligned and almost touching. He went there on foot, leaving his coachman free until four o'clock, when he was to drive him back to Paris.

As he walked along, Nicolas sketched out a plan of action. It was clear that the young woman must have gone to Paris to attend her betrothed's funeral at the church of the Theatines.

She would not be back in Versailles until four or five in the afternoon. That would leave him enough time to question the servants or the neighbours. He was surprised by how modest Mademoiselle de Sauveté's house looked, because she was said to be wealthy. What stood before him was no more than a modest country villa, a sort of hunting lodge or one of those gatehouses to be found on either side of the grandiose entrances to great estates. The one-storey building was surrounded by a large garden enclosed by a wall. The overall effect was one of neglect: dead leaves were strewn over the lawn and in the flowerbeds unpruned rosebushes still bore their last blooms, withered by the elements. He pushed open the gate and walked towards the house. A large French window was open; he went closer. It opened on to an old-fashioned drawing room with heavy, elaborately turned furniture. The walls were hung with red damask that had faded and was torn in places. The colours of the threadbare carpets had also faded. Like the outside, the room had a sad, neglected look.

He was about to go inside when he sensed a presence behind him and at the same time he heard a shrill, grating voice.

'What's this? Where do you think you are and what are your intentions, Monsieur?'

He turned. A woman stood before him, her right hand resting on a long stick. A full-length dark cloak, in an indefinable colour, almost entirely covered a shapeless purple dress. Her face was hidden by a large muslin veil, which hung over a straw hat; beneath this screen she wore dark glasses, of the sort used by people with failing eyesight. What ghostly creature is this? wondered Nicolas before this shapeless apparition of indeterminate age.

She must surely be Mademoiselle de Sauveté's housekeeper or a relative. He introduced himself.

'Nicolas Le Floch, police commissioner at the Châtelet. I beg you to forgive me but I was looking for Mademoiselle de Sauveté to discuss some matters concerning her.'

'I am Mademoiselle de Sauveté,' said the grating voice.

Nicolas was unable to conceal his surprise. 'I thought you were in Paris, Mademoiselle. Your betrothed ... Please accept my condolences.'

She struck the ground with her stick. 'That will do, Monsieur. You have the temerity not only to enter my house but to presume to mention my private affairs.'

Nicolas felt a growing sense of annoyance. 'Where can we talk, Mademoiselle? It so happens that I am empowered to question you and I warn you that—'

'Question me, Monsieur? Question me? And for what reason, I pray?'

'The death of the Vicomte de Ruissec.'

'He killed himself while cleaning a weapon, Monsieur. That does not justify your request.'

He noted that she seemed well informed of the official version.

'The circumstances of his death have attracted the attention of the police. I must hear your evidence. May we go inside?'

She barged past him. He caught a whiff of her perfume and followed her. She sought refuge behind a large Spanish leather armchair. He observed her two gloved hands, tensely gripping its back.

'Come, Monsieur. Let us conclude this quickly. I am listening.'

He decided to precipitate matters. 'Why is it that you are not at the church of the Theatines?'

'Monsieur, I have a migraine, I have failing eyesight. I have little taste for society and besides, I did not know Monsieur de Ruissec, having only met him once.'

How absurd! thought Nicolas. Was this a joke at his expense?

'Are you trying to tell me that you saw your betrothed only once?' he asked. 'You will understand that I find that strange and hard to believe . . .'

'Monsieur, you are interfering in family matters. The intended union between us related to private agreements in which personal acquaintance had little place. I should add that such arrangements are not your concern.'

'Very well, Mademoiselle. So I will remain within the boundaries of my function. Where were you on the evening of . . . your betrothed's accident?'

'Here.'

'Alone?'

'Yes. I live alone.'

'What about servants?'

'I have a gardener a few days a month, a housemaid twice a week.'

'Why do you live in such isolation?'

'I like solitude. Am I not free to live my life as I wish without someone constantly asking me to give explanations?'

'Did you know the Comte de Ruissec?'

'I was no better acquainted with him than with his son. Our affairs were decided between lawyers.'

'What are their names?'

'That is no business of yours.'

'As you wish. Do you have any family?'

'I am on my own.'

'But you have not lived in Versailles all your life, I assume.'

'I come from Auch originally, and two years ago I settled here to take up an inheritance.'

'And where did that come from?'

'From my family. Monsieur, that is enough. Please withdraw. My poor head can take no more.'

She made a strange gesture as if she had wanted to offer him her hand to kiss only to restrain herself at the last moment, after realising the incongruousness of the idea. He bowed and left. He could tell that she was watching him until he pushed open the gate. Only then did she slam the French window shut.

The vision of this strange creature stayed with him. Nicolas could not stop thinking about this being with her ill-defined outline and unbearable voice. The face was indistinguishable, with the gauze veil and thick ceruse. The dark glasses added to the disturbing overall effect. *The angel of death with her sunken eyes* ... It beggared belief that the Vicomte de Ruissec, the noble scion of an illustrious family, should have linked his destiny to a scarecrow who was as ugly as a witch. Nicolas could now really understand why the vicomte sought amorous adventures in the boudoir of a sultry actress, who at least, as he knew only too well himself, could provide grace and laughter as well as a dash of vindictiveness in her love-making. None of this made any sense. What miracle or what mad compulsion had led the Ruissec family to seek a union between its elder son and this screeching harpy? Could it be that money alone was the reason for this absurd mismatch? Nothing seemed to indicate the lady's vaunted wealth, or else she was plumbing new depths in dissembling and miserliness. Around Guérande Nicolas had met rich country gentry who liked to disguise the extent of their wealth, earning the contempt of other wealthy landowners for whom ostentation was the rule. Perhaps this explained Mademoiselle de Sauveté's behaviour.

In any case it was clear that she was completely indifferent to the vicomte's death. This unclassifiable being had made such an impression on him that he could not take his mind off her, especially her voice with its shrill, false-sounding notes. He must find an explanation for her union with the Ruissec family. Monsieur de Noblecourt's advice was certainly right: Nicolas would write to the intendant of the generality of Auch to find out more about the lady's past.

He was walking away deep in thought when a sweet little voice attracted his attention.

'I say! Have you found what you were looking for? May I offer you my help?'

A prettily dressed little old lady, with porcelain-blue eyes beneath a goffered lace cap was standing on the doorstep of the house immediately next to Mademoiselle de Sauveté's.

'In what way, Madame?'

'I saw you talking to our neighbour. Are you one of her friends or someone who . . .' She hesitated. 'Well . . . is connected with the police?'

Nicolas was always surprised by the perceptiveness of ordinary people. He was evasive.

'No, I don't know her. I just needed a piece of information.'

She blushed and hid her hands beneath a starched pinafore.

'Oh, good! That's much better. She's not liked, you know. She doesn't speak to anyone. And she always dresses the same way. It's frightening!'

'Does she have servants?'

'None, Monsieur. We find it disturbing. Never a visitor. Whole days go by without her appearing. Sometimes she comes home in a carriage when we haven't seen her go out.'

Nicolas smiled. 'Perhaps you just missed her.'

'Oh, come now! I'm sure you're from the police but you're right to be discreet. And I understand why you don't want to tell me. If I'm so definite about her it's because my husband and I take it in turns to watch because we're so intrigued. What did she tell you?'

She put her wizened little face closer to him, at once apprehensive and inquisitive.

'Nothing that could interest or worry you.'

The old woman huffed. She had been hoping for more than this but Nicolas had already bid her farewell and hurried away. By sheer good fortune he had learnt something without having to ask. Everything he had just found out fired up his desire to learn more. So Mademoiselle de Sauveté had no servants, whereas she had claimed the opposite. Had she thought it would be that easy to get rid of him? She would soon discover the price of trying to fool the police. The Vicomte de Ruissec's betrothed was added to the long and growing list of mysteries that had been building up since the beginning of this investigation.

*

Nicolas was once again on the vast Place d'Armes. He returned to his carriage, unsure what to do next. He did not know how to find Truche de La Chaux. He was giving this some thought when his coachman handed him a small note. It was a brief message from his friend La Borde. Sartine must have informed him of Nicolas's arrival and La Borde had then sought out his carriage to leave him this note. In it he asked Nicolas to go and see him as a matter of urgency. A royal page would be waiting for him at about five o'clock at the entrance to the apartments to act as his guide. The prospect of this unexpected meeting calmed Nicolas somewhat. It would soon be time. He went through the palace's second set of gates and entered 'the Louvre', the innermost precinct of the chateau.

VIII

MADAME ADÉLAÏDE'S HUNT

I roam the forest night and day,
Where king and nobles come to play
But then I hear the hunter's cry,
The fateful sign that I must die.
JACQUES DU FOUILLOUX

In the guardroom Nicolas noticed a royal page with fair hair, whose sharp eyes were examining every new arrival from head to foot. He realised this was his guide. He was immediately taken in hand and whisked off through the usual maze of rooms, corridors and staircases. Would he ever manage to find his own way around this palace? The expedition took them to the very top of the building. He knew that Monsieur de La Borde had been given a small suite of rooms under the eaves, a special favour granted by the King. The royal page opened a door without knocking, as he was a member of the Household; he stepped aside to let Nicolas enter. He was immediately taken by the peacefulness of the drawing room, with its roaring fire in a garnet-red marble fireplace. On the pale oak panelling were small depictions of hunting scenes and above the hearth a magnificent framed map of France. A library set into the wall but also extending either side of a door contained row after row of pocket-books that further contributed to the overall effect of pleasant intimacy. Wearing a chintz dressing-gown but no cravat or wig, Monsieur de La Borde was lounging on a sofa upholstered in a large red floral design on a cream background, and was engrossed in reading a document. He looked up.

'Ah, my dear Nicolas, here you are at last! Thank you, Gaspard,' he said to the royal page, 'you may leave but do not go too far away. We might need you.'

The young man turned on his heels and, after a cheeky little bow, disappeared.

'Make yourself at home, my friend. You will liven up my dreary afternoon. I was compiling the writs from my creditors.'

He showed him the heap of papers beside him.

'There's no worse way to spend one's time,' said Nicolas.

'No indeed. But enough of that. Nicolas, enlighten me. What stage have you reached? I found out you were at Versailles from Sartine. It seems that you won over the minister this morning. My compliments, he's not an easy beast to tame! I hear you are now someone who can command respect.'

'And why is that?'

'Because you are armed with those ready-signed *lettres de cachet*, of course!'

'You may rest assured, my friend, I shall not be using them against you.'

'If the service of the King required it, you would not hesitate and you would be right.'

Once again Nicolas was struck by Monsieur de La Borde's ability to pick up news. By virtue of this mysterious gift he shared a liking for secrecy that was the outstanding characteristic of his royal master.

'So you were looking for me, were you?'

'Indeed I was. Monsieur de Sartine asked me to inform you that Madame Adélaïde has invited you to her hunt on Monday morning. I can shed no further light on this event, but you need to make arrangements immediately.'

Nicolas showed his surprise. 'To what do I owe this unexpected honour?'

La Borde gave a wave of the arm as if he were brushing away a fly. 'Don't worry your head about it. Either it is a sheer whim of the princess's after hearing mention of you ...' He paused and looked at the clock. 'Or there is something in the air and the summons – I mean the invitation – has another meaning. You will find out on Monday.'

'I am honoured,' said Nicolas, 'but I am not equipped to take part. What can I do?'

'This is where I can help you, my friend. I am leaving Versailles for two days; I have business in Paris. Accept the modest hospitality I can offer you here. You will be doing me a favour. If anyone asks for me, be so kind as to let me know, at this address.'

He handed him a sheet of paper. Nicolas noted that La Borde had been so sure of his response that everything had been prepared down to the smallest detail.

'I don't know whether I can accept such a generous offer ...'

'Not another word. For your equipment I have the answer also. You know that Madame, on her father's orders, hunts neither the stag nor the boar. She restricts herself to deer, game that is considered harmless. No special uniform is required for this type of hunt; a jerkin is enough, together with a jacket and boots. We are more or less of the same size. My men will provide you with everything. So that should reassure you.'

La Borde explained to Nicolas that the First Grooms of the King's Bedchamber commanded authority over all domestic arrangements in the palace and had at their own disposal a large staff of servants: a cook, a major-domo, a footman and a coach-man. They could also eat from the King's table because there was always too much food and the leftovers were shared out.

'I must quickly go and dress and leave for Paris immediately. Make yourself at home. Any questions?'

'I'm looking for a Life Guard. In your opinion where might I find him?'

'In his barracks or else tomorrow in the Hall of Mirrors while the King is hearing Mass. Gaspard will help you. He's a cunning little rascal.'

As he was about to open the door, he stopped and turned.

'Oh! One more thing. The meeting place for the hunt is in front of the palace, facing the park. You are on the list. Make yourself known and get into the carriage. It will take you to the assembly point where you will be given a horse –' he rushed over and took something from the mantelpiece, '– in exchange for this note. Be generous with the whippers-in, it will stand you in good stead this time and next: they are the ones who choose the horses! There is nothing for you to worry about – my men have been informed. Gaspard will not leave your side and will tell your coachman to come back on Monday. Lastly, my library is at your disposal.'

He left the room. Shortly afterwards he reappeared dressed and bewigged, and, after a friendly wave to Nicolas, who was reading, he left.

This was a special moment for Nicolas. He found it hard to believe that he was in the royal palace. He had never known such splendid surroundings, so far removed from the austerity of the garret in Guérande or even from the good taste of his room at Monsieur de Noblecourt's house. Even the ancient splendours of the chateau at Ranreuil paled in comparison with what was around him. He had glanced at the titles of the books assembled here, delighting in the look and feel of the bindings. Their subjects included music, history, travels and libertine literature.

Nicolas suddenly remembered the royal page. He opened the door on to the corridor and found him sitting on a bench. Knowing the sort of person he was dealing with, he gave him a few coins that were pocketed without thanks but with a satisfied grin. He told him he would not be needed for the whole evening, but that on Sunday morning he was relying on being taken by him to the Hall of Mirrors, when the King would be passing through and where he hoped to find Truche de La Chaux.

Gaspard reassured him. He slept only a few yards away and Monsieur de La Borde had given him clear instructions to watch over Nicolas and to remain at his disposal. Nicolas questioned him about whether it would be possible to meet the Life Guard.

'I can assure you it will be. He's much in demand.'

'Do you mean that someone else is also looking for him?'

'Was looking for him. On Monday or Tuesday . . . no,

Tuesday. Monsieur de La Borde was away in Paris for the day; he was due to attend a performance at the Opéra. Towards eleven o'clock or midday I happened to be in the Princes' Courtyard when an individual asked me to deliver a note to Truche de La Chaux.'

'So you know him, do you?'

'Yes, by sight, like the others.'

'And did you hand him this note?'

'No, not directly. When I reached the guardroom he wasn't there, but when one of his friends in the French Guards, a lieutenant, heard me enquiring after him, he took the note and promised to hand it over as soon as he saw him.'

'That's interesting. Do you want to earn a few extra *écus?*'

'I'm at your service, Monsieur.'

He held out his hand, which Nicolas filled appropriately.

'Had you already seen the person who gave you the note?'

'No, he was a valet without livery.'

'Can you describe him to me?'

'To be honest I didn't look at him closely enough. His face was hidden by a hat.'

'What about the lieutenant?'

'He was a lieutenant like any other; the uniform makes them all look alike and they don't like royal pages much.'

'Thank you, Gaspard. We'll talk about this again another time. Good night.'

He went back inside and remained deep in thought for some time. So the day the Vicomte de Ruissec was murdered, a note was sent to Truche de La Chaux by an unknown person – a note that by all appearances ended up at midday in the hands of a lieutenant in the French Guards, who might easily be the vicomte. Was this connected to the murder? He suddenly went back out into the corridor to call Gaspard. The boy reappeared immediately.

'My friend, you must tell me everything. This note that you took to Truche de La Chaux . . .'

'Yes, Monsieur.'

'You must understand that this is important and that I shall be able to reward . . .' He waved another gold coin. 'Did you read it?'

Gaspard was fidgeting, looking embarrassed. All his cheekiness had vanished.

'Well, yes. It wasn't sealed, only folded. I didn't think . . .'

He looked crestfallen, resembling more and more a young lad caught stealing apples.

'It will have been a good thing that you did,' said Nicolas with a smile. 'What did it say?'

'It was to arrange a meeting in front of the fountain with Apollo's chariot as soon as the note had been received. I thought it was a lovers' tryst.'

'Good. And what did the lieutenant do? I'm sure that you kept a discreet eye on him.'

'He did the same as me, read it, then rushed out.'

Nicolas threw the gold coin, which was caught in mid-air. When he returned to the apartments an obsequious manservant had set up a small table with venison pâté, a brace of partridges and a bottle of chilled champagne, not to mention a few sweet delicacies. Nicolas did justice to this feast and, after reading for about an hour, found the bedroom had been made ready for him and the bed warmed. Amidst such delights he fell asleep peacefully without thinking of the day's events or what was to happen in the days to come.

He woke very late and, after quickly washing and dressing in a small, well-appointed closet, he breakfasted on hot chocolate served by an impassive manservant. He read for an hour or two, then called Gaspard, who was waiting in the corridor. Truche de La Chaux would be on duty in the Hall of Mirrors and Nicolas would take advantage of this to see the King go past on his way to Mass.

He was surprised by the noisy bustle of the crowd. In the Hall of Mirrors and the War Drawing Room, those present were lined up along the window side. From the Throne Room onwards they were positioned well inside the rooms to allow free passage through the enfilade of doors. He was positioned by Gaspard not far from where the sovereign would emerge from his state apartments. He found himself amidst courtiers and provincial noblemen who had come to see their master. The mirrors in the hall multiplied the crowd and made it seem enormous. Nicolas saw the King emerge and had eyes for nothing else. Etiquette required each person to remain still. One was not supposed to bow but to keep one's head erect. Thus the King could be seen by everyone and could see everyone.

When he went past Nicolas, his brown eyes with their vacant stare seemed to brighten and the young man felt he had been noticed and recognised. He became quite convinced of this when, after the procession had passed, a group of talkative, inquisitive people formed almost a circle around him. This did not suit his purposes at all: he was not supposed to make himself conspicuous. He melted into the crowd, hoping that Gaspard would find him. And indeed soon there was a tug at his sleeve and, weaving in and out of the crush, the boy led him along to the War Drawing Room. There, near the brown marble bust of a Roman emperor, Nicolas spotted a Life Guard, whom he immediately recognised as the man from the tavern in Choisy, and whom he had come across again after his audience with the Marquise de Pompadour. So the man he was looking for was connected with two areas of his investigation. There had to be some explanation for this. His immediate concern was to appear to have not recognised him. There was no point in arousing his suspicions; he would soon see how the fellow would react.

The man gave Nicolas a half-smile as he approached. From the featureless face with its pallid complexion and fair beard Nicolas could tell it was the man from Choisy. He drew closer to him.

'Monsieur Truche de La Chaux, I presume.'

'At your service, Monsieur. And you are . . . ? But did we not meet only recently in Choisy?'

The man was putting his cards on the table and Nicolas had not been expecting this.

'I am a police officer. I would like to speak to you about the Vicomte de Ruissec. I believe you know him.'

'I know that he is being buried today after his unfortunate accident. Had I not been on duty—'

'You knew him, then?'

'We all know one another here.'

'What about his brother, the vidame?'

'I know him, too. We have had occasion to play cards together.'

'At the Dauphin Couronné?'

For the first time the man looked surprised. 'You are asking the questions and giving the answers.'

'Does he lose much?'

'He gambles like a madman and never bothers to count his losses.'

'And do you help him pay his debts, like a good friend?'

'I have done so.'

'Did you give him a ring to pledge, for example?'

'It's a family heirloom.'

'That you simply handed over. That's hard to believe.'

'What would one not do to help a friend? It could always be redeemed. Are you one of those spies from the Gaming Division?'

Nicolas did not rise to this provocation.

'Where were you last Tuesday afternoon?'

'In Choisy. At the chateau.'

'Do you have any witnesses?'

He gave Nicolas a contemptuous sneer. 'Ask you know who. She will confirm it.'

What could he say in answer to this rejoinder, which put the two men on an equal footing? It was obvious that Truche de La Chaux was trying to trip him up and associate him in his own deviousness. What then did the King's favourite have to do with someone of that ilk, who also happened to be the common factor in a criminal investigation?

'I'm afraid I do not understand what you mean. Do you know the Comte de Ruissec?'

'Not at all. I know only that he is a member of Madame Adélaïde's entourage. And with that, Monsieur, I must leave you. My presence is required for the end of Mass in the chapel.'

He bade farewell and strode off. Nicolas watched him go. He was not satisfied with this conversation. It had produced nothing new and was merely confusing the issue. It had even created a new problem by hinting at secret connections between Truche and Madame de Pompadour. What was more, the Life Guard seemed very sure of himself. Was he innocent or protected by a higher authority? In any case, what could he be accused of except being involved in various aspects of the investigation, with the apparent exception of the Comtesse de Ruissec's death? The fact remained, however, that some unknown person had arranged a meeting with him and the plan had been thwarted by a lieutenant in the French Guards.

Gaspard was waiting for him. Nicolas thought he should let the young man go. It did not prove so simple; the royal page did not want to leave him, no doubt because of the clear instructions he had received from Monsieur de La Borde. Besides, after Nicolas's generosity it was a matter of honour for him to prove his worth. Nicolas eventually succeeded in convincing him, assuring him that he wished to visit the gardens and the ornamental fountains and that he would meet up with him later in the First Groom's apartments; he knew his way around now and could manage on his own. He simply had the boy show him how to get to Apollo's Chariot. It was child's play, Gaspard told him. He only had to keep in line with the palace and walk straight on.

*

The park revealed itself to be a source of surprise and wonder to Nicolas. Struck by the grandeur and beauty of the gardens, he crossed the water parterre, admired the Fountain of Latona and the Basins of the Lizards, and walked straight ahead until he finally reached Apollo's Chariot in the middle of its ornamental pond. He wanted to see the place that had been chosen for the mysterious rendezvous. He did not know exactly what he was looking for. In the midday sun a gentle breeze lightly ruffled the surface of the water.

He decided to go and see the Grand Canal, which began just behind Apollo's Chariot. He went through the Sailors' Gate, which was guarded, and was surprised to see a dozen or so boats moored on the bank of the Grand Canal. He carried on walking. As he went along the immense waterway, his attention was suddenly caught by an eddy. His first thought was that it had been made by a giant carp leaping out of the water: it was in fact a child struggling and desperately waving his arms about. He kept opening his mouth but no sound came out. He clearly had no strength left. Nicolas hastily removed his coat and shoes and plunged into the water. He swam swiftly towards the child, took hold of him, lifted his head out of the water and brought him back to the bank.

It was only then that he could examine the creature he had just saved. He was a puny-looking boy, aged between ten and twelve, dressed in rags. There was a scared look in his beautiful eyes and his mouth continued to open and close without producing any sound. He kissed Nicolas's hand. After a few minutes of puzzlement Nicolas realised that he had saved a poor deaf-and-dumb boy.

With the aid of gestures, they eventually managed to hold a conversation of sorts. The child had been fishing, had fallen in and, not knowing how to swim, had been swept away by the choppy water. He had been on the point of drowning when Nicolas reached him.

Nicolas drew a house in the gravel. The child stood up, took him by the hand and led him off into the untamed countryside of the great park. They walked for a long time through the thicket before coming to a large hedge covered with brambles, which concealed the entrance to a long building made of logs. The child now became agitated and strangely anxious. He suddenly pushed Nicolas back towards the forest, kissed his hand again, smiled and then motioned him to leave.

Nicolas found himself in the forest once more. Hours had passed and night was about to fall. He had some difficulty finding his way again but thanks to his country upbringing he knew how to plot his bearings amidst the tall trees. With the help of the distant light of the stars he found the Grand Canal and went through the Sailors' Gate. There the same guard recognised him. Nicolas questioned him and was told that many fountaineers' workshops were allowed in the Great Park, and the one he had seen probably belonged to Jean-Marie Le Peautre, who had set it up only a few months ago with his helper Jacques, a young deaf boy.

On reaching the chateau he discovered Gaspard pacing up and down, waiting for him. He went up to La Borde's apartments where, after getting changed and drying off, he read until supper time. When he returned to his bedroom an outfit had been laid out on an armchair: jerkin, cravat, jacket and braided tricorn, together with a pair of boots and a hunting knife. He asked the manservant to wake him early in the morning.

Monday 29 October 1761

The manservant woke him at the crack of dawn. The meet was arranged for ten o'clock and the carriages were due to leave half an hour earlier. Nicolas took his time, getting ready with particular care, and was only satisfied once he had seen a flattering reflection of himself in the pier glass above the fireplace. At the appointed time Gaspard appeared, his sharp-featured little face now cheered by a kindly smile showing that he had adopted Nicolas, and advised him to set off.

The carriages were assembling in front of the North Wing. A host of vehicles was waiting. A valet examined the note that Nicolas handed him and pointed to his carriage where a young man who did not introduce himself eyed him up and down and then turned away. Nicolas did not take offence at this and lost himself in contemplation of the gardens, then the park. After passing through a gate, the carriages quickly entered the forest pathways. He saw again the great park where he had walked the previous day. The countryside became increasingly wild, with fields, fallow land, spinneys and tall trees. Three-quarters of an hour later the caravan arrived at the meet. The guests alighted from their carriages and, following his neighbour, Nicolas once more presented his note to the whippers-in. He remembered to tip one of them, who, with a knowing wink, showed him a tall dappled grey gelding. He preferred to give a favourable interpretation to this gesture of complicity. The animal in question, after bucking and rearing a few times to test him, realised that it was dealing with an experienced horseman and bowed to his will. For a horse used by so many different riders Nicolas thought it obeyed the bit rather well and that they would prove good companions. He felt in high spirits. A few paces away a young lady in a green riding coat was talking loudly. Nicolas recognised her as Madame Adélaïde, who was listening to an elderly master of hounds giving his report. He was showing her deer droppings on some leaves.

'Long, Madame, well formed and shaped. A good-sized male.'

'Did you see it, Naillard?'

'I went out beating in the early morning, I headed it back, then saw it feeding. A fine tall beast with palmed antlers. I followed it with my dog back to its lair in the thicket, where it went to ground again. Then I marked the spot with broken branches.'

The princess appeared satisfied and the troop of riders moved off again in the midst of the barking pack.

To begin with, Nicolas simply enjoyed the exhilarating experience of once again riding a contented mount. The two of them were as one, both filling their lungs with the pure forest air. He had always loved to gallop and forget all his cares. He was, however, forced to slow his pace, for fear of overtaking the head of the hunt. Besides, Madame Adélaïde had just put her horse into a walk and did not seem eager to hurry things along until the animal was started and the pack at its heels. Just as the hunters were entering a large clearing she suddenly left the main group and went into the shade of the trees. The unpleasant person who had travelled in the same carriage as Nicolas came up to him and, with a wave of his hat, requested him to join the princess. Now it was Nicolas's turn to enter the shade of the trees, amidst the dried and reddish ferns. Madame had halted her horse. He came closer, jumped down and, removing his tricorn, bowed. She gave him a kindly look but did not smile.

'They speak well of you, Monsieur.'

There was nothing he could say in reply. He simply adopted a modest expression. Who could 'they' be? The King? Sartine? La Borde? All three, perhaps. Certainly not Saint-Florentin, whom the King's daughters hated.

'They say you are wise and discreet.'

'I am Your Royal Highness's humble servant.'

That went without saying.

'There has been some troublesome business in my Household, Monsieur Le Floch. My poor Ruissecs have been struck by misfortune, as you know . . .'

She meditated for a moment. Nicolas even thought she was praying. Then she seemed to brush aside some annoying thought.

'Still . . . I also have recently discovered some very unpleasant thefts from my caskets.'

He dared interrupt her. She smiled at him in surprise. She was a beautiful young woman with an imperious charm.

'Jewels, Madame?'

'Yes, jewels. Several jewels.'

'Would it be possible for Your Royal Highness to have a list drawn up by one of your most trusted servants describing the missing items?'

'My people will see to it that you are provided with the list.'

'Would you permit me, Madame, to put some questions to your servants, under the guidance of a member of your Household?'

'Do as you please. I am relying on you to solve this matter.' She smiled once more. 'I knew your father. You resemble him.'

A horn sounded from not very far away. A loud voice shouted, 'There it goes!'

'I believe, Monsieur, the deer has been started for the dogs. It is time to go. Good hunting.'

She spurred her mount, which whinnied and set off. Nicolas put his hat on again, remounted and followed at a canter. He could hear blasts on hunting horns and the hunters shouting. There was considerable confusion. It looked as if the hunted animal was doubling. A whipper-in could be heard calling in the dogs: 'Tally-ho! This way!' and alerting the hunters. Amidst this commotion Nicolas's mount became nervous and bolted. Before he could bring it under control it had carried him away from the hunt. Deafened by the rushing wind, he did not hear two riders come up from behind. By the time he felt their presence it was already too late. Turning round, all he could see was a black cape stretched between them that struck him, knocking him to the ground. His horse fled in panic. His head hit a tree stump, for a moment everything was a blur and then he passed out.

He felt a dull throbbing in his head. He should not have dispatched his supper and wine so eagerly. And besides, the bed was very hard and the bedroom cold. He tried to pull up the sheet and felt the buttons of his jerkin. He gathered his wits and then recalled the attack. He really had been set upon by two strangers.

Where was he? Apart from a sore head, he seemed to have no broken bones. As he tried to stretch he realised that he was bound, hand and foot. A familiar odour told him where he was being held prisoner. That musty smell and the reek of extinguished candles and incense could only belong to a consecrated place, a church or monastery. There was no light at all, just darkness. He shuddered. Was he locked away in a crypt or the dungeon of a monastery, where no one would ever find him? He had a growing feeling of suffocation and anxiety.

One detail kept coming back to him, although it seemed trivial given the gravity of his situation: he had not thought of informing Monsieur de Noblecourt that he would be spending several days in Versailles. He could imagine how worried his friends would be. In the end this nagging thought helped him forget his predicament. Time passed.

After several hours he heard a noise. A door opened and the light from a lantern dazzled his sore eyes. When he opened them again he could see nothing; someone had gone behind and blindfolded him. He was picked up, carried almost, and dragged outside. He could feel steps underfoot, and then fresh air on his cheeks. He heard the crunch of gravel. Another door opened and he had the impression that they were going back indoors, and was struck by the same church smell. He was made to sit on a straw-bottomed chair, which he could feel under his fingers. His blindfold was removed. His eyelids were swollen and there was a searing pain in the nape of his neck.

The first thing he noticed was a large black wooden crucifix on a white wall. An old man in a cassock sat at a table, hands clasped, staring at him. His eyes gradually became accustomed to the light. A single candle was burning on an earthenware plate. He stared at the elderly priest. There was something familiar about him but the years had taken their toll on a face he had known in another life.

'My God! Father Mouillard! Is it really you?'

By what twist of fate did he find himself in the presence of his former master from the Jesuit college in Vannes? He was astonished at the transformation of that lovable man into this wild-eyed and lost-looking figure. And yet it was only a few years since they had last met.

'Yes, it is I, my son. And I am sorry to meet you in these circumstances. You recognised me but I cannot recognise you. I have lost my sight and I thank God for granting me this grace, which spares me the pain of seeing these wicked times.'

Nicolas understood why his master's features had changed. In the dim candlelight his eyes appeared almost white and his lower jaw trembled constantly.

'Father, what have you to do with my abduction?'

'Nicolas, Nicolas, one must go through certain trials to reach the truth. It matters little to me how you come to be here; I have no part in that. Go down on your knees and pray to the Lord.'

He knelt down himself by leaning on the table.

'Even if I wanted to,' said Nicolas, 'I could not. I am bound, Father.'

'Bound? Yes, by the error of your ways. You are determined to ignore the right path, the clear path, the one I taught you and from which you should never have strayed.'

'Father, please explain to me why I am here and why you have come. Where are we?'

The priest continued to pray and replied only after standing up again.

'In the Lord's house. In the house of those who are unjustly threatened and persecuted and to whose enemies you lend the support of your office, to your eternal shame.'

'What do you mean?'

'The damned of the Court have charged you with the task of investigating so-called crimes. Your role is to level false accusations against our company, the Society of Jesus.'

'I am merely doing my duty and searching for the truth.'

'You have only one duty: you must obey that inner grace that in all things and all ways abides by God's glory. You have no other rule of conduct than His divine commandments. You must reject all tyrannical power and repudiate the reign of the evil one, be he even crowned.'

'Am I to conclude from your words that your society is involved in the appalling crimes I am investigating?'

'What we want from you, what I, poor old man that I am, have been instructed to command you is to give up an investigation that may harm an institution from which you have received everything and to which you owe what is best in you.'

'I am the King's servant.'

'The King is no longer lord of his domain if he abandons the holiest of his servants.'

Nicolas realised that it was pointless to argue. The old man's infirmities, and the orders he had received, had obviously so confused his mind that he had lost the even temper that had made him the most respected master at the college in Vannes when Nicolas was a student there. He knew that regretfully he must now lie to Father Mouillard.

'Father, I have difficulty believing you. But I shall meditate upon your teaching and reflect on my actions.'

'My son, that is good and I know you once more. "Whosoever will save his life shall lose it; and whosoever will lose his life for my sake shall find it." Listen to the word of the Lord; you can never meditate upon it enough. In all things one must not show so much concern for what the world thinks. By seeking to save ourselves in the present we damn ourselves for eternity. I bless you.'

Nicolas had never imagined he would have to dupe his old master, but he knew that beyond his venerable person there were other less saintly and more unscrupulous interests that had to be deceived. Father Mouillard fumbled for the candle, which he snuffed out, plunging the room into darkness. Nicolas heard a door open. Someone came up to him and blindfolded him again.

An unknown voice spoke: 'Has he agreed?'

'He is going to reflect on it but I think he will do so.'

Nicolas felt sick at heart at the old man's confidence.

The voice went on: 'In any case, it's just a first warning.'

This sounded like a serious threat. Nicolas was again bundled off into a carriage, which immediately set off at full speed. He had now fully recovered consciousness and tried to calculate the distance travelled by counting the minutes. After an hour the carriage stopped and he was pushed out. They untied his hands and threw him unceremoniously into a ditch full of dead leaves and stagnant water. He heard the carriage drive off. He took off his blindfold. Night had fallen. He tried to free his legs. He managed to do so only after half an hour's struggle, thanks to his penknife that miraculously was still in his jerkin pocket. It was eight o'clock in the evening by his watch, which had also survived unscathed.

He had been well and truly knocked out, then abducted and must have remained unconscious for many hours before coming to. Where he had been held did not really matter. The important thing was that, without making any secret of the fact, the Jesuits or some Jesuits had had him abducted and had used a poor old man to try to influence him and blackmail him into abandoning his investigation into a case that seemed to threaten the King's safety.

What was more, they had not hesitated to use the opportunity of the King's daughter's hunt to carry out an outrageous assault on the person of a magistrate. There had to be serious and significant interests at stake for people to go to such lengths. One way or another, he thought as he followed the dark verge of the path, there was a connection between the Society of Jesus and this case. Whether directly involved in the murders or not, the Society feared the result of the investigation and seemed prepared to do anything to hamper its progress. Some seemed to be relying on his loyalty and gratitude. It was true that he had never added his voice to the almost unanimous chorus of critics of the Society. Because of his gratitude for the education he had received and because of the respect he still felt towards his former masters, his feelings towards it had never changed.

He knew perfectly well that the Society was under threat. On 2 August the King had made it publicly known that he would not pronounce on their fate for another year. However, there had been a series of damning judgements against the Jesuits in cases of bankruptcy. In the Paris Parlement, Abbé Chauvelin had painted a terrifying picture of the Society, depicting it as a hydra with the Old World and the New in its grip. He claimed that its existence in the kingdom was based only on the principle of tolerance and was not an absolute right. By the end of November the French bishops were due to submit their recommendation to the King. They were said to be divided on what position to assume. All this justified and explained why the Jesuits feared a scandal in which they might be implicated and which could have a decisive effect on both public opinion, already deeply hostile to the Society, and on the King's final pronouncement.

Nicolas eventually reached a small village. He knocked on the door of a cottage and asked an astonished-looking peasant where he was. In fact his wanderings had not taken him very far from Versailles: he was just between Satory and the royal town. He enquired whether it would be possible to find a carriage to take him back to the palace. After much discussion, dithering and confabulation, which strained his patience, it was arranged for him to be taken back to the palace by a fat farmer who owned a cart. One hour later he was on the Place d'Armes.

Having followed his instructions to come and collect him on Monday evening, his coachman was there with Gaspard, who was asleep on the box of the carriage. Worried by the rumours of his disappearance, the royal page had come to wait for him to take him back to La Borde's rooms, as it was difficult to gain access to the palace after the doors and 'the Louvre' had been closed. Nicolas simply said that he had fallen from his horse and had got lost in the forest.

He went up to La Borde's rooms to wash and to clean the ugly bump on the back of his head. He left a message of thanks for his friend, in which he gave a concise account of the day's events and their consequences. Gaspard accompanied him back to his carriage. They were firm friends by the time they left each other, the young man offering to do him a thousand favours whenever he came back to Versailles.

The return journey to Paris was a dreary one. Nicolas was in pain from his injury and very sad that Father Mouillard had been used so wickedly in his declining years to exert pressure on his former pupil. The lasting memory he would have of that day was not the conversation with the King's daughter, nor his first hunt with the Court, but the distressing picture of the old man.

When he arrived at Rue Montmartre very late that evening, the house was in turmoil. Marion, Catherine and Poitevin were in the pantry waiting for news. Monsieur de Noblecourt was pacing about in his rooms. When they saw Nicolas they all shouted out at once. The procurator, alerted by his dog, hurried downstairs as fast as his old legs would carry him. This welcome and the anxious questions with which they bombarded him soon restored Nicolas's spirits, and he was immediately forgiven as soon as they learnt what he was prepared to tell them of his adventures at Court. He reserved for Monsieur de Noblecourt's ears the one incredible detail.

IX

UNCERTAINTIES

Omission to do what is necessary
Seals a commission to a blank of danger.
SHAKESPEARE

Tuesday 30 October 1761

Nicolas woke early. His stiff, aching body was painful proof of
the treatment he had received the previous day. The throbbing
pain from the bump on his neck was excruciating. He remembered similar mornings in his youth, the day after a game of *soule*.
This violent sport in which players were constantly exchanging
blows usually ended in an epic brawl and then a hearty feast,
washed down with sharp cider and apple brandy, at which
everyone became friends again.

Washing and dressing was a long and painful process. He
walked slowly down to the pantry where Catherine saw his sorry
state. She assessed the damage and decided to take him in hand.
For many years she had been a canteen-keeper and seen her fair
share of battles, marches, brawls, soldiers on the spree, strained
muscles, wounds and bumps. This experience had taught her a
number of practical remedies and a knowledge of poultices,
which added to what she had learnt from her peasant childhood in
Alsace.

She rummaged around in the depths of a cupboard and took out a carefully sealed earthenware jug. It was, she claimed, an all-powerful remedy that she kept in store for special occasions: a concoction of herbs in plum brandy. A 'witch' from the area of Turckheim, who happened to be her aunt, had bequeathed her a few jugs of it. She guaranteed its miraculous effect.

Ignoring his protests, she made Nicolas undress, chiding him for being so shy in front of an old woman who'd seen all this before, and worse, when she was with the army. She then rubbed him down vigorously with her magic potion until his skin felt hot. The warming, stimulating effect of this rough and ready application seemed to relax his muscles. To complete her treatment she poured him a small glass of the liquid: initially it made his throat burn but as soon as this wore off he felt its benefits. A feeling of warmth welled up inside him, which extended and speeded up the lotion's effect.

Now, according to Catherine, he must get under the bedclothes and sleep until he was completely rested. Nicolas scolded her for not giving him the remedy on his return the previous evening. She replied that muscles need to stiffen before they can be loosened properly and that yesterday, so soon after his misadventure, he would not have been able to work off the pain as he had this morning. Catherine treated herself to a small glass in anticipation of ailments to come, then carefully put the jug back in its hiding place. The rest of the household was still asleep, exhausted from the waiting and dramatic events of the previous night.

*

Back on Rue Montmartre Nicolas sensed something unusual. He put it down to his physical state and to his nervousness following the assault and abduction of the previous day. He decided to keep to his usual precautions and discreetly went down Impasse Saint-Eustache.

Once inside the church he hurried into a gloomy chapel and hid himself in the corner of an altar. He heard footsteps and saw a man in grey, who was obviously following him and who, having lost sight of him, was walking rapidly towards the main door. Nicolas was able to escape the same way he had come in and jumped into a sedan chair waiting for custom. So the hunt was continuing: he was now no longer the hunter but the game.

When he reached the Châtelet, Bourdeau, who knew from the coachman some of what had happened at Versailles, informed him that Sartine had been detained by the King after his weekly audience and that he would not be returning to Paris until after High Mass on All Saints' Day, the day after next.

'That certainly does not help matters,' said Nicolas. 'Though I have to go back to Versailles in any case.'

He gave an account of his audience with Monsieur de Saint-Florentin and how he had been given *carte blanche* to continue his investigation. He described the strange Mademoiselle de Sauveté and the violent end to his invitation from Madame Adélaïde, but he made no mention of the incident in Saint-Eustache, so as not to worry the inspector unduly.

'I do respect your feelings as a former pupil of the good fathers,' said Bourdeau, 'but these people really are a menace. I agree with Abbé Chauvelin. These priests take orders only from their general. They are bound together by their vow of obedience. But I don't think they have much of a future. What you describe sounds like the death throes of a wounded animal. Do you know what people are singing? Loyola was lame and Abbé Chauvelin is a hunchback. The whole of Paris is humming this song.'

He began to sing it himself in a deep voice:

> *Oh company of evil,*
> *A cripple was your founder,*
> *A hunchback's now your curse.*

Nicolas gave a sad smile. 'I'm not following you down that path, Bourdeau. You know my sense of loyalty towards my teachers. But I think there are bad shepherds and I bear a particular grudge against those who dragged Father Mouillard into this reckless adventure.'

'In any case it proves how well organised they are. Did they bring him from Vannes at the drop of a hat, just to debate with you?'

'He's not from Brittany. He must be living out his last years in one of the Society's houses.'

'But notice how well informed they were. I can't imagine Sartine, La Borde or Madame had a hand in this ambush.'

'Of course not. But, Bourdeau, tell me what you found out at the service in the church of the Theatines.'

'It was a fine ceremony, all very dignified. There were not many family members present and even fewer friends. The Comte de Ruissec was prostrate with grief. Apart from how distressed he looked, three other things struck me. First, as you know, the vicomte's betrothed, Mademoiselle de Sauveté, was absent. As I don't know her, I made sure I found out about her. Secondly, the vidame was there, a very charming young man and very definitely left-handed! We knew that but I was able to check it when he sprinkled holy water on the coffins. But that's not all: Lambert, the manservant, is also left-handed . . . The aspergillum again. Thirdly and lastly, the family kept the vidame out of things. He did not go with the Comte de Ruissec to his mother and his brother's final resting-place. Isn't that surprising for a young cleric, albeit a libertine?'

'We've talked about him for far too long. I really must go and question him.'

'You're right. And we now know something useful about him. After the service was over, I followed him. He went back to his home on Rue de l'Hirondelle, a small street that runs between the Place du Pont-Saint-Michel and Rue Gilles-Coeur. He came back out quite quickly and do you know where he led me?'

'Oh, Bourdeau, I'm too tired for guessing games.'

'To the corner between the boulevards and Rue de Richelieu, where Mademoiselle Bichelière lives. He only stayed there a moment, two or three minutes, no longer. He got back into a cab and dashed away. I passed myself off as a tradesman and after paying my due to an ape-faced woman on the door, I found out from the maid that her mistress was not at home but at the theatre.'

'At the theatre, so early in the morning. That's very strange . . .'

'I questioned the creature and she confirmed the young man with clerical bands often came to hear the pretty actress's "confession". She told me that with a horrible grin full of innuendo that could not be misunderstood.'

'This is vitally important, Bourdeau. So the vidame knows his brother's mistress very well. We shall see what he has to say about all this. Perhaps he'll be more inclined to speak to us than his father. From now on we must draw up our plans, work out and verify all these people's movements and cross-check our findings. In the end we'll discover the weak spot. We already have two left-handed men involved in this case. We can almost state as certain that Lambert was in the wardrobe and that he took part in the murder, as well as in transporting his master's body. He's an accomplice in the suicide cover-up. We are missing a second culprit. There's no reason why it might not be the vidame.'

'How shall we proceed, Nicolas? I'm not happy to leave you on your own from now on.'

Nicolas finally decided it would be wiser to tell the truth.

'I didn't tell you that I was followed this morning. My old trick in Saint-Eustache worked wonders, but I'm going to have to be even more watchful. However, this is too large a task for us to stay together all the time. But I might resort to one of my disguises to mislead our enemies. For the time being I would like you to find out all you can about La Bichelière, Lambert, Truche and La Sauveté. What are their backgrounds? For heaven's sake, we are the best police force in Europe! If need be, write to the intendants instructing them to reply by return. I want answers by the end of the week, so that we can know everything about them.'

'I forgot to tell you that the Minister of Bavaria's coachman has been arrested.'

'I shall have to see him. Monsieur de Sartine is bound to ask about him again, as soon as the plenipotentiary next shows himself. I didn't say a word about my suspicions. This is a chance to verify them.'

'Where are you going to begin?'

'I'm sorry to leave you with all this paperwork but we can't avoid the detail if the case is to succeed. As for me I'm going to get changed and hurry off to question one of our jeweller friends on Pont au Change about the ring pledged by Truche de La Chaux. Then I'll try to pin down the vidame. Don't forget we're having supper at Semacgus's this evening, in Vaugirard. I'll spend the night there and leave early tomorrow morning for Versailles to investigate Madame Adélaïde's household.'

A few moments later an elderly, portly bourgeois leaning on a stick and carrying a leather bag stepped out of the Châtelet and climbed into a carriage. Nicolas had spoken to old Marie for several minutes without the usher recognising him. Reassured by this test, he was driven to a shop on Pont au Change belonging to the jeweller Koegler, to whom the Lieutenant General of Police often turned in cases involving stolen jewels. He was welcomed with the enthusiasm reserved at such places for wealthy customers.

In a faint voice he requested the master craftsman kindly examine an item that he wished to acquire but whose provenance might, he also feared, be dubious. He added that a friend of his had given him this address as a place where the workmanship and the hallmarks would be properly checked.

Suitably flattered, the jeweller adjusted his magnifying glass and examined the fleur-de-lis ring that Nicolas had confiscated at the Dauphin Couronné. The examination was slow and meticulous. Monsieur Koegler shook his head. His advice was not to buy the item and even to inform the police. The ring was extremely old and carefully made. The gems were remarkable for their water and for their size but – and here the man lowered his voice – there was every reason to believe from various observations, which he kept to himself, that the item belonged to the Crown Jewels and that it had been stolen from a person of royal blood. There was only one thing to do: to rid oneself of it by handing it in as soon as possible to the appropriate authorities, on pain of being accused of possessing stolen goods, which in this particular case would be tantamount to the crime of lese-majesty. Nicolas took his leave, assuring the jeweller that he would follow his advice and that he was going to hand over this compromising item to the right person.

Although the Vidame de Ruissec's home was not very far from Pont au Change, Nicolas ordered his coachman to take him first to the Comédie-Italienne. He did, however, suggest a few detours, in order to check that he was not being followed. He made the coachman drive into a blind alley and wait a moment. Feeling reassured, he gave the order to carry on. He closed the curtains in the cab and quickly changed his appearance: he spat out the tow lining the inside of his mouth, removed his false white eyebrows, wiped off the ceruse covering his face, took off the wadding that gave him an artificial paunch and pulled off the bourgeois wig to reveal his own hair. He took a firm grip of the apparently harmless stick whose hollowed-out interior contained a well-tempered sword.

At the Comédie-Italienne the washers and scrubbers were still at their morning work, toiling away with bucketfuls of water. Above this tide stood the tall silhouette of old Pelven, who in his time had swabbed many a deck on the vessels he had served on. His craggy face lit up when he saw Nicolas. He immediately wanted to drag him off to celebrate their reunion with a few glasses of his favourite beverage or even by sharing his repast, whose pleasant smell was already wafting through the corridors of the theatre.

Short of time and mindful of the effects of his last foray into sailors' cuisine, Nicolas succeeded in politely declining the invitation without the doorkeeper taking undue offence. He enquired as to what brought Nicolas there, and immediately answered his questions.

No, of course, La Bichelière had not set foot in the theatre all day Saturday, nor indeed since. She was really going too far and the exasperated director never stopped complaining, threatening to increase the fines for her repeated absences. The actress's punctuality often left a lot to be desired and her frequent failure to turn up had disrupted the performances and resulted in the use of understudies who were often under-prepared and less popular with the public. Had it not been for her charms and how they attracted the swells, she would have been only a strake[1] away from being thrown out on to the street, which was where she belonged. That would be her just reward for idling around to no purpose.

In answer to another question, Pelven assured Nicolas that a young cleric had turned up on Saturday afternoon asking for the pretty miss. Annoyed at being told she was not there, he had become so insistent and so unpleasant that Pelven had slammed the grille in his face. The old salt added that the welcome given the young man had been all the chillier because he had made no attempt to mollify the doorman's surly temper by greasing his palm.

This hint was not lost on Nicolas, who gave him due reward for the precise and plentiful information received. He cut short Pelven's show of friendship by asking him if he could leave by the back of the building, having told the coachman to wait on Rue Française in front of the leather market. The place was bustling with activity and he would go unnoticed. He was taken to a small door that opened on to a corridor leading into an alleyway between the houses. A great lover of the byways of Paris, Nicolas memorised the route.

He crossed the Seine again on his way to Rue de l'Hirondelle. He was worrying about how he would broach matters with the vidame until it struck him that the best approach was the one that would seem the most plausible. Truche de La Chaux had unintentionally offered him the solution: to pass himself off as a representative of the police Gaming Division and question the young man about his visits to the Dauphin Couronné.

Would the vidame have been warned about him? That was unlikely, given his bad relationship with his father. Nicolas could use these family quarrels to encourage the younger son to speak out, now that a new future lay ahead of him after the death of his brother.

The vidame's house looked nondescript, neither luxurious nor humble. It was an ordinary bourgeois house in an ordinary street. There was no doorkeeper to block Nicolas's path and it took him only four strides to reach the mezzanine. He knocked on a pointed-arched door, which was opened almost immediately by a young man who stood in the doorway looking intrigued rather than annoyed by Nicolas's incursion. Wearing breeches and a shirt with neither tie nor cuffs, and with one hand on his hip, he gave Nicolas a quizzical look, thrusting out his chin. He had bushy eyebrows that arched over deep blue eyes and protruding, pouting lips. His hair was loosely tied in a knot on the verge of coming undone. This first, pleasant impression gave way to one that was more disturbing. Nicolas noticed the pallor of his complexion, the prominent, flushed cheeks, the rings around the eyes; his whole face was bathed in sweat. Purple blotches accentuated yet further the crumpled look of a man who in Nicolas's opinion had not slept for some time.

'Monsieur de Ruissec?'

'Yes, Monsieur. And to whom do I have the honour of speaking?'

'I am a police officer, Monsieur, and would like to have a few words with you.'

His face turned bright red, then paled. The vidame stepped aside and invited Nicolas in. The accommodation consisted of a large, low-ceilinged room with little natural light. Two semi-circular windows at floor level looked on to the street. The furniture was elegant but not overly so, and there was nothing to suggest the occupant's religious calling. It was a bachelor's establishment, that of a young man more intent on leading a life of pleasure than one of spiritual meditation. The vidame remained standing with his back to the light and did not invite Nicolas to sit down.

'Well, Monsieur, how may I help you?'

Nicolas decided to strike fast and hard.

'Have you repaid Monsieur de La Chaux for the loan he gave you or rather the pledge he entrusted to you?'

The vidame blushed again. 'Monsieur, that is a personal matter between him and me.'

'Do you realise that you frequent a place where gambling is forbidden and that as a result you are liable to prosecution?'

The young man raised his head in a defiant gesture. 'I'm not the only one in Paris who goes around the gambling dens and as far as I'm aware the police of this kingdom don't make a fuss about it.'

'That, Monsieur, is because not everyone is intended for the priesthood, and the example you are giving—'

'I am not going into the Church. All that is in the past.'

'I see that your brother's death has opened up your career!'

'That is a needlessly offensive remark, Monsieur.'

'The fact is that not everyone in your position stands to benefit from the death of a close relative.'

The vidame stepped forward a pace. Instinctively his left hand went to his right side in search of the hilt of a missing sword. Nicolas noted the gesture.

'Be careful, Monsieur. I shall not allow insults to go unpunished.'

'Then answer my questions instead,' Nicolas said curtly. 'I am going to be frank with you and I would ask you to take due account of my openness. I am also and more importantly investigating the death of your brother, whose murder your father, the Comte de Ruissec, has succeeded in covering up. Not only his, but your mother's.'

Nicolas heard what sounded like a sob.

'My mother's?'

'Yes, your mother was savagely killed and thrown into the well of the dead in the Carmelite monastery. Your mother, who wanted to confide to me what was troubling her and who died because of this secret. It was in the interest of certain people to silence her before she spoke. This, Monsieur, is what authorises me to treat you as I do, I, Nicolas Le Floch, police commissioner at the Châtelet.'

'This is too much to bear. I have nothing more to say to you.'

Nicolas noticed that the news of his mother's murder did not seem to come as a surprise to the young man.

'That would be too simple. On the contrary, you have plenty of things to confide in me. To start with, do you know Mademoiselle Bichelière?'

'I know that she's my brother's mistress.'

'That's not what I'm asking you. Do you know her personally?'

'Not at all.'

'What, then, were you doing at her home, early yesterday afternoon? Don't deny it. You were seen there. Three reliable witnesses are prepared to swear so in front of a magistrate.'

Nicolas thought that the young man was about to burst into tears. He bit his lip until it bled.

'Not having seen her at my brother's funeral service, I was going to—'

'Oh, come now! Are you trying to say that this young woman would have been allowed to attend the funeral service for your brother and mother? Think of something more convincing to tell me.'

The vidame fell silent.

'I should add,' Nicolas continued, 'I have statements from witnesses saying they met you several times at the house of the aforesaid young woman. You're not going to make me believe that you don't know her. Please explain yourself.'

'I have nothing to say.'

'That is entirely up to you. Then can you describe your activities on the day your brother died?'

'I was walking in Versailles.'

'In Versailles? Versailles is big. In the park? In the palace? In the town? Alone or in company? There are plenty of people in Versailles and you must have come across someone of your acquaintance.'

Nicolas disliked being so brutal but he wanted to make the young man react.

'No, no one. I wanted to be alone.'

Nicolas shook his head. The vidame was in the process of turning himself into the main suspect. Nicolas could not allow him to remain free. Whatever uncertainty there might still be about his possible guilt, locking him away would enable matters to progress. With the young man looking on in consternation, he took out of his pocket one of the *lettres de cachet* that Monsieur de Saint-Florentin had given him. He wrote down the vidame's name without any hesitation. It was the second time in his career as a police officer that he would take a suspect to the Bastille. The first time it had been Dr Semacgus, but that had been for his own safety and he had come away cleared of all suspicion. This precedent strengthened Nicolas's ability to take the serious step of imprisoning a fellow human being with a certain degree of composure.

'Monsieur,' he said, 'by order of the King I must conduct you to the Bastille where you will have ample time to meditate upon the disadvantages of remaining silent. You will doubtless be more talkative the next time we meet, or so I hope.'

The vidame drew closer, looking him straight in the eye. 'Monsieur, I beg of you, listen to me. Whatever I may be accused of, I am innocent.'

'I should point out that if you claim to be innocent it is because you know a crime has been committed. I could turn your remark against you. I assure you no one wishes you to be innocent more than I. But you must give me the means of getting closer to the truth. I am convinced that you possess a share of it.'

He thought that this sensitively spoken exhortation was going to break down the young man's defences and that he would at last speak. It was a wasted effort. The vidame seemed to be on the verge of giving in but he collected himself, shook his head and began to dress.

'I am at your disposal, Monsieur.'

Nicolas took him by the arm. He was shaking. He put a seal on the door of the dwelling, which would later be thoroughly searched, then they went out to the carriage. The coachman was ordered to head for the state prison. The young man remained silent for the entire journey and Nicolas respected his unwillingness to speak. There was no further information to be had from him. A few days in solitary confinement might make him less reluctant to talk and bring him to a realisation of how grave the accusations against him were as a result of failing to explain himself.

At the Bastille Nicolas went through the formalities for the admission of a prisoner. He took the chief gaoler to one side to put in a good word for the young man. His imprisonment had to be kept absolutely secret and no visits were to be allowed without Nicolas's prior consultation. Lastly, and he laid particular emphasis on this point, the prisoner was not to be left unsupervised, lest he commit suicide through the negligence of his warders. Nicolas had in mind the death of the old soldier who had hanged himself in the Châtelet because they had forgotten to take away his belt. He left a small sum of money to cover the cost of meals to be brought to the prisoner from outside.

He was relieved to leave the ancient fortress behind. He found its grey stone bulk oppressive. Inside the dank, dark maze of staircases and galleries, the creaking of keys turning in locks and the slamming of wickets increased his unease yet further. The cheerful bustle of Rue Saint-Antoine with its crowds and its carriages comforted him.

Nicolas reflected on the consequences of the vidame's arrest. It remained to be seen whether the Comte de Ruissec would intervene as energetically to have this son freed as he had done to recover the body of his murdered elder son. Nicolas was nagged by doubt: there was too much evidence against the vidame. The motives were blindingly obvious: rivalry in love, thwarted ambition, and perhaps other more materialistic ones. It was also plain to see that Lambert was a likely accomplice. What made Nicolas more hesitant and gave him grounds for doubt was the idea of brother killing brother. It was true that there were precedents. A few months earlier one particular case had caused a sensation. A nobleman by the name of Aubarède had killed his elder brother. He had shot him in the head with a pistol and finished him off by stabbing him and beating him with an iron bar before fleeing to enlist in an enemy army. Monsieur de Choiseul had had a missive sent to the ambassador in Rome containing a description of the murderer so that he might be arrested.

Nicolas had a sudden inspiration. As they needed to delve into the suspects' pasts he ordered his coachman to drive him to the Hôtel de Noailles, on Rue Saint-Honoré, opposite the monastery of the Jacobins, the home of Monsieur de Noailles, the most senior of the marshals of France. This was the location of the offices of the Court of Honour, which had been had set up by the marshals to judge contentious cases. Under the presidency of their most senior member, their jurisdiction applied to all noble-men, civilian or military, and dealt with insults, threats, assault and battery, gambling debts or challenges to duels. Their knowledge of military staff was extensive. The secretary of this institution, Monsieur de La Vergne, liked Nicolas. When the young man had still been working for Commissioner Lardin, by making full use of his spies and network of informers in the world of receivers of stolen property, he had managed to recover a snuffbox stolen from the Maréchal de Belle-Isle, the Secretary of State for War, who had died in January of that year. Monsieur de La Vergne had put his services at Nicolas's disposal and had promised to reciprocate if the opportunity arose.

The man had a vast knowledge of senior officers' careers; there was no one better placed to give Nicolas information about the Comte de Ruissec. He found his office without difficulty. Luckily Monsieur de La Vergne was there and received him straight away. He was a small, slim man with a smooth, pale face and smiling eyes, but his blond wig failed to make him look any younger. He welcomed Nicolas warmly.

'Monsieur Le Floch. What a surprise! Or rather congratulations, Commissioner Le Floch. To what do I owe the pleasure of your visit?'

'Monsieur, I need the benefit of your knowledge with reference to a most awkward matter.'

'Nothing is awkward between us, and as a friend of mine and as a protégé of Monsieur de Sartine you may count on my help.'

Nicolas sometimes wondered if the day would ever come when his own qualities would suffice to warrant the help he was offered. When would he stop being the prisoner of his relationship to Sartine? He was annoyed with himself for this puerile reaction. Monsieur de La Vergne meant no harm; it was a compliment of sorts. Everyone asserted their status in this society by their birth and by their talents but also by their connections and their protectors. Monsieur de La Vergne belonged to this society in which it was impossible to disregard such considerations. Well then, he would give proof of his own impressive contacts.

'The minister, Monsieur de Saint-Florentin . . .'

The secretary of the marshals bowed.

'. . . has given me the task of resolving a most confidential matter concerning a former senior officer, the Comte de Ruissec, who has just . . .'

'Lost his son and wife. Rumour spreads quickly, my dear fellow. It has to be said, the man was not well liked.'

'Precisely. Would you be kind enough to enlighten me on his career? I have been given to believe that he left the army in somewhat unusual circumstances.'

Monsieur de La Vergne waved towards the boxes lining the walls of his office. 'There's no need for me to consult my archives. I've heard this story. As you know we receive a large amount of information. It sometimes helps us in the matters we deal with. This Ruissec of yours was a brigadier general and a former colonel in the dragoons, was he not?'

'Exactly so.'

'Well, my dear fellow, in 1757, a dreadful year, our troops invaded Hanover under the command of the Prince de Soubise. There were an ever-increasing number of complaints about your man. He was said to be in league with commissaries and traffickers. That was nothing new and he was not the only one. They scrimped on food and meat, and added dirt to the flour to make up the weight. The result was that the hospitals were the worst affected and the soldiers left to rot there in inhuman conditions. Vile broth, rotten meat and vermin-infested carrion, and all for the sake of making savings if not profits. What was even more serious was that for months the paymaster made cash payments to Monsieur de Ruissec for both men and horses that existed only on paper. Unfortunately that also is common. He would in normal circumstance have survived this.'

'Then what happened?'

'I'm coming to that. A lieutenant complained about these breaches of the regulations and even attempted to expose them.

Straight away Ruissec convened a court martial. We were up against it with the enemy at the time. The lieutenant was found guilty of cowardice and hanged immediately. But he had friends and this time the rumour spread. Further corroboration of these reports reached Versailles. His Majesty was informed but made no pronouncement. Everyone understood that other influences were at work and that the King would do nothing more. However, the comte left the army. I have always found it surprising that he should have insinuated his way into a position at Court with the Dauphin, who is such a virtuous prince, and with Madame, thanks to his wife!'

'Do you remember the name of this lieutenant?'

'No, but I shall look it up and let you know. But I have not yet finished. They say that damning evidence has been assembled against the Comte de Ruissec. From time to time new documents reach the Minister of War or are sent here to the Court of Marshals. But it's all so disjointed and fragmentary that it would be impossible to use. It would appear that some unknown correspondent is trying to keep this business alive in people's minds. But why? We do not know. It is said that the Comte de Ruissec has in his possession compromising evidence against the Prince de Soubise himself. What do you think of that? And when people say Soubise . . .' he lowered his voice, 'they mean Paris-Duverney, the financier. And when they say Paris-Duverney they mean Bertin, the Secretary of State for Finance, Choiseul's rival and the friend of . . . of . . .'

'Of a certain good lady.'

'You said it, not me. The father of that same person, Monsieur Poisson, was a clerk to the Paris-Duverneys.'

'That makes things both clearer and more obscure at the same time.'

The little man waved his hands about. 'It is a matter that must be handled with care, my dear fellow. With the greatest care. The Ruissec is a many-sided coin.'

He looked pleased with himself and chuckled with satisfaction at his joke. Nicolas felt puzzled as he left the secretariat of the Court of Marshals. The conversation with Monsieur de La Vergne opened up many new lines of inquiry. All the signs were that the mystery was considerably deeper and more complicated than anything that Nicolas might have imagined. Nicolas took comfort from the fact that the secretary of the marshals of France had proved to be friendly and helpful, and he realised once more how important it was for his job to have acquaintances in different circles, a list of people he could call on to help him.

He decided to call in at Rue Montmartre before going on to Vaugirard. He was eagerly looking forward to the supper, which had been arranged some time ago. At the Noblecourt mansion Catherine asked him to take a pear and marzipan tart that she had made for Awa, Semacgus's cook. She inundated him with advice and made him promise to remind her counterpart to warm it up in the front part of the oven just before serving it but not to leave it in for too long or it would get dry, and lastly not to forget to serve a jug of whipped cream that should be liberally poured over the tart. She finally remembered that the master of the house wished to see Nicolas, if only very briefly. Cyrus was already showing him the way, going back and forth like a tireless dispatch rider between his master's command post and the outbuildings of the mansion.

When he entered the bedroom Monsieur de Noblecourt was playing chess, looking fresh-faced and ruddy-cheeked and sitting snugly in his large armchair, from where he could keep a watchful eye on the busy street. He was staring hard at one of the pieces.

'Ah! Nicolas . . . I'm playing against myself, my left hand is playing my right hand. I won't last out. I know myself only too well. There's no surprise about the outcome, it's skilfulness against laziness! What would you try with this knight here?'

Nicolas was careful not to indulge in one of those swift moves that were more intuitive than calculated, even if sometimes appropriate, because they annoyed the elderly magistrate, who favoured a more thoughtful and slower game.

'I would attack. It's threatening both a bishop and another knight. These two opposing pieces are caught in a pincer movement but the knight is protected on either side.'

Monsieur de Noblecourt blinked and bit the side of his lip. 'Hm . . . I still have my queen. That's precisely why I asked you. The queen with the queen, on both sides.

'You are being very enigmatic. What do you mean?'

'I've been thinking a good deal about all that has happened to you. The Court . . . dissembling and distrust . . . the scourge of all virtuous enthusiasm . . . The great are polite but hard; that does not preclude, moreover, a brutal frankness that can conceal duplicity. Sophistry allied to natural wickedness, sheer horror.'

'I am becoming increasingly worried about you. You sound like the Pythia prophesying on her tripod. This black mood . . . this bitterness, it's really not like you. You have an attack of gout coming on, no doubt. I was wrong to tire you with my investigation. It's my own fault.'

The elderly procurator smiled. 'Certainly not, certainly not. I feel as fit as a fiddle, as right as rain. But I am worried, Nicolas. In the words of my old friend Voltaire, the most prickly of men when people try to humour him, "It's not you who are giving me a headache but the concern I feel for you at this difficult juncture." As for the gout, that she-devil has well and truly forgotten about me.'

'So?'

'So, Mister Always in a Hurry, I've spent a good part of the night thinking.'

'You really shouldn't have!'

'No, a night without pain is a good night for an old man. It's an opportunity for his mind to be fresh and alert.'

Nicolas suddenly thought that every man really was an island unto himself, and that his elderly friend disguised the ravages of time more often than he should, apparently out of vanity but in reality from a sense of dignity and as an expression of that exquisite politeness that required such things to be concealed from one's friends. Only the gout could not be hidden.

'And well-tempered insomnia put to good use is not time wasted but time regained. I thought about the Queen, the one in Choisy and the one in Versailles. And then I thought about your Truche. A very self-assured fellow, that one! I could see your good lady pulling the strings from a distance but not lifting her little finger if it meant becoming involved herself. As for this charade with the Jesuits, there are no two ways about it: either they were behind it and for once it proves their panic but not necessarily their guilt; or they are not behind it, which would be even more serious and the mystery deeper and the danger more acute. I'm surprised you got out of it safe and sound.'

'Pardon? What do you mean?'

'Make no mistake. No one can have been taken in by your forced and unconvincing compliance with the demands of your elderly master. But it's quite clear that the mysterious power that held you in its grip did not wish to crush you. To put things a little more bluntly, the pressure put on you seems somewhat feeble. In any case you have presumably not changed your line of investigation, have you?'

'I have continued along the same route. This morning I arrested the Vidame de Ruissec. The evidence against him and his refusal to explain his actions seemed sufficient grounds for having him temporarily imprisoned in the Bastille.'

'My, my!' said Noblecourt, shaking his head doubtfully.

'Is that meant to imply that my actions were dictated by someone else?'

'I'm not implying anything. Only later will you be able to tell whether this last judicial decision suits or works against your mysterious assailants. Are we to have the pleasure of your company at supper this evening?'

'Unfortunately not. I am invited to Semacgus's. I simply called in to tell you the situation. I shall sleep in Vaugirard and first thing tomorrow morning I will return to Versailles, where I have to meet someone from Madame Adélaïde's household.'

'I repeat, Nicolas: take care. The world of the Court is a dangerous one. I shall certainly play this bishop.'

Nicolas left his elderly friend and rushed off to put what he needed into a portmanteau. As he went back downstairs he carefully placed inside it what Catherine had taken so much effort to prepare. Early that morning he had asked for a carriage to be waiting for him on Impasse Saint-Eustache. All seemed quiet but as an extra precaution Rabouine had been sent to the area and told to keep a close watch, with explicit instructions to foil any attempt to shadow him.

For the first time since the beginning of the inquiry, Nicolas let his mind wander. Even Monsieur de Noblecourt's disjointed and unsettling words had not been able to affect his mood. Without daring to put them down to age, he did not take them too seriously, even though some of them would doubtless give him food for thought. He soon gave in and, lulled by the movement of the carriage, fell asleep.

When he awoke he had passed the toll-gates, and the pink and gold of the western sky signalled the end of the day across a horizon broken occasionally by the tall, dark outlines of wind-mills. In the meantime it had rained and from his seat he could see the earth and sand pockmarked by the drops. The ground was riddled with gullies and tiny channels. Soon the massive bulk of Semacgus's residence loomed up, with its large wall on the street side, its carriage entrance and its symmetrical wings around the main dwelling. It gave an impression of solidity, further empha-sised by the fact that it was a single-storey building. The central rooms were brightly lit. Through the pantry windows he recognised the stocky silhouette of Bourdeau and the taller one of the doctor; they were in shirtsleeves around a table. In the entrance hall he came upon Awa, Semacgus's black servant. She greeted him with kisses and peals of laughter, asking in her warm, guttural voice for news of her friend Catherine. The offering of the tart enabled him to get away and join his friends. He went towards the kitchen. The two companions were talking and laughing.

'Doctor,' shouted Bourdeau, 'make sure not to squash the chestnuts. You need to find large pieces that break easily when you eat them. Be careful!'

'Here we go. It's the police showing off in front of the medical profession. Chop up your bacon and sweat it gently. Make the little devils sing! And one piece of advice: take care not to brown the garlic. As for the cabbage—'

Nicolas interrupted, imitating Catherine and her Alsace accent: 'Above all be careful to blanch it well and to throw away the first water. Then let it simmer so that the whole thing stays a little crisp.'

The two companions turned.

'Well, if it isn't Nicolas joining in!'

'I hope,' Bourdeau added, ' he's not hungry. We'd never have enough in that case!'

They burst into laughter. Semacgus poured some wine. Nicolas enquired about the menu.

'We're having braised partridges, spit-roasted loin of pork and fricasséed cabbage with diced bacon and chestnuts: a combination that I've devised and that will have you licking your lips. The sweetness of the chestnuts marries with the slight bitterness of the cabbage, spiced with pepper and cloves, then wrapped in the bacon fat. It's softness and tenderness combined. And Bourdeau has brought us a basket of bottles of Chinon.'

'Well, well!' Nicolas exclaimed. 'You can add to the menu a pear and marzipan tart from good old Catherine.'

Supper was soon ready and served by Awa, who was wearing a dazzling damask boubou from her native St-Louis for the occasion. The table set up in Semacgus's study was a haven of light and cheerfulness amidst the books, the skeletons, the fossils, the specimen jars and the myriad curiosities that the master of the house had brought back from his distant expeditions. Nicolas had rarely seen Bourdeau so jolly, ruddy and tipsy. He had a repertoire of bawdy tales that was second to none, to the delight of the surgeon, who was a great lover of saucy stories. The climax came with the gargantuan fit of laughter that greeted Semacgus's telling the story of the stuffed *kumpala*.

'Imagine,' he said, 'the bishop inviting us to dinner, the governor and myself, and so impatient to have us appreciate the talents of his cook, a very attractive mulatto, far too young to be working for a cleric. She had planned to make *kumpala*.'

'What sort of creature is that?'

'Imagine a crab that can climb trees.'

'I think it's the Chinon that's going to your head.'

'Not at all. The *kumpala* climbs up coconut trees during the night. That's where people catch it. Then you have to starve it like you do snails, to purge it of the nasty plants it may have eaten. Then you plunge it into boiling water and add local herbs and the hottest type of pepper you can find. The whole thing is then put in the oven and it's a dish that . . .'

'. . . gets men going!' shouted Awa, showing her beautiful white teeth.

'She knows the story,' said Semacgus.

'So what?' said Nicolas, failing to understand.

'So then,' said Semacgus, 'well, the following morning the

bishop was discovered in bed with his servant; it's a dish that would have given Monsieur de Gesvres an erection!'

The evening ended very late, around the traditional decanter of vintage rum. Bourdeau was carried to bed by his two friends but just as he was falling unconscious he tried to speak to Nicolas. With a glazed look in his eyes and raising a finger, he attempted to explain himself.

'Nicolas . . .'

'Yes, my friend.'

'I've seen the coachman, the Minister of Bavaria's coachman.'

'That's very good, my friend.'

'He saw a thing or two . . . The face . . . the face . . .'

He collapsed without finishing his sentence. Soon the house resounded to the snores of the three men, while Awa was busy until late into the night putting everything back in order.

X

THE LABYRINTH

What apparitions did I see!

All cross that fatal stream, said he.

However sweet may seem this place,

Death here doth show its grisly face.

HENRI RICHER

Wednesday 31 October 1761

Waking up was something of a struggle, even though the excesses of the previous night, combined with Catherine's vigorous treatment, had miraculously relieved Nicolas of his aches and pains. He restricted himself, however, to his usual chocolate, resisting Semacgus and Bourdeau's tempting offers. They remained fervent believers in a glass of dry white wine as the best way to clear your head the morning after a supper washed down with too much wine. The carriage was still there, the coachman having slept on the hay in the shed after being copiously plied with food and drink by the welcoming Awa.

The morning was sharp and clear, and the sun accompanied Nicolas on his journey to Versailles. Would this trip prove as eventful as the previous one? Would he uncover new evidence to further his investigation? After a while he remembered that he had not questioned Bourdeau about his ramblings of the previous evening. Hadn't he said something about the Minister of Bavaria's coachman?

Now the vital thing was to gain access to Madame Adélaïde's apartments to find the person who was to give him the details of the stolen jewels. Nicolas had often observed that the aristocracy had total contempt for detail and practical matters. On issuing an order or an instruction, they simply left you to carry it out without offering any helpful information about how it should be done. He could of course call on Monsieur de La Borde but he felt a certain reticence at having to turn to him yet again. Perhaps he could prevail on the kindness of the quick-witted royal page, who seemed to know everyone and everything, to direct him to Madame's apartments.

On the road to Paris, with its fine view of the palace, Nicolas suddenly decided to take a quick look at Mademoiselle de Sauveté's house. While the visit would also allow him to stretch his legs, dropping in unannounced could sometimes produce unexpected results. He made the cab stop and strolled casually up to the house, where he was immediately spotted by the old woman who had spoken to him four days earlier. He had not believed her then, but in fact she did seem to be permanently on the lookout. He smiled, thinking that it was a harmless enough activity.

Her small blue eyes regarded him kindly.

'I knew it! I knew it! You want to know more about the lady, admit it . . . But she's not at home. I'm sure this time; we saw her leaving.'

Nicolas felt that there was no point in disguising his interest.

'When did she leave?'

'Yesterday afternoon, at about two o'clock.'

'Perhaps she went for a walk?'

'She hasn't been back since.'

'Are you sure?'

She gave him a withering look. 'Do you think we're so unobservant we wouldn't notice her?'

'No, I don't think that, but on Saturday you told me several times that you hadn't seen her go out.'

Disgruntled she went back into her garden, and slammed the gate in his face. Nicolas felt that he would never have such a good opportunity again. The gate to Mademoiselle de Sauveté's house was not fastened, only pushed to. He walked through the sorry-looking garden. The large French window was closed and its inside shutters drawn. He continued right round the house. At the back a worm-eaten door seemed suitable for his purposes. He took his little picklock out of his pocket and his skill soon enabled him to free the lock. He gave the door a gentle push with his shoulder and it creaked open, bringing a thick cobweb down on his head. He shook himself, shuddering. It must have been a long time since the entrance had been used.

The pantry also seemed abandoned: loose floor tiles wobbled as he walked on them and the dirty windows barely let in the daylight. He came to a corridor. The rest of the house was in a similarly desolate state. He went into the drawing room where he had questioned the Vicomte de Ruissec's betrothed. The cupboards were bare, their musty interiors infested with all sorts of creepy-crawlies. He discovered a bedroom looking slightly more inhabited. The mattress was folded away in the alcove but a coffee pot and a cup had been left on a pedestal table. He examined them.

In the wardrobe he found some unbleached sheets, without embroidery or initials. Two singlets were hanging up, faded, outmoded affairs. Three well-made wigs of different shades were poking out of a chest of drawers. He smelt them at length. Then he looked closely at three pairs of shoes, intrigued by their size, and noted down the details in his black notebook. The house had yielded up all it could offer. He put everything back in place, carefully relocked the door and returned to his carriage.

The old woman reappeared on her doorstep, sneering, and stuck her tongue out at him.

In the end everything went as planned. It did not take him long to find Gaspard, who seemed to spend all his time keeping a sharp eye on everyone's comings and goings.

Thanks to one of his fellow pages, Gaspard had ready access to Madame Adélaïde's apartments, near the King's. After having Nicolas wait in the Marble Courtyard, he came to take him to a small room lit by a round window, overlooking the reception rooms. A man of indeterminate age, dressed in black, awaited. He introduced himself as the princess's intendant and showed no surprise that the policeman was so young. It was clear that Madame Adélaïde had told him what Nicolas required and had instructed him to answer any questions about the stolen jewels. The official did not look directly at Nicolas, instead observing him obliquely in a mirror.

'Sir,' Nicolas began, 'Her Royal Highness will have told you that I urgently need information in order to complete the investigation she has charged me with.'

Without answering, the man took out of his pocket two folded sheets of paper tied with a pale blue ribbon and handed them to him. Nicolas glanced at them; it was the list of the stolen jewels. They were described down to the smallest detail, and beside each description was a small painted sketch. He immediately recognised the ring with the fleur-de-lis in its setting of turquoises. The intendant was wringing his hands and looking embarrassed. Nicolas had the feeling he would have liked to tell him something but could not bring himself to do so. He decided to be direct.

'Is there anything you wish to add? I have the impression that you are hiding something.'

The man looked at him distractedly. He opened his mouth several times before replying.

'Sir, I do have something to tell you in confidence. But please understand that I was unable to do so before. However much the princess trusts me I would never wish to overstep the mark. One must know one's place. But neither do I want to conceal a fact that may bear on your investigation, Commissioner.'

Nicolas gestured for him to continue.

'Sir, I have a suspect in mind – someone who has access to Madame's Household and could have committed these thefts . . .'

'Who is it, sir?'

'I am truly reluctant to name him. But the secret will be safe with you and you will doubtless know the right thing to do. He is a Life Guard, one Truche de La Chaux. Our good mistress, always so kind-hearted, has taken him under her wing; he is a young man without family or connections.'

'Is there something particular about him that justifies the princess's interest in him?'

'Monsieur de La Chaux used to be a follower of the so-called reformed religion – he has since converted. Madame likes converts. You know how devout she is. She interprets the renunciation of religious error as a sign of God's handiwork. Now the man comes and goes at will in her apartments at all hours of the day.'

'And you don't think he's trustworthy?'

'I have thought long and hard about the possible culprits but I have gradually eliminated them; he is the only one left who could have committed such a crime.'

'And did you tell anyone your theory?'

'Unfortunately yes, sir. I told Monsieur le Comte de Ruissec, gentleman-in-waiting to the princess, in confidence. He assured me that he would oversee the investigation and that justice would be meted out swiftly if the Life Guard were found guilty.'

'And what happened?'

'Well, sir, the extraordinary thing is that he never mentioned the matter again. So I took it upon myself to bring it up and was given short shrift. I was told that the theft was nothing to do with me, that the princess was no longer to be pestered about it and that it would be resolved privately. Lastly he told me not to make false accusations against Her Royal Highness's servants: my suspicion was unfounded and Monsieur de La Chaux had nothing to do with the disappearance of the jewels.'

'So was the matter resolved, in your opinion?'

'I might have believed so had I not since observed a strange collusion between the Comte de Ruissec and Monsieur Truche de La Chaux. From then on they were frequently engaged in lengthy conversations, whereas previously they never spoke to each other. The Comte de Ruissec, a very grand nobleman, would not normally deign so much as to look at the Life Guard. I began to suspect a sort of complicity between the two men. I don't want to say any more but that was my overwhelming impression.'

'Sir, I am immensely grateful to you for having confided this to me. Have you noticed anything else out of the ordinary?'

'Indeed I have, sir. On several occasions a young messenger, a deaf-and-dumb boy, carried messages to or from Monsieur de Ruissec. I followed the child once and saw him enter the great park, only to disappear.' He hesitated for a moment. 'I even thought I recognised the name on one of these missives ... Monsieur Truche de La Chaux.'

'Sir, I must congratulate you on the relevance and precision of your observations. They will no doubt be extremely useful and perhaps even decisive for my investigation. Reassure the princess. I believe I will soon have found her jewels.'

As he bade Nicolas farewell, the intendant at last looked him in the eye. He seemed relieved and, bowing frequently, led him back to the Marble Courtyard, where Gaspard was whistling as he waited for Nicolas. The day had certainly been full of surprises: the illusive Mademoiselle de Sauveté pretending to live in what was actually a run-down house, and now mysterious connections between the Comte de Ruissec and Truche de La Chaux. Lastly, by an accident that Nicolas ascribed either to the hand of providence or his own good fortune, the person linking Truche, Ruissec and other mysterious figures had turned out to be the deaf-and-dumb boy he had saved from drowning in the murky waters of the Grand Canal.

As Gaspard looked on in bewilderment at his apparent

incoherence, Nicolas began mumbling through his clues. He suddenly remembered Madame Adélaïde's ring, which he could feel in his pocket next to his watch. What was Monsieur de Ruissec up to? Clearly he had rescued Truche de La Chaux from a very tricky situation. Nicolas was well placed to judge the Life Guard's real character and to confirm that he had acted suspiciously. There was no doubt about his dishonesty. So how could he have convinced the Comte de Ruissec of his innocence? Or rather, for what particular reason had the comte not denounced him, preferring to use his influence to protect him?

Nicolas pictured Monsieur de Noblecourt's wrinkled, mischievous face and his reference to 'the queen on both sides'. He suddenly remembered how their conversation had continued: Madame de Pompadour could also be described as 'queen'. Everything revolved around Madame Adélaïde's stolen ring. The King's favourite, like the Comte de Ruissec, knew Truche de La Chaux. His presence at Choisy was no accident. Nicolas was more and more convinced of that. Besides, the Life Guard had made no secret of having been at La Pompadour's chateau the day the vicomte was murdered, and had even boasted about it. This was his way of implying that the favourite could, if necessary, vouch for his presence at Choisy. So, Nicolas thought, the only way of piecing together the puzzle was to find out more about the relationship between Madame de Pompadour and Truche de La Chaux . . .

Gaspard was patiently waiting for Nicolas to finish his train of thought. Then, as no instruction was forthcoming, he asked if his services were still required. Nicolas replied that for the moment what he most wanted was to see Monsieur de La Borde to request his help. Nothing could be simpler, the page told him. The First Groom was to be on duty the following day, so at this very moment he would be in his rooms, having gone to bed very late, or rather very early. Gaspard winked as he said this. Respect was not the scamp's strong point, but that was one of his charms and a small price to pay for his loyalty.

Monsieur de La Borde welcomed Nicolas warmly. He immediately dressed, asked Nicolas to wait for him and disappeared, preceded by Gaspard. He returned quite quickly to report that, wishing to take advantage of the beautiful weather, the marquise had gone for a walk in the park's maze. She would see Nicolas there and La Borde would arrange to have him taken to her immediately. It was not very far away and could be reached by going back to the palace terrace in front of the gardens, crossing the Southern Parterre in the direction of the orangery and turning off to the right.

Nicolas had never been to the labyrinth before and was struck by its strange beauty. Two statues representing Aesop and Cupid stood opposite each other on pedestals of coloured stones and shells. An enormous fountain topped by a latticework dome on pillars depicted a lifelike representation of a multitude of flying birds. The lead figurines were decorated in authentic colours, and the statue of a fierce-looking eagle-owl dominated the ornamentation.

A valet in the favourite's livery awaited him. He pompously explained that the labyrinth, designed by Le Nôtre, contained thirty-nine fountains on animal themes, all inspired by Aesop's

Fables interpreted by La Fontaine. He told him to go past the Partridge and the Cocks, the Hen and the Chicks; he would eventually come to one of the openings of the maze. He was to meet Madame de Pompadour by the central basin.

When he arrived he did indeed see a woman standing there motionless. She had her back to him. She seemed to be wearing something enormously thick but then fashions did favour an exaggeratedly crumpled and untidy look. Nicolas felt that this did not flatter the female figure. The aim seemed to be to demonstrate how many bits and pieces could be used in the making of a single garment The size of the panniers added to the general overblown impression. He had a momentary doubt that this was the Marquise de Pompadour, but on hearing his footsteps on the gravel, she turned and he recognised her. Beneath her dark green satin cape she wore a bottle-green bodice embroidered with silver thread, trimmed with chenille and the looped bows that the favourite had made fashionable. Embroidered silk florets stunningly set off the whole. A light muslin veil discreetly protected the marquise's face.

'I see, Monsieur Le Floch, that you have wasted no time in following my advice. You wished to speak to me and here I am.'

'Madame, forgive this intrusion. I wish that I could have spared you, but I have reached a stage in my investigation that requires me to account to you.'

'You mean to inform me . . .'

'I have made some progress, Madame. A solution is in sight, but I still need to order the details into a coherent whole, rather like those children's games of patience where each card represents a part of a map.'

She lifted her veil. Her eyes were strangely cold, with no flicker of benevolence. She looked tired.

'I have no doubt that you will succeed, however hard it is. You bring to the task the methodical approach you have previously demonstrated and I find this very reassuring.'

There was no real feeling behind these words. Nicolas took Madame Adélaïde's ring out of his pocket and handed it to the marquise. She gazed at it without taking it.

'A handsome item.' As Nicolas said nothing she continued more quickly, 'Why are you showing it to me? Are you offering it for sale? I do not wear rings.'

'No, Madame. I would like to ask you a question.'

She pulled down her veil again and walked away a little, looking exasperated.

'Madame, I must insist. Forgive my audacity. Have you seen this ring before?'

She appeared to reflect a moment, then imperceptibly relaxed and began to laugh.

'You are a redoubtable adversary, Monsieur Le Floch. When one sets you a task, there is no point in hoping that something might slip past you.'

'I am at your service, Madame, and that of the King.'

'Well, as I have no choice but to come clean, I admit that I do know this jewel. It comes from the King's collection. He showed it to me several years ago, when he made a gift of it to his eldest daughter.'

'Is that all, Madame?'

Her foot, beneath her voluminous gown, crunched the gravel.

'What more could there be, sir?'

'That's what I am trying to find out, Madame. Might you have seen the jewel again since His Majesty showed it to you?'

She was unable to conceal her impatience. 'You are starting to annoy me, Monsieur Le Floch. Are you trying to read my thoughts?'

'No, Madame, I am striving to prevent a dishonest man compromising you, as indeed he has already begun to do. At the moment I am the only one to have seen through him.'

'Compromising me? Me! You forget yourself, sir. To whom are you referring?'

'A man I came across as I arrived at your chateau in Choisy. A man who apparently stole this ring from Madame Adélaïde. A man who seems to be in league with the King's enemies and yours, Madame. A man, in fact, who has the audacity to use your name to provide himself with an alibi for a crime. That, Madame, is what prompts me to remember your benefaction and to do my utmost to be worthy of it.'

He had the impression that he had gradually raised his voice but that in doing so had given his words a warmth and persuasiveness that she could not fail to respond to. In any case after this outburst there was no way out. She immediately put a brave face on it; with a charming gesture she took his hand.

'All right, I give in. Let us make our peace. It is no more than I deserve and it will teach me to turn to a sleuth of your calibre. It is obvious that you would not let such a thing go.'

'Madame, what I am doing, everything I do, is dictated by what you asked me to accomplish: to be fully informed in order to serve and protect you better.'

'I understand. It was wrong of me not to have told you the

whole truth. Here is what happened: I came to know Truche de La Chaux while he was serving at Court. One day he offered to sell me a piece of jewellery, the ring you showed me. I immediately recognised it as belonging to Madame Adélaïde and saw that I could make use of this discovery. I also knew that he had ready access to Madame's apartments. He was originally a Protestant, although he has since converted. The princess, who is still besotted with religion, loves neophytes. I offered him a deal: either he worked for me or I would reveal what he had done.'

'I am sorry to tell you, Madame, that there is every chance that he has done the same with your enemies. For the same reason that you have a hold over him, the Comte de Ruissec had him in his power. He had discovered that he was responsible for stealing from Madame's jewellery collection. I suppose that knowing that the Life Guard had free access to your chateau, the comte did the same as you. He used him for his underhand schemes. I am almost certain that the tract you passed to me was put in your apartments by Truche de La Chaux. To cut a long story short, caught in a bind and also probably for financial gain, he became a double agent and it is impossible to tell where his loyalties lie or even if he has any!'

'Sir, you have earned my gratitude a second time. I will think about what you have told me.'

'If I may be so bold, Madame . . .'

'By all means, sir. I have every confidence in your good sense.'

'Continue to pretend to Monsieur de La Chaux. Treat him exactly as before. If you have a trusted servant make sure he keeps a careful watch on him when he is in your houses. Do not warn him until this affair is resolved. I think he is only a minor figure in it . A crook and a thief, certainly, but a minor figure.'

'You have set my mind at rest, sir. I shall follow your advice. Goodbye.'

She smiled, arranged her veil, gathered up her voluminous dress and disappeared, taking the same path he had used. Nicolas, not wishing to appear to follow her, set off in the opposite direction.

He lost his way amidst the alleys, went round in circles several times and eventually came upon a small square dominated by the figure of a large lead monkey. Finally, he found a way out. He thought that his journey through the labyrinth was symbolic of his investigation. He found himself in a broad avenue lined with hornbeams, at the far end of which he recognised Bacchus's Basin. From there he reached the central prospect of the palace and walked back towards it.

He had still not recovered from his encounter with Madame de Pompadour. He sensed that their relationship – if that was the right word – would never again have the same frankness. He had overcome her defences, made her disclose one of her secrets and in addition had almost forced her to reveal her own meddling in the Household of the King's eldest daughter. For a brief moment she had allowed herself to appear before him stripped of all her authority, but, if this were to become known, her situation would be very delicate and greatly weakened.

In addition, Nicolas had still not made up his mind about Truche de La Chaux. He was small fry but involved in serious matters, and evidently careless and heedless of the danger of his actions, and of the indiscretion of his words.

Just as he was coming out into the central area of the gardens Nicolas recalled the little deaf-and-dumb boy. He felt that he would never have a better opportunity to check whether the child he had rescued really was the one who carried Monsieur de Ruissec's messages.

The weather was fine and clear, and it would be pleasant to walk in the park. In the distance the heights of Satory, topped with a bluish haze, were tinged with gold and crimson. He walked briskly to the Sailors' Gate, near the Grand Canal. There he questioned the guard, who was not the same one as previously but was able to tell him the way to the shed belonging to Le Peautre, the fountaineer. It was no easy task to cross the uncultivated land through the tall trees and thickets. The workshop was in a part of the park that was still very nearly in its original wild state. Nicolas's heart began to race when a wild sow, followed by its young, burst out of a coppice right in front of him. Further on, a large solitary stag was belling, a column of steam rising above it in the dim light of the undergrowth.

Shortly before reaching the shed he heard strange noises, an irregular banging followed by a long creaking sound. He headed towards them and discovered that they came from the log door of the shed as it slammed in the wind. After making sure that his sword moved easily in its sheath, Nicolas knocked. As there was no reply he went inside.

To begin with he could make out little. A small opening cut into the thick wall let in only a glimmer of light. He dimly perceived a heap of disparate objects. The building was narrow but surprisingly long, and Nicolas continued forward, still disconcerted by the banging and creaking of the door that accompanied his progress. He was startled by a distant whinnying and was immediately on his guard. He was now in total darkness. He became aware of something else that added to his unease at being in the dark: a metallic smell he knew only too well.

He took a few more steps and felt a viscous substance beneath his feet. He bent down and touched it with his hand, then recoiled in horror and immediately ran back towards the light at the entrance to confirm his fears. His hand was covered in blood. His heart began to beat so fast that he was suddenly short of breath and nearly keeled over. What new horror must he face now?

At first sight the place seemed deserted but he had to make sure. He tried to remain calm and to act like the King's servant he was. He would have to deal with this alone. It was no doubt connected with his investigation but it had happened in the royal domain, in the great park, which meant that if he went to seek help immediately it would become public knowledge. He felt that it was important to keep the matter secret and avoid any scandal.

He looked around for something he could use to make a torch. He found the resinous branch of an old pine tree and gathered some dry moss, which he moistened with the sticky sap. He struck a light and, by blowing gently, managed to ignite the moss, which produced a short yellow and blue flame. The pungent smell of the resin mingled with the autumnal forest scents.

Nicolas went back inside the workshop and at first could see nothing but a heap of logs and bars of lead piled one on top of the other. The torch was guttering and giving off as much smoke as light. On a workbench littered with tools he found a candle stuck into a crudely fashioned lead holder. He lit it and stamped out the torch. His field of vision was now wider. He advanced towards the far end of the workshop and immediately spotted the apparently huge dark pool of blood. Then he heard murmurings and whispered words. Fumbling his way forward, he eventually discovered a low door at the far end of the workshop. Cautiously he turned the knob, pulling it towards him. A narrow passage a few yards long led to another door behind which people were talking. He listened, pressing up against the door, all senses alert.

'Will you finally tell a dying man what all this means?'

Nicolas recognised the voice of the Comte de Ruissec. His words were interspersed with rasping croaks. Why on earth was he here when he was supposed to be accompanying the funeral cortège of his wife and son?

Another voice spoke. 'I have been waiting for this moment for a very long time. Here you are at my mercy at last. First the son and the wife, now it's the turn of the father and husband . . .'

'But what treachery is this? Did we not have common cause?'

The second voice mumbled something that Nicolas was unable to catch. The Comte de Ruissec let out a loud cry.

Nicolas was about to leap forward to open the second door and had already placed his hand on the hilt of his sword when he was struck a violent blow on the back of his head. He fell senseless to the floor.

He could hear Bourdeau's voice distinctly and clearly, yet it seemed unreal. He felt about with his hands, finding grass beneath them. This, and the smell of the vegetation, brought him back to reality.

'Look, Doctor, he's coming round.'

Nicolas opened his eyes to see both the inspector and Semacgus leaning over him, anxiously studying him.

'He's a strapping lad and it's not the first time he's been knocked out. Nor the last, probably. Bretons are headstrong.'

'That'll teach him to be so reckless,' Bourdeau added.

Nicolas straightened up. A small, clear flame was flickering before his eyes. He touched the back of his neck and could feel a bump the size of a pigeon's egg.

'Are you two proposing to render me senseless again by smothering me with your chatter?' he said. 'Or are you going to tell me what you're doing here and what happened?'

Bourdeau nodded, satisfied. 'Thank God, he grumbles; he must be alive! Monsieur de Sartine, who values you more than he chooses to show, gave me instructions not to let you out of my sight. So the doctor and I followed you here. As we came inside we saw you lying unconscious in this wretched passage-way. Two people fled on horseback. We were sick with worry after wading through all that blood.' He showed his blood-stained shoes.

'Thank God you're safe. I asked Dr Semacgus to take you outside and I searched further. Behind the door where you were I discovered the Comte de Ruissec's body. He'd been killed by a pistol shot. He had his sword in his hand but he stood no chance: a bladed weapon is no defence against a firearm. However, the struggle must have started in the workshop and his opponent dragged him into the room behind. It looks as if he was able to wound his assailant before dying. A trail of blood led to the vegetable garden where the horses waited.'

'Nothing else?' said Nicolas, taking in all this.

'Who do you think attacked you?'

'It wasn't the man I heard talking to the Comte de Ruissec. I'm sure of that.'

'So there were three people here: the comte, his assailant and the person who hit you.'

'And there's something even more alarming,' Bourdeau added. He waved a sheaf of papers. 'I found an old chest in the loft. It contained an impressive number of documents obviously only left behind in the haste of their escape: new plans of the palace, even more detailed than those found in Grenelle, tracts against the King and La Pompadour and the draft of a declaration announcing the death of the "tyrant Louis XV".'

'So we're right to suspect a plot,' said Nicolas.

The three friends began a thorough search of the workshop from top to bottom. They carried out their task methodically, examining every tool and every nook and cranny of the cluttered room. Although they found several funnels still contained shining traces of molten metal, this was not definitive proof that the Vicomte de Ruissec had been murdered here; they could just be the normal tools of the trade of the fountaineer. But in current circumstances their presence was nevertheless incriminating. A sort of leather litter fitted at the four corners with metal rings reminded Nicolas of the vile mattresses on to which Sanson's assistants strapped their victims during torture sessions in the

Châtelet. Again that was not conclusive, and Nicolas could not allow himself to read too much into it, but there were certainly questions to be answered.

Dr Semacgus examined the Comte de Ruissec's body. The wound to the heart had indeed been inflicted by a pistol shot. The amount of blood spilt tallied with a bullet severing the main vessels at the base of the lungs or in the region of the heart. It was not yet clear whether it was murder or suicide, and there was no indication of motive. Nicolas found nothing of note when he searched the dead man's pockets.

The nature of the documents discovered, Nicolas thought, should be considered in conjunction with the volumes justifying tyrannicide in the Vicomte de Ruissec's library. It meant that there was a real danger of an attempt on the King's life. What was the Comte de Ruissec doing here? He had obviously slipped away from the funeral cortège he was supposed to be accompanying in order to ride back at full speed to Versailles. But was he an accomplice or a victim? Or an avenger? Was his death the settling of scores between accomplices?

It was too early to answer these questions. For the time being Nicolas gathered up the most telling documents and, after a last glance at the comte's mortal remains, left the workshop, asking Bourdeau and Semacgus to ensure that no one entered it.

By the time Nicolas returned to the palace it was three o'clock in the afternoon. He immediately headed for the Ministers' Wing and asked for an audience with Monsieur de Saint-Florentin. He was quickly shown in. The minister listened to him in silence, carefully sharpening a quill with the aid of a small silver penknife. As usual, Nicolas strove to be clear and concise, describing things without embellishment and avoiding unsubstantiated theories. He cautiously suggested that the comte's body should be removed by some of the King's officers in the utmost secrecy and taken to the Basse-Geôle. It was essential that the murder remain secret. In any case, no one would be looking for a man known to be taking his place in a funeral cortège. As the comte had left the convoy he had probably given good reasons for doing so; his household would not therefore be immediately worried about a prolonged absence and would not sound the alarm for a few days, if at all.

Once he had settled the problem of the body, Nicolas asked the minister to give him a week to complete his investigations. He said that he felt confident of being able to reveal the truth by then. Finally he ventured to suggest that further measures should be taken to improve the safety of the palace and the protection of the King.

Monsieur de Saint-Florentin broke his silence to approve the suggestions that had just been made. He too was of the opinion that the new development should be kept secret because it would give the police time to act and Commissioner Le Floch time to complete his task. He was due to receive Monsieur de Sartine that evening, so would pass on to him the latest information and the state of his deputy's investigation. He added that he was extremely satisfied with Nicolas's work.

In addition the minister would immediately write to the intendants of the provinces to place Le Peautre on the wanted list, noting that he was probably accompanied by a deaf-and-dumb child. Finally, as an extra precaution all workshops unofficially set up in the park, whether they belonged to fountaineers or others, would be put on record. It was important to regulate this practice, to carry out the necessary checks and no longer to tolerate through laziness the illegal occupation of the royal domain without due title or authorisation.

Monsieur de Saint-Florentin added that once the Ruissec case had been solved he wanted Le Floch to devote some time to studying arrangements at Versailles for the protection of the King, the princes of the blood and also ministers. He ordered Nicolas to draw up a report the conclusions of which would be closely examined to decide how to proceed.

As for the case of Truche de La Chaux, the minister seemed somewhat embarrassed and merely made a vague reference to the need to take into account the wishes of a person whom Commissioner Le Floch knew, as well as the minister himself did, could not easily be overruled.

Nicolas did not press the matter. He was convinced that although the deceitful, shallow Life Guard was guilty of dishonesty and theft, he was not implicated in the murders.

The minister rang for one of his trusted officials. He ordered him to assist the commissioner to arrange the collection and transport of the body. But when the man suggested that it would be better not to rely on the King's officers, who were notoriously indiscreet, Monsieur de Saint-Florentin cut him short by sitting down at his desk and beginning to write as though no one else was there. Nicolas and the official silently left the room.

*

It took some time to get the bearers together, find a vehicle and work out from a map of the park a discreet route to the fountaineer's workshop. Guarded by Bourdeau and Semacgus, the place was found as Nicolas had left it, and placing the body in a temporary coffin the bearers loaded it on to a cart.

The procession emerged from the park near Satory and joined the Paris road. Nicolas followed in his own carriage. They passed through the city toll-gates a little before nine o'clock. Nicolas had sent an officer ahead on horseback to warn the Châtelet of their arrival. The coffin was taken down to a vault in the Basse-Geôle behind the room where bodies were put on public display. Once the formalities were complete, and after Semacgus had left, Bourdeau suggested to Nicolas that they went for a meal in their usual tavern in Rue du Pied-de-Boeuf. They could go by carriage, which would then take them home. Nicolas had eaten nothing since his morning chocolate and he was starving after such an eventful day so he willingly agreed. He was worn out by all that had happened that day, weary from the effort of keeping his nerve and his temples were throbbing. He was in need of sustenance to revive his spirits after the successive ordeals of facing a defensive Madame de Pompadour, the shock of discovering a dead body and the nervous tension of the meeting with the minister.

Now sitting at the rickety old table where they felt so much at ease, he was happy to let the conversation between Bourdeau and the innkeeper wash over him.

Their host suggested stewed eels caught in the Seine, and Bourdeau, his fellow countryman, said teasingly, 'What, you mean one of those monsters that feed off our customers in the Basse-Geôle?'

'They may have a nibble when there's nothing more appetising around, but actually, Mr Know-it-all, their preferred diet is beech-mast and whitebeam. What could be healthier?'

'What about something from the clear waters of the River Vienne and the River Loire? Something that hasn't been near the butchers' shops whose blood runs into the river?'

'But, Pierre, perch and pike, even if they look more attractive, don't give up their flavour easily . . .'

'That may be, but eel is far too heavy on the stomach.'

'Not the way I make it.'

'And how is that?'

'Well, it's true, the flesh is fatty, gelatinous and viscous so I gut and skin it, season it with spices and grill it for a short time before letting it simmer in wine. This dissolves the parts that are hard to digest and makes the dish lighter. Served with sautéed mushrooms freshly delivered from Chaville, and a bottle of our local wine, which I also use in the sauce, you'll have nothing to complain about. All I add is some *beurre manié*, just for a little extra flavour.'

The two friends, deciding to trust their host's advice, were served an enormous eel in a piping-hot terrine. The morsels of fish were firm but tasty, and for some minutes they concentrated on the food in silence. Then after their initial hunger had been satisfied Nicolas gave Bourdeau a detailed account of his visit to the fountaineer's workshop.

'So it appears,' said Bourdeau, 'the Comte de Ruissec set out to eliminate an awkward accomplice and ended up falling into a trap.'

'That would mean that it was the Comte de Ruissec who

arranged his son's murder. I just cannot imagine that, whatever the causes of their disagreement might have been. Have you forgotten the horrible circumstances of the vicomte's death?'

'But you couldn't imagine a brother killing his elder sibling either, though such things have happened since the dawn of time, and there are numerous examples in the legal records.'

Nicolas reflected on the inspector's remark.

'By the way, Bourdeau, there was something you wanted to tell me the other evening but the rum had slurred your speech somewhat.'

'I don't see . . .'

'Yes, you mentioned a face . . . You repeated the word several times.'

Bourdeau slapped his forehead. 'My God, I'd completely forgotten. But it's an important detail. I'd told you that the Minister of Bavaria's coachman had been found. As I knew you were very busy I thought it was right for me to question him.'

'It was indeed. So what happened?'

'He told me a very strange story. When he drove his carriage towards the bank of the Seine at Pont de Sèvres to tend to the foot of one of his horses, he really did see the scene described by the footman: two men plunging someone unconscious into the water, saying that it was one of their friends who was dead drunk. But what the footman had not noticed but which struck our coachman was the drunkard's face. It still made him shudder, the poor devil. His description exactly matches the description of the Vicomte de Ruissec's face when he was found. He was still trembling at the memory of those sunken cheeks. He had indeed drunk something – it was lead. And he was certainly dead.'

'Do you know, that had already occurred to me. The smell of wet clothes, that obtrusive smell, really did come from the river and the stagnant water near its banks. They wanted to dump the body in the river. Weighted down like that it would have sunk straight to the bottom. Enough to satisfy the appetites of the fish you were talking about earlier.'

Bourdeau suddenly pushed away his bowl of eels.

'I've always thought it was suspect,' he muttered, 'fishing in big cities.'

'But,' Nicolas went on, continuing his train of thought, 'our fellows were interrupted on the job and one of them, probably the manservant Lambert, worked out the diabolical plan of taking the body back to the Hôtel de Ruissec. He or his accomplice.'

'The vidame?' said Bourdeau.

'Perhaps, but there are other candidates.'

'In any case this clears up certain points and opens up new possibilities. I've had the coachman put in solitary confinement. He's a prime witness and it's a shame he didn't have a better look at the other two rogues but perhaps he was too frightened by the look on the face of the so-called drunkard.'

Nicolas and Bourdeau stayed on talking for some considerable time and got through a good few bottles as they prepared their plan of campaign. By now Nicolas was calm and composed. Though he did not yet have all the cards in his hand he felt confident that he could keep his promise to Monsieur de Saint-Florentin to bring the guilty parties before him by the following week. He needed to wait for the information requested from the provinces, then collate and check it, hope that Monsieur de La Vergne could find the name of the lieutenant who had fallen victim to the Comte de Ruissec – this detail might prove important – and above all close in on the protagonists with his network of spies and informers.

XI

REVELATIONS

'If Justice has been depicted with a blindfold over her eyes, then
Reason needs to be her guide.'
VOLTAIRE

Wednesday 14 November 1761

Since All Saints' Day the city had been cold and foggy. The
Lieutenant General of Police made his entrance into the Great
Châtelet with his hands in a warming muff. With the help of old
Marie he attempted to extricate himself from his thick fur-lined
cloak. He muttered in exasperation at the usher's clumsiness.
Nicolas and Bourdeau observed the scene. The inspector was
leaning back against a wall, as if trying to be inconspicuous.
Nicolas for his part felt a twinge of emotion at being back in the
office where several years earlier he had met Monsieur de Sartine
for the first time. The contrast between the ancient medieval
walls and the splendour of the furniture never ceased to strike
him. This dull, grey morning the room was illuminated by a vast
number of candelabra whose flickering gleam added to the
radiance of the banked-up fire blazing in the great Gothic
fireplace. Monsieur de Sartine was known to be sensitive to the
cold, hence the need to warm the high-ceilinged room in which
the magistrate appeared only once a week, on Wednesdays, to

preside symbolically over the hearing in his nearby courtroom. In fact he usually had someone stand in for him. He leant his elbows on the back of a chair, lifted his coat-tails and warmed himself against the fire. After a moment's reflection he signalled to Nicolas to begin.

'Sir, I wanted to speak to you today with Inspector Bourdeau in attendance to offer you the conclusions I have come to concerning the criminal deaths of the three members of the Ruissec family. I have asked your permission for this session to take place in the privacy of your study so as to preserve the secrecy and confidentiality of a case whose ramifications go right to the heart of the monarchy and the State.'

'I venture to hope, sir,' said Sartine with a smile, 'that this degree of secrecy will not extend to concealing the names of the guilty parties.'

'Rest assured, sir, they will be revealed. I should like to go back to the strange beginnings of this case. From the start intervention from above deflected the course of the investigation. I will not go so far as to say that justice was impeded but it was encouraged to look in a certain direction. From the moment we reached the Hôtel de Ruissec, before we knew anything, suicide was spoken of. Monsieur de Ruissec's violent reaction towards you, his contempt and reluctance to answer my questions, could admittedly be ascribed to his fear of scandal but I sensed there was something else. Numerous obstacles were put in our path, clues seemed contradictory and various interventions impeded my enquiries.'

Monsieur de Sartine drummed his fingers on the back of the chair.

'That is all well and good, Nicolas, but please explain what it was that convinced you from the very beginning that we were dealing with a murder when the room was locked from inside.'

'There were several clues. The state of the wound gave all the appearances of having been inflicted by a firearm *post mortem*. Then there were the corpse's hands. As you know, when someone fires a pistol, especially a heavy cavalry type like the one used in this case, the hand pulling the trigger, and sometimes even the face, is spattered with black powder. However, the Vicomte de Ruissec's hands were clean and well cared for. In addition there was the terrifying appearance of the face.'

'Yes, I witnessed that,' said Sartine, shaking himself as if to dispel a haunting image.

'Other incomprehensible facts added to the confusion. For example, the smell of stagnant water coming from the dead man's clothes and some fragments of a powdery, coal-like substance that I found stuck to his boots. But it was the evidence found in the room that proved vital. A farewell note had been written, in capitals. The position of the lamp on the desk, the armchair, the quill and inkstand, and even the paper all convinced me that the person who had written those lines was *left-handed*.'

'But perhaps the Vicomte de Ruissec really was left-handed. You didn't know.'

'Indeed, but what I could see was that the shot from the pistol had struck the base of the neck on the left. It would have been difficult, not to say physically impossible, for a right-handed person to inflict such an injury on himself.'

Monsieur de Sartine fidgeted.

'I don't understand. Who is left-handed and who is right-handed?'

'Let me explain,' said Nicolas. 'A right-handed person cannot fire a shot at the base of his head on the left-hand side without extraordinary contortions and at the risk of missing. A little later I happened to discover in the dressing room a mother of pearl and silver-gilt dressing case, carefully placed on the right-hand side. There was further confirmation later: *the Vicomte de Ruissec was indeed right-handed*. But the question still remained: did the person firing the shot do so without taking this into account or had he cleverly *tried to make it look as if the murderer or the person who wanted to make it look like a suicide were left-handed?*'

'Why should anyone want to make it look like a suicide when so many factors argued in favour of a murder?'

'Perhaps someone was trying to draw attention to the fact that it could not possibly have been suicide. They were trying to send a message; it was a warning.'

'Commissioner Le Floch is once again leading us into a labyrinth where he alone knows the way through!' sighed Sartine.

'There were many other clues. A manservant in stockinged feet who claimed just to have got out of bed but whose cravat was perfectly positioned and knotted, and who gave no sign of emotion at the sight of the body. You witnessed that, sir. He was doing everything, more even than he needed, to substantiate the theory of the vicomte's suicide. He made great play of his master's gambling debts and melancholy. After you left I examined the dead man's library and was intrigued by the titles it contained. The dead man's hat thrown upside down on to the bed shocked me: you know the superstition . . .'

From the shadows Bourdeau could be heard expressing his amusement.

'Questioning Picard, the major-domo, confirmed my doubts. The man could hardly see. He had not seen the vicomte clearly when he returned. He described him as infatuated with a manservant who exerted an evil influence over him. On the other hand, Picard too mentioned that the young man was anxious, depressed and preoccupied by a serious matter. Finally in the garden of the mansion I noticed footprints and a ladder, though I could not immediately see what this all meant.'

'So you had not at this point solved the mystery of the locked bedroom, had you?'

'No, sir. The revelation came when Bourdeau and I went on an undercover visit to Grenelle. An unexpected visitor forced me to hide in the wardrobe and I then understood what had really happened. Lambert, the manservant, dressed in his master's clothes, goes past the half-blind major-domo, up to the first floor, closes the door behind him and opens the window for his accomplice. The two of them bring the vicomte's body up the ladder and stage the suicide scene. Lambert hides in the wardrobe and reappears when all our attention is focused on the dead body in the semi-darkness. It was a risky game, but worth the candle.'

'What about the Comte de Ruissec? What was your initial impression of him?'

'His reaction was not quite what I would have expected. He seemed to come to terms with the idea of an autopsy on his son's body very quickly, as if he knew full well that it would not take place. Monsieur de Noblecourt later shed some light on the comte's complex personality. His past, his ostentatious piety, his reputation but also his position at Court with the Dauphin and

Madame Adélaïde suggested there was much to learn. He also told me about the vicomte's younger brother – intended for the priesthood, but leading a profligate life and spending money like water. Going back to our evening visit to Grenelle: as we were about to leave, the major-domo brought me an envelope purporting to come from Madame de Ruissec, asking me to meet her the next day in the Lady Chapel of the Carmelite monastery so that she might "seek my advice".'

'But as usual your witnesses perished. First the son, then the mother, leaving only the father!'

'That's nothing to do with me, sir. The undoubted murder of Madame de Ruissec proved that someone involved was left-handed, either genuinely or by pretence. The doctor who made the preliminary examination, in the presence of Monsieur de Beurquigny, one of your commissioners, confirmed that. As you know I decided to keep this new crime quiet because it could quite easily be passed off as an accident. Today, sir, I would like you to hear the evidence of a man who no longer has any reason to remain silent. He's a decent fellow, a former soldier. I gave him my word that he would not be prosecuted. All he is guilty of is a silence that could be interpreted as loyalty to his masters. Bourdeau, bring in Picard.'

Bourdeau opened the door of the Lieutenant General's office and motioned to the usher who invited the old man to enter. He seemed to have aged even more and was leaning on a stick. Nicolas made him sit down.

'Monsieur Picard, you are a soldier and an honest man. Are you prepared to repeat here what you have already told me in confidence?'

'Yes, sir.'

'On the evening in question did anyone else enter the Hôtel de Ruissec before the vicomte returned?'

'Yes, indeed, sir, and I hid this from you. Monsieur Gilles, I mean Monsieur le Vidame, came while his parents were accompanying Madame to the opera. He had arranged to see his mother and went up to wait for her in her rooms.'

'So she would have found him there when she got back home, would she not? When the comte accompanied his wife to her rooms did he see his younger son?'

'No, sir. The comte did not go upstairs and, in any case, Monsieur Gilles had instructed me not to tell the general he was there. In my opinion he would have been hiding in case his father did go upstairs.'

'Did the comtesse join him immediately?'

'Not to my knowledge, sir. When we reached the first floor to break open the door she passed out, so I believe, and she returned to her rooms only much later.'

'Could anyone have heard the conversation between mother and son?'

'Definitely, sir. There are many double doors and the back of Madame's rooms gives on to a corridor that leads to the servants' quarters.'

'Why did you conceal from us that the vidame was in the house?'

'I did not consider it important and he had asked me to be discreet. He was afraid of his father.'

After Picard had been shown out, Monsieur de Sartine began his habitual pacing, before stopping in front of Nicolas.

'Where does that get us? You do not know what was said between mother and son.'

'You are quite wrong, sir. We know everything. Bourdeau will explain how. It is always possible to discover something if you investigate thoroughly. All that's needed is to search and listen.'

The inspector emerged from the shadows. He seemed caught between the satisfaction of playing his role and the embarrassment of being brought to the fore.

'Sir, Commissioner Le Floch can tell you that we carried out a very detailed assessment of what everyone was doing that evening in Grenelle. Neither Picard, the major-domo, nor Lambert, the vicomte's manservant, could physically have been near enough the comtesse's rooms to know what was said. On the other hand, I did learn that someone had heard the conversation.'

'A *deus ex machina*!' exclaimed Monsieur de Sartine.

'Simpler than that, sir, the comtesse's chambermaid was in the adjacent boudoir when the conversation began. She did not really understand what was happening. The exchanges were virulent. The comtesse accused the vidame of having killed his brother.'

'Why did she make such an accusation?'

'Apparently she thought the vidame was jealous of his elder brother and that in addition they were rivals in love. The comtesse did not believe her son had committed suicide. There was a terrible argument. The vidame eventually managed to convince his mother he was innocent by referring to a plot involving his father and elder brother. He begged his mother to intervene and convinced her to speak to the police. It was at this point that she wrote a note to the commissioner.'

'Is the chambermaid implicated in any way?'

'No, except that, courted by Lambert, she was in the habit of repeating to him in all innocence the secrets of her masters' conversations and probably related word for word the incomprehensible exchange that she had overheard between mother and son.'

'That is always the problem when servants are led astray,' said Sartine.

Nicolas resumed, 'At the Discalced Carmelites, who was in a position to attack Madame de Ruissec? Not her husband, who was in Versailles. Some doubt remains concerning the vidame. We do not know Lambert's timetable but we now know that only he and the vidame knew about the meeting and the reasons for it. Up until that point the case might only have been a private matter, a family drama. But from then on everything suddenly changes; other factors come into play and soon the authorities themselves decide or pretend to give up the investigation.'

Monsieur de Sartine began to cough and he quickened his obsessive pacing about the room.

'You are surely not claiming that the son killed his mother, are you?'

'I ruled out nothing. At that moment I was wondering what to do. Should I let things drift and risk losing the tenuous thread that guided me or should I carry on until the end, working on the basis of the few things I was certain of? Covering up the Comtesse de Ruissec's murder was simply a tactical ruse. One thing obsessed me: the gruesome way in which the vicomte had been killed. In the Basse-Gêole we discovered for certain that he had been choked with molten lead. Why such a horrible death? Monsieur de Noblecourt happened to mention that this was the punishment meted out to counterfeiters in Russia. This set me thinking. It looked as if the vicomte might have been killed by an accomplice as an example to others, to strike fear into their hearts. I concentrated my enquiries on the trades that use lead.'

'What do you mean by an example to others?'

'To the other conspirators and accomplices I gradually came to believe were involved, as further disturbing evidence emerged that this was not simply a private matter. A second question intrigued me: why execute someone in such an extraordinary way, a way so difficult to organise, so risky, and which at first sight seems excessive? It is thanks to you, sir, that I answered that question. Whilst there is an element of madness in all this, as well as it being the revenge wrought by a secret society on members who have betrayed the cause, there is an additional and, so to speak, a practical explanation too.'

'Why thanks to me?'

'Does the mention of the Minister of Bavaria, whose carriage was intercepted for smuggling at the Porte de la Conférence, mean anything to you, sir?'

'What it means to me is two insistent letters from Monsieur de Choiseul and three extremely tedious conversations with the pompous minister, who's obsessed with his diplomatic privileges.'

'Statements from various witnesses confirm that two men were caught immersing a body in the water near Pont de Sèvres on the evening of the vicomte's death. One of the witnesses, the minister's coachman, was terror-stricken at the sight of the face of the man, who was said to be dead drunk. Well, I maintain that the two men were trying to dispose of the vicomte's lead-weighted body and that it was the failure of this attempt that then led them to stage the so-called suicide. However, this could only be successfully achieved by someone with perfect knowledge of the layout and habits of the Hôtel de Ruissec.'

'This is all very complicated and unconvincing.'

'The murderers could not dispose of a body in the great park at Versailles. At the first hunt a dog would have discovered it. They wanted to immerse it in the Seine, weighted down with lead, but that failed. This immersion explains the smell of stagnant water clinging to the dead man's damp clothes.'

'That's typical of our Nicolas, always an answer for everything.'

'The Comtesse de Ruissec's death also produced another vital piece of evidence: a ticket for the Comédie-Italienne. The murderer clearly wanted to direct me towards Mademoiselle Bichelière. Why? Was it to point the finger of suspicion at her? No. Everything was intended to attract my attention to her entourage instead. The actress had the reputation of being flighty. Though she was the vicomte's mistress, she also had other admirers. She displayed, or feigned, a violent jealousy towards Mademoiselle de Sauveté, her lover's betrothed, but more from self-interest than hurt feelings.'

'So you were still no further forward?'

'No, but another aspect of the case emerged. A lady, a lady of high rank, a lady with influence in the highest quarters . . .'

Sartine went nearer, pulled up an armchair and sat down. Nicolas lowered his voice.

'. . . sent for me. She wanted to tell me her fears concerning you know who and to give me a scurrilous and offensive tract. She also warned me against the Comte de Ruissec's intrigues. That meeting brought me nothing tangible. However, while at Choisy I spotted a person I had already heard was a friend of the vicomte's, a certain Truche de La Chaux, a Life Guard at Versailles. He seemed to have ready access to the lady's chateau. Continuing my investigation, I questioned La Paulet, an old acquaintance of ours, whose establishment, despite the bans, still enjoys the reputation as the best haunt for illegal gambling. That meeting did prove fruitful: I discovered that the vidame betted heavily here with Truche de La Chaux and *that he was left-handed*. After his companion had lost an excessive amount of money the Life Guard had pledged a jewel that intrigued me by its appearance and which I officially confiscated on the spot. La Paulet also had plenty to say about the looseness of La Bichelière's morals. That same evening, our undercover visit to Grenelle, apart from providing us with the solution to the problem of the locked bedroom, enabled me to lay my hand on the documents and tracts that confirmed the threats against the King's life. As a result sir, the minister gave me *carte blanche* to see the matter through to a successful conclusion.'

'I can assure you that we always approved the very appropriate measures you took and the general conduct of your investigation. I was constantly pestering the minister to authorise you to act officially.'

Nicolas thought to himself that it would have been nice to know this, when he had been agonising about his superior's reactions to some of his initiatives.

'In Versailles,' he went on, 'I met the vicomte's betrothed. She was a strange character and the intended marriage was even stranger. I noted that she seemed extremely well informed since she knew that her betrothed had been killed while cleaning his weapon. Who had told her this? Why was she not attending the vicomte's funeral service, being held that day? Since then Bourdeau has looked into the wedding contract drawn up by the notaries.'

'A one-sided contract,' said Bourdeau, 'which bestowed preposterous advantages on the bride-to-be. It looked more like an attempt at blackmail than an arrangement between two families. The Ruissecs were falling into a legal deathtrap. I was told that the dowry was for an excessive amount. If the vicomte happened to die before his wife, or even before the wedding was celebrated, she received a fortune. The agreement had already been signed.'

'My visit to Versailles,' said Nicolas, 'also afforded me the opportunity to meet Truche de La Chaux. That swindler tried to spin me a tale about the ring that he'd left as a pledge at the Dauphin Couronné. He seemed sure of his impunity and made no secret of the fact that he enjoyed the protection of the great lady we spoke of earlier. Chance always has a role to play in any investigation and I happened to discover that on the day the vicomte died, someone had had a note sent via a page to Truche de La Chaux: he was to meet a mysterious person near Apollo's Chariot. However, this note, which was intended for the Life Guard, was intercepted by the Vicomte de Ruissec.'

'How do you think that happened?' asked Sartine.

'I assume the vicomte knew the sender of the note and that by taking the place of Truche he intended to find out more about the plot. The following day, during the hunt, Madame Adélaïde informed me of the disappearance of several of her jewels. The hunt had just begun when I was knocked unconscious, thrown to the ground, abducted, taken to an unknown place and confronted with one of my former Jesuit teachers, who attempted to make me give up my investigation.'

Monsieur de Sartine stood up and went to sit behind his desk, where he began to move the items around, always a sign of puzzlement or annoyance.

'Sir,' he said, 'I have had that investigated and it has only a distant connection with our case. *Someone* has been overzealous. *Someone* has press-ganged an elderly man into an insane scheme. *Someone* now realises that it's likely to work against the interests that *someone* wants to defend. But I guarantee you that the guilty parties have nothing to do with the people I should like you at last to bring before me.'

Nicolas reflected how this investigation produced surprise after surprise ... Faced with the mysterious workings of power he still sometimes felt like an apprentice.

'Now will you finally explain the truth about all this?'

'You must realise that we are confronting not *one* intrigue but several schemes being carried out at the same time for different reasons. To complicate things further, the protagonists are connected and their actions and movements affect one another. Yes, sir, there are several plots: a private plot that I shall call an act of vengeance against the Comte de Ruissec, a secret plot that I call a political conspiracy against the King's life and lastly the intrigue of a great lady who, as you know, manipulates individuals of little consequence.'

'There you go again, flying off at tangents!' exclaimed Sartine. 'All those tales of chivalry that you once told me had fascinated you as a child have gone to your head. I'm prepared to believe there was a plot but don't mix everything up.'

'Sir, I'm not mixing anything up,' Nicolas replied with a hint of annoyance. 'The Comte de Ruissec was part of the Dauphin's innermost circle. He was gambling that the Dauphin would soon be king. Of course the heir to the throne knew nothing of these intrigues; people were merely acting in his name. In circumstances that are not as yet clear the comte became involved in a conspiracy intended to eliminate the King. Don't forget that he hated the King for blocking his career in the army. He succeeded in convincing his son, a lieutenant in the Life Guards, to join the conspiracy. Lastly, though formerly a Protestant, he had adopted, either through conviction or ambition, the views of the pious party, which protected him from the consequences of his past actions that might otherwise have jeopardised his position at Court.'

'There goes your imagination again!'

'Sir, would you like to hear what Vidame Gilles de Ruissec, whom I have had brought from the Bastille, has to say?'

Without waiting for Sartine's answer, Bourdeau showed the prisoner in. He was deathly pale, but his whole bearing evinced a certain determination.

'Sir,' said Nicolas, 'please repeat to the Lieutenant General of Police what you told me this morning.'

'Certainly, sir. As my father is dead there is no longer any reason for me to conceal the truth.'

'Why did you not speak up earlier?'

'I could only vindicate myself by implicating him. I was suspected of having murdered my brother. In fact, on the day of his death I attempted to see my mother at Versailles. For months Lionel had seemed desperately sad. He eventually told me what was eating away at him, swearing me to secrecy. Our father had dragged him into a conspiracy. Lionel was convinced that it was an act of madness, that it would cost him both his honour and his life and that our family would never recover from it. My mother was preparing to accompany Madame Adélaïde to Paris to the opera; she was unable to see me and arranged to meet me that same evening in her rooms in Grenelle. When she arrived she thought for some reason that I was responsible for my brother's death. I eventually managed to convince her of my innocence. She decided to seek advice from the police. I had no alibi. Later I did not know what the prevailing theory was. It was Lambert who told me that the police suspected it was murder. I had no reason to distrust him at that point, having no idea he was part of the conspiracy; my brother had not warned me against him.'

'What was your relationship with Mademoiselle Bichelière, the actress at the Comédie-Italienne?'

'She was my brother's mistress. On Lambert's advice, after he assured me that she was a decent girl and would do anything to please me, I thought it would be a clever idea to ask her to swear that I had spent the evening with her. She had such a reputation for . . . She refused. I just didn't know what to do. When you came to arrest me I couldn't bring myself to talk. My mother was my only witness and she was dead.'

'I'm going to put to you the decisive question: were you Mademoiselle Bichelière's lover? You were often seen at her house in Rue de Richelieu.'

'The people who make that allegation are lying. It was the first time I'd been there. And even then it took Lambert to persuade me to go.'

Sartine intervened. 'What was the purpose of the conspiracy your father and brother were implicated in? Do you know?'

'For a long time my brother refused to tell me. Its aim was to kill the King, to bring the Dauphin to the throne and create a governing council around him.'

'Thank you, sir. We shall have to see what is to become of you. Your frankness will be taken into account.'

Bourdeau led the vidame back out of the study.

'So, Nicolas, now where do we stand?'

'I think, sir, that the main actor in this drama is the person best placed to reveal its mysteries. Let me introduce you to an extraordinary couple.'

At a signal from Nicolas, Bourdeau opened the door of the study and clapped his hands. An officer appeared, followed by Mademoiselle de Sauveté in shackles, wearing a russet dress and dark glasses. Immediately afterwards two other officers put a stretcher on the floor on which a pale-faced man lay, his head resting on a straw bolster. His eyes were bright with fever and his almost shorn head was reminiscent of that of a galley slave or a monk. Nicolas forestalled Sartine's request for an explanation.

'Sir, you no doubt recognise Lambert, the Vicomte de Ruissec's manservant. Or rather I should say Yves de Langrémont, the son of Jean de Langrémont, a lieutenant in the dragoons, executed some time ago for cowardice in battle. Before dying from his bullet wound the Comte de Ruissec had time to inflict on him what the doctors consider to be a mortal wound. Monsieur de Langrémont wishes to explain himself before he appears before the Almighty. I should add that he was arrested in Versailles at Mademoiselle de Sauveté's house.'

'And who is this lady?' asked the Lieutenant General of Police.

'May I introduce you to Mademoiselle Armande de Sauveté, or rather . . .'

He removed her spectacles and her wig to reveal the pert face of Mademoiselle Bichelière.

'Mademoiselle de Langrémont, arrested yesterday as she was leaving Mademoiselle Bichelière's house in Rue de Richelieu.'

'What is the meaning of this charade?' asked Sartine indignantly. 'Are you trying to tell me that La Bichelière is the sister of Langrémont, alias Lambert, and that the vicomte's betrothed never existed?'

'It is indeed a strange and dreadful tale, sir. Monsieur de Noblecourt advised me to delve into my suspects' pasts. It's as well that I took his advice. Many years ago the Comte de Ruissec had one of his officers executed. It was a blatant injustice. For years documents and statements from witnesses have been emerging about the episode. Who was behind this? Until today it has remained a complete mystery. A few days ago I learnt the name of the lieutenant executed: he was called Langrémont and came from the diocese of Auch. The reports from the intendant of the province also enlightened me and I remembered that on two occasions that town had been mentioned in the course of my investigation. It then became clear that various diverse facts in my enquiry were related. The strange Mademoiselle de Sauveté had been brought up in that area. My unexpected visit to her house was illuminating. Beside the fact that she had shoes of different sizes and wigs with various fragrances, there was a coffee cup with a mark that could only have been made by someone *who held it in the left hand.*'

'There he goes with his obsession again,' said Sartine.

'Well, it so happened that I knew Mademoiselle Bichelière's fragrance very well and even the . . . size of her foot.'

Nicolas blushed. Bourdeau emerged from the shadows and hurried to his rescue.

'The commissioner, sir, has a very good nose and the gift of recognising smells.'

'Does he indeed?' said Sartine. 'And a well-trained eye for recognising ladies' feet. Strange, strange!'

His sudden imitation of Monsieur de Saint-Florentin's quirk of repeating words and the slight involuntary twitching of the eye revealed the magistrate's barely suppressed amusement.

'Well,' Nicolas continued unperturbed, 'the two fragrances were identical . . .'

'It's about time you reached your conclusion, Commissioner,' said Sartine, who appeared weary at having to furnish so many expressions of surprise at Nicolas's carefully constructed narrative.

'I'm getting there, sir. We are confronted with a machination in which filial piety and perverted ideals were accompanied by a devilish desire for revenge.'

Suddenly the wounded man coughed and, attempting to clear his throat, began to speak. Lambert's slightly coarse tone had now given way to another more natural way of speaking which seemed to betray an innate distinction, adding to the mystery surrounding him.

'As I am about to appear before God,' he began, 'and submit to

His judgement, the only one that matters to me, I do not wish to leave anyone else the task of explaining my actions. Commissioner Le Floch has just used a term that touches me greatly: filial piety. May my actions, however dreadful they seem to most people, be truly represented.'

These opening words had exhausted him. He attempted to sit up because he was short of breath. Bourdeau helped him to find a more comfortable position. As he had become agitated the blanket had slipped down and his half-open shirt revealed a blood-soaked dressing wrapped right around his chest.

'I was born Yves de Langrémont, in Auch. My father, a lieutenant in the Comte de Ruissec's regiment, was executed for cowardice in action . . . Cowardice!' A stifled sob interrupted his words. 'My mother died of grief as a result. I was twenty-five, leading a dissolute, wasteful life. We were immediately thrown on the street. My sister could not stand our new way of life for long and ran away with a troupe of travelling players . . . Only a Jesuit priest, my former teacher, tried to help me. He was a tormented spirit, interested only in ideas. At school he despised the mediocrities, those who, in his words, floundered because of their own inadequacies. His colleagues and pupils found the iciness of his anger disconcerting. He could see that I had received an outstanding education and had acquired a great store of knowledge but that I also surrendered to wild outbursts, driven on by a vivid imagination, always liable to be carried away by ideas and fancies. How could I be taught to reconcile so many contradictory qualities?'

He asked for some water. After glancing at Monsieur de Sartine, Nicolas handed him a glass.

'I discovered from one of my father's comrades the exact circumstances of his execution. He also brought me a bundle of papers proving the Comte de Ruissec's wickedness. I used some of them to prepare a report that I gave to the Minister for War, along with a petition to the King asking that one of his noblemen be brought to justice. Nothing came of it and I even received threats from various quarters and was ordered to keep quiet. My father's friend died and left me a considerable fortune as his heir. I decided to use it to take revenge by my own means. My former teacher had been driven out of his order by a decision of the bishop's court. He was forced to flee and magistrates issued a summons for his arrest. He did indeed hold subversive views about the legitimacy of assassinating kings who transgress the rules. His idols were Clément,[1] Ravaillac and Damiens. His zealousness threatened the Society of Jesus. Before going into hiding abroad he convinced me that the sovereign was responsible for the misfortunes that had befallen my family. So to the hatred of my father's assassin was added the hatred of the person in whose name innocents were killed.'

He was breathing with increasing difficulty. Monsieur de Sartine went closer to him.

'Sir, now tell us how this infernal plot was devised that has caused the death of so many people.'

'I decided to come to Paris to find my sister and to gain access to the Ruissec family. Unfortunately —' he tried to turn towards Mademoiselle Bichelière — 'our misfortunes had led her into a type of life that despite all my exhortations she refused to give up. She would not concede to me on this matter. She merely agreed to help me to see that justice was done. Here I solemnly wish to declare that she knew nothing of my plans and played only a passive role in the situations I set up without understanding their consequences.'

'We shall see about that later, sir,' said Sartine.

'It was not difficult for me to gain access to the Ruissec family. I paid the vicomte's manservant to give up his position and immediately took his place. It was just as easy to gain the confidence of the young man and his brother, whose frenzy for gambling gave me the advantage of seeming to be a willing, discreet lender. It did not take me long to realise that the comte also sought vengeance. Having been befriended by the malcontents and the pious, they had recruited him to their conspiracy. I gained his confidence and became his secret factotum. Gradually I passed myself off as the agent for a clandestine group preparing the new reign. In this way I built up two intrigues, one for the benefit of my personal vengeance, and the other, just as real, to punish the King for his injustice. I did not want to bungle my plan. I had to entangle and ensnare the comte so that he had no possible way out. He was implicated in a plot. His sons were in my hands. A judicious use of certain documents forced him to consent to the marriage of my sister – Mademoiselle de Sauveté – whose true identity he still did not know.'

'But,' said Nicolas 'you yourself pretended to be Mademoiselle de Sauveté. In her house in Versailles I found unusually large women's shoes and a tow-yellow wig, as well as your fingermarks on left-hand side of a cup. Not to mention the clerical bands under a bed, which you presumably used for pretending to be the vidame.'

'I was indeed free to move around in different guises, acting various roles. In the midst of my preparations I came across a galley slave who had served his time and was wandering about accompanied by his deaf-and-dumb son. He was a former fountaineer. His experience enabled me to enter Versailles to prepare subsequent events.'

Nicolas, who could not help feeling an element of pity for the man, remembered just in time that the subsequent events included a long series of increasingly cruel murders and the King's intended assassination.

'Everything was coming together as I wanted,' continued Langrémont. 'The Ruissecs were in my grip. The comte was conspiring in the belief that he was part of a secret and fearsome organisation whose chief communicated with him via me, and whose hide-out was in the fountaineer's workshop. However, it so happened that the Comte de Ruissec, convinced of the treachery of a Life Guard called Truche de La Chaux, asked for him to be executed as a traitor to the cause and a threat to our interests. Why and how the Vicomte de Ruissec took his place, I have no idea.'

Monsieur de Sartine turned towards Nicolas. 'You can no doubt throw some light on that.'

'Yes, sir. The Vicomte de Ruissec intercepted a note intended for Truche de La Chaux. When Lambert saw the vicomte and not the Life Guard arrive at Apollo's Chariot for the meeting he no doubt considered that providence was delivering up to him his enemy's son for him to wreak his revenge upon, and the most dreadful thing of all was that it was the Comte de Ruissec himself who had given the order for the person coming to the meeting to be killed. So the father signed his own son's death warrant!'

'How can you be so sure of this?'

'A search carried out in Grenelle amongst Lambert's belongings turned up, carefully hidden away, the note brought by the page and intercepted by the Vicomte de Ruissec. Its content is harmless enough: "Be at Apollo's Chariot at midday." But it has the great merit of being in the Comte de Ruissec's handwriting.'

'Was it not strange and foolish to have wanted to keep such a compromising document?'

Lambert raised his voice; it was firmer, as if telling the story of his vengeance had strengthened it.

'On the contrary, it was proof that the Comte de Ruissec was guilty of the trap that had cost his son his life. It was a useful protection for me, and also served as a means of blackmail. But there is one essential point about which you are mistaken, gentlemen. I did not know it was the Vicomte de Ruissec. The man who was due to come was masked for reasons of security. It was only after . . . the execution . . . that I realised it was my enemy's son and, as God is my witness, however much I may have hated that family I swear that I would never have allowed what happened, had I known it was the vicomte.'

'It's easy to say that now,' Sartine butted in. 'That doesn't explain why the comte wished to be rid of Truche de La Chaux.'

'Oh! There were plenty of reasons for that,' Nicolas went on. 'Truche de La Chaux had stolen Madame Adélaïde's jewels. He was being blackmailed by the comte, who had discovered what he had done and was threatening to denounce him if he didn't obey the comte's instructions.'

'What were those instructions?'

'His task was to spy on the great lady we have referred to. His function gave him access to her apartments where he was to leave the scurrilous tracts that the conspiracy kept producing against her and the King. However, it is more than probable that the comte had had wind of the ambiguous attitude of his spy because he had other agents spying on the great lady. All Truche was interested in was his own advantage and he took it where he found it. When attempting to negotiate the sale of one of Madame Adélaïde's rings with the great lady, the latter recognised the jewel and, having caught out Truche, she ordered him to serve her and inform her about the intrigues of the coterie surrounding the Dauphin and the King's daughters, whose influence she feared. So, the Comte de Ruissec, convinced of Truche's double dealing, and fearing his dangerous influence over his sons, decided to do away with him and ordered his execution.'

'What about the second murder, the killing of the comtesse?'

Lambert closed his eyes at the mention of this death.

'I am the culprit. I slipped into the convent of the Carmelites before Commissioner Le Floch arrived, broke her neck and threw her into the well of the dead. The comtesse's chambermaid had told me she was meeting Le Floch and I wanted to prevent that meeting at all costs.'

A coughing fit overcame him.

'None of this would have happened had we not been caught at Pont de Sèvres as we were about to immerse the vicomte's body in the Seine. That was when I had the idea of forcing the comte to see his son's dead body to make him understand that he had caused the death. To show him how his execution of my father had now been avenged by his killing his own son. Nothing could stop me now. I have fulfilled my mission. I have avenged my father. Just before he died I revealed myself to the comte so that his dying vision was of his victim's son. His family is decimated.'

He sat up, let out a loud cry, a stream of blood spurting from his mouth. He fell back unconscious. His sister would have hurled herself upon his body had she not been restrained by an officer. While Bourdeau was arranging for the stretcher to be removed, Mademoiselle Bichelière was taken back to solitary confinement.

Monsieur de Sartine stood stock-still, gazing at the slowly dying fire in the great fireplace.

'He does not have much longer to live. Perhaps that is better for all concerned. As for his sister, she will end her days in some convent dungeon, or its equivalent now that that system no longer exists. In some nunnery at best, or in the depths of some state fortress at worst. I have three questions, Nicolas. First, how did you know the vicomte had been killed in the workshop in the park? We have the confessions now, but before that?'

Nicolas opened his black notebook and took out a small sheet of tissue paper folded in four. Sartine, came closer and saw what looked like black gravel.

'Sir, I collected this from the hem of the vicomte's cloak: coal. Where does one find coal other than near a forge, or in a workshop where metal is melted down? I found the same dust in the workshop of Le Peautre, the fountaineer in the great park.'

'My second question is this: why those dark glasses?'

'My guardian, Canon Le Floch, had an irrational dislike of eyes of differing colours. Though I do not share his sentiment I always notice this feature, especially because when I first arrived in Paris I had my watch stolen by a robber with such eyes. Look at Lambert. He had to conceal his eyes if he was not to be recognised. When he disguised himself as Mademoiselle de

Sauveté he used those dark glasses. And when his sister played the role of the same person, she did likewise.'

'My last question, Nicolas: do you have any hope of arresting Le Peautre?'

'A letter from the intendant of Champagne informed me yesterday that his body had been found near Provins, half eaten by wolves. Before that he had entrusted the little deaf-and-dumb boy he used as a messenger to one of the monasteries in the town.'

'Man works in strange ways. This was a difficult investigation and you have carried it out very well. There remain Madame's jewels. Do you expect to find them?'

'I have not given up hope. We already have the ring.'

'What about Truche de La Chaux?'

'His is not a hanging offence and besides, the good lady protects him, but my intuition leads me to believe that the man will eventually be caught in the web of his own intrigue.'

XII

TRUCHE DE LA CHAUX[1]

'Kings are subject to alarm . . .'
ÉTIENNE JODELLE

Sunday 6 January 1762

The royal supper was about to take place according to time-honoured ritual. For the past two months Nicolas had not left Court. Monsieur de Saint-Florentin had kept the young commissioner at Versailles, much to the chagrin of the Lieutenant General of Police. Nicolas's task was to check the security of the palace and prepare the report requested by the minister, still anxious about threats to the King's life. The revelations concerning the outcome of the Ruissec case had only strengthened his fears and he trusted Nicolas implicitly. The commissioner stayed initially with Monsieur de La Borde, thanks to whom he had been able to find lodgings in the palace, in a loft close to the rooms of the First Groom of the Bedchamber.

It was the first Sunday of the year. Three times a week the King took supper in state with the royal family, following a tradition established by Louis XIV, even though he disliked appearing in public. Louis XV's personal preference would have been to take supper privately with his favourites and the Marquise de Pompadour, but he was bound by his duties as King.

Nicolas, who was now closely involved with Court ceremonial, stood at the door to the first antechamber of the royal apartments, where tables had been set up in a horseshoe-shape. The King and Queen would sit at the top and members of the royal family down the sides. La Borde whispered the details of the protocol in Nicolas's ear. The first meat course was already on its way from the kitchens in a long procession, preceded by an escort of two guards, carbines at the slope, and followed a few paces behind by the footman carrying the candelabrum and the rod, the Master of the Household with his baton of office, the Superintendent of the Pantry, the Comptroller General, the Comptroller of Provisions and a dozen or so other officers of the Household, each carrying a dish, and finally by two more guards bringing up the rear. The Master of the Household paid obeisance before the silver-gilt *nef* containing the scented napkins. Each officer then tasted the meat to ensure it had not been poisoned. The first course of soups and entrées had been elegantly laid out on the table. The result of all this ceremony was that the King ate his meat cold.

The arrival of the royal procession had been heralded by a clicking of heels and a shouldering of weapons as well as by the murmur of the throng of people crowding the antechamber. Preceded by an usher, lit by his pages and followed by a captain from his Guards, the King reached his chair just as the Queen arrived. They were given napkins to wash their hands. The rest of the royal family, the Dauphin and his sisters, had taken their seats. Nicolas now observed the crowd, kept at some distance, who scrupulously followed the progress of the supper. Nobles were lined up, often squashed against one another, behind the

King's chair. They were listening attentively, straining to catch a few words or perhaps a sign of acknowledgement from the august presence.

Eventually the King broke the silence and asked the Dauphin, who had just returned from Paris, for the news from town. The Dauphin mentioned the fears sweeping Europe and circulating in the capital about the Tsarina's state of health. Everyone was anxiously awaiting news from St Petersburg. The winter and the difficulties that the snow and frost created for the mail-coaches cast further doubt on already contradictory or fanciful reports. No one knew what to believe any more. The Dauphin described the fainting fits that were worrying the Tsarina's doctors, leading them to fear apoplexy. These medical details captured the King's attention and he turned to his physician for further information. The Dauphin added that according to certain sources there was great dismay in Russia, although not amongst the uncouth, barbaric and heartless populace. It was at the oriental court that everyone was in a ferment, not for love of the reigning monarch but rather for fear of the Tsarina's successor. This thoughtless remark darkened the King's mood and he fell into a sullen silence, despite the Queen's timid attempts to restart the conversation.

As the table was being cleared and the meats were arriving, a clamour arose outside the antechamber where the supper was taking place. At first it was only a rustle, the patter of hurried footsteps, weapons clattering to the floor, voices being raised and people calling out. Unable to reach the heart of the commotion because of the large crowd of people, Nicolas tried to make out the cause, but in vain. An officer from the Guards suddenly fought his way through the mass of courtiers, managing to reach his captain and whisper something to him.

Outside the scene was one of increasing confusion. The officers of the Household and the members of the King's family looked at one another in disbelief. The sovereign remained unperturbed, even though he looked impatient at the disruption to the ceremony. Rumours were spreading through the gathering. Everyone was talking loudly to their neighbour. Nicolas heard the words 'horrifying assassination attempt' and saw Monsieur de Saint-Florentin give Sartine an interrogatory, flustered look, though the minister stopped pulling faces when the captain of the Guards informed him what was happening. Many people now seemed aware of what had taken place and wore suitably grave expressions. Annoyed by the dull, ever-increasing disturbance around him, the King pursed his lips and looked questioningly at his entourage. He finally displayed his displeasure.

'Where is this commotion coming from? What is the meaning of it?'

No one dared reply but the look on people's faces said it all.

'What is it? Why is everyone looking so embarrassed? What could possibly have this effect? Is my life under threat again?'

The princes and the King's family all started to talk at once so that the King could not understand what was being said. Their replies were so evasive and confused that, far from reassuring the King as intended, they alarmed him further.

'What have I done?' he said suddenly, rising from the table and flinging his napkin to the floor. 'What have I done to deserve these enemies?'

A murmur of consternation and dread ran through the

assembly. The royal procession hurriedly formed up again and the King withdrew to his private apartments. Swept along by La Borde, Monsieur de Saint-Florentin, Sartine and Nicolas followed behind the procession. The King, turned round momentarily, noticed his minister and pointed a threatening finger at him.

'Tell me exactly what happened. Don't try to deceive me, just explain.'

'Sire, Your Majesty may rest reassured, the matter is under control and there is no danger now.'

The fateful word had been spoken and the King immediately seized on it.

'So there was indeed a danger! Sir, enlighten me forthwith.'

'Sire, here is what happened: Truche de La Chaux, one of your Life Guards, was stabbed on the staircase by two villains with a grievance against you. The two evil-doers fled but your guard is at his last gasp.'

The King leant on the captain of the Guards' arm. He looked pale and Nicolas noticed sweat pouring from his forehead and red patches appearing on his face.

'Monsieur de Saint-Florentin, take good care of my poor guard. If he survives I shall reward his zeal.'

The procession formed up again and the King left. Monsieur de Saint-Florentin gathered his men, all except La Borde, who had followed his master. They went off to the minister's office and there everyone turned to Nicolas, the only one to know Truche de La Chaux. He was bombarded with questions. Could someone whose deceit was well known be trusted? Was it possible that the dishonest gambler, thief and double agent had transformed himself overnight into a heroic defender of the throne? Nicolas responded that it was impossible to tell without knowing all the details of the assassination attempt on the Life Guard. The first reports were coming in but they were either incomplete or made little sense. In exasperation, Monsieur de Sartine ordered Nicolas to go himself to find out what had happened, providing the minister did not object.

The Life Guard had been taken to the lower part of the palace, near the kitchens. He was lying on a mattress on the floor of a gallery dimly lit by torches, waiting for a surgeon to arrive to dress his wounds. A police officer whom Nicolas knew told him what he knew of the assassination attempt.

'Monsieur Truche de La Chaux was apparently on guard in the palace. As the King was beginning supper in state, between nine and ten o'clock, he is thought to have left his post in the guardroom to go to buy some tobacco.'

'Which way did he go?'

'From the guardroom he went to "the Louvre". After going through the Princes' Gallery he then went down a very long corridor leading from the offices of the Comptroller General of Finances, which allows you to go out more or less opposite the Grand Lodgings. It was in the extremely badly lit passageway that he was discovered, lying unconscious on the ground.'

'Who discovered him?'

'One of the servants. He found him covered in blood with his sword broken, so he immediately called for help. I believe Monsieur de Saint-Florentin and the Grand Provost of the palace, his deputy, were informed. The Provost made the initial enquiries and drew up a report in the presence of two Life Guards.'

Nicolas noted inwardly that the Grand Provost could have made all this known to the minister earlier.

'So the man had regained consciousness, had he?'

'Yes, he regained consciousness almost immediately. He spoke to the guards and gave them the story of his mishap.'

'Can you try to tell me what he said, in exactly the same words?'

'I'll do my best. I'd just arrived, so I heard everything. He spoke in a weak, faint voice as if he were about to die and said that he had been the victim of an assassination attempt. His very words were, "Make sure the King is safe. I was stabbed by two wretches who wanted to kill him. One was dressed as a priest and the other in a green coat. They promised me a considerable sum of money if I would let them into the royal supper or into the King's apartments."'

The man looked at the notes he had written on a small piece of paper.

'He went on: "I was not tempted by that offer and refused to let them in. Whereupon they rushed at me and stabbed me. They declared it was their mission to deliver the people from oppression and to strengthen a religion that has almost been destroyed."'

These phrases had a familiar ring to Nicolas. The text of the tract found in Madame de Pompadour's apartments reflected the same philosophy. But then all these tracts sounded more or less the same.

'Is that all?'

'He didn't say anything else. He was taken away and brought here.'

The surgeon called to tend to the wounded man had just arrived. He was tall, wiry and stern-looking, with delicate, astonishingly long hands. As Nicolas looked on, he leant over Truche de La Chaux and pulled back his clothes in order to study the wounds. The man was struggling and shouting, screaming with pain. After a few moments the surgeon searched in his bag for a revulsive and some lint. Annoyed by the wounded man's protestations, he held him down firmly so that he could do his work.

'Sir,' he said disdainfully, 'you are making a lot of fuss about very little. You are screaming as if you were in great pain but you are not badly wounded; all I can find are scratches.'

The surgeon asked who Nicolas was and why he was there, and then asked him to be his witness. He thought the incident was a ruse and was determined get to the bottom of it since there were such serious implications.

'Look, Commissioner, at the wounded man's coat and jacket. No one would seriously believe this was an assault.'

He leant over and shook the coat of Truche de la Chaux, who moaned faintly.

'You think, sir, that there has been an attempt at deception?' said Nicolas

'I do, and I can prove it! He must have wounded himself. Look, the holes in his coat do not at all match the superficial grazes he has.'

Defenceless and bewildered, the man was like an animal caught in a trap, desperately searching for a way out. In the end he went into nervous convulsions and began to weep like a child.

Nicolas went up to him. 'I think it would be best for you if you were to tell us the truth.'

Truche looked up and recognised him. He grasped his hand as if he had found a saviour.

'Sir, please help me. I shall tell you everything. I did not want to harm anyone. I withdrew between nine and ten in the evening to one of the staircases and there I broke my sword and took off my coat and jacket. I slashed them in several places and stabbed myself in various parts of my body.'

Nicolas was surprised that the man confessed so readily to a capital offence.

'Did no one see you?'

'I put out the lights so that nobody saw my preparations.'

The man now seemed perfectly calm, as if he had accepted the idea of being found guilty of an imposture.

'Then what?'

'Then I put my coat and jacket back on, lay down on the floor and plaintively called for help.'

'Why did you do it?'

'Sir, one has to make a living. I wanted to obtain a pension from the King, at whatever cost.'

Nicolas left the Life Guard in the hands of the magistrates. He rushed off to report to Monsieur de Saint-Florentin, who instructed him to keep a close eye on the case. It was very late by the time Nicolas saw Monsieur de La Borde, who had stayed with the King. The sovereign was preparing to spend a restless night. Some people had concluded that because one of the aggressors was said to have been dressed as a priest, it had been a Jesuit plot, and recommended that the members of the Society should be immediately driven out of the kingdom. Nicolas informed his friend how far the investigation had progressed. The Jesuits could still sleep peacefully: they were in no way involved in the insignificant impostor's pathetic charade. The King's favourite on the other hand, Nicolas thought, was likely to be racked with anxiety when she learnt of the potentially serious incident that compromised one of her clandestine servants.

The following day the news of the crime reached the capital and the reaction was either fear or scepticism. But as the investigation continued and uncovered new evidence, everyone was soon agreed that the Life Guard was a calculating rogue. The close interrogation to which he was subjected proved that he had conceived his evil plan as early as the previous October. It was discovered that he had had a scraper sharpened by a cutler from Versailles, and had used that to slash his clothes and inflict the cuts on himself. Those who were better informed put it about that the spineless brigand belonged to Madame Adélaïde's innermost circle, since her weakness for converts from Protestantism made her incautious. At no point did Nicolas hear mention of any possible collusion between Truche de La Chaux and Madame de Pompadour. That whole aspect of the case seemed cloaked in secrecy.

On 10 January, Truche de La Chaux was imprisoned in the Bastille, then transferred from the state prison to the Great Châtelet for his trial. In fact the procedure should have taken place before the Grand Provost in Versailles, where the crime had been committed, but taking him to the Bastille had removed him from normal jurisdiction. There were no witnesses produced nor confrontations of the accused. Precedents were quoted: in 1629 a soldier had been broken on the wheel for the same offence; in the reign of Henri III another man found guilty of the crime had been beheaded. Truche did not make use of his letters of nobility in order to be judged by another court. The Parlement of Paris by its decree of 1 February 1762 sentenced him 'to be placed in a tumbrel in his shirt, with a noose around his neck, a torch in his hand and a notice to front and back bearing the words: "The impostor who fabricated an attack on the safety of the King and loyalty to the Nation", to be paraded in this state in different districts of Paris, to make the *amende honorable* in front of Notre-Dame, at the Louvre and the Place de Grève, and having been subjected to preliminary torture to be broken on the wheel.'

The day after this sentence was passed Nicolas received a messenger from Monsieur de Saint-Florentin giving him verbal instructions to visit Truche de La Chaux, who was in the Conciergerie awaiting execution. The commissioner was somewhat surprised by the manner in which he received the order, which contained no explanation. He returned to Paris. His work at Versailles was in any case over and he now had to draw up his report about the King's safety in the palace. The study had become even more important since recent events had revealed disturbing deficiencies in this area.

At the Conciergerie he made his presence known but was received as if he had already been announced and his visit expected. Jangling a bunch of large keys, the gaoler led him through the dark passageways of the prison. They stopped in front of a heavy wooden door reinforced with iron and fitted with a wicket. The locks were unbolted and he was let into the prisoner's cell.

At first he saw nothing: only a dim light penetrated through a window protected by a grid of bars. Nicolas asked the gaoler to bring him a torch. The gaoler was reluctant: it was not the custom here and he had not been given orders to that effect. Nicolas overcame the man's reluctance by offering him a coin; the gaoler hung his own torch on a ring in the wall and withdrew after shutting and locking the door. Nicolas could then examine the cell. To his left, on a bed covered with straw, lay a human figure, his feet clamped in heavy chains, the ends of which were fastened to the wall. His arms were also shackled by lighter, slacker chains that allowed the prisoner to sit up and move his hands. Nicolas remained silent for a time. He could not tell whether the man lying there was asleep. Going closer, he was struck by the change that had come over the Life Guard. Without a wig, his few strands of hair were plastered to his head, his face was greyish and hollow, and he had aged several years in a few weeks. His face wore an expression of deep despondency. His mouth was open and his drooping jaw trembled.

He opened his eyes and recognised Nicolas. He nodded with the semblance of a smile and tried to sit up, but Nicolas had to help him by taking him under the arm.

'So, sir, you have been allowed to visit me. Despite everything.'

'I can't see why I might have been prevented from doing so. You are forgetting my function.'

'You don't know what I'm referring to. Are we alone?' He looked anxiously towards the door of the cell.

'You can see we are. The door is closed and the wicket is shut. No one can hear us, if that is what you are afraid of.'

La Chaux seemed reassured.

'Monsieur Le Floch, I have every faith in you. I sense that you do not believe that my offence is as great as all that. You had the opportunity to arrest me before the event, before I committed my crime. You refrained from doing so, you took everything into consideration . . . That is why I asked to speak to you.'

'Sir, I do not exonerate you from your crime. Make no mistake about that. Your offence is a serious one but I think you acted out of fecklessness rather than the desire to do harm. For the rest, I am at your disposal and ready to listen, provided that what you have to say does not impede the discharge of my duties.'

'Can we make a deal?'

'You are in no position to dictate conditions and I am not allowed to negotiate with you.'

'Sir, do not be in such a hurry to say no. Grant a man who has only a few days, perhaps only a few hours, left to live, the favour of listening to him and, hopefully, with a little compassion, of understanding him.'

'Speak, sir, by all means. But I make no promises.'

'First of all I wish to prove my good faith. I imagine you are still searching for Madame Adélaïde's jewels, are you not?'

From Nicolas's startled reaction he could tell he had struck home, and the commissioner was annoyed with himself.

'That may be so, sir.'

'I regret what I did. The princess was always kind to me and my betrayal of her trust is inexcusable. Monsieur Le Floch, you already have the fleur-de-lis ring but the remainder of the stolen jewels are in the Life Guards' barracks. Go there and dig into the plaster behind my bunk, under the wooden crossbeam of the cob wall; you will find them there. Will you now listen to what I have to say, sir?'

'Certainly, but I cannot promise you anything.'

'That hardly matters now. I have nothing left to lose. Would you agree to take a message from me to the Marquise de Pompadour and to guarantee its safe delivery today?'

He lowered his voice as he mentioned her name. Nicolas remained impassive. What did this request mean? Could Truche have a last wish to express, a favour to ask? Knowing the relationship between the favourite and the condemned man, Nicolas wondered where his duty lay. He was not fearful of the consequences, but he did have the distinct feeling that acceding to this request might be beyond his remit. On the other hand, could he deny Truche de La Chaux, about to die a terrible, shameful death, his last request? He thought that he could not refuse. He also aware that he was in this prison cell not because he had chosen to be here but because Monsieur de Saint-Florentin had instructed him to come. He wondered how close the minister and the marquise were. Perhaps they had agreed that he should be their messenger to the condemned man on the eve of his execution. What did he risk? He would rather take the responsibility of passing on the information than have on his conscience remorse at having refused a man his last request.

'Very well, sir. How do you wish to proceed?'

'I am not allowed writing materials. Do you have any on you?'

Nicolas searched his coat pocket. There were the usual items: his black notebook, a black lead, a penknife, a piece of string, a handkerchief, a snuffbox and some sealing wafers.

'Will a page from my notebook and this pencil do?'

'Yes, they will.'

Nicolas tore off the fragile paper as carefully as possible, smoothed it out and handed it to the prisoner, together with the lead. Truche put the paper flat against the wall, and after wetting the tip of the pencil, began writing in very small characters. Nicolas noted that he did not hesitate as he wrote; he must have thought out well in advance what he wanted to say. He produced about twenty closely written lines, then carefully folded the sheet of paper like a letter. He gave Nicolas an embarrassed look.

'Monsieur Le Floch, please do not misinterpret my next request: I only wish to protect you. It is better for you not to know the contents of this message. I know that I can trust you in this matter, but the recipient may not. So how can I seal my message?'

'Very easily. I always carry sealing wafers and can give you one. You will close the message and sign across the seal.'

Truche sighed as if a great weight had been lifted from him. It seemed to Nicolas that in adversity the man had taken on a new dignity. Instead of an ordinary, rather vulgar person Nicolas now saw someone who was suffering but facing his destiny calmly. It was time to say farewell. Nicolas put the note in his coat. As he was leaving the cell, he spoke to the prisoner one last time.

'Why me?'

'Because you are an honest man.'

Nicolas knocked on the door. The key turned in the lock. The gaoler reappeared and retrieved his torch. The visitor turned and bowed to the prisoner, whose form had already merged into the shadows.

*

Nicolas had been afraid that some difficulty would arise, preventing him from seeing Madame de Pompadour, but it was not the case. As soon as he asked Monsieur de Sartine if he might see her, having given a full account of what had happened, everything was arranged for him. Without pretending to have to refer the matter to his minister, the Lieutenant General of Police urged him to go immediately to the chateau of Bellevue, where the favourite was in residence. He was certain that she would receive him immediately. He advised him to choose the fastest horse in the stables of the Hôtel de Gramont and to hurry to Sèvres as quickly as possible. Nicolas, by now well aware of the practices of those in power, suspected that behind the haste and the help afforded him in his mission lay the desire to conclude successfully some scheme whose meaning remained a mystery to him.

As soon as he arrived at the chateau of Bellevue he was shown into the marquise's apartments. The lady received him in a white and gold boudoir, far too hot for his liking because of the roaring fire. She sat in a large *bergère* swamped by her flowing grey and black dress. Nicolas remembered that the Court was in mourning for the Tsarina Elizaveta Petrovna, who had passed away in St Petersburg the week before. When she saw him she languidly held out her hand, only to withdraw it immediately as she was seized with a violent coughing fit. He waited for her to recover.

'Sir, I must congratulate you on the case that you have solved so successfully. You are entitled once more to our gratitude. Monsieur de Saint-Florentin has told us the story in detail.'

He made no reply but bowed, noting the 'we'. He wondered if this included the King . . .

'You wished to see me, I am told.'

'Yes, Madame. Monsieur Truche de La Chaux, a Life Guard who has just been sentenced for the crime of lese-majesty in the second degree, asked to see me. In the course of our meeting he handed me a letter to be delivered to you. I did not think I could refuse a favour to a man who was living his last hours.'

She shook her head vigorously. 'Is it not extraordinary, sir, that such a faithful servant of the King should agree to be the go-between for such an undesirable person?'

But a man desirable enough for the Marquise de Pompadour to entertain him, Nicolas thought. He needed to tread carefully now, but he felt the favourite was being disingenuous. He decided to challenge her.

'The fact is, Madame, that this person acted for you at certain times in certain missions.'

'This is too much, sir. I will not allow you—'

He interrupted her. 'I therefore felt it to be in your interest, and that of His Majesty, for me to agree to pass on to you the note in which the guilty party might reveal some useful information.'

She smiled, patting the arm of her chair. 'Monsieur Le Floch, it is a pleasure to cross swords with you!'

'I am at your service, Madame.'

He handed her the letter. She examined it carefully without opening it.

'You know what it contains, do you not, Monsieur le Floch?'

'Certainly not, Madame. I gave Monsieur Truche de La Chaux the means to ensure beyond any question that its contents remained secret.'

'So I see.'

She opened it with a flick of her fingernail and immersed

herself in reading it. Then with a sudden gesture she threw it into the fire, where it burnt instantly.

'Monsieur Le Floch, I thank you for everything. You are a loyal servant to the King.'

Without holding out her hand, she nodded farewell. He bowed in turn and withdrew. As he galloped along the banks of the Seine he had the feeling that it would be some time before he saw the favourite again. The burden of what had not been said would now weigh too heavily upon them for any future meeting to have the same levity and openness as in the past.

Tuesday 5 February 1762

Nicolas was drinking chocolate with Monsieur de Noblecourt, who was reading a newssheet, his spectacles perched on his nose. Cyrus sat on his lap, trying unsuccessfully to get between his master and what he was looking at.

'What are you reading?' asked Nicolas.

'Ah! My dear fellow, it's the *Gazette de France*. It's a new publication that first appeared on 1 January and now comes out every Monday and Friday.'

'What's it about?'

'Well, it's supposed to inform the public what's going on and about all sorts of discoveries, and secondly it's supposed to provide a collection of memoirs and accounts for the historical record. That at any rate is what the prospectus claims.'

'And what information is there today?'

'There's one item that will particularly interest you. Your Truche de La Chaux, Nicolas, was granted a rather strange privilege. In the end his sentence was commuted and instead of being broken on the wheel he was merely, if that's the right way to put it, hanged . . .'

Nicolas was startled. 'I told you in confidence about my last meeting with him. I am still convinced that he had a secret agreement with Madame de Pompadour. You know how everything was made so easy for me. Perhaps she pleaded on his behalf. Oh! Not directly, of course . . .'

He could not bring himself to go on. For days a terrible suspicion had been haunting him. Nicolas had thought long and hard about the real role played by the favourite in the whole business. He had been struck by the way in which the Life Guard had immediately confessed to his heinous crime. Everything had happened as if he had felt sure that he would not be prosecuted and that his crime would be overlooked. Or perhaps he entertained the hope of obtaining a pardon from a higher power. It was likely that the message that Nicolas had taken to the favourite had resulted in indulgence of a kind, if it could be considered any kind of indulgence to be hanged instead of broken on the wheel.

In what final act of bargaining had Nicolas been the innocent go-between? Truche de La Chaux must have known that although he could not save his life the circumstances of his execution were still negotiable. But it was terrible to harbour a suspicion deep down that the Marquise de Pompadour might have organised behind the scenes a fake assassination attempt against the King. Spurred on by her hatred of the Jesuits, driven by her jealousy towards the King's young mistresses and sincerely concerned about the real threats to her lover's life, she might have been trying to pin the blame on the Jesuits and the pious party.

Yes, that was just possible. He tried to banish these dreadful thoughts from his mind and concentrated on what Monsieur de Noblecourt was saying.

'He might have revealed something incriminating; torture does make even the most hardened talk. That is perhaps the secret behind the lessening of his punishment. Anyway, the Ruissec case and the derisory attempt on the King's life are not going to make the Jesuits' situation any easier. People say their fate is sealed, and even if they are innocent in this, calumny will do its work!'

'There is a great deal of unfairness in the criticisms levelled against them.'

'I agree. There is more enlightenment in them than amongst all those musty Jansenists who have been addling our brains for the last forty years. They will be driven out of the country, Nicolas, you'll see. Their educational work will be destroyed. And we are all their pupils! In the end the person to benefit will be the King of Prussia.'

'In what way?'

'Consider the great-grandfather of our present king. He revoked the Edict of Nantes. What was the result? The most brilliant and the most useful young men of the reformed religion went into exile, in Prussia in particular. You'll see, the same will be true of the Jesuits. They will go recruiting in the lands of the North and will teach generations to come to hate us.'

'Who will replace them in France?'

'That is a pertinent question, but I fear it is not the one that will be asked . . . But, Nicolas, you were at Versailles yesterday. Tell me about it.'

'Monsieur de Sartine took me to see Madame Adélaïde, so that

I could give her back in person the jewels that we found in the Life Guards' barracks.'

'That was a noble gesture on the part of the Lieutenant General of Police and one that does not surprise me coming from him. What of Madame?'

'Madame was very kind. She invited me to her hunt.'

'Good gracious! You are on the way up! Provided,' he said with a smile, 'that you manage to stay in your saddle.'

Nicolas was gazing at Rue Montmartre, which was gradually filling with the morning crowd. The sounds of passers-by and carriages in the street reached them. He thought of all those individual destinies. He himself would soon forget the protagonists in this sinister case, even if the sad figure of Truche de La Chaux in his cell would long linger in his memory. Soon the old capital would be alive again with the masks of Carnival. Other tasks awaited him. He finished his chocolate. The final mouthful had a bitter-sweet taste, much like life itself.

Sofia, July 1997–February 1999

NOTES

CHAPTER I

1. It was submitted to Louis XV on 30 November 1761.

2. Victoire de France (1733–1799), the second daughter of Louis XV and Maria Leszczyńska.

3. The names given to the two opposite sides of the auditorium where supporters of the French or Italian styles of opera gathered at the time of the 'quarrel of the corners'.

4. The comic sequence of the opera *Les Paladins* that was strongly criticised at the time.

5. A tragic opera in five acts by Jean-Philippe Rameau, first performed on 5 December 1749, in which, amongst other innovations, the composer replaced the prologue with an overture.

6. This suggestion of Nicolas's was in fact implemented by Sartine in 1764.

7. Lenoir, the Lieutenant General of Police, improved the lighting of Paris by introducing streetlamps to replace candle lanterns.

8. See *The Châtelet Apprentice*, Chapter I.

9. A fine, hard-grained limestone.

10. It was common practice at the time to send precautionary letters to the Lieutenant General of Police.

11. The morgue, situated in the cellars of the Châtelet (cf. *The Châtelet Apprentice*).

CHAPTER II

1. Saint-Florentin (1705–1777), Louis Phélypeaux, Comte, then Duc de la Villière, Minister of State in charge of the King's Household, a department that included among its responsibilities the administration and the policing of the city of Paris.

2. Cf. *The Châtelet Apprentice*.

CHAPTER III

1. 'Formerly in France, one who held lands from a bishop as his representative and defender in temporal matters' (*Oxford English Dictionary*).

CHAPTER V

1. Literally 'Pickpocket Street' (Translator's note).

CHAPTER IX

1. '[T]he breadth of a plank used as a unit of vertical measurement in a ship's side' (*Oxford English Dictionary*).

CHAPTER XI

1. Jacques Clément, a Dominican friar (1567–1589). A fanatical member of the Catholic League, he assassinated Henri III.

CHAPTER XII

1. The author reminds readers that Truche de La Chaux is an historical figure. The circumstances of the fake attack in Versailles on 6 January 1762 are recounted by the memorialists of the time, Barbier and Bachaumont. He was indeed hanged after his trial.

ACKNOWLEDGEMENTS

First I wish to express my gratitude to Sandrine Aucher for her competence, carefulness and patience in typing the text. I am also grateful to Monique Constant, Conservateur en Chef du Patrimoine, for her unfailing help and her discoveries in the archives of the period. Once again I am indebted to Maurice Roisse for his intelligent and detailed checking of the manuscript and for his useful suggestions. Finally I wish to thank my publisher for the confidence he has shown in this second book.

The First Nicolas Le Floch investigation

THE CHÂTELET APPRENTICE
Jean-François Parot

Translated by Michael Glencross

France 1761. Beyond the glittering court of Louis XV and the Marquises de Pompadour at Versailles, lies Paris, a capital in the grip of crime and immorality . . .

A police officer disappears and Nicolas Le Floch, a young recruit to the force, is instructed to find him. When unidentified human remains suddenly come to light, he seems to have a murder investigation on his hands. As the city descends into Carnival debauchery, Le Floch will need all his skill, courage and integrity to unravel a mystery which threatens to implicate the highest in the land.

'A terrific debut . . . brilliantly evokes the casual brutality of life in eighteenth-century France' *Sunday Times*

'Jean-François Parot's evocation of eighteenth-century Paris is richly imagined and full of fascinating historical snippets . . .'
Mail on Sunday

'Has all the twists, turns and surprises the genre demands'
Independent of Sunday

'An engaging murder mystery that picks away at the delicate power balance between king, police and state.' *Financial Times*

GALLIC BOOKS

Paperback February 2008

978-1-906040-06-2

£7.99

THE OFFICER'S PREY

A Grande Armée murder featuring Captain Quentin Margont

Armand Cabasson

June 1812. Napoleon begins his invasion of Russia leading to the largest army Europe has ever seen.

But amongst the troops of the Grande Armée is a savage murderer whose bloodlust is not satisfied in battle.

When an innocent Polish woman is brutally stabbed, Captain Quentin Margont of the 84th regiment is put in charge of a secret investigation to unmask the perpetrator. Armed with the sole fact that the killer is an officer, Margont knows that he faces a near-impossible task and the greatest challenge to his military career.

'Combines the suspense of a thriller with the compelling narrative of a war epic' *Le Parisian*

'Cabasson skilfully weaves an intriguing mystery into a rich historical background' *Mail on Sunday*

'. . . an enthralling and unromantic account of Napoleonic war seen from a soldier's perspective' *The Morning Star*

'. . . vivid portrayal of the Grande Armée . . .' *Literary Review*

'Cabasson's atmospheric novel makes a splendid war epic . . .' *The Sunday Telegraph*

GALLIC BOOKS

Paperback October 2007

978-1-906040-03-1

£7.99

WOLF HUNT

A Grande Armée murder featuring Captain Quentin Margont

Armand Cabasson

May 1809. The forces of Napoleon's Grande Armée are in Austria. For young Lieutenant Lukas Relmyer it is hard to return to the place where he and fellow orphan, Franz were kidnapped four years earlier. Franz was brutally murdered and Lukas has vowed to avenge his death.

When the body of another orphan is found on the battlefield, Captain Quentin Margont and Lukas join forces to track down the wolf who is prowling once more in the forests of Apern . . .

Winner of The Napoleon Foundation's fiction award 2005

GALLIC BOOKS

Paperback May 2008

978-1-906040-08-6

£7.99

THE SUN KING RISES

Yves Jégo and Denis Lépée

1661 is a year of destiny for France and its young king, Louis XIV.

Cardinal Mazarin, the prime minister who has governed throughout the king's early years, lies dying. As a fierce power struggle develops to succeed him, a religious brotherhood, guardian of a centuries-old secret, also sees its chance to influence events.

Gabriel de Pontbriand, a young actor, becomes unwittingly involved when documents stolen from Mazarin's palace fall into his hands. The coded papers will alter Gabriel's life forever, and their explosive contents have the power to change the course of history for France and Louis XIV.

Fact and fiction combine in a fast-moving story of intrigue, conspiracy and love set in seventeenth-century France.

'. . . has all the life, spirit and momentum of the best historical novels'
Le Figaro

'The heroes of the book are the stars of the era: Molière, La Fontaine, Colbert . . . a book to savour'
Paris Match

'A suspense-filled mystery, a cross between the Three Musketeers and the Da Vinci Code'
Europe 1

GALLIC BOOKS

February 2008

978-1-906040-02-4

£7.99